"Mary Sheehan Ronan is the kind o[f]... Jane Kirkpatrick did a stellar job o[f]... grave and onto the pages of *Beneath the Bending Skies*. It takes a woman of courage to stand up to a manipulative father and marry the man she was clearly meant to be with. As the wife of the 'White Chief,' Mary's ministry to the Salish Kootenai Natives and friendship with Shows No Anger in Montana during times of unrest between Natives and non-Natives is one of inspiration. This story celebrates the ties that can and do take place between cultures in the past and present. A story that will linger in your thoughts and heart for years to come."

Carmen Peone, award-winning author of *Lillian's Legacy*

"Jane Kirkpatrick never fails to take us away on unforgettable journeys. Her carefully crafted layers of colors, textures, music . . . transport us to eras of history that we might otherwise miss. Mollie and Peter's story is no different. What amazing lives they led! Their resilience and love was a legacy that lives on—thanks to Jane's gifted storytelling!"

Melody Carlson, author of Westward to Home (historical series)

"Jane Kirkpatrick's latest book is about the struggle between a father and daughter and the challenges of seeking a better life during the 1800s. Jane's story shows a sensitive and compassionate approach to the coming-of-age of a daughter and the conflict between two men who love her. I will not easily forget *Beneath the Bending Skies* nor the eloquent prose used to connect the reader with the characters. I will recommend this book to all my customers, friends, and family, and look forward to discussing the book with them."

Judi Wutzke, owner/manager of ...and BOOKS, too!

"Jane Kirkpatrick's *Beneath the Bending Skies* is one of the best novels I've read in a very long time. Set primarily against the backdrop of Montana's Big Sky country, the story narrates the life of

Mollie Ronan. At times tragic, yet always compelling, it is overall the uplifting account of a woman's struggles to find her place in life, within her extended family, and in the arms of the man she's loved since childhood. Told with warmth and respect for the land and its people—especially her relationship with the Salish, Kootenai, and Pend d'Oreille tribes—*Beneath the Bending Skies* is a fascinating journey and a worthwhile read."

Michael Zimmer, author of *The Poacher's Daughter*

BENEATH
THE
BENDING SKIES

Also by Jane Kirkpatrick

BENEATH THE BENDING SKIES

A NOVEL

JANE KIRKPATRICK

Revell

a division of Baker Publishing Group
Grand Rapids, Michigan

© 2022 by Jane Kirkpatrick

Published by Revell
a division of Baker Publishing Group
PO Box 6287, Grand Rapids, MI 49516-6287
www.revellbooks.com

Printed in the United States of America

Library of Congress Cataloging-in-Publication Data
Names: Kirkpatrick, Jane, 1946– author.
Title: Beneath the bending skies / Jane Kirkpatrick.
Description: Grand Rapids, MI : Revell, a division of Baker Publishing Group, [2022]
Identifiers: LCCN 2021062756 | ISBN 9780800736125 (paperback) | ISBN 9780800742195 (casebound) | ISBN 9781493438716 (ebook)
Subjects: LCSH: Ronan, Mary, 1852–1940—Fiction. | LCGFT: Biographical fiction. | Western fiction. | Novels.
Classification: LCC PS3561.I712 B46 2022 | DDC 813/.54—dc23/eng/20220114
LC record available at https://lccn.loc.gov/2021062756

Scripture used in this book, whether quoted or paraphrased by the characters, is taken from the King James Version of the Bible.

This book is a work of historical fiction based closely on real people and events. Details that cannot be historically verified are purely products of the author's imagination.

Published in association with Joyce Hart of the Hartline Literary Agency, LLC.

Baker Publishing Group publications use paper produced from sustainable forestry practices and post-consumer waste whenever possible.

22   23   24   25   26   27   28   7   6   5   4   3   2   1

Fairy tales are more than true: not because they tell us
that dragons exist, but because they tell us that
dragons can be beaten.

—Neil Gaiman

Desire accomplished is sweet to the soul.

—Proverbs 13:19

Dedicated to Jerry,
one more time

⩫ Cast of Characters ⩫

Mary "Mollie" Sheehan—an Irish daughter
James Sheehan—Mollie's father
Patrick, Ellen, and Mary Sheehan—Mollie's cousins
Anne Cleary Sheehan—stepmother to Mollie
Kate Sheehan—half sister
Jimmy Sheehan—half brother
Peter Ronan—(Row-NAN) editor, friend of James Sheehan
Jules Germain—student in Mollie's Montana school
Father Van Gorp—Helena priest and matchmaker
Richard Egan—*alcalde*, mayor of San Juan Capistrano,
    friend
Martin and Louise Maginnis—congressman, friend, and
    partner of Peter Ronan; and his wife
Harry and Mrs. Lambert and Grace—agriculturist at the
    agency and his family
Hanna Hoyt—cook and sister of miller
Dr. E. L. Choquette and Hermine—agency physician and his
    wife
*Shows No Anger and son Paul—Salish friends of Mollie

Chief Arlee—Salish chief at Jocko Agency of Flathead Nation

Chief Charlo—Bitterroot Salish chief, non-treaty Flathead Nation

Chief Michelle—chief of Pend d'Oreille of Flathead Nation

Chief Joseph—Nez Perce warrior

Chiefs Looking Glass, White Bird, Sitting Bull, Eagle of the Light—part of Nez Perce War of 1877

Elizabeth Custer—widow of General Custer, author and speaker

Michel and Maria—blind interpreter and his wife

Children of the Ronans—Vincent, Mary, Gerald, Matthew, Louise, Katherine, Margaret, Isabel, Peter

*fully imagined characters, not a part of historical record

≋ Prologue ≋

I loved my father, but that didn't mean I understood him. Nor that I ever pleased him, much as I tried. His disappointment shone in his Irish eyes like that of a teacher whose star pupil gives up academics to file a mining claim in Montana, choosing to wear pants instead of petticoats. My escape into fairy tales helped me face the trial between him and the other love of my life. "Your mother is turning in her grave that that man of yours has taken you into Indian wars," my father told me. It was a painful time.

But I think my mother would have said, "Trust your husband, Mollie, until he gives you reason not to." I last heard her lilting voice in 1858, when I was six. I remember her fanning my hair as long as Rapunzel's out behind me to dry as we lay together on her Irish linen. We stared at cloudless Kentucky skies, her belly mounded with my soon-to-be-born brother. What she did say as I chattered about what I wanted to be when I grew up were these words: "Whatever you do, be kind, Mollie. Notice what others' needs are and try to meet them."

"You mean fetch Pa's pipe before he asks?"

"Like that, yes." She smiled and whispered her fingers across my forehead as we rested in the shade of an umbrella magnolia. How I wish she'd lived to see Montana. And San Juan Capistrano. And her son. And mine.

She stood, helped me up. She rolled up the linen.

"Let me, Mama."

She nodded, watched, her hands on either hip, stretching her back. "I believe this child will arrive today." She sighed, hugged my shoulder to her side. She smelled of lavender. "We'll keep your papa happy. I'll make that serviceberry pie he likes. That might please him."

"Be kind."

"Yes." She smiled, then added, "To yourself, too, Mollie. And remember to be brave."

I'd have done better with her advice if she'd been there to show the way.

ONE

MAKING HAPPINESS OUT OF MUDDLE

Once upon a time there was a place, a people, and a love as astonishing and rare as a blood moon over a Montana peak. I—Mary "Mollie" Catherine Fitzgibbon Sheehan—was forced to leave that place and love behind in 1869, complying with my father's wishes without understanding why. But I never abandoned hope that one day I'd find my way back to that happy ending cherished in Ulster fairy tales, if not often in real life.

But my growing up occurred in a turbulent time. The War between the States raged. My father brought his brother and his three children from Ireland. My younger brother passed away, as did my uncle. We left Kentucky, reached Missouri, where my father said goodbye, leaving us on a cousin's plantation in the midst of turmoil.

It was his first leaving of me. The almanac read 1861—I was almost ten.

After months of my wondering if he'd return, he did. Within days, we left again, heading toward the gold rush gulches of Colorado, my feelings mixed, leaving cousins behind. He didn't smile as much as before. I wondered that he held something back or had I upset him? I tried to please him now. I sat beside my father on his freighter wagon led by six mules we called the Gems: Agate, Amber, Amethyst, Pearl, Jade, and Jasper. He'd sing Gaelic songs and, in the evening around the campfires, had me read to him. I did my best. He brought a cat along for company. Often while we plodded between towns, the feline would jump on the back of Amber, the mule closest to the wagon's dashboard.

"I think Puddin doesn't like your singing, Pa," I said.

"Or she wants another view."

I could see that the cat might want to gaze at the wide expanse of mountain peaks touching skies as blue as my father's eyes.

Then he told me he'd be leaving me behind once we reached Colorado. That secret revealed.

"Why can't I go with you?" A child's question of her only parent.

"Don't you worry, Mollie." He patted my knee. "I'll come back to get ye."

Would he? He always had returned, though months would pass. Months, filled with my wondering if he had found another child to love. Our reunions were tainted that way, my feeling orphaned even with him beside me as he was now. The wagon rattled down a ravine, then up the other side, toward a cluster of buildings in the shadow of mountain peaks.

My father—James Sheehan—was literate, did not drink, and was quick with numbers rumbling in his head. He was an honest man, though being Irish he wasn't always assumed to be so. He wasn't a big man in western country where physical bigness carried power beyond intelligence. He couldn't afford to be hunched over or broken further by his grief.

I knew that grieving effort. I had little memory of my mother except for a sweet voice, a set of Irish linens, and a square of Irish lace she'd worked on that I kept in a precious box. And a green parasol with black fringe. I could almost see her face behind that edging when I opened the brolly against the hot sun, miles from where I was born and where she had died when I was six.

I knew I was supposed to be obedient and kind. Still . . . desire pushed me to disagree with my father's plans.

"I can heat the stew now," I said. "And I could carry the collars to you." I showed him my almost-ten-year-old muscled arm, puny as a cat's back leg. I could drag the heavy yokes to where he harnessed the mules. Or rub oil into leather at night around the campfire to keep them pliable, and him near.

"Travel to those camps has its risk, Mollie. Bandits. Indians bent on revenge. No. You'll be safer where I've arranged." Then he added the promise I'd hang on to: "I'll come back." His blue eyes pooled tears. "We'll be together again."

My father pulled up before a framed house. A flower box spilled vines. "You need to stay here for a little bit, lass," he said.

He didn't tell me the town.

The couple who came out to greet me looked like the father and stepmother in "Hansel and Gretel." Short and round, they wore smiles of pity. What did they think of me that my father would leave me behind? I cried as the wagon rolled down the dusty road. The woman put a pudgy arm around my shoulder and offered me a cinnamon roll, which I accepted.

My father wouldn't say he abandoned me. After all, I had a roof over my head and a woman who smelled of comforting sauerkraut. She fed me and taught me needlework too. But I was alone, as sure as an orphan. I stayed quiet, shy, and watched in silence every sunrise, praying I would see my father's wagon coming back, giving me another chance to be his dutiful daughter. My world spun still.

THE STRANGERS PUT ME to work doing tasks a little girl could do. I learned to hem there, practicing on my landlord's shirttails, warming at the praise for my precision. My mother had taught those little fingers to knit, but she'd died before I learned to stitch. Looking back, I wonder if I worked for room and board; perhaps I also earned a wage that my father garnered—as fathers were allowed to do.

In the early morning, before my German keepers were awake, I'd wander the streets looking for the familiar Gem team of mules. I never saw them nor my father.

The one reward in that time of separation was that the German couple one evening took me to a play. I thought it strange to call something that seemed so real a "play," but I loved the splendor of the stage, the words the actors spoke, the music. For that time, I didn't think of my father or my mother, only of the costumed people prancing across the stage, making people laugh and clap and wet their cheeks with tears. They took me to another world where all turned out well in the end. I hoped for that, as I had no magic wand to make happiness out of muddle, nor to bring my father back.

TWO

THE BALLAD OF ANNE

My father never wanted me to cut my hair, my mother wouldn't want that. I could sit on tresses the color of earth and autumn oak leaves that others often commented on about its shine and waves. The German woman suggested cutting it. I resisted, and she helped me braid it instead. When I was with my father, he'd weave it into one long plait. At night, he brushed it.

I don't know how long he'd been gone—but my father returned, picked me up, swung me around, then sent me to get my things. I wasted no time tossing my little valise into the wagon and climbing up onto the smooth board seat, stroking the cat's arched back as I waited for him to finish some transaction with the Germans.

When we made camp that night, I was quick to show my father how helpful I could be. I gathered buffalo chips and with both hands carried the bucket full of water from a rushing stream. The air smelled fresh, dust lying quiet. Mules munched and I knew contentment, though it was not a word I'd understand or use until years later.

We traveled between snowcapped mountains, in lush, green valleys, wild horses lifting their heads as our wagon approached, then fluttering like colored ribbons across the meadows out of view. Streams trickled against stones, and I said how pretty it was. "Wait until you see the land around Denver and the rise of mountains, so many clustered together like a family of white-haired elders."

Toward the end of our journey—he said we were but days away—he sang a new song. Or rather he created new words for an Irish tune called "Gentle Annie." "It's a mournful Irish ballad," he said.

I wasn't sure what a ballad was and asked.

"A dance song, from long ago. But the English, they turned it into poems that tell stories of real people and events. Some are sung, some just recited."

"I like stories." The fire crackled before us. I heard the mules stomp at their tethers, ripping at grass. "Cousin Ellen showed me the library in Missouri. My reading is much better. I like to recite poems. Shall I?"

"Not now."

Something troubles him. "I like the fairy tales best." I kept my voice light. I so wanted to please him.

He scoffed. "Don't get too attached to such as those. One has to stay in this world, not run off into dreamland."

I hadn't thought that "Hansel and Gretel" or "Cinderella" were dreams so much as hopeful stories that said life could get better. But he took me from such musings with his "Gentle Annie" ballad he now began to sing.

> "She is the sweetest woman in the town
> Warm and wise and willing
> To take on a man and family
> To keep my heart from chilling."

He paused, stared at me.

I was puzzled. "Is that all of the song?"

"Oh, I've given it many verses, but this first is enough to share for now." He cleared his throat and I thought he might sing more, but instead he said, "You see, Mollie, there is a real Anne."

"You said the ballads talk of real things." I poked at the fire with a stick.

"I did." He cleared his throat again. "And this Anne I sing of is Anne Cleary. Or she was. Now she is Anne Sheehan, my wife, and your new mother."

AT THE CAMPFIRE with sparks lifting to the starry night, I tried to understand my new tumbled world. It wasn't to be just "the two of us," my father and me, again, ever. While I'd been pining for my father's return, he'd gone off and found a forever companion. Now, I understand his loneliness, his sorrow for having lost my mother. But for me, as a child, it was as though my mother had died again, would be replaced, and my father was now adored not just by me but by this woman, this "warm and wise and willing" Anne.

"You'll like her, Mollie. She's a sweet woman with a smile to melt your heart."

Your heart.

"And she's a hard worker, helping your ol' pa. Why, even now she's watching the store." He closed his eyes, remembering, I imagined. "Say something, Mollie." He brushed his hands through his wavy hair.

The store? We have a store?

My father was a handsome man, something most children claim for their fathers, but for the first time I understood that others might see him that way too. As for speaking to him, I just couldn't then. I could hear in his voice how much he cared for this Anne and knew my silence scraped at that happiness. Puddin started purring and stretched up against me while I petted him in silence.

He sighed. "Let's turn in, lass." With a blanket, he brushed away any snakes or critters that might have crawled beneath the wagon where he now began to roll out our bedding. A full moon rose and it was almost as day. "Does it look like rain to you, Mollie? If not, we can sleep beneath the stars. What do you say?"

I knew what he was doing, trying to make me be his companion in decision-making, as though he needed me for that now. Had he ever needed my childish opinions? I was a small boat in a large pond, alone, without an oar to paddle.

I do remember lying beneath a bright shining moon. My father snored beside me as tears seeped from my eyes. In silence, I spoke childish prayers that when we reached Denver, there might be another story, a different ending. I didn't wish Anne ill, but maybe she would change her mind about living with us. Maybe if she had a brother, he'd come to take her back to wherever she had come from—if she had a brother. And then I imagined myself as a child-sized Sleeping Beauty whom a wicked queen sent to slumber. I just needed a Prince Charming to wake me up.

In the morning, my father cheered me awake. He'd already made johnnycakes and had a tin of grape jam he said he'd spread on mine. Bacon sizzled in a pan; its aroma made me think of Cousin Ellen and how she never liked the taste of it and never wanted any on her plate. I wished that she was with me now, someone I might talk to about my change of fortune. He sang as he worked, and after we had eaten, he asked if I'd like him to braid my hair. "'Tis the color of sunset, lass. Shiny and beautiful." I shook my head. Strands were loose, but I didn't want his hands on my head, his pretending nothing had changed.

I helped clean up the dishes, rolled up our bedding, and did my father's bidding as he harnessed the team. I'd be dutiful in my silence. Throughout the day, my father sang, told stories he thought would make me smile. I took cold comfort in resisting his efforts to cheer me. I still had my prayer that things might be different once we reached our destination.

And so they were.

THREE

FAULT OR FAVOR

Our wagon filled with boxes of supplies rattled into Denver. The landscape looked ground-up like chunks of pounded meat. "The leftovers," my father named the tailings composed of mounds of gravel pushed through sluice boxes where men sought gold. I watched miners with pans slosh water round and round to uncover the heavier metal, shining bright. Men banged about inside a kettle of chaos, everyone rushing.

This new terrain was so different from the tobacco farm of Missouri or what I remembered of Kentucky. My father said we were nearly a mile high into the sky and that was why it might take a bit to catch our breath. The steep sides of the gulch looked like a giant cat had cleaned its claws on them, scraping long trenches in the soil. Tree stumps abounded, evidence of logs taken to form crude houses and small stores such as the one we pulled up in front of. Snow-drenched mountains shimmered in the background.

"Annie!" my father shouted. "I'm back." He leapt from the wagon and started toward the cabin, then turned back—an afterthought—to reach for me and help me down.

Then there was Anne. She held a baby in her arms.

"Ah, Anne, love," my father gushed. "How I've missed ye."

She laughed, a gentle sound. "You've only been gone a week."

The German family had not been too far away. He could have come to see me at least. Once. But there Anne stood, holding a baby, small and pink as ham.

Anne was as my father, maybe five foot eight or so. She blushed at my father's kiss right in front of the store. She looked over his shoulder beyond him to me and said, "And this must be Mollie, the apple of her father's eye."

His rotten apple he has tossed aside.

"That she is. Mollie, come meet your little sister, Kate." He lifted the child Anne held in her arms and brushed her porcelain forehead with a kiss. He smoothed her copper-colored hair.

"This is Mollie," he told the babe and then to me, "Would you like to hold your sister?" I shook my head, afraid that I might drop such a fragile thing. Small children—like my little brother Gerald—I knew could break and even die.

"Maybe later. When Mollie's rested," Anne said.

She stepped aside to let a man leave the store. He wore an apron around his middle and shook hands with my father. The two then unloaded the wagon goods while I followed Anne and Kate into the dark interior of my new home, a log structure without windows.

Anne wore her hair in curls the color of coffee, piled atop her head. She had lush eyebrows that balanced over blue eyes. Her face was the shape of the oval frame that housed a photograph of my father and Anne that sat upon a shelf. It must have been their wedding picture. I had no image of my mother. I didn't know what to call the feelings swirling inside a lost child's heart.

I didn't know what to call my father's wife, either. *Mother* wasn't possible. I ached for her. "Your pa sure speaks highly of you, Mollie. He says you're smart as well as pretty. I can see the pretty part by looking at you. And I'm sure as we get to know each other, I'll see the smart part too." She smiled then as she caressed Kate in her arms.

I guess I could have called her *Anne*, but that seemed too grown-up for a child addressing what was to become a familiar adult. It might be disrespectful. Or *Mrs. Sheehan.* But what rang in my ear was her calling my father *Pa.* I'd call her *Ma Anne* to go with Pa. When I used the name some days forward, my father didn't marvel that I'd finally spoken but instead corrected me and said, "*Ma* will be sufficient. No need to add the *Anne.*"

SHE WAS A KIND SOUL, Ma was. She never raised her voice nor complained about my silence until at last it seemed unkind to keep my voice from her. It was then she encouraged me to recite little poems, prayers, Irish stories that, when I finished my recitation, she applauded. Little Kate clasped her tiny fists and kicked her feet with joy. For discipline, when I left a candle burning low or lost myself in a book and didn't hear Kate cry, the most Ma did was swat me with her apron strings, no willow switch allowed. Once while I was to watch Kate, I instead dressed up in Ma's gown, pretending to be "a lady" and took Kate around to show off to the neighbors. When Ma returned, she scolded, the first time I ever saw her angry as she held up the muddy hem of her ruined favorite dress. "Mollie, you will not ever play the lady again."

She was a marvelous cook and a natural organizer, managing the household and the store after my father's employee left for the gold rush in the Black Hills. She was patient with her only step-child, eventually coaxing conversation from me in part by saying that Kate would learn how to talk if she could hear me speak. I soon found that she was not like the stepmother of Ashley Pelt, the Ulster version of "Cinderella," but more like the fairy godmother, trying to bring magic into a young girl's life, especially when my father left on freighting trips and we were there together—with little Kate—without him for months at a time.

I suspect all the aloneness wasn't what she had imagined for a married life, but she was "agile," that's what she called it. "It's our work to find ways around the boulders in our lives," she told me as she rolled out the dough that would be the braided bread I loved. She added anise to it or rosemary when we had the herbs. "We Irish make life a dance, and must be light on our feet, Mollie. Agile, finding ways." She might have said those things to convince herself, but I heard them, and soon found I was less afraid to speak to her, at first just answering questions but finally asking them too. And so I had words years later to help myself and then another, my little sister Kate.

WHEN SPRING CAME to our high-altitude home, wildflowers washed the hillsides. Fireweed, mule's ears, lupine, and larkspur grew as tall as me. Ma and I with Kate in her arms would climb the steep hills where we could look down on the mining operations as well as gaze across the ridges to vistas far and wide. We'd pick blooms to grace our table with, bringing a bit of spring inside. A school chum and I would carry our floral prizes to the boarding-houses whose owners often paid us in wisps of gold dust gleaned, they said, from laundering a miner's pants. We took the flowers to the saloons, too, where our bouquets would be accepted with perhaps a sweet for payment before we were hustled out.

"You will not do such a thing, selling flowers like a common scamp. Did you know she was doing that?" my father growled when I proudly showed him my earnings.

"I didn't see the wrong in it," Ma said. "Flowers are a blessing."

"No child of mine will act the waif and sell flowers paid for out of pity."

His words stung. It was true I'd done it, but it didn't seem a sinful thing to bring a little beauty to a humble miner's table. What would he say if he knew I'd also sold to the saloon, those "halls of sin and degradation" as I heard the traveling preachers call them.

And I had shared the benefits, the sweets and gold dust, just like I shared what my friend and I found in the sluice boxes we were allowed to brush with the owner's consent. I didn't tell my father about that, either, but Ma knew. Perhaps that's when our alliance truly began, when she didn't betray me to my father.

And I began to love her when she seemed to understand my disappointment that upon his return my father should find fault instead of giving favor. My flower-selling disgusted him. Ma patted my back and suggested I take Kate out for a walk and track Puddin hunting mice. I nodded and slipped by my father, who had not hugged me but sat at the slab table—wildflowers gracing the center in their tin vase. My father held his head in his hands, and while I grieved my own hurt feeling from his sharp words, I also felt his suffering for failing him yet again.

I BEGAN TO FANCY MYSELF as someone that I wasn't. I saw it as a way of being agile, as Ma said. I would set aside my father's disappointment and instead put on the mask of certainty. I would practice it in school—when we had a teacher. Standing behind the façade of confidence and surety, I could proclaim and bring comfort and enthusiasm to an audience of school chums. Shakespeare's words, Elizabeth Barrett Browning's writings, the Psalms. I thought I might find self-assurance in that recitation world, a belief that standing behind words could take me from my sadness and with it my confusion over my father's sweetness or chastisement.

In school, we could pick whatever composition or poem we wished. One day I chose the Indian Chief Black Hawk's speech. I loved seeing the faces of my peers sneering first at my speech choice, then through my declamation, help them see Black Hawk the man differently and themselves too. President Jackson meant to humiliate that Indian and his son as they toured the country as a defeated enemy. But the chief was agile. He spoke those words to audiences that made them see him closer to themselves, a man who in defeat was worthy of remembrance. Enchantment, transformation, entertainment: that's what I could do with words. As a performer, I wore a mask and became someone other than what I was. Best of all, the applause could cauterize my wounds. Especially those made when I disappointed my father.

"DID YOU GET THE AUGER?" We'd been in Denver more than a year, and I'd made one friend—Carrie Crane. She was skinny as a wagon tongue, but we could laugh together. I followed her lead at doing things my father would not have approved of. That cold winter day, I nodded and handed her the tool. One advantage of being the child of a father freighting supplies into mining towns across the West was that a determined girl could find any tool she wanted. I either looked in the store where we sold such things as saws beside bags of flour, or in the musty, smelly shed behind the log store. It was dusk and February's cold and snow still kept the miners from their sluice boxes and into saloons, of which there were many.

Standing in crunchy snow pushed up against a clapboard building, we augered into the Miner's Roost. Icicles hung from the rafters as slippery and slender as snakes. Piano music rose from the stage where we imagined that girls danced and men downed drinks of whiskey, fruit, and rock candy—the real reason our store stocked that sweet. We heard the hooting, and men stomped their feet for more, sounds that muted our drilling efforts.

We augered two holes, giggling. And when I put my eye to one and watched through smoky haze, I was transformed. I loved the music, smiled as the skirts that rose above the women's ankles with a flourish sometimes showed a fine knee. Their dancing seemed to elevate the women, make them taller, brought a flush of perspiration to their faces. They looked happy, not how I'd seen such women on the streets. One dance brought the house down when three Irish girls—they must have been Irish because they knew how to clog—lay their hands across each other's shoulders and with straight backs lifted their knees and danced the jig, their heavier shoes throbbing around the wooden stage.

They all wore ribbons with their names on them. Melody's sash was red. I'd seen her in the daylight on the muddy streets, eyes averted. "They think because they're saloon girls, they aren't good as us," Ma told me when I asked why certain women looked away. "They feel shame. But they needn't. Every soul has merit. They're just doing what they can to get by in these overnight-and-gone towns."

"They're agile."

"You could call it that, yes."

Melody didn't look forlorn. She smiled all the way to her eyes.

"What are you two doing?"

The voice came behind us, a smooth cadence. Both Carrie and I twisted, pushed our backs up against the saloon wall. "You girls shouldn't be here. Something bad could happen to you."

He had a handsome face, thick eyebrows not unlike my father's. "Aren't you James Sheehan's girl?"

"Don't tell my da, please."

He smiled. "Wouldn't think of it. Such pretty hair," he said and stroked it. I squeezed tighter against the logs as he stepped closer. I smelled tobacco on his breath. My heart pounded. I felt a thrill with this wisp of danger.

"Hey, you let her be." Carrie spoke up. "I'll tell her pa you looked out for us, Mister . . . what's your name?"

He dropped his hand. "Not necessary. This'll be our little secret. Get on home now."

He walked away, his gait crooked as though the pistol on his side made him off-center.

"That was close." Carrie's teeth chattered as she talked, plugging the holes we'd made. Frantic moves.

"Who was that?"

"Bart Davidson. He's nasty, my pa said. A road agent."

"Thanks for distracting him." I flapped my mittened hands to get them warm.

"You've got to be careful of men like him, Mollie. Stand your ground."

I grabbed the auger. "Until tomorrow night?"

"Don't be a coot. We're lucky he didn't take us by the ear and drag us home. Or worse."

I'd encountered a dangerous man. One who had touched my hair and I hadn't even tried to stop him. Carrie was right—and so was my father: I didn't always make the best decisions, didn't recognize danger even when it was so close I could smell whiskey on its breath. What I could do—and did—the next day was leave a bouquet of flowers for Melody. An act of kindness that I hoped would be a path toward better choices in my future.

FOUR

THE SMILE THAT CONCEALS

When my father took me to see *Hamlet*, I heard the words that one may "smile, and smile and be a villain." I sometimes smiled to cover my awkwardness. Smiles can be deceiving, and villains can be difficult to identify. Perhaps we are all villains in our own stories at various times. At least I think I was.

My father didn't invite Ma Anne to *Hamlet*. I failed to ask if she might like to go, but there was Kate who needed looking after. She likely told him no when he extended her an invitation. Still, I could have stayed with Kate and let the two of them enjoy an evening out. He hadn't asked me; had told me we were going.

My father acted pleased to have me beside him. He touched my hair in its long braid; introduced me to others in our theater box as "my precious Mollie." I vowed to tell Ma all about the play so she wouldn't feel badly to be left behind. It was an early foray into how to diminish guilt for being happy while someone else was not.

NOT LONG AFTER the performance of *Hamlet,* my father announced that we would be moving again, this time to the newly formed Montana Territory. The gold strikes had petered out, he said. Like miners with their pans, we followed gold veins too by bringing supplies to hopeful men. I would have liked to stay in Denver. I had a friend there. The store was to be left in the hands of a hired man, and my father would now freight to the Montana sites. He'd build a mercantile for sales or storage, I wasn't sure. What was clear was that we would be uprooted.

I wrote to Cousin Ellen, and having prepared her for the delights of Denver and the plays and circus and school she would attend when my father finally brought her and her two siblings to us, I now had to share that we were off to a new town. I was prideful of my penmanship that teachers commented on and didn't think then of what Ellen might be going through with the war much closer to her than any of us. Her letters back were sporadic, with paper a premium in Missouri. And there were other struggles she had that we didn't. *"More slaves leave to join the Union army. When will Uncle James come and get us?"* I didn't know, and when I questioned my father he would say, "Time will tell." I wondered then if he ever would or if my cousins would be letter-people all my life. Another loss.

Ma Anne packed and did a large washing the day before we left Denver so we wouldn't have to take a laundry day along the way. We'd have clean sheets and clothes when we arrived in our new abode. There was a cabin there waiting for us, my father said. I put on a happy face, deciding it was a way I could manage disappointment, pretend it was different than it was.

The stage of every day; the smile that concealed.

Ma and I hung trousers and linens on the line, the ever-present wind flapping the wet, lye-scented sheets against my face as I placed the wooden pegs. I hung our wrappers and little Kate's nappies, though she was nearly free of wearing them and toddled after me as her big sister. I kept Kate from the steaming washbasin, always remembering the fragility of children.

I could remember when my cousins' da had left my little brother Gerald sitting on a stump near where oxen grazed while he walked away to talk with someone. The oxen, curious, lumbered toward my brother and bumped him with their wet noses and big heads. He was barely two. When he fell to the ground, it was but seconds—everyone later lamented—before he was trampled to his death. I suspect my uncle thought himself a villain, though his part in the plot of our story was unintended. Tragedy trailed us Sheehans.

My cousins' da died not long after, though he had not been ill. I overheard my pa tell Ma Anne that he thought his brother had died of a guilty heart. I didn't want such a weight on my soul, so I watched Kate closely through the opening between the pegged sheets. In the morning, we would fold and finish packing those clean clothes into trunks.

When the sun rose on the day we'd head to Alder Gulch, it was Ma who shrieked, "The sheets are gone. Everything, gone."

Did I not secure them properly?

Frazzled for the first time I ever saw, Ma grabbed hold of the clothesline. She looked left and right, to see if the wind might have whisked those sheets into trees or maybe they were caught in brush or stones nearby. But no. Someone had come in the night and taken them. She sank to her knees.

Those were my mother's linens.

The night before, we'd laid out our dresses and underthings. I had taken in a table runner of my mother's that was already dry, and so we had it for that later dressing of the altar. But now, the day before our grand departure, all was gone with no time to sew up more nor seek out the robbers. I felt naked even though I still had nightclothes and the smock I'd planned to travel in. Thieves steal twice: the objects taken and the well-being that the victim once enjoyed.

"Nothing to be done now," my father told us. He glared at me, one eyebrow raised as when he accused. "Let's finish packing and head out."

How had I failed him? I didn't know.

THE TRIP NORTH took us through ravishing country. It was July, and oh, how the flowers marveled at their surroundings. At rushing streams, my father would make camp while the sun was still high in the sky. I helped hobble the Gems, then gently touched their velvet eyelids, whispered of my confusion about my father's changing moods. Pa took his pole and returned within an hour with fish enough for supper and for breakfast too. He was restful on these camping trips, would sing or read to us while we washed our dishes. Those trips were a different kind of time with outside demands on him put aside, and he'd wax eloquent about current affairs gleaned from a recently read newspaper, about the railroad pushing through the West and how that would change all our lives. He would dream out loud, saying he would one day soon bring the cousins north. "And I'll send Mollie back to the States for a proper schooling. Anytime now. When things are a little more financially stable."

"You will?"

"Aye, though I'll miss ye wretchedly, my lass."

"Desolately," I offered. Would he see my response as correct-ing him?

"Hmm, desolately? No, I think wretchedly says it best."

"I'm sure you're right, Pa."

Ma was busy flouring the fish.

Though the idea of more schooling appealed, I had no interest in traveling to the States, leaving him and Ma and Kate. I had no confidence that I'd ever be secure in a city like Chicago or St. Paul.

It did surprise me that he could be so calm on this journey to another town. We had all our worldly goods with us—less what the thieves had taken from the clothesline—and I saw that he wore a money belt beneath his loose shirt where he carried currency and gold. Even after we'd arrive at a new place, he usually kept his trea-sures on himself, until a bank was built and large vaults ordered to be installed. He'd bid on the contract to meet the railroad at its farthest point west and haul the treasuries to the towns—when roads were passable—such heavy freight a challenge. I felt sorry for the Gems.

With the campfire crackling, he spoke of his successes. The world seemed small enough to fiercely love not only each other but every leaf and rippling stream. We were all together, and I would once again vow to do everything I could to please my father, knowing he did so much for each of us.

WHISPERING PULLED ME from my sleep, and before I could clear my eyes and sit up, a shot rang out. No one groaned but my father shouted, "Hold your fire! Who's there? What do you want?"

"Just your gold." The voice, gruff.

In the dawn I pushed back the dust-scented tent flap. I could see there were two strangers on horseback. They wore masks so only their eyes were visible beneath their black brimmed hats. My father looked small and vulnerable in his long johns.

"I haven't any gold. We're just a family moving to Alder Gulch. Household things. You can see for yourself." He nodded toward the wagon. "I'm going to put my hands down. Don't shoot. There are children here. And my wife." My father had his hands in the air. "Don't wake the cat. He'll scratch ye." He grinned.

One of the men peered into the wagon box. "He's right, Bart. Nothing here worth shooting over." He turned to my father. "You got any bacon and eggs? I'm starvin'."

"That we can do. Would you like my wife to fix them for you?" His voice shook a little, but if one didn't know him, they wouldn't recognize the tremble.

The man holding the gun scoffed. "Clever trying to get us to show our faces. No, just give us what you got and we'll be on our way. Fix it ourselves." His voice was distinctive with its smoothness and its tone. *Familiar?* "Best get yourself a dog if you travel out. Be a little more wary as you've got women and a pretty lass with you."

I stepped back toward the tent Kate and I shared. *I know that voice.*

"There are dangerous villains roaming these roads," he said.

My father nodded as he helped Ma gather eggs and the side of bacon and two of her big cinnamon rolls. I hated to see the latter go.

"Get back in the tent, lass," my father ordered as Ma put the groceries in a canvas bag and handed them up to Bart, who had remained mounted. "Thank you, Missus." Bart's voice was deep as a cellar. "Lass." He tipped his hat at me, bushy eyebrows over glinting eyes. They rode off.

"Ye should have stayed hidden, Mollie. I don't like how that Bart looked at ye." My father wiped his forehead of perspiration, and I realized then that he'd been worried, maybe even frightened.

"We should have a dog," I said. "He would have warned us."

"Something to consider." My father put his arm around my shoulder, squeezed. "We're safe. Don't you be afraid, lass." He stroked my hair, released me. He patted his stomach over his money belt.

Ma stood behind him. "I kept some eggs back." He didn't hug or kiss her. Kate slept through the whole adventure.

We behaved as though it had been a normal morning as we ate our vittles. But I'd remember that it was a day when I didn't see my father comfort Ma as he had me—and when Bart Davidson didn't give away that he'd seen me once before.

FIVE

WAYS TO PLEASE

We reached Alder Gulch in Montana Territory, exhausted. Pa moved us into a cabin without any windows clinging to a steep hillside, but which gave a view of all the activity going on to get the stream or ravine to give up their gold. I noticed my breath came shorter than when in Denver. We were at a higher altitude, my father said. Ruby Creek ran close by. I prayed this would be our home forever.

Already hundreds of miners had made their way to this gulch, ripping the landscape with their sluice boxes and the other accoutrements of placer mining. But it had been my father who had broken the road to this latest rush, bringing in the first load of supplies to those miners who had gotten the news of a gold find. He'd been doing that while Carrie and I had augered into the saloon.

This new gold find promised to be a good place for my father's business of setting up a store while he freighted supplies between towns or drove south to where the railroad ended to pick up goods. His judgment was critical, though. He'd be leaving hired men to watch the operation, handle money and consumers, deciding who to lend credit to and who not. But my father did have such judgment. He was clever. Hadn't he talked his way out of road agents bent on thievery?

I always wondered, though, why he didn't have Ma and me run his store. Ma managed to take care of our little family while he was gone. She had a good head for money too. And he could trust her. I suspect it was our gender and that having a wife in "the trades," as he called it, would speak poorly of him, suggest that he wasn't the provider an Irish husband and father was expected to be.

We'd settled ourselves that first night. Ma fixed a supper very much like when we'd broken our fast the morning after the attempted robbery. We feasted on bacon and eggs. We'd finished when my father made his next big announcement. "I leave by week's end."

Ma stiffened at the basin where we two washed dishes. Kate played on the dirt floor with Puddin, who rolled over for her to scratch his belly. "So soon?" Ma said.

"Yes, 'tis soon, but you'll be happy when I return."

"I'm always happy when you come home, Husband." I realized Ma always was, greeting him with a happy face, maybe even a little bow when he stepped off the wagon seat. She never raised her voice to him as I heard neighboring women often do to their wayward men. And even though she had no way of knowing when he'd return, she always looked as though she did. Coffee-colored strands of hair wisped at her oval face. A touch of pink colored her welcoming cheeks. She wore a clean apron every morning.

She was beautiful, I thought, backlit by the window light. And dutiful. She never questioned what my father asked of her. She did everything to please him. Only later in my life did I realize when she took such care of herself, that she wasn't only pleasing him; she was treating herself with kindness when there wasn't anyone else to do it.

"I wish you didn't have to go away again." I pooched my lower lip out.

"When I'm back this time, I won't be alone. I'll bring back Patrick and Mary and Ellen with me. We'll be our old family at last."

"You'll bring the cousins?" I danced around the room, pulled my little sister's hand up to swirl with me. "The cousins are coming, the cousins are coming." I hugged my father then. "You didn't forget."

"Not for a second, but until now, I couldn't afford it. They'll come partway by train and then I'll pick them up along with freight. It'll be two months or more, you understand."

I was envious that they'd get to ride a train.

"Get a dog," Ma said. "We should have one here too." I heard a modest bite in her words. Perhaps he had surprised her too with the knowledge that her family would soon grow by three.

"I'll have me knife with me." He emptied his pipe into a tin. "I'll see about a mutt. The Gems don't always take to little things."

My father left by week's end. Ma set about making the dark cabin into a home. She stretched a hide across the dirt floor holding it with wooden pegs. She rolled tree stumps inside and made little pillows stuffed with straw both for color and to soften the hard, backless seats. Ropes crisscrossed from the corner for the bed that we all shared when my father was gone. When he was home, we girls slept on straw and quilts on the floor. My father had provided a cookstove and a table to gather round. A smaller table near the stove was where Ma prepared the meals, and a still smaller one beside the door held a washbasin and a matching white pitcher painted with roses. In the evening, sitting in a rocking chair beside the washbasin, a lantern shedding light, Ma sewed. New bedding. New clothes. Mending. I would read out loud to her and Kate, who would say, "Again, Sister. Again." Especially to any offerings from *Grimm's Fairy Tales*.

The second day after my father left, Ma baked. Then on the third day, she put on her hat and, with us in hand, knocked on the neighbor's door, to introduce ourselves and offer up cinnamon rolls. They were the size of a man's hand. The aroma was heavenly.

"It's my experience that people fill an empty space. I help fill it with the truth," Ma said as she braided my hair before our visiting day. I considered cutting it, but I knew my father would object. "It's important to let your neighbors know a bit about you," Ma continued, "so they won't make up stories that might upset them later."

"What kind of stories?"

"Oh, about where your father might have gone, thinking he deserted us. Or that we were fleeing the law. Or that I was a witch or a sorcerer of some kind." She'd changed her voice to sound scary. She laughed. "Once years ago, when an old man died after I visited, his family made that suggestion. This was before I met your pa. But it was the neighbors who assured his children I'd been helpful to their father—whom they'd abandoned, I might add." She scoffed. "Knowing the people around you is as preventative of trouble as taking saleratus for your tummy before eating sauerkraut."

One of our new neighbors was a scholarly looking man. His wife was a Salish Indian woman, and they had a baby who slept in a little hammock hung in the corner. I loved to come by and swing the infant while its wide brown eyes watched me. The baby's father wrote at his desk. He wore a vest and jacket and store-bought pants and fine dress boots, while his pretty wife padded about in moccasins wearing simple calico with a beaded belt.

"Why did you marry an Indian woman?" I asked him one day.

"I'm an odd sort of fellow," he told me. "A white woman might argue with me to make me change my ways. Rides-a-Fine-Horse is sweet tempered, never raises her voice."

"Does she? Ride a fine horse?"

He smiled. "She did."

When I told Ma about my new information, she said, "Mollie, it's not polite to ask such personal questions. Ladies don't do that. Why people marry is no business of others."

I surely wanted to be a lady.

"Should I say I'm sorry?"

Ma seemed thoughtful. "You might take a gift to his wife. I'm sure she'd appreciate being noticed."

I thought for days about what to take and then decided on knitting a yarn ball for their baby. Even then I noticed that babies were special to Indian parents—just like I was special to my father, even if I didn't please him as often as I wanted.

But the larger lesson was of "neighboring," I called it, and Ma's approach to what truly made a home safe.

SUMMER ASSAULTED US with its beauty and heat. I held my hand to shade my eyes and watched a hound-like yellow dog with a long skinny tail jump down from my father's freighter. Apparently, the Gems team took to this dog, as he wove his way between the mules' legs and bounded toward me.

"His name is Dange," Pa shouted as he jumped. "Short for 'dangerous.'" The big dog's tail nearly knocked Kate down with its exuberant wagging. I thought I knew why he'd garnered the name. I wrinkled my nose.

"Dange means stinky." Pa laughed.

"He does like to roll in raccoon scat." The young woman who stepped down looked so much older than when I'd last seen her that I didn't recognize her as my cousin Ellen. She was seventeen. "Look at you." Dange wandered over to sniff Kate and then Ma Anne, who scratched his head. "You're a proper young lady, you are," Ellen said. "Twirl around. Let's see the back of that fine dress."

"Ma Anne made it."

"I love the yoke."

Mary, younger than Ellen, settled her hat that had come ajar when she jumped from the back of the wagon, her dark curls bouncing as she raced toward me. She was heavier than her sister or me but with the Sheehan dimples in her plump face.

The last sibling, Patrick, tall and slender as a slice of bacon, sauntered forward. He'd been driving a second freighter wagon he'd pulled up behind Pa's.

41

"Do you have a fellow?" Mary asked. She was fifteen. Girls her age—and even mine at eleven—claimed friends of the opposite sex, and some were even noticed by older men in their twenties. It wasn't uncommon in the mining towns for girls—women—as young as fourteen to marry.

"No, she doesn't," my father barked. "And neither should any of you. You're too young to be courted." But Ellen, at seventeen, would be sought after soon, I was certain. And she was old enough to choose a fellow even if my father disapproved. I anticipated the stories she would bring into our little cabin, filling the space when my father was gone.

Ellen greeted Ma Anne then. "I've heard a lot about you, Mrs. Sheehan." Ellen curtsied. "Uncle James speaks endlessly of your many virtues."

"Oh, pshaw." Ma dismissed the compliment, but I could tell she liked hearing it. "And it's Anne to you. Come here, my latest kin." Then she reached for Ellen and Mary and held them in her embrace. From behind, I could see my cousins' shoulders sink into the comfort of this older woman, saw the shaking then as each began to cry inside her shelter. Ma let them. Finally, she stepped away and offered up a handkerchief, then dabbed at her own eyes too. I brushed my cheeks of tears. She reached for Patrick next, who was taller than her and who sported a thin mustache. Patrick let Ma hold him in her slender arms, his shoulders only slightly lowered to her comfort. Then, like herding little chicks, she said, "Inside." She motioned them forward into the cabin. "We'll have something to eat and drink after your long journey."

I didn't follow. I hadn't greeted my father yet. He'd been gone for months.

He reached for Ma next, swirled her about, then swatted her behind as she stepped through the cabin door. She laughed, hesitated, then followed the cousins inside.

My father picked up Kate and kissed her, set her down, and then he turned to me and opened his arms. "Ah, my Mollie. A sight for these sore Irish eyes." He hugged me, kissed the top of my head. The scent of tobacco lingered as we walked arm in arm inside. Happiness reigned with his arrival.

It never occurred to me until I was older that it was Ma who should have been the one he walked with after such a long separation.

My father didn't stay long before he and Patrick headed out to gather more supplies. Patrick's team of mules all had flower names. They were a fine set of animals. But before he left again, Pa secured a two-room cabin for us on Wallace Street just down the ravine. Ma set about to make it into a home. We all four girls slept in the large bed but had our own cup and saucer for morning tea.

Ellen, it turned out, was like Ma, a marvelous cook. Her choke-cherry and dried peach pies brought neighbors to our door, and miners too. With the men gone on freighting trips, we women—I counted myself as one now—took the interest in our table fare and began charging a small fee for the larder. It didn't take long before we thought of our cabin as an "establishment." Not a sleeping place, food only.

Neither Ma nor I mentioned how Pa might feel about our venturing into the trades. We needed the money. We were only being agile.

Ellen, small and quiet as a wren, wore a ready smile and seemed to enjoy the attention of those taking meals at our table. She was a star attraction. But so was Kate with her copper-colored hair and delicate freckles. Many of the miners missed their own children, and a child with Kate's red hair never failed to garner comments. As did my long tresses and the recitations I spoke from memory as after-dinner entertainments. Mary could talk to anyone, and she did, making the meals friendly gatherings as she served.

We heard the latest gossip of the town, learned about new

strikes or claims jumped and talk of fights and vigilantes. There was no law to speak of in the territory, no one to turn to about disputed boundaries or stolen goods. Vigilantes, self-imposed arbiters of right and wrong, had formed in other gulches, and it wasn't long before Alder Gulch saw its dark side rising. Gunshots could be heard at all hours. And when Ma sent me to the butcher down the steep slope, she'd say, "Don't be afraid, but run, run." Once I rounded a corner where the blacksmith singed his iron rods into water in the shade of a man's body swinging from a nearby tree. I'd startled and stepped back.

"Teaching other would-be thieves what fate they'll find if they rob another of his goods," the farrier said, nodding toward the spectacle. "Happened yesterday. Run along, now."

I stumbled on by but couldn't release from my memory the man's boots, all wrinkled, the tragedy of lost life. The smell. I told Ma.

"I'd heard that these hangings were happening. You'll have to slip by, Mollie. Don't dawdle on your way." Then when she saw my tears, she brought me into her arms and let me cry. "I'm sorry you had to see the costs of disputes."

"But what if he wasn't the real robber? What if someone else did the deed?"

She held me for a time, then said, "In established towns, ones that grow up and have sheriffs and judges and juries, there's a better chance that the truth will rise above the fray. We can hope for that here or your father can move us to another place where vigilantes don't rule."

I thought she affirmed my concern and I vowed to ask my father about it when he returned. After a school chum and I witnessed yet another hanging, this time of four men, I thought the likelihood of another move might happen soon. Wouldn't a protective father want to take his family away from robbers and vigilantes or the quick justice of a mob? Even my father might get caught up with someone thinking he cheated them in a transaction. I once overheard someone say he had a temper.

I TRIED TO PUT DANGER from my mind and watched instead how Ma handled our guests, how she'd make light of miners pushing limits at our establishment. "Now don't you be taking your fingers from your spoons or someone else will have your dessert," she'd say as she laughed and brushed away a man's hand reaching for her aproned hip. "You don't want to miss Ellen's dried peach pie." She'd swirl away, making sure not to make fun of the man in her rebuff and kept her repudiations light. If someone got rowdy, the others eating at the table would intervene and send him on his way. But Ma would take the blame for his misbehavior saying, "I thank you, boys. I should have noticed that he'd imbibed too much and not opened the door to him." A rule of the establishment was that no one would be served if they'd been drinking. We women set the rules and we enforced them mostly by ourselves. Ma didn't want to be beholden to anyone for help in case they expected payment of whatever kind. "I wish your pa was here," she sometimes sighed after everyone had left for the evening. It was the most she ever complained. She seemed to know she'd made this bed and could either lie in it or change the linens.

WHEN HE WAS AROUND, my father took me again to plays. I especially loved *One Touch of Nature*. The plot was of a separation of a father and a daughter and all that went on to keep them parted and then a final, loving reunion. I could become quite dramatic, imagining these tribulations being between my father and me and the great joy of restoration when our trials brought us back together. I'd imagine us on a stage playing the parts of a real father and daughter in *One Touch of Nature* and the great joy of that final reunion. We both had good memories for lines and would repeat portions of the performances for Ma and the cousins, only later acknowledging the eye rolls. Pretending wasn't everyone's "cup of tea," as Ma told me once, but it was a brew that made my father happy.

SIX

The Plot Thickens

"When did you get here?" I asked.

My friend Carrie Crane appeared, her father, an attorney, having moved the family from Denver to Alder Gulch. "A week or so ago," she said. "I saw your ma and knew you wouldn't be far away."

I hugged her. We chattered like squirrels, and I told her of my newest gulch activity: finding gold.

"You've filed a claim?"

"Nothing like that. Here, I'll show you." I took two hairbrushes saved for this purpose and a little scraper and demonstrated how to clean out the sluice boxes after the miners had taken their gold at the end of the day. "The miners let me."

We brushed the dust onto cloth and took it home, dried the mud and gravel in the oven, then used our blowers to get the gold dust out. "I put my dust in this inkwell."

"The store owners will take it?"

"Buys me rock candy and trinkets," I told her. It became a regular occupation with my friend, another activity I didn't share with my father.

One day Carrie and I worked on a sluice owned by that miner named Peter Ronan. I wore a new hat Ma had made me with a chambray valance, the weave as tight as denim. I took it off to keep it tidy while we brushed the box, believing Mr. Ronan had finished for the day. Instead, a splurge of water poured down the lumber chute, washing my new hat into its stream.

"Hey!" I shouted up to him. He sprinted down, looking worried. He might have thought we'd been hurt. "Look what you've done to my hat. See if I ever clean your sluice box again!"

He grinned, which made me twice as angry, even when he said, "I'm sorry."

I took my hat home and Ma helped me clean it up. She smiled when I told her of my threat to Mr. Ronan.

"I'm sure he's contrite." Then, "There's talk that he's going to start a newspaper, so you might not have his sluice box to ransack in the future anyway."

"He should be more careful."

"He's one of the kindest men I've ever met. And he's friends with your pa, did you know that? They share books."

"He should have taken more care of his surroundings and my hat." I brushed the chambray of the mud.

"It's a gift he lets you take his gold," Ellen said. "The damaged hat is a small price to pay, I should think."

Ellen's observation annoyed. "I should think of it as just a minor trial and tribulation?"

Ellen nodded, but then I laughed. "I've made a pun." Mary scrubbing a pan beside her looked confused. "A minor miner," I said. "I might forgive him for giving me such fun with words."

I took my share of the gold Carrie and I recovered to a jeweler in Virginia City, a mile down Alder Gulch, and had a little ring made. I thought about giving it to Carrie but wasn't sure it was something she might like. She'd always spent her gold dust on food. I decided I'd just wear the ring when my father wasn't about.

I DON'T REMEMBER that Peter Ronan ever came to the establishment. But men well-known began to dine with us. A lawyer. A sheriff recently elected. A judge sent to preside over a trial—law and order arriving. An eastern investor. I suspect it was their presence that allowed the establishment to continue even after my father was told of it when he returned. Their presence—and the steady income Ma Anne handed him.

What was certain was that we women were an attraction, especially Ellen, who found a regular admirer in William Tiernan. Ellen barely reached his chest, he was so tall and she so small. He had a big black beard and owned the "upper discovery claim," as it was known, in another nearby gulch. I watched with wonder how Ellen blushed and fluttered when William came for supper. Ma also let him be the last one to leave, he and Ellen sitting at the table talking while Mary and I cleaned up and Ma prepared for the next day's meals. We were their chaperones. Which, after Christmas Day, 1863, weren't needed when Ellen and William were married, the first wedding in Virginia City.

Ellen began her married life in some chagrin because my father disapproved. Not of her choice. William was a hard worker and had plans to put his earnings into valley land where they could have a farm with "cattle and kids."

"You are not my pa," Ellen told my father when he objected to her wedding. "You've been as one to me, good and kind and caring. But now I'm old enough and I have prayed my prayers and feel certain William is the one meant for me. We'll have an official to speak the words, maybe the newly elected sheriff or a traveling judge. And when a priest comes through, we can affirm our vows."

"It's the way it was done years ago." I spoke in her defense. "Large gatherings, sometimes for six hundred or more when a priest came to fur trappers' gatherings. Our teacher tells us. A marriage blessing for the men and their Indian wives, years after they spoke their vows in front of family or even just the two of them. It's the frontier way, Pa."

"Don't *you* get any ideas, Mollie. You'll do as I permit. Honor your father and mother, don't you forget." He actually shook his finger at me.

How I missed Ellen though she was but a few miles away. She was in a married world, one I could not pretend to be a part of. The world Ma Anne and my father possessed. A world without me.

THE DAY I FIRST HEARD his voice at the establishment, I knew it sounded familiar. My skin prickled when he commented on my hair. Then someone called him "Bart." *We have a road agent among us.* He was always polite and only once alluded to that day when he had attempted to rob my father by commenting about the nourishment of having fresh "bacon and eggs." My father wasn't around to hear that said, but Bart looked at me with knowing eyes, wondering, I suspect, if I remembered or what I'd do if I did. He was charming. Charm could get one welcomed into many different settings. Danger had its intrigue, though I'd never say any such thing to my father.

TWO THINGS CAUSED our lives to change a year after Ellen's wedding. The gold discovery of Last Chance Gulch was one. It drew hundreds to an area in western Montana Territory that gave up one of the largest payouts in all the country. We didn't know that then. It began as just a rumor about four miners who were headed back east, defeated, when they stopped at a promising stream. "Let's give it one last chance," they supposedly told each other and did, striking it big.

But I think equally important was my father's decision to move us a few miles to Last Chance Gulch not just to service the new town but to shut down the establishment. "We are moving because of the rise of the vigilantes and my women being exposed to more hangings and citizen justice."

But I thought it was something more. He recognized Bart Davidson one evening when he took a meal with my father at the table. I had told him who I thought Bart was, though I had no proof, of course. I said nothing about the night he'd touched my hair. The rumors that Bart might be the chief road agent—who could get vicious with his victims—had reached my father's ears during his deliveries. He looked alarmed when I told him who I thought that cunning road agent might be.

Earlier that evening, I had presented my after-supper recitation, this time Chief Black Hawk's farewell speech followed by a love sonnet.

"Such a beautiful voice." Bart cast his smile upon me as I finished. He leaned back in his chair, chewing on a toothpick he'd whittled from a stick. "Spoken by an angel with such glorious hair."

I saw my father's face turn red above his beard.

That evening Mary and I overheard him telling Ma that he didn't think it proper for his daughter to "parade in front of grown men, performing Shakespeare's sonnets."

"I don't see the harm," Ma said. "We're all right there, seeing everything. It gives Mollie some pleasure."

"She can find pleasure by helping in the kitchen. It's safer for her there." He'd paused. "In fact, I don't think we should have the establishment anymore at all. I can support us. No need for you to bring in money."

But I saw it as something more. My father didn't like the compliments Ma's cooking garnered. He felt protective of Mary, too, and how the men enjoyed Mary's sometimes raucous patter back and forth as she served the miners their coffee. And he surely didn't warm to my receiving praise from other than him—rare as that was. The men were treating us as grown women. That's what worried him.

And soon Last Chance Gulch became our newest home, about

one hundred miles north from Alder Gulch. Ma said that she hoped it would be our last, that gulch-hopping was taxing.

"I have to go where the gold shows up," Pa defended.

"Why not stay and run the store and have Patrick get the supplies here," she told him. She set his venison stew in front of him, with flaky biscuits on a side plate.

"He's just a boy and it's dangerous work." He dipped a biscuit into the gravy.

Patrick kept his head lowered while he ate and let them talk about him as though he wasn't there.

IN OUR NEW HOME, Dange the dog stayed close but Puddin had taken to roaming, sometimes bringing us plunder. The dead mice Ma didn't mind. But a child's mitten? A paintbrush? "Who do these belong to?" She shook her head, putting the items into a basket. "We own a thieving cat."

"We'd better not let the vigilantes know," I said.

Ma frowned. "Let's not joke about them."

A new group had formed and once again were meting out their justice. My father said miners had nothing to fear if they were honest. There was a sheriff now and a territorial judge too.

Bart Davidson, though, was still in our world and shocked us by being named by the new sheriff as his deputy. We could read about the activities in the *Montana Post*, a newspaper started by one of my teachers. A rival paper—the *Daily Gazette*—carried the stories too. I hadn't heard if Mr. Ronan had turned to journalism and was covering these Montana activities, though Ma said he too had left Alder Gulch to discover his Last Chance. Secretly, I thought the frightening work of the vigilantes or the crimes they were hoping to suppress would keep my father close to home, to protect his women. But they didn't. I never wondered how it was Ma knew of Mr. Ronan's latest move.

PETER RONAN APPEARED one evening while Pa was in town. I answered his knock on the door of our house on Clore Street. He held a letter from Mother Vincent of the Leavenworth, Kansas, Sisters of Charity. "I wrote asking if they might come north to start a school."

"From Leavenworth?" Pa put his newspaper down, picked up his pipe.

"I have some history with the Sisters." Peter sank into the horsehair chair beside Pa. "I was jailed for running a southern-leaning newspaper a few years back, in Kansas. The Sisters brought me food and even did my laundry while I was jailed. I think they had something to do with my release. I thought you might be interested in a school, James. For your girls."

He nodded toward me and later said it was the first time he began to see me not as a schoolgirl but as a young lady worthy of more notice in my white smock dress, embroidered by my own hand.

I noticed him differently that day too. Warmth from his eyes spread through me. He had the longest eyelashes. My heart beat a little faster each time he looked at me while my father prattled on about a proper school where I wouldn't have to go to the States. My father never noticed that new bridge forming over him between Peter Ronan and his daughter.

The Sisters started their school many months later, and Pa's name was on the letter requesting that two priests be sent to the Helena mission too. That's what folks were calling the gulch now—Helena. We were all there when the first mass was said in the little Catholic church built at the top of that Last Chance gulch.

Later, with neighbors—some who were not Catholic—I'd walk there to vespers and we'd sing together in the choir. I think now that such activities were a cloak that kept me from the harshness of the vigilantes and the mining life. I was surrounded instead by the kinds of people who turned to faith in times of peril. Peter Ronan was such a man who, with my father, affirmed that if I followed the commandments, all would be well. According to my father, I was to pay special attention to the fourth one, "Honor thy father and thy mother." And so I would. Still, I began to imagine Peter Ronan as a Prince Charming, a mix of fairy tale and faith.

WE'D BEEN A YEAR in Helena when I overheard my father telling Ma, "I can keep ye here, but to do it, I've got to leave for a longer time. There, there." My stepmother must have been crying. "I've already signed the contract with the railroad." She said something I couldn't hear, and my father answered. "Could be a year or more before I see your face again."

It disturbed me that my father could just announce things without ever consulting Ma or his offspring. If the father in "Rumpelstiltskin" had conferred with his daughter, maybe she and her family wouldn't have been in such peril. But it was the way of things. Wives did what their husbands told them to do. Daughters did the same.

We spoke our goodbyes. I no longer cried when he left. But each time I watched the wagon head out the road—Dange now running beside—I was reminded that life was fragile and a parent must do whatever he could to keep his family, if not together, then at least believing they were whole despite the miles between them. I stroked old Puddin, knowing it wouldn't be long before he too would leave us. I was tired of loss and took to practicing my sonnets in front of the mirror, planning my future on the stage.

Our days were different with Pa gone and no hope that he'd return for a year or more. I missed the activity of the establishment and cooking for a dozen every day. We didn't even have Dange to chase from the house when he snuck inside. Ma sewed, patched miners' jeans and shirts. I expanded my stitching, too, making dresses for Kate and me and Ma. We subscribed to ladies' magazines that we carried in our store. At Christmas, missing our da, I sang a solo at the Christmas pageant and warmed at the compliments that followed, especially from Peter Ronan. He lingered outside the church and Ma invited him to Christmas dinner. Thus continued a fantasy I nurtured about that man and me. A schoolgirl play forming in my mind that didn't include my father.

SEVEN

STEALING

In the year my father was gone—1866—a neighbor gave us a black puppy. We had it only long enough to have someone take it from us.

After searching one morning and calling until I was hoarse, I told Ma, "I'm going to go to the *Rocky Mountain Gazette* and post an ad."

"Brute probably just ran off." Mary tied on her work apron. She proved a natural at the counter at our store even though she wasn't supposed to be working in "the trades." My father might not be happy when he learned of it, but she wasn't his daughter. She could get by with contrariness. "I'm not sure with all the strays around that anyone would actually steal a dog."

"They might take this one," I said. "He has a distinctive look."

I walked the mile or so to the booming business district. Survey offices, an apothecary, eating houses, two hotels, saloons, and other stores seemed to appear overnight. Hammers pounded on the theater being built for winter entertainment. And more people called the town Helena, named after the hometown of one of the founding miners, Saint Helena, Minnesota.

The newspaper office was in a building on the corner. Puddin followed me, sniffing the September air and disappearing around piled garbage to look at various treasures along the way. I walked in the office and there sat Peter Ronan.

Something inside me smiled, though I don't think my face did. He looked up from his desk where he'd been writing and said, "Good morning, Mollie. What can I do for you?" Bits of paper peppered the floor. End cuttings, I decided, of the latest issue.

I blurted it out, sounding like a mere child. "I've lost my puppy."

"Have you." His kind eyes held no mirth. When he combed his mustache with his fingers, I noticed that he didn't wear an ostentatious ring made out of a nugget or a showy necklace formed of gold as many successful miners did.

I should give him that ring. I made from his sluice box.

"That must be awful." He stood as though I was a lady.

"He was stolen. At least I think he was."

He sat down again and set aside what he'd been working on. He asked for a description and wrote while I talked. I gave him all the details. The puppy's black color, his size smaller than a raccoon, his fur fluffy with white markings only on his tail. "And he recently had a bath. I think he's a Labrador. I've seen pictures of them."

"We'll see what we can do." His blue eyes held mine.

I didn't really want to leave.

"Did you get that hat I messed up in the sluice box taken care of?" he asked, allowing the departure to be prolonged.

"Ah, you remember. Yes. And I should apologize for my outrage. My stepmother noted that it was your property Carrie and I were . . ." I didn't want to say stealing from him since he knew we did it.

"Ravishing?" he offered.

"That seems not quite right." I paused, a finger to my lip. "Pilfering, maybe?"

"Pinching? Nicking?"

He plays a word game. "Nicking will do." I smiled. "Though you were only trying to clean up the last bits that the earth gave up. You've left that claim?"

"It played out and my brother had enough to tend to his family and I had enough to invest in another newspaper. This is my second."

"You said the first was in Leavenworth."

"I'm humbled you remember that."

"I eavesdrop," I said. "And I have a good memory." I felt my face grow warm. *Pride is a sin.*

"I think my placer days are over and I'm plunging into printing. Got a couple of partners, so I'm not on my own." He fiddled with a pencil. His fingers were ink stained. "Have you heard word from your father? How are things going in Utah with his railroad contract?"

"It hasn't all been good. He wrote that on the way he met some men who knew him who asked why he'd sold out his store back in Alder Gulch. He tried to find the man he'd left to run it, and the scoundrel had sold all the stock and headed downriver. Pa went after him but never found a shadow of him anywhere, nor of his money."

Peter Ronan shook his head. "This country is full of thieves. I'm glad he's got the railroad contract even though I miss seeing him around."

"We do too." I was probably taking up Peter's valued time, though he made no mention of it. "I hope things go well for you," I said.

"And you. That you find your puppy."

With reluctance, I headed back up the steep street. It felt good to be taken seriously by this man.

Ma showed me the newspaper the next day, and there was a paragraph chastising whoever had stolen the unique black puppy of Mollie Sheehan and to be certain to return it. "See, he thinks it was stolen."

"He's just being a good newspaperman, reporting as his interviewee told the story," Mary said. She'd leaned over my shoulder to read.

Whatever the reason, I was certain the thief would return the dog with such an eloquent admonition. But more, I wondered when I might have occasion to talk with Mr. Ronan again.

Puddin gave me the chance when a pencil—very much like the one Mr. Ronan had fiddled with—landed on our doorstep. "Our thieving cat," Ma said.

So of course, I had to return it and apologize.

But Peter wasn't at the *Gazette*'s office. "I'll tell him you were here, Miss Sheehan," his partner, Mr. Maginnis, said.

"Please thank him for running the paragraph. I'm sure it'll bring results."

"We aim to please," his partner said. He looked at me for a moment before adding, "I think Peter especially hopes to please you."

My face felt hot and I worked those words over in my mind as I left. I wondered what they could mean. Wanting to please me because I was the daughter of his friend? I thought to ask my stepmother, but something kept me from it. I could cherish the fantasy that this learned man with kind eyes, whose presence made me happy, cared about me. Just me. I didn't want reality to tangle up the story I was building in my head.

WINTER WITH ITS STINGING COLD and brazen winds and snow made everything we did more work. I took on the task of chopping wood to fit the firebox while Mary helped in the store. Ma shoveled snow and the cabin smelled of wet wool drying near the fire.

"I think we deserve a little outing now and then," Ma Anne told us one evening after a washday that demanded everyone's hard labor.

"A picnic." Kate clapped her hands. "In the snow."

"Come spring, yes. But for we women of this house, we will go to a dance." She tapped Kate's nose. "Your father wouldn't approve if I went alone, so we'll all attend. Besides, it's good exercise." We'd read about keeping healthy with stretches and bends. We'd laughed, wondering about women with so little to do they had to plan to move. "Let them survive a laundry day," Mary said. "That'll get their hearts pumping."

My father had taken me and my stepmother to dances in the past. I learned the squares, as some were called, the touching of men and women during them sanctioned, being arm to arm. Sometimes the callers had two men make a chair of their forearms that a woman sat on while they spun in circles. Sweat beaded on their brows while hair ribbons flared out and laughter abounded. They weren't the chaste reels mentioned in the ladies' magazines, though there'd sometimes be waltzes that slowed the pace.

Mary and Kate came, too, and we took turns looking after our littlest sister until she fell asleep beside the other youngsters in the corner of the dance hall, sleeping in a giant bed made of quilts. With so few women in Helena, I was approached by men to be a partner. The first few times we attended, I looked around for Peter Ronan but didn't see him. Perhaps he wasn't the dancing kind. He had a paper to get out three times a week and might have preferred sleep. But there were others there to treat me like a lady, and I enjoyed the attention, my long hair swinging in a single braid across my back. Cousin Ellen and William sometimes arrived through deep snows, and they'd stay with us a few days afterward. Other times, there'd be a meal served early in the morning to send people on their weary way. Ma often brought her cinnamon rolls to share. It was a way to spruce up winter, take us into spring. We wore costumes for the Saint Patrick's Day dance that even visiting priests attended.

At one of the last dances before spring work took away the musicians and the dancers, I chattered with Ellen at the punch bowl. She'd been "agile" keeping miners' money bags inside her mattress, charging interest until those men could take their wealth to the nearest bank in Salt Lake. We Sheehans were a resourceful lot.

"Will you be my partner, Miss Sheehan?"

I turned to the charming voice. It was Bart Davidson. "Well, I—"

"She's promised this dance to me."

A nervous laugh escaped me as I put my hand in Peter's out-stretched palm and turned my back on Bart. The music began. Ma had a partner in that square too. We do-si-doed and faced the sides across from the men and Ma smiled her approval. We danced a half dozen squares before the fiddler and the caller took a break. I expected Mr. Ronan to bow and make his way outside for fresh air but he didn't. He took my elbow and escorted me to the punch bowl again. "A gentleman always returns a lady to the place where he first encountered her," he said.

"That would be in your news office."

"That would be your father's cabin long ago in Virginia City."

"Would it? I'm surprised you'd remember me. I was just a child."

"A very determined one as I recall." He looked past me.

I turned and saw that Bart Davidson wasn't there anymore. (Soon he wouldn't be around at all, his corruption bringing about his trial and a hanging.)

Peter brought my thoughts back. "But I was thinking more of this evening."

"Oh, of course." Dancing squares required little talking, for which I was grateful. But now, the old shyness threatened.

"Did you ever get your puppy back?"

I shook my head, then, "Did you get your pencil? My cat's a thief."

He laughed, reached around me to get a donut from a plate piled high, and I caught the scent of him, a cologne of perspiration and ink. "I did. I was sorry to have missed you."

"And I, you." *Is this how Snow White flirted?*

"Would you consider going for a ride with me, Miss Sheehan? I could get a wagon or maybe you have a horse?"

"My father has one. He's kept at the Henderson ranch."

"Sunday afternoon, could I come by?"

"I'll have to ask my stepmother."

"I already have. She said if you were inclined, it would be fine with her. She mentioned you have a mind of your own."

OUR COURTSHIP BEGAN that simply. I was fourteen, he was twenty-four. In those days, age really didn't matter. My father had been ten years older than my mother at their marriage. Our first ride out toward Spring Meadow Lake eased us into conversation. We could talk of horses and deer we watched cross our path. I had my mother's silk parasol with me to ease against the sun that could be hot in spring. I was careful to wear gloves and long sleeves to keep from burning like a commoner.

Peter brought a book. I'd packed a picnic lunch of cucumber sandwiches, dried peaches, and big jugs of water, with rock candy for sweets. I'd had Ma bind my hair in ribbons crisscrossed to keep it from blowing all over, contained, to flow like a long baguette down my back.

We'd spoken of our pasts—mine so uninteresting, his so intriguing. And then he'd gotten the book out of his vest pocket. "Your da likes 'Lady of the Lake.'"

I bristled with the mention of my father. I wasn't sure why.

"Byron's work too. I like his sentiments. Don Juan's exploits, his references to heroes. He fought in the war in Greece. And there's a song of an affair ending." I dropped my eyes. *Why am I chattering so?*

"'When We Two Parted.'" Peter nodded. "That's a sad poem. I never liked it. I don't like separations."

"But there is emotion in them, and the hope for a reunion. It reminds one that they're alive. Juliet's 'Parting is such sweet sorrow' is sweet only because she knows she'll be seeing Romeo again." The romantic in me was pontificating. *What do I know of partings?* I was pretending to be wise while he looked in the book for the page he wanted.

"Separations are even worse between people who love each other, not just between parents or friends or even leaving a landscape," I said. I'd surprised myself by bringing up the word "love" in conversation with him or any man.

The sun beat down and I got the umbrella out to shade us. "Lady of the Lake" was the first poem Peter ever read to me. After that, we took turns sharing poems and talking about them, my head speaking of regional affairs while my heart pounded, feelings I'd never known before racing through my veins.

He'd brought along a copy of his newspaper. "It's not a daily yet, but I have plans. One of our partners up and quit within the first week, though. Set us back."

"My stepmother has kept up the subscription," I said. "I read all four pages."

"Maybe you would write a piece or two for us."

"What about?" I couldn't imagine what I had to offer.

"A book review."

"That I could do."

"Or a review of the plays performed at the theater." He leaned back, his arms behind his head.

"It would be a reason to go to the performances." Imagine having a reason to disappear inside a play. Thinking of making a little money, I asked, "Would you pay me?" I squinted into the sun, shifted the umbrella.

"Of course. A workman's worth his wage." He motioned for me to join him. He didn't put his arm around me. We lay side by side, separated, hands clasped upon our chests. It reminded me of when my mother and I had watched clouds beneath the bending skies. I blinked back tears. I felt so safe.

"You could write about your experiences as a young woman in a mining town."

"I met Bart Davidson once."

"Did you?"

"He sometimes ate at our establishment. But he nearly robbed us once too. And one time, when Carrie Crane and I looked through peepholes into a saloon, he caught us." Peter sat up, resting on one elbow. I saw concern in his face. "He didn't do anything. He touched my hair."

"Your pa must have been furious."

"Oh, he never knew. Doesn't know. I won't be writing about that." I laughed. A magpie jabbered in the nearby alder tree. "My father thinks I should open a school, put all my learning to work, so he writes to my stepmother. But I just like the reading, learning new things."

"You'd be good as a teacher I should think."

"I'd have to pretend every day that I knew what I was doing," I said. "Deceive the students into thinking I knew more than they did. My own teachers that I love, Professor Dimsdale, for example—who edited your rival, *The Montana Post*—he not only held more knowledge than we students but knew how to impart it in such a way that we cared about knowing too. I'm not sure I have the skills to do that."

"But it would please your da?"

"Yes, I'm sure it would. He *wouldn't* like for me to do what I might really want to do, go on the stage."

"You fancy being an actor, do you?"

"It's how I'd have to think of myself as a teacher. Put on a mask of confidence, impart someone else's words."

He didn't say anything for a time. He'd lain back down, stared at the sky. A bumblebee dropped by, landed on the coverlet I'd placed over the food. "Only do it if it pleases you," he said. "'To thine own self be true—'"

"'And it must follow, as the night the day, thou canst not then be false to any man.'"

"*Hamlet*, act 1, scene 3. A father's blessing to his son, on how to behave while the boy heads off to the university."

"Or maybe his daughter," I said. "If girls went to university."

"I'd want any daughter of mine to go on to higher education," Peter said. "Wouldn't you?"

"Yes. My father says he'll send me to the States for schooling, when he has the money to do that."

"You'd leave our happy territory?" He got up on his elbow again and looked at me. "I should miss you," he said.

Something in the way he spoke the words warmed me. I looked into those kind blue eyes. "And I should miss you as well." Despite my inexperience in affairs of the heart, it was in that moment that I knew that Peter Ronan had captured mine. He kissed me then, chaste and gentle as a breeze upon a lily.

And thus began my struggle to honor my father while falling in love with his best friend.

EIGHT

MIRROR, MIRROR ON THE WALL

I'd been in school the day we learned of Mr. Lincoln's assassination and my chums had pulled their skirts up and danced a little jig. "Come on, Mollie. You're from Kentucky. You must be glad that Mr. Lincoln is gone," one of the students said.

We lived in Virginia City then, before Helena burst out of the hillsides into her own. I joined in, reflecting their glee. When I told my father about our schoolgirl dance, he admonished me. "Oh, Mollie, no. Mr. Lincoln's death is a tragedy. I care about the South, but I am always for the Union and was for Mr. Lincoln." I learned then we were Union Democrats, something Peter told me he was too. Their politics joined them.

Shame had washed over me at my disappointing my father.

But the war was over now, my father's railroad contract finished, and I was wiser and able to resist the push of pals, not simply do what someone asked. Unless the request came from my father.

MY PA CONTINUED his departures and my ma nurtured my independence. I came to appreciate a benefit of my father's absences. Peter visited our cabin often, chatting with Ma Anne, who like me enjoyed his company. He chopped wood for us, fixed a leather hinge that had come loose on the back door. She always thanked him for his help, but she also saw what passed between us in the looks we shared.

"Your father won't be pleased. That doesn't mean you shouldn't allow your feelings to grow for Peter. But you must be aware." Ma Anne had sat me down after Peter left one evening. He'd taken an oyster meal with us, and I picked up handwork, a dress Ma helped me cut out and now stitched together. "Be prepared. I've always thought a woman must know her own way and have the courage to walk it."

"But Pa likes Peter."

"And that can have its complication too. Are you ready to fit?" She motioned toward the material in my lap. I nodded and stood. With care she lowered the cloth over my head, lifted the bulk of my hair, and started adjusting the precious pins that marked the seams.

"Do you think I can convince him that I'm old enough to know my own mind?"

"I'm not sure," she said. "Your father is very attached to you."

"But he has you," I said.

"He does." She paused. "Wait a moment while I check the stew I've started for tomorrow." Though we didn't have an establishment anymore, we still ate well and often served neighbors and friends, including Peter. I once teased him that he joined us for Ma's cooking rather than for my company.

"It's not a deterrent," he'd said, winking.

Ma returned and moved the pins, holding them between her lips the way seamstresses do.

"I was thinking I might start that school Pa is always encouraging," I continued. "He might see me as more grown-up, able to make my own way. I'm sixteen."

"I can't imagine anything worse than running a school," Mary said. She and Kate were playing a board game where my seven-year-old sister could spin the teetotum. And when the sphere covered with numbers stopped, she'd read the top one that told her how many moves to make. We didn't have dice; my father said it was too much like gambling. He said life was so much of a gamble, one didn't need to make it a game.

"It isn't what I'd want to do, the teaching part," I told Mary. "But it would prove to Da I'm an independent woman, responsible and all that. And maybe it is my calling, to teach, until I'm old enough to marry."

"It's a respectable profession," Ma agreed. "It's just that, somehow, I don't see you enjoying it. Speaking in front of others, that I can imagine. But you can't lecture all day or stand behind a character, like an actor on the stage." I blinked. She knew more about me than I thought she did. "In teaching, one has to be genuine and think of others. It was my teachers' care for me as much as what they knew that gave me gain in school." She sighed. "I wish I'd been able to stay in school longer."

I felt a pinch of censure in her words, as though I didn't pay attention to others as I might. Her words reminded me that once she'd come into my room while I was practicing a portion of a Shakespeare soliloquy and had gotten lost in my own image before the mirror: pretending to put color on my lips, raising my eyebrows, tossing my hair. Childish, really.

"Vanity," she'd said. "It's not attractive, Mollie."

I looked at her reflection. I'd been so absorbed, I didn't even see her until she spoke.

"Remember the queen in 'Sleeping Beauty'?" she said. "The mirror told the truth—perhaps because it tired of seeing the queen and having to answer her question over and over. The queen went wild the day the mirror had to tell the truth—that she was no longer the 'fairest of them all.'"

Ma Anne had told my father that night that she was worried

about the pride I showed in my person. He'd rebuked me, and said vanity was a menial sin for which I should seek absolution. But without a priest around, how could I? Instead, I carried the weight of disappointing him.

Just remembering, I felt my face get hot.

"I'd have to prepare for many readiness levels," I said, lowering my arms to get the sleeves pinned correctly. "I don't think I'd have time to declaim much. But I would have to pretend that I liked being there when I'd rather be on the stage." I said it like a tease, to make her smile, but she didn't. I did notice others, but I compared myself to them, envied them, wanted their ease in interactions.

She motioned for me to raise my arms, and she carefully lifted the dress up over my head. "We can use the money if you decide to teach. The mail did not come through again, so your father's allotment didn't arrive. And there was another robbery on the road."

I wondered if it was Bart.

"The supplier for the store must have been held up too." Mary moved her game piece. "The storeroom is getting sparse." She'd been keeping time, as she called it, with a farrier who was teaching her to nail shoes onto horses and mules. She was a strong girl and not very tall, features her beau said were perfect for horseshoeing. She had nuptials in her future. And she paid more attention to what was happening in the store, how much things cost, keeping track of what customers wanted and urging the manager Pa had hired to order those items in. She knew her numbers well.

"Shelves always get low through the winter," Ma said.

"I don't get to count the day's take," Mary said. "But it seems like we should have ordered in several things that never arrived."

"I'll write to James about allowing you to do more in the store, Mary."

I wasn't as skilled in numbers as Mary was. I would have to learn. I'd be forced to be a student in my own school. But it would give me reason to spend more time with words and exchange books and ideas with Peter Ronan.

I WOULD THINK of my school teaching as a play in three acts.

Act 1: I had Peter make up an announcement for the paper about the school.

Mollie Sheehan, well-read daughter of James Sheehan, successful freighter and owner of Last Chance Gulch's premier store, to open school. Return interest to the Gazette, Box 12.

In short order I had ten students ranging in age from several four- and five-year-olds on up to ages ten and twelve and even one as old as me, sixteen. I got slates from my father's store, and a house my father owned next door wasn't rented, so I commandeered it for my school. I set the fees at $1.25 per pupil each week.

Act 2: I prepared lessons, pretending I knew how my teachers had done it, but I wasn't as organized nor had I really studied how they did what they did. I hadn't paid as much attention to subjects like geography and math as I had to reading and writing. But I applied myself, and with Ma's and Mary's help, offered arithmetic problems that challenged but didn't frustrate. Parents paid in gold dust and seemed satisfied with their students' progress.

Act 3: The fun parts. We had a full house for the Christmas play we'd rehearsed for and performed. The children generated their own script, and even the reticent ones shone and hugged me when they succeeded. I had hoped my father would make it home for that event and for the celebration of the Christ child's birth. He'd missed last Christmas. I longed to tell him about the success of the school and that he'd been right about my being a good teacher.

SNOW HALTED SCHOOL in the new year, making it too difficult for children to attend, and the little stove didn't push out enough heat for comfort anyway. But school-less days meant parents and children, dance hall girls and bachelors held oyster parties and took sleigh rides in the valley. So did Peter and I, once turning a sleigh over with squeals and laughter, pitching us into a snowbank. Those in other sleighs stopped and pushed us back onto the runners, and we were off again. And on those rides, we'd sit bundled beneath buffalo robes, the night a chaperone that kept us chaste against the cold. And then, sitting side by side, Peter put the reins in their keepers, and he turned to me and lowered his face to mine. My heart welcomed him. I wanted to unmuff my hands and reach up to hold his face. He kissed my nose, inhaled deeply. "I'd better get you home."

"It's only my nose that's cold. My lips are warm."

"They are." Then, like the Prince Charming I knew he was, he kissed me deeper, as a man would kiss a woman. My father never entered my thoughts. Peter pulled away. "Ah, Mollie," he said. "Now I must surely get you home and protect you from the elements. And me."

PEOPLE LIVING HIGHER UP in the gulch would ride down on spruce limbs, using them like sleds, laughing all the way. When we decorated for a Valentine's party, there were several large spruce limbs we hadn't used, and the oldest student asked if I'd like to ride the limb.

"It seems scary," I said, but I liked that the older students were willing to approach their teacher and invite me to join the fun.

"I'll support you on one side and we'll get another for the other side. You can stand up. We can catch you if you fall."

"Why not," I said and stepped on the limb.

Little Jules, the youngest boy in my school, appeared at my side. "I can hold you, Miss Sheehan."

The bigger boys laughed.

I glared at them and knelt in front of Jules. "It might be dangerous. If I survive, I'll do another and you can be my guardian then. I'll walk back up the hill and find you, all right?" He lowered his head and nodded agreement. The larger and older lad then stepped in front of him, and he stumbled out of the way.

The boys on either side of me held my mittened hands, then began to run down the snow-covered hill. The spruce-limb sled whizzed past children hauling real sleds uphill. I saw others dragging limbs, but they were blurs. True to their commitment, my big students didn't let me fall. I was exhilarated by the racing wind. At the very bottom I plunged into the arms of Peter Ronan.

"Whoa!"

It was the first time he had ever held me fully, not sideways, his arms around my shoulder, nor side by side as in the sleigh. There'd been no repeat of those kisses that took my breath away. But here, out in the open surrounded by students and other sledders, he held me. And there I was all bundled in a bear coat, the fuzzy fur turned inside out to be against my body, and only my pink cheeks exposed to the elements.

I was laughing so hard and enjoying Peter's arms around me with such glorious pressure that I failed to see my father standing there beside him until he spoke.

"Where's a father's greetin', lass?"

"You're back." I left Peter's arms and moved into my father's. Later I'd recall how reluctantly I made that transition. "Oh, Da, we've missed ye," I said, the Irish lilt rising to the front.

"Just so, Mollie. Anne said you were decorating. I didn't think you'd be doing foolish things like standing up to take the hill."

"My students took good care of me, didn't you?" Both boys nodded, then headed off, worried from my father's tone that they might be in trouble. "Thank you for that bracing ride," I called after them. I looked for Jules but didn't see him. He'd apparently wandered off, maybe to find his own limb to sit on and slide down.

My father put my arm through his and turned me toward our home.

"When did you get back? Are you able to stay for good now? How was your journey?"

71

"Just today. Not for good. The latest journey was fraught with trials, but God was with us, Patrick and me." He changed the subject. "Anne tells me you've started a school. Good for you." He chattered on, and I realized he had not seen the intensity of Peter's embrace nor my response. Peter was just his friend who walked on the other side of me.

That was how Peter came to join us for St. Valentine's Day dinner later that evening. We heard my father tell his tales, granted him the honor he was due for being with us. Patrick had returned as well. And that evening, Mary's beau, Jacob, joined us too—a big, burly man as tall as Peter and much rounder.

My father had brought ready-made valentines he distributed to each of "his girls." He also supplied the store to sell them. Kate loved hers, a blotch of color small enough to hold in her small palm. Ma smiled at hers and kissed my father on the top of his head. "Thank ye, James." Her face glowed with the joy of his presence. The aroma of the Irish stew Ma had prepared filled the happy room. Puddin lay curled beside the stove.

I treasured the valentine my father gave me—but not as much as the one Peter slipped to me while Ma and Pa and the others chattered and went out to watch for shooting stars.

Peter had my valentine printed at the newspaper. It was a heart that he had carefully placed red bars across, to look like the heart was in jail. By lifting up each bar, it loosened a puffy material beneath. I started to lift the little bars when he motioned for me to stop, nodding toward my father who, having stepped back inside, handed cigars out to the men. "Patrick, Peter, time for a smoke."

So it was alone, later, in the privy beneath the lantern glow when I lifted all the other valentine bars and inside found a gold necklace with a tiny heart. On the card he'd written: "*You've made my heart your captive, Valentine. Please wear this to set me free.*" He'd signed it with "*Love, Peter.*"

The card I made for Peter included a portion of the Irish lace that had been my mother's. I'd thought of her all the while I made it, imagining her approval—that I had a profession, a way of contributing to the family. That I was a good daughter as I remembered her asking me to be. "Your father will need you, Mollie. Do your duty." But most of all, I thought she'd be pleased that I'd found my truest love, the way she had found hers. I wasn't really giving away the last piece of Irish lace of my mother's. For when the time came to marry, I knew I'd get it back. Peter was my one true love and surely he'd save that valentine just as I saved his. I'd wear the necklace from then on. And we'd live happily ever after.

NINE

LESSONS LEARNED

During the month that the school was closed for weather and my father was with us, we walked to tend the mules like old times. He told me more stories of close calls, one in which Dange had failed to warn him and he'd been accosted while in his tent. He never saw his assailant, but my father had a knife, and he stabbed and stabbed through the canvas into the man until he left him— and any assets—behind. "I went into the nearest town to tell them that I might have killed a man. At least wounded someone. They said there'd be no charges."

"Were you hurt?"

"Mostly bruised. And carrying the weight of someone who might have died at my hands."

"But it was self-defense."

"I'd like to think so."

"Perhaps you could speak with Father Van Gorp."

He'd turned to look at me. "That's a good idea. What would I do without my wise little girl? Ah, Mollie, I miss my girls so much when I'm gone." He squeezed my shoulder. "You most of all."

I gave the mule named Jade one of the carrots I'd brought and the other Gems mules came closer. My father stepped back and let me feed them and then we headed home. "I've been thinking, Mollie. We ought to have our pictures made. There's a photographer in Helena now. I could take your image with me that way. Yes, that's what we'll do."

"And Ma Anne and Kate and Mary too?"

"What? Oh, yes, of course. Such a kind heart, ye thinking of my having their images as well."

As much as I loved my father being home, I also found his presence a burden. I couldn't break away to ride with Peter, to talk over little trials at the school, to hear Peter read to me. I wondered if my father ought to be sharing his limited time back more with Ma Anne. I knew he was looking after his daughter, but still, it seemed he'd want to spend more private time with his wife, wouldn't he?

I suppose Peter and I could have just told him about our growing care for each other. Ma had accepted it and approved. But I think we both knew that my father would object. Our age difference the major factor. Or so I thought.

Now and then, Peter walked me home from school or he stopped by. He returned a book, exchanged another. Ma would invite him to stay for supper and he always did. My father seemed to enjoy his company as they spoke of politics, religion, and local affairs.

Neither Ma nor Mary nor even little Kate commented about when Peter and I had "stepped out." I held my breath through dinner discussions, the meals not as carefree as they'd once been as I worried about our relationship becoming a subject.

There were entertainments. My father took me to a lecture given by the famous General Thomas Francis Meagher, an Irish nationalist who traveled and gave lectures. "Won't you come too, Ma?" I asked.

"I'm sure you and your father will enjoy it," she'd said. Had he even asked her?

As a newspaperman, Peter was there, making notes in the back. The lecture inspired. The general spoke of passion for a cause.

"Do your duty," he had said. "As all men must." We went back-stage afterward, and I was thrilled to meet this man my father so admired. I thought Anne would have liked the fanfare too.

My father did invite Ma—and the rest of us—to the first winter dance of the season. The mines were shut down by snow and cold and Pa was home. Ma beamed with my father as her partner, his dimples marking grins that spoke the same about his being able to dance with her. He didn't notice how often Peter and I were partnered. If I wasn't with Peter, I was dancing with my da or at the punch bowl, serving others.

"Good to see you back, James," one of the stalwarts of the dance hall told my father. He was a caller for the squares. Ma and Pa, Peter and I had stepped outside, joining several others already there, the crisp air chilling us of our dance perspiration. The stars above looked like jewels one could pluck and pop into a celestial basket. "Your girls were missing you," the square-dance caller continued. "'Tis good to see them with their preferred escorts."

"We should go back in." I took my father's arm.

"Oh, they liked their partners all right, but I never saw the grins they have with you here dancing with your missus and your daughters."

My father frowned, said, "Good to know. Yes, good to know."

We left soon after, Pa rushing us out the door. Back at the house, he ranted, stomped around the table we women sat at, heads bowed. "You went to dances. Without me? What were you thinking, woman." This to Anne. "You're responsible for these girls. And for yourself, to act like a wife and mother." He raised his eyes to the ceiling. "Holy heavens, what kind of damage to your reputation—and Mollie's and Mary's and even little Kate's—have you rendered here?"

"Kate rarely went," I said. "And when she did, she slept in the corner with the other children."

"Where you should have been," he snapped. "You're just a child, Mollie." He glared at Anne. "I hold you accountable for this disgrace."

She had tears on her cheeks, but she didn't defend herself, didn't say, "After all I've done to take care of your family and my Kate and your nieces; after how we survived making decisions—dozens— without you here to ask or direct; selling my sewing and mending when your currency didn't come through. Pleasantries like dancing, hearing music, laughing with one's neighbors, how can that be considered sinful?"

I didn't say it either, though I should have.

"Peter Ronan often saw us home," Ma finally said. "We were in no danger."

"Danger of losing your reputation, that's all. I'll thank Peter for his diligence, but I forbid you to attend dances without me. I shouldn't have to say it."

"I understand, Husband." She wiped her eyes.

I held my breath, hoping he wouldn't turn to me and say, "That goes for you as well, Miss Mollie Sheehan," though I knew it's what he intended.

When he and Anne headed to the second room where they went to bed, I breathed a sigh of relief.

"I bet you were waiting to see if he'd order you to stay home, too, to keep you from dancing with your Peter," Mary whispered while I brushed Kate's shiny hair.

"He'll expect Ma to be sure that I behave. I hope she might still see her way to let me be with Peter. At least he didn't forbid sleigh rides or horseback rides or picnics."

"Because he didn't know those were going on."

"Exactly." I slipped into bed, pulled the covers over my shoulder.

"So will you do what he wants even though he doesn't forbid it?" Mary donned her nightdress and crawled in, her weight making little Kate, in the middle, roll toward her.

I didn't answer. Ma was on my mind. I prayed that Pa would ease his temper toward her. She carried on without him with such grace, finding ways to keep us together while he was gone for months—years—with only letters now and then for reassurance. She was the perfect mate. My father failed to see it.

SPRING CAME AT LAST with wildflowers dotting the hillsides, the mountains white with snow so bright we squinted at their tops beneath blue skies. Yes, mud caked on our boots and melting snow streams cut down the gulch while miners went back to work filling their sluice boxes, sloshing gold in metal pans, taking out riches, defending their claims. Shootings happened. Hangings too. I was glad Peter had a safe occupation behind a desk.

My father and Patrick headed out once again too. No telling how long they'd be gone. I felt relief tempered with guilt. I'd be able to see Peter without the fear of my father intervening.

School was back in session and I had a better handle on arithmetic. Peter, Ma, and Mary had given me instruction. I tried to make a game of it with the younger students, using dominoes for counting and sticks for measuring tables. I got them to imagine how many cakes a table could hold. Kate sometimes came, but if paying students filled all the seats, she had to sit on the floor. Walking past a miner's camp, I saw a folding sort of chair and asked Mary if we could have them for sale at the store. Liking a problem to solve, she said she'd see what she could do. Kate soon had her own chair to bring to school.

My biggest challenge was introducing numbers to the younger children. Little Jules struggled to remember that one plus one made two, and the other sums as well. "It'll become easier when you've grown taller," I told him. Fortunately, he didn't ask what his height had to do with his memory. I just didn't want to see him discouraged. His parents were separated and I felt a special concern for the river of life he was on.

We had taken an afternoon recess where the boys rolled hoops and the girls stood in clusters, chattering. Five-year-old Jules came over and held my hand.

"You may take your toy horse from the cubby," I said, referring to the sluice-box-like structures I'd put in the back for children's precious things when they brought them to school by mistake.

"It ain't there no more."

"Isn't," I corrected. Then, "Something happened to your horse?" He nodded. "Did one of those big boys take it from you?" He lowered his eyes. "If they did, I'll get it back." I sounded fierce, but I wasn't sure how I'd find it.

"I'm tired, Miss Sheehan," he said after a bit. "May I go home?" He lived in the St. Louis Hotel with his mother. His father, the proprietor of the International Hotel, lived down the street.

It was early, but his leaving now would save me from teaching the youngest ones their numbers. I would hold the lesson until the next day when he was back. And it was a cold but sunny day. I considered letting all of school out early. But I had lessons to cover and assignments of recitations to hear, and so I soon called everyone back inside.

"Why don't you finish the day with us, Jules." He shook his head, then waved and wandered down the path.

I let him.

Once inside I made a little speech about stealing and thievery. "If any of you have Jules's wooden horse, I suggest you leave it in his box. I won't pursue who took it, but one of the great commandments is 'Thou shalt not steal.' I wouldn't want the wrath of God coming down on me for having violated that commandment. Just leave it where he can find it in the morning." I saw fidgeting and looks pass between students as I proceeded with the lessons.

I stayed later after all the children had gone home. It was easier for me to plan the next day without the distraction at our cabin. I'd prodded Kate to leave, and she had, carrying her little chair. I noticed Jules's wooden horse returned to its stable, satisfied I'd solved that problem. So it was dusk by the time I brought in the wood for the stove, should we need any the next day. Splitting wood was one of my duties, and mornings were always brisk, so I liked having a stack ready at my arrival. I locked the door and was startled by voices from behind me.

"Is Jules still here?" It was his father asking.

"Why, no. He said he wanted to go home. At least two, no three hours ago."

"He doesn't come," his mother said. She had a German accent. "He should arrive by now, *ja*. I thought his father takes him, but no."

I felt my heart start to pound. "We must look for him."

"We alert the neighbors."

"I'll—I'll get my ma and cousin, and ask if anyone has seen him. Maybe he took another path and you missed him."

"Ja, we asked up and down the road."

"Then the sheriff. He'll help, get up a search party. I'll go now."

The sheriff was out of town, but a deputy began gathering up people walking the streets as he strapped on his holster.

"What's happened?" Peter had seen me scurrying by his door and not even stopping. He caught up and fast-walked next to me.

"Jules Germain is missing. He left the school but didn't make it home."

"Maybe he's stopped to see a friend," Peter said. "How old is he?"

"Five. He's so young, Peter." I stopped. "I should have kept him at school." I saw Ma Anne and Mary ahead, so someone must have alerted them.

"Come," Peter directed. "Let's follow the usual trail and then branch out. I'll light the lanterns."

The night sky smelled of kerosene. People held their tins aloft, some carried torches made of straw and burning tar, the black smoke smelling like evil. Peter held my hand, and with others we formed a long line to try to cover every space. But the fallen trees, branches, and brambles proved daunting in the dark. The men conferred and decided to end the search and gather in the morning.

Peter walked me home, Ma and Mary behind us. I shivered.

Jules would be so cold. "Maybe a puppy found him and he curled up next to it to keep warm." I prayed for that.

But in the morning, my prayer was for his parents in their grief. Jules's body had been found a few feet in from the edge of a prospector's pond. It was well off his usual path. We'd never know if he got lost or just wanted to take another way home and stumbled and fell into the icy grave. It was a deep pond with no gradual incline to its depth.

"He was always being turned away," I said after Peter brought me the word. I'd canceled school so older students could assist in the search and had been helping Ma bring food to the searchers. It was high noon when they gathered, no longer a rescue; now a grieving. I thought of my own little brother dying his tragic oxen-trampling death. Grief grabbed at my throat.

Peter held me, right in front of others, as I wept. I didn't care who knew. Life was limited and one must love it while one can.

All the students attended the funeral at the St. Louis Hotel. We marched in two by two and around the casket hastily made. We sang, my own voice choking on the words. "I want to be an angel and with the angels stand / A crown upon my forehead, a harp within my hand." My mother's death came to me.

After the funeral, I gave Jules's little horse to his parents. They appeared to be comforting each other and thanked me for it. I didn't tell them that the toy had been missing. Privately I wondered if its loss had so discouraged little Jules that he had walked into that pond. I shared that fear with Peter, wondering if I should have anticipated such an ending to a small child's disappointments. Once, after my mother died, I had thought of doing such a thing to ease the knife-cut to my heart. My father had seen my despair and kept me close to him and gradually the pain eased. Or at least I carried the weight of it—with my father's help.

"It isn't your fault, Mollie."

"Isn't it? I didn't mind Jules leaving early that day. That was selfish of me."

"You encouraged him to stay, didn't you?" I nodded. "Kids have left early at other times, haven't they?"

"Yes. But Jules was so fragile."

"It was likely an accident." We stopped at a large rock and sat for a bit. "You allowed children to make choices. That's a good thing, Mollie." He handed me his handkerchief.

"The ten-year-olds are always asking to have more and longer recesses," I said, dabbing at my tears. "Especially the boys. And sometimes right after they've just come inside from one."

"You see." Peter smiled. "You're teaching independence and how to negotiate. They'll be lawyers and politicians one day. Wise parents. Which is good."

I failed to see any goodness in my teaching at that moment. But I savored this man's efforts to bring me comfort. Later that evening I made another decision. I wondered what my father would say when I told him I would close the school at the end of the term. I thought of it as the end of act 3. I'd pretended I knew how to teach, but all I'd done was act in a play without a happy ending.

TEN

THE TURNING POINT

My father said I could name the son born to him and Ma. I looked at Anne and she nodded as she held the infant in her arms. "James," I said. "For you, Pa. And Francis as his middle name, the same as General Meagher, your hero."

We called him Jimmy. He'd been born with a veil over his face, said to be a sign of greatness. "He comes to bring us joy," Ma told me. After the midwife removed the fragile film of skin from Jimmy's brow and cheeks, Ma Anne had it framed behind glass. Jimmy was special in her heart.

Special in my heart was Peter Ronan, who took me riding on a blustery autumn day and changed my life forever. I'd brought my mother's umbrella with us and rode my father's horse, a big sorrel named Buster who didn't mind the fluttering or flapping of the silk. We rode east into a broad valley away from the Continental Divide, a ridge that kept serious storms at bay. We'd ridden here before, making our way through wooded areas that opened into vistas that always marveled. We stopped beside Prickly Pear Creek to watch the water flow. There was no need to talk with Peter. Just being with him always filled me up. I never had to pretend with him.

It did seem he was nervous, had started to speak, then silenced himself. Finally, "Mollie." He cleared his throat. Our horses ripped at grass, stomped against flies. "I . . . I'd like you to be my wife. Not right now," he was quick to add. "You're young."

Did he just propose? "I'm sixteen."

"I know. And old enough for an engagement, I believe."

A light rain began, and I wrestled with the umbrella while Buster stomped and turned about, not being the calm horse he usually was. Peter lifted from his pocket a little box.

"Will you marry me?" No hesitation now.

The umbrella wasn't cooperating. Peter took it from me then, offered me the box in its place, then flared the parasol and held it over our heads. The silk would do little to prevent rain for long. "Please, open it," he said, nodding toward the box. "Before we get drenched."

My pa's horse chose that moment to spread his hindquarters and let loose a spray.

"Not the most romantic moment I had in mind," Peter said.

I looped the reins over the horn and lifted the box lid. Inside was a ring, set with a cluster of three diamonds.

I gasped. It was beautiful. I looked up at him. Hadn't I rehearsed in front of my mirror something grand to say when Prince Charming declared his love and begged for me to wed? I tried to find something profound to say but all that came out was "yes."

He threw his head back then and laughed. "I confess, I feared you wouldn't." He leaned in then to kiss me, the savoring kind that awakens every nerve and fiber in one's being. At least it did mine. He took the ring from the box and placed it on my finger, the umbrella tilting.

"My Prince Charming, riding on his steed. I'll wear it always." I held it to my breast, wondering if I should remove it once my father returned. Maybe wearing it would be the best way to tell my father that I had found my truest love. I'd have to plan out what I'd say.

The rain let up and we folded the umbrella. I tied it by the strings to the saddle while we spoke of our future, the ring sparkling. A few more kisses and then the wind picked up and Peter said we'd best return before the weather made such a glorious day a misery.

We cantered a distance, the wind pushing at our faces, blinking against the moisture, the horses ready to run. Invigorated, that's how I felt, the ring on my finger the beginning of a longed-for chapter.

We arrived back at the house wet enough to welcome the warmth of the stove inside.

"Ma Anne, see what I've gotten." I showed her the ring. "Peter's asked me to marry him and I will, one day."

"It's beautiful."

"You approve?" I asked.

"Peter is a good man." She nodded to him. "And he talked to me before he gave it to you, as a proper suitor should. Of course, your pa will have the final say."

"Whenever he gets home," I said. *My father loves me. He'll give his blessing.*

I hugged Anne. She was a shaft of sunshine in a day when foul weather threatened. Almost as gratifying as if my mother had been there to share the joy.

"I'll take good care of her."

"Wait," I said. "I have something for you too, Peter." I went to my precious box and took out the little gold ring I'd had made from the tailings of his sluice box all those years ago with Carrie Crane. "I pledge my troth to thee with this," I told him.

He slipped the circle of gold onto his little finger. "I will wear it always," he said.

"I've supper ready. Will you join the family, Peter?"

"With pleasure, Mrs. Sheehan." He made a little bow to her.

He stroked Jimmy's copper-colored hair as he lay in his cradle. Ma went forward to tell Mary and Kate to leave the store now and come for supper. "I'd like a half dozen of these," he whispered when we were alone, and Jimmy pushed his tiny fists against Peter's palms.

I think I loved him even more as I watched his tenderness toward children.

"And you shall have them," I said. "God willin'."

The horde returned and Mary marveled at Peter's ring almost more than mine. Kate asked if she could wear it, just for a moment, and Peter let her. I laughed. "So much for 'I'll wear it always.'" His cheeks turned red, but I loved how he treated Kate. Ma served up venison and the potatoes Kate had dug earlier from our garden. And we shared our first meal as the future Mr. and Mrs. Ronan.

The only thing to mar the day was when Peter returned after taking the horses back to the livery. "Did you bring your mum's umbrella in with you?"

"No. Was it not with the saddle?"

He shook his head, no. "I was afraid of that. It must have come loose. I'll ride out next chance I have, to see if I can find it."

I went to bed that night happy, gazing at my ring while my sister and cousin readied for bed. But I carried a tint of sadness at my having lost my mother's umbrella. Still, it had sheltered the moment when Peter had proposed to me, and I would always keep that memory with me, that my mother had been there and blessed the union . . . in her way. And wasn't it so in Greek fables that it was best on happy days to have something erroneous happen lest the gods get jealous of mere mortals?

I OFTEN SPECULATED about what happened after Ashley Pelt's foot fit the shoe that would change her life forever, Ashley being the Irish version of Cinderella. What kind of relationship did they have with their respective families, Ashley with her father and stepsisters? But one has to imagine what went beyond the "happily ever after." I imagined my father would be pleased, setting aside the gnawing in my stomach.

HE HAD GONE to check on one of his stores left in the hands of a hired proprietor. He returned in an angry mood. Once again, he'd been taken advantage of, the man he'd contracted with to manage things having sold the goods, kept the money, and absconded to parts unknown. "The deputy says there's nothing he can do but put out a warrant, send posters out. Where are the vigilantes when you need them."

"James," Ma chided him.

He sat at the table, a mug of coffee in his hands. Ma put a piece of pie in front of him. The aroma filled the house with scents of home and hearth.

"It's just so maddening," my father continued. "I work hard, think I know the character of a man and entrust him with my business, and unless I'm right there to watch—which I cannot be—he takes advantage." He took a bite. "At least the Helena store is in good hands."

"I'm not so certain of that, Uncle James." Mary bit into her pie, wiped the oozing apple juice from her lips.

"What are you saying?"

"I sometimes help there. I stock shelves and talk to customers."

"A woman ought not be in the trades," he said.

"I don't have access to the till, of course, but it seems to me that what Mr. Bland gives to Ma is a small portion of what it ought to be."

"I'll check the books," he said.

"You should just let us women run it," I said.

"You can trust us," Mary agreed.

I sat across from my father. "You do work hard, Pa. Maybe Patrick could do the freighting and you stay here and work the business."

"What's this?" He pointed to my hand. I had forgotten to remove the ring.

I swallowed. I had planned a little speech to give for when Peter stood beside me. I took a deep breath, laid my hand out, and spread my fingers. The diamonds caught the sunlight and reflected it. "It's my engagement ring."

"Engaged! I think not. You're too young." He thrust his napkin to the table. "You have schooling to pursue."

"We don't intend to marry for a while yet, maybe next year. When I'm seventeen."

"And who is this boy who thinks he's man enough to support my daughter?"

"It's your friend Peter Ronan."

I saw the color fade from his face and then return to blossom red. The room had gone still when he stood, turned to my stepmother. "You knew of this?"

"Yes. Peter's a good man, James. He's been good to her. And to us."

"My friend, taking advantage, hoodwinked my women, my Mollie. No." He glared at me. "You will return that ring. At once. This so-called affair is ended, now." He stormed out of the room.

In my actor's voice, cheerful, I said to the stunned audience before me, "I can change his mind."

"He's upset about the business." Ma brushed at her apron, then raised her eyes to mine. "But I doubt he'll allow your engagement to continue. I'm sorry, Mollie."

"But they're friends. How can he not see this is the best husband I could ever have or want? He knows him well."

"That may be part of what upsets him. He had no idea that his friend had fallen for his greatest love after your mother. You." *She doesn't put herself before me?* "It's his duty to protect you." Ma motioned for Jimmy to crawl toward her.

"Protect me? From his best friend?"

"Will Pa come back?" Kate asked.

"Of course," Ma told her. She picked Jimmy up. "Let's get you fed."

"I'm sorry," Mary said. She patted my shoulder as she stood to clear the dishes.

"What's wrong with you all? He'll change his mind, I know he will. He wants my happiness. Every father wants that for his children. It was just a surprise. The timing was wrong. I'll get it right. I'll go tell Peter. It'll be fine." I had blinders on my imaginings.

ELEVEN

No Magic Wand

It was not fine.

I ran to the *Gazette*'s offices, certain I'd find Peter there, hard at work setting type, running the press if need be, bundling the papers to go out for distribution. But he wasn't there. Peter lived a few streets over. I'd been there once with my father when he'd returned a book. I started up the street when I saw Peter walking a brisk pace through dirty snow. He smiled and waved. My father hadn't gotten to him. At least I thought that was where my father had rushed off to.

"Have you seen my pa?"

"No. He's back? What's wrong? You're shaking." He put his arm around my shoulder. Others walked around us on the boarded walkway.

All my bravado at my kitchen stage had disappeared. I couldn't be separated from this man. I wouldn't survive.

"I had my ring on and he saw it and he's furious about my being engaged but became enraged when I told him it was you. Why would that be? You're his best friend."

"Was, apparently." He turned me back toward his business.

"Let's find him. I knew I should have told him. He feels betrayed, I'd guess."

"Betrayed? Why isn't he happy for me? Shouldn't a pa be happy when his child has found the one she'll be devoted to for life?"

"Not if he thinks the man too old for her."

"Ten years. When I'm thirty, you'll be forty. Who will notice or care?"

He pulled my gloved hand through his elbow, patted my fingers. "We'll ask him to meet with us and Father Van Gorp or Mother Vincent. They'll help him understand."

I hadn't thought of enlisting the priest or sisters. "Yes, that's perfect. Let's go to the church now. See if they can come with us to the house."

But when we arrived, there was no need to go back home to find my father. He was there, his fists clenched when he saw Peter beside me. Father Van Gorp put his hand gently on my father's shoulder. "Calm now, James. You don't want to harm another, especially not in front of your child."

"JAMES," PETER SAID. "I'm so sorry I didn't tell ye that I love Mollie, more than I can say."

"She's a child," my father barked at him. "You've taken advantage of a child." We were all inside the church, the altar candles waiting to be lit for vespers later, the smell of candle wax permeating. ·

"I'm not a child," I said. "I'm sixteen. Mama was barely more than that when she married you."

"You leave your dear departed mother from this discussion. You disgrace her."

I jerked back as though he'd struck me. *Disgrace my mother?* Peter moved to step in front of me, but I pushed my way beside him again. "How . . . how have I done such a thing?"

"Your father believes you have broken the fourth commandment." Father Van Gorp's soft voice broke into my despair. We turned toward the priest. "That you have dishonored him by not seeking his permission to be courted by any man."

"Boy. She could be courted by boys. I allowed that, didn't I?"

I nodded, though those walks home after school had been of no significance: a fellow student carrying my books. I remembered my father trimming his beard as I waited for a boy to come by in a sleigh. I'd been nervous about going out on the cold night with someone from school I barely talked to. I'd been twelve or maybe thirteen. My father had joked about my worry. "A little outing is good for a little girl." It was only Peter who provoked his ire.

"Now that I'm older, an outing is also good for a young woman, which I am. Peter has been only a gentleman—kind, like you, Pa. He loves books. And he loves me."

Peter put his hand on my shoulder, and my father's eyes narrowed. I saw anger there. And hurt.

But I couldn't speak to his emotions when mine were being rattled like hail pounding a tin roof. "How can you not see the gift of your daughter marrying a man you know well, a man who calls you friend." I pleaded, wished we'd gone to the school where Mother Vincent could have spoken to Peter's good character better than this new priest.

"No friend of mine would make a child fall in love with him."

"I love him on my own, Pa. He didn't make me do anything."

"He made you violate the commandment. A sin."

"It is so," Father Van Gorp said. "He worries over your soul and his own lack of protection against potential harm."

"You're against me too? Peter brings no harm."

"Remember these words, Mollie," the priest said. "'The Lord shall open unto thee his good treasure, the heaven to give the rain unto thy land in his season, and to bless all the work of thine hand.' Deuteronomy 28:12. You must trust the Lord, Mollie, and his plan for you. In due season, Peter might yet come into your life in a way your father approves of."

I wanted Peter to contradict the priest, but by his own depth of faith, I knew he wouldn't. He believed the priest. "God's good treasure, Mollie. In due season," Peter said. *He's backing out.*

I cried then, deep, heavy sobs, brushing Peter's hand off my shoulder. I would go to confession, receive absolution for violating the commandment. I knew this. But only if I obeyed my father now and broke the engagement, waited for the right season.

Peter had tears in his eyes when he turned me to him, wiped my cheeks with his handkerchief. "We must honor your father, Mollie. Otherwise, you'll bear the wounds of having hurt him. Carrying such a weight would pummel our love in time. I'll wait for you," he added. "Until you're older."

"Oh, now you act the noble man." My father wiped the spittle from his mouth with his wrist and stepped forward. *Does he want a fight?*

"James." Father Van Gorp shook his head and my father stepped back, bowed his. The priest said, "Perhaps, in time, your friendship can be restored with Peter."

"Never."

"Mollie and Peter, when you are older and no longer under the shelter of your father, you may find your love has endured through your separation." The priest's voice with a Belgium lilt was hopeful, though I could not imagine how I'd survive without Peter in my life, even for a year. Or two. Or forever, if my father had his way.

"All must be severed." My father spoke then to Peter. "You get no gains from saying you'll wait. This engagement never should have happened in the first place."

"But Ma Anne—"

"Don't you blame her," my father shouted at me. "I'm your father. I set the rules for you. You must have known I would not approve of Ronan or you would have told me of your . . . court-ship. Truth is the greatest honoring. Anything less dishonors."

Anger rushed into me. Anger at Peter for not standing with me; at my father for his demand. At myself for not being strong enough to do what Ellen did, marry despite my father's approval. I was still a child who wanted her father's blessing. And I wanted to never disgrace my mother's memory by being disobedient.

"Find a time when the engagement ring can be returned. You'll allow such a meeting, James?" Father Van Gorp waited for my father's nod of agreement. "Excellent."

Then my father grabbed my arm and pulled me toward him, pinching me as I trembled out of the church. There'd be no hap-pily ever after.

MA LET ME CRY when we returned to the house. Pa patted my back. "Ye've done the right thing, Mollie. Ye never should have taken up with him. Why, he's almost an old man." To Ma he said, "I can't imagine what you were thinking of, Anne, to allow this engagement, this fiasco."

"You weren't here, James. Peter looked after all of us. I could see his love for Mollie was genuine. He treated her as a fine lady."

He snorted. "You must give the ring back and any other gifts he gave you. Courting a child." The disgust in his voice made me sob harder on my stepmother's shoulder.

He left the room and Ma dabbed at my eyes with her apron.

"How will I live meeting Peter on the street," I told her. "Seeing places where we had happiness together. I'll have to pretend." The ache was something I'd never known, not even when my mother died. "Maybe he'll move." I started to sob again.

"Maybe we should," Ma said.

And before the month was out, such plans were made. Pa closed the Helena store and sent word that the Virginia City store he'd reopened would be sold too. "Things are booming in San Diego," he told us as we sat around the table. "Anne always wanted to go to California, didn't you, luv?"

Ma nodded. "They say it's summer all the time there. No worry over snow."

"Now's the perfect time. We'll leave after the Saint Patrick's Day dance. We'll all want to go to that, now won't we?" He rubbed his hands together with glee, his wanderlust made richer because his "girls" and Jimmy would be with him.

Such cheerfulness was an aggravation, like a little stone in the bottom of one's shoe. My father had won. He knew I would obey.

THE SAINT PATRICK'S DAY dance was a costumed affair. We had loaded everything on the wagon the day before. Patrick was staying in Helena with the Flower team of mules, running his own freighter operation. Mary had elected to remain too. So we were saying goodbye to family. We were to spend the night in the St. Louis Hotel and leave from there the next day. I was to give the ring and all the gifts back to Peter the morning after the dance. I had negotiated that concession at least, that we would have time alone to say our last goodbyes. Ma Anne had helped.

"She's entitled to a private goodbye, James. She may be young, but the heartache is no less than you or me separating."

I heard them in the second room. I'd thank her for standing up for me when I hadn't stood up for her after the dance episode.

"You've seen her. Her eyes are blood red from crying, those tears are genuine. Do you really want Helena's finest to see what you've caused?"

"I've caused? Ronan caused."

"Not all will see it that way."

"Some public place, then," he said, and so the morning after the dance in the hotel had been agreed to.

In my room, I packed up treasures Peter had given me. The gold necklace and heart, the "Lady of the Lake" book, the ring, of course. But there was also a scrapbook that Peter and I had decided to keep together. We planned to put articles from the paper in it, ones he was especially pleased about, like his piece about camels coming to town, or social events we had attended together. Our valentines were to be pasted in. He had given me the scrapbook just before the explosion—as I thought of the night of my father's return—so there was as yet nothing in it. I opened the flowered cover and wrote in pencil these words:

> *To Peter Ronan*
>   *Other skies may bend above you,*
>   *Other hearts may seek thy shrine,*
>   *But none other ere will love thee,*
>   *With the constancy of mine.*
>
>> *Your friend,*
>> *Mollie Sheehan*

Was I being disobedient to my father in writing such words? I tapped my lip with the pencil, the very one Puddin had stolen from Peter's newspaper office that he'd returned to me. I read the words again. Yes, I was being disloyal.

And so I erased them.

FOR THE SAINT PATRICK'S DAY DANCE, I wore a white swiss dress. I'd covered it with dozens of green shamrocks for decoration. Kate had helped me stitch on the paper leaves. A green satin ribbon slashed across my left shoulder, fastened at my waist. I wore a gilded crown. I was to be allowed one dance with Peter. That next morning, all would be returned to him and anything I'd given him was to come back into my possession.

I was grateful that a neighbor had gifted me with *Beadle's Dime Ball-room Companion and Guide to Dancing* that Mary and I had used to practice waltzes and the schottische. My feet didn't have to think about what to do. The one dance allowed was a waltz.

Peter's costume was that of an Irish guard, a banner across his chest, an old dragon on his hip. He reminded me of General Meagher. He wore my gold ring I'd given him on his little finger. The very touch of his hand felt like fire against my ribs, my heart an ache so sharp I could barely take a breath. The music started. My fingers trembled inside his palm, blood at my temples pounded. "Mollie," he said, his voice deep and cracking. He put his cheek to mine. "I shall miss ye."

I had no words.

At least it was a waltz, not a galop or a polka, but a social dance some said was too sensuous, taking people from arm's length to permit a chaste embrace. There were other couples dancing, but soon they stepped away. People moved off the floor to circle around us as though Helena wrapped us in their care. Everyone knew our story, knew that here in Last Chance Gulch a love had bloomed, one both beautiful and strong like the wild rose bush that survived to color the deep ravines. It was a love that promised to overcome great trials. But not this, not when a father set the rule. Here there was no last chance.

I was being as devout as I could be, dancing in the arms of my Prince Charming, spurning the kiss that had awoken me, all to honor my father . . . and my mother.

Mining towns could be rough with guns and knives and fights and death. But they were also filled with good, kind people who had taught me how to play the organ, who joined with me in choirs. People who wouldn't let a lady be injured, who now watched this one last dance between loves. I was safe in Peter's arms as he shepherded me around the wooden floor. I could feel the audience around us wish that there would be a shaft of light to break through this wretched ending.

"Will you write, Mollie?" Peter's voice choked, words whispered against my ears as he pulled me closer, the fiddle forlorn in playing "The Girl I Left Behind."

"My father has forbidden letters. And you must not write to me as well, it isn't allowed."

"Not a hope for one day?" His voice trembled. "I love you so."

"We are finished and—"

The fiddler ended the dance and my words. My father stood by the musician. He had stopped the dance that might have gone on longer than usual. While people applauded, Peter bowed, then escorted me to my father, who nodded his head at Peter. He took my elbow, and with Ma on his other side, carrying Jimmy, and with Kate behind us, he ushered us out.

IT HAD BEEN ARRANGED that the next morning, my parents and Kate and Jimmy would head out with the Gems, and they would make an early evening camp. I would be brought later by a family friend—John Sweeney—to catch up with them. John had helped build the Catholic church and was "trustworthy," according to my father. I had begged for one last time for a private goodbye, one without the town viewing. I'd be allowed to be alone with Peter, in a public place, and have a last hour to return his gifts.

We had to say goodbye to Mary too. She would stay at the hotel and work until such time as she would marry. Puddin, old and frail, would remain with her. "He can be our resident mouser," Mary said. "And he won't have to travel far to find things to steal."

"Those poor guests," Ma said and we laughed. It felt good to laugh.

I thought maybe we'd come back for Mary's wedding and I might see Peter once again. I didn't say such a thing but did encourage Mary to get her beau to set the date.

"Maybe next year," she said. "He wants a nest egg, he calls it, but they're hard to brood in a big-and-bust town."

"I think Helena's here to stay," Pa told her. He gave her a hug, then released her to Ma and Kate and finally me.

"You'll be missed, Mary," I said.

She whispered in my ear, "I'll pray for you and Peter."

I blinked back tears.

And then my parents and Kate and Jimmy climbed up onto the wagon and headed southwest. Mary went to work. Looking back now, I think it rather odd my father conceded to let me meet with Peter alone. In some ways it prolonged my agony and Peter's too. Perhaps he allowed it as a test, to see if I would follow through or perhaps run off with Peter. Or maybe he felt some guilt for having brought such unhappiness to his precious daughter.

Big ferns in ceramic pots made borders in the oversized room of the St. Louis Hotel lobby, giving us some privacy. I could see the mourning wreath for little Jules still hanging on the front door as I chose a big horsehair divan where we could sit, side by side.

The wreath was fitting. I was in mourning too. I arrived early, dressed in a simple tunic, gone the gilded crown and Irish banner. On my lap sat a wooden box holding the scrapbook, necklace, and books he'd given me. And of course, the diamond ring. Puddin purred on the floor at my feet.

"I wanted to be late, to put our final meeting off," he said when he arrived a few minutes after 9:00 a.m., our appointed hour to meet. Handsome, that aquiline nose, those sparkling eyes—looking dull this day. He never failed to make my heart leap whenever I saw him. He wore the new higher-heeled boots that stayed in the stirrups better, a suit complete with vest, and a watch fob draped across his chest. "I tried to conjure up a good fairy with a magic wand to make this departure, this . . . severing all go away."

I motioned for him to sit beside me. "I imagined one too. But there is no magic wand. Our faith demands this separation."

"Your pa demands it." He held his hand up as I started to defend. "Let it just be a leave-taking, only for a time."

"My father says it must be a severing." I made a motion as though I held a knife. "One that can't ever be restored."

He bowed his head. His hands were clasped between his knees. "I talked to Father Van Gorp and prayed—oh, Mollie, how I've prayed that your father's ire toward me would be removed."

"Me too." I sighed.

He looked at me then. "I won't ever forget you. Never."

"It's better if you do." The words came in a whisper.

He took a deep breath and pulled from his pocket a book I'd given him written by General Meagher. "Read this book again, Mollie," he said. "Please." I nodded, though I didn't understand his intensity that I reread a book I'd already finished. He handed me another book of poems, and another that included "Lady of the Lake," the first poem he'd read to me.

I'd given him mostly books, I saw. The valentine with my mother's piece of lace he handed back, fingering it for a moment before he did. "I rode back out to try to find the umbrella. I know it was your mother's. I'll keep looking."

"One more thing of hers left behind," I said. "There are only a few brooches now, that Ma has. But I have the memory of that parasol on the day you proposed. Maybe its being lost is just another moment I won't have to be reminded of. Should you ever find it, keep it," I said.

I handed him the scrapbook then and the other gifts. I blinked back tears, each returned gift like a sliver piercing in its stead. "And here's the ring." I took it from my finger where I'd placed it that morning for the last time.

"Could you not wear it, but have it?"

I shook my head, no. His eyes were pooled with tears.

"And here's the ring you gave me." He tugged at the circle of gold.

"No." I put my hand on his and whispered, "Keep it until I ask for it."

I stood then and rushed up the stairs into my room, leaving him standing. I knew he watched me go.

My last-minute decision to let him keep the ring was a violation of my father's order, and I suppose I did it in an act of defiance, small as it was. I wanted to imagine Peter wearing it, being reminded of what we once had. But it also symbolized a tiny glitter that might sparkle in the future. Not a magic wand, but a golden ring to rub that might unleash a genie who could grant three wishes. I only needed one fulfilled: that Peter Ronan would come back into my life. Prayers, my mother would have said, would offer more, and that was what I turned to.

TWELVE

TENDING
AND BEFRIENDING

John Sweeney arrived at the St. Louis Hotel at noon as planned. "How are you doing, Mollie?" The hotelier had come to take my overnight case. I carried my reticule and the wooden box of treasures Peter had returned. I didn't answer John. "A hard morning for you." John was thin as a noodle; wiry, my father called him. "I saw Mr. Ronan outside, don't you know."

"He's still here?" I didn't think I could bear it if I had to pass by Peter. I chastised myself that I hadn't stayed with him until John came. I could have had that time with him but forfeited it as punishment for telling him to keep the ring. Was that a pattern I was fomenting? Punishing myself for any small act of disobedience to my father?

"No, no, Mollie. He's gone. He just wanted to be sure I arrived. Looking after you, he was."

John helped me step into the buggy drawn by two horses, stomping and ready to move. The sun hurt my eyes that were red and puffy from crying. I wished I'd had a cucumber slice to put on them, but a part of me did not care how I looked. Vanity's mirror, that Ma once worried over for me, had cracked.

As we neared the hill where the church was, John said, "Let's go inside and say a prayer, that your journey would be safe and that all may turn out well and happily for you."

He helped me from the carriage.

We knelt and silently put out our petitions, and as I prayed, a kind of peace settled over me. I didn't understand why this painful time had come upon me, but I prayed for Peter, for acceptance of what was, for his happiness. I thought of the priest quoting, "The Lord shall open unto thee his good treasure." It was a promise I could claim when I was a loyal, obedient daughter. If only I could remove the mix of hardness I felt growing toward my father.

"Thank you for that, Mr. Sweeney," I said when we were back in the buggy.

"Always good to pray, Mollie," he said. "And call me John. The Lord works in mysterious ways, don't you know?"

"I'll count on that."

I tried to pay attention to the scenery, for final goodbyes to the landscape as well as to my heartache. I loved this Montana Territory. I'd climbed Mount Helena, walked through meadows of lupine and syringa, even fished a stream or two. Horseback rides on Buster; meandering and swift races gave distinctive memories of where we'd picnicked, lost an umbrella while gaining a love. I'd made journeys with my father and with Peter who had helped me turn the ugly placer mining tailings into memories that included a little gold ring drawn from a sluice box at Alder Gulch. I was leaving all behind.

We met my parents at dusk. John Sweeney spent the night, and in the morning after breakfast, he turned back and we went forward.

I didn't know how long the trip to San Diego would take and my father was vague about it. I soon realized there was no rush to arrive. He rather liked the camping out with Ma and me cooking through the dust and bugs. And he had a few surprises. "We're not far from Ellen and William's place, in the Ruby Valley," he said. "Let's stop by. You'd like that, wouldn't you, Mollie?"

I nodded. I hadn't talked much, going inside myself as my best defense against the pain.

And so we did, discovering that Ellen was due to have a baby in a month or so and we were invited to remain. Bill—that's what she called her husband now—had his valley ranch and would soon have his "kids and cattle." It had been a couple of years since we had seen Ellen, but she was the same wren-like cousin who now sported a baby's promise. She'd had two ruptured pregnancies "early on," she said. "But this one is doing well." She rubbed her abdomen. "I prayed I'd find a good midwife and here you are."

"It worked out well that we were leaving Helena when we did," Ma said.

"Tell me everything about that town," Ellen said, expecting happy stories of our time there, the theater, how Mary was. We spoke of that. But when Pa and Bill headed outside to tend the Gems, I shared my sad story of Peter Ronan and me. She put her arms around me and let me cry. "You'll be seventeen this July. That's how old I was when I married Bill. Uncle James will surely allow it then."

I shook my head. "No. He said I must sever it forever, that Peter betrayed his friendship and I betrayed Pa by suggesting a man of Peter's age could love me. Or that I was old enough to love deeply. I'm not a child."

My voice must have raised, as Ma shushed me, then left to put Jimmy down for a nap in another of Ellen's rooms in her three-room home.

"Well, I'm not a child," I said. "But he insisted I define my life by the fourth commandment, to honor thy father and thy mother." I sighed. "I wish my mother was here." I was grateful Ma was in another room. I didn't want to hurt her feelings.

"We'll take your mind off . . . things. You can go riding with Bill. And your friend Carrie Crane, remember her?"

I nodded as I wiped my eyes.

"She lives on Wisconsin Creek, not that far at all. Maybe a couple of miles."

Carrie's name brought back Alder Gulch and our sluice box cleaning. That took me to Peter's ring. I didn't see how my broken heart would ever mend, with every memory of Peter tearing out the stitches.

I would have to make new memories, without him.

Carrie Crane wasn't Crane anymore, it was Spencer. And she was happy to see me. She'd moved away before I began my school. I'd lost touch with her, but Cousin Ellen hadn't. Two children ran out from the ranch house that, like Ellen's, had three rooms, considered "substantial." The valley offered milder winters, and Carrie said the government granted free grazing on public land, so they'd been building up a herd of longhorns brought up from Dallas, Texas. "Once the railroad's complete, we'll ship them to Chicago. It's a two-month drive to the rail terminus at Salt Lake and there are Indian problems, so it'll be good to have the tracks come closer."

My father rarely spoke of Indian troubles. Those of that race that I'd seen in Helena once or twice looked tired and would be of little threat, I thought. Carrie was well-versed on cattle commerce, and she quilted too.

"You must come by often," she said. "During Ellen's waiting. We'll stitch and tell stories. Remember when you got mad at— what was his name? That miner who ruined your chambray hat?"

"Peter Ronan," I said. "I was engaged to him."

"Oh, la. He was an old man."

"Just ten years my senior. How much older is your husband than you?"

She laughed. "Nineteen years. I guess Mr. Ronan looked older when we were rascals cleaning out his sluice boxes." She picked up another patch from her basket. "You said you were engaged. What happened? Did he die?"

"No. My father decided I had broken a commandment by agreeing to marry without his permission, though my ma concurred. He didn't say it, but he doesn't allow for a woman's opinion." I bit the words out, made the sign of the cross over my heart, and silently asked forgiveness for my unkind thought. "And then when he realized it was his best friend—former best friend—who loved me, he stubbornly refused to let the engagement stand. It's why we left Helena."

"That's awful," Carrie said. She reached across to hold my hand.

"It is." There wasn't anything more to say.

DURING THE TWO MONTHS we stayed at the Tiernans', I saw Carrie often. I rode out with Bill until I knew the route on my own. It was a lush and massive country, mountains embracing meadows, rushing streams so clear one could see the trout nesting on the rocky bottoms. Many ranchers raised horses to sell to the military. Bill and Ellen's ranch boasted such fine horses too. The animal I'd been given to ride was a big sorrel gelding with a soft mouth. He took little reining, and I rode sidesaddle like a lady.

The sorrel, Duke was his name, took me through the herds of longhorns Carrie said were driven north by a wealthy neighbor. "Six hundred brought up over the Bozeman Trail." Carrie's husband had bought twenty of the unusual cattle and was building up their herd. I thought maybe Pa would be drawn to cattle country, possible free grazing. Maybe we'd stay in this valley. He and Bill Tiernan got along well. We wouldn't be that far from Helena. We could subscribe to the *Gazette*. I could make my way back east like those miners from Minnesota seeking one last chance.

Ma and I sewed for the new baby, and I kept up with soap and

candle-making, housework, and the eternal wash. My father let me
attend country dances at the Spencer ranch, a reward for helping at
Ellen's. I danced the reels and squares but declined any who asked
for a waltz. I found that standing behind the cookies, sandwiches,
and punch table worked best for me where I could wear my mask
of pleasantness to cover up my sorrow.

ELLEN'S BABY ARRIVED without difficulty, for which we all sang
praises. Ellen named her Elizabeth and asked if I would be her
godmother. It was a singular joy to hold that infant and imagine
what her life might become. Ellen beamed and Bill gave out cigars
at the next country dance when Ellen was well enough to attend
with Pa and Ma while Kate (with Ellen and her baby close by)
watched over Jimmy sleeping in the corner. Fiddlers played and
the high-heeled cowboy boots stomped the wooden floor. Once,
eight-year-old Kate was even asked to be a partner. I remembered
how I'd loved being a "grown-up" for the squares.

My father didn't take to my idea that we consider remaining
in Ruby Valley.

"Your ma's got her heart set on San Diego," he said.

Before we left, Carrie held a quilting bee for me. Some of the
women I'd met at the dances, ranching wives, attended, as did
the local schoolmarm, as she was called. Many looked to be my
age and some already had a baby at their breast. Carrie was a
hospitable person, welcoming her guests, smiling, introducing me
to newcomers. Ma and Ellen and Kate came, too, and it felt good
to be a part of an affair of fun and food. People complimented
me on my hair, how shiny it was and long. I could sit on it. We
talked about the time it took to dry. But mostly, I found it easiest
to pitch in, have a task like serving food where I could listen, ask
others about their dress or child but not have to reveal much about
myself. I watched the banter back and forth of these women whose

hands showed calluses from ranch work but that also threaded a needle with grace. I could be among them as a wife one day. But without Peter, it might be the spinster schoolmarm who represented my fate.

As a gift that day, the Ruby Valley women gave me a Tree of Life quilt. The triangular blocks formed green branches I could wrap myself inside of for comfort or use to divide a single-room cabin into two. I took with me even more their gift of acceptance. I enjoyed the pleasure of women gathering, telling stories, participating in the daily life of meeting children's needs and friendship-tending and befriending. I thought of how little of that I'd done in Helena, especially after Carrie had moved. The quilting bee on Wisconsin Creek had taken my mind from Peter. I would have to seek more friendships if my heart would ever mend.

THIRTEEN

THE ACTING DAUGHTER

Write to me, Mollie." Ellen hugged me goodbye. "And I'll keep you abreast of your godchild's growing."

Pa patted her back as she hugged him, and he shook Bill's hand. "You take good care of my Ellen," he said. "And if you didn't know it, there's a priest and Catholic church in Helena now, so you could get your marriage blessed."

"Something to consider," Bill told him, "though I think it's been blessed already." He gazed at his first child.

All the goodbyes spoken, we stepped up onto the wagon led by the Gems, with Buster and another good riding horse trailing behind. Our route was across parts of the old Bozeman Trail toward Sheridan, Montana, and then we headed south toward Corinne, Utah, where Pa had spent that long year away, allowing me time to give my heart to Peter.

I turned seventeen as we traveled. We rarely celebrated a birthday, but that July I marked a day, choosing the first. But being seventeen gave no reason to believe it would change my father's mind about his daughter's eligibility for marriage. And it didn't.

We celebrated the Fourth of July with my father singing Irish songs while Ma and I washed dishes at a stream bank somewhere in Utah.

CORINNE, UTAH, BOOMED. At the north end of the Great Salt Lake, the town on Bear River wasn't growing due to gold but from supplying what was needed for the Union Pacific Railroad nearing its terminus. My father saw a chance to replenish his funds and hired on to drive our mules to haul timbers for railroad ties. He would be home each night. We set up our big tent and unloaded the wagon, and it looked like we'd be there for a while. He even bought a separate tent where Ma said, "Your father's decided we should open up another establishment." Soon my Tree of Life quilt became a divider between kitchen and tables where we served railroad men.

I was tall (maybe five foot six), slender, and with that same long hair that so attracted attention—attention my father didn't seem to mind this time. The railroad workers—except for the Chinese who bowed and kept to themselves when they occasionally entered our tent—were brasher than the miners we'd served in the establishment in Alder Gulch. A kind of tension filled the air when the rowdies arrived. Sometimes they'd stand at the Chinese table, poke fun at them, and mock their clothes or speech. When they weren't harassing them, they grabbed at my hair, pinched my bottom, and made raucous comments.

"Can't I cook, Ma? Let me wash dishes so I don't have to serve."

"You bring in paying customers," Pa said. He tacked a gap in the quilt to keep cooking smoke away from those paying souls. "Kate's too young to serve and she has to watch Jimmy, and Anne's the better cook."

"I guess there's no concern I'll be reciting sonnets after supper. You wouldn't want me getting attention for that."

"I'm here to monitor such antics. Things won't be happening here as they did with Ronan."

WE'D BEEN IN CORINNE a month, San Diego still far away. I considered getting on Buster's back and riding him to Helena. But I wasn't sure Peter—listening to the priest—wouldn't turn me back around. I couldn't trust the people who said they loved me, neither Peter nor my father.

"How'd you like to take the train to Salt Lake City? A pleasure trip." My father finished his Irish stew, then leaned back in his chair.

"All of us?"

"No, just you and your pa. Anne said she'd as soon stay here, keep the tent open."

I looked at her as she vigorously cleaned the table. She didn't look back at me.

"How long would we be gone?"

"Just a day or two. They're building a tabernacle there, the Mormons are. I'd like to see that. Walk the streets they say are wide as the Missouri and ten times as clean. Maybe have our photograph made."

I didn't say much, thinking of Ma's not looking at me.

"Don't let your enthusiasm overwhelm you." He sounded disgusted. "They have a theater."

It didn't seem right that I would get a train ride, visit a city with real streets, and maybe go to a play. A show with Tom Thumb and his wife had come to Corinne, but railroad workers found pleasure in the saloon tents with the hurdy-gurdy girls, not actors and actresses wearing masks.

"Will you be alright alone?" I asked Ma.

"I'm accustomed to being alone," she said. She smiled. "You go. Have a good time." Her generosity and good wishes seemed genuine. *Does she wear a mask too?*

If I said yes, I would please my father. But I didn't want to give him that satisfaction. I'd had few words with him since we'd left Helena.

"Take Ma. Or Kate."

Ma shook her head. "Don't cut off your nose to spite your face, Mollie. You love performances. Enjoy. Even if it does please your father."

She made good sense. "Alright." Maybe we would talk and I'd understand why he so opposed Peter.

My father clapped his hands and kissed Ma. "Thank you, Gentle Anne. I'll bring you a pretty."

And so I boarded a train for the first time.

I paid attention to the landscape, mountains and flatlands, desert and meadows, and the imposing lake with darting seagulls. Salt Lake City rose up orderly, not like the mining camps. We ate in restaurants. My handsome father laughed with the serving girls who flirted with him.

I thought of generous Anne.

"I'd like to talk about Peter." I toyed with my fish baked in a buttery sauce.

"We won't spoil a nice dinner with talk of him."

"But what is it about him that—"

"I said no talk."

I sighed. There'd be no chance to change his mind.

Later we stood outside of the tabernacle where hammers broke the pristine air. My father said, "I think that's Brigham Young." There were other men beside the Mormon leader and one woman who was dressed in red with rouge on her cheeks. My father turned on his charm and was introduced to the men and to the woman said to be an actress.

My ears perked up. She looked directly at me. I wanted to speak to her, to ask if being on stage would be a way to set aside one's sorrow. But I didn't approach. I was adrift.

We found a photographer's studio, and he posed my father and me sitting on a settee, my father with his elbow across the back, looking past me toward some distant place. Ireland, perhaps. He wore a suit with striped pants. I was posed looking past him as well, a side glance to the camera's lens. I held a Bible in my lap, the book provided by the photographer.

"Let's have your wife sit to your right."

My face grew hot and my father bristled. "She's my daughter."

"I beg your pardon." The photographer seemed nervous after that.

I wore a dark blue velveteen dress my father had just bought me, along with a ribbon and a brooch at my throat. The brooch was new too. My hair was parted in the center, and while one could not see it, it flowed down my back. I sat on it. Strands lay across my breast.

The photographer commented on my hair as so many did.

"She's never cut it," my father said. "She listens to her pa about such as that."

That evening we went to the theater in a structure with white Doric-style columns placed for the dramatic entrance. It was well lit that evening and the chalky plaster fairly glowed. Inside there were enough seats to fit fifteen hundred people, or so the usher told us as we took our seats. The play was *One Touch of Nature*, the very play we'd seen back in Denver about the father and daughter that I had once imagined my father and me performing. I no longer thought it something I would want to do, dwell on a story of a father-daughter separation and reunion.

The next morning as we were boarding the horse carriage to take us to the train to return to Corinne, the rouged woman of our Brigham Young encounter of the day before sat on the hotel porch. While her cheeks were colored, she carried herself with the grace of a lady, her gown flowing. "I saw you yesterday, my dear. You're quite striking. Did you enjoy the performance last evening?"

"That was you? Playing the daughter?" I was sure I would have recognized her in that role, even though we were far from the front.

"No, it wasn't. I saw you in the audience. Here." She handed me a book, *Lucile*. "It's a lovely story, different in its format. But I thought you'd like it. There is a dramatic flair about your person," she said. "Do you perform?"

"Mollie is not an actress," my father said. "She's much too young. And, present company excluded, it is a profession with some . . . heavy freight to carry. I thank you for the gift." He had taken the book from my hand, and I thought he intended to give it back, but instead he said, "It speaks to your good character that you keep company with Mr. Young and have a liking for books. Mollie will enjoy it, I'm sure, though I'll read it first to determine its suitability."

"I've heard of this author, Owen Meredith," I said. "Thank you so much for thinking of me."

"I see acting in your future," she said. "Something about your countenance." Her diction was precise, as though she herself was on the stage at that moment. "Acting offers several avenues for personal advancement as well as entertainment for the audience, no matter the size." The ends of her sentences lingered. "It might only be for one."

Pretend that all is fine and perhaps it will be so.

I READ THE BOOK while my father slept, lifting my eyes often to gaze upon the landscape. I had yet to be in any western place where mountains and streams and the vastness of the valleys didn't take my breath away. They never failed to lift my spirits and give me hope.

Dange wagged his tail in greeting while Pa changed his clothes and went right to work. In the family tent, I told Ma I had some plans to deal with the rowdies who came into the establishment.

"Something you discovered in Salt Lake?"

"You might say that."

In the morning, I put on my dress, but instead of my slippers, I wore my boots. And when the rowdies came in, before they could say a word to me about my girlish figure or ask if I wouldn't want to spend a day with them, I spoke loudly first. "How did your mules work today? Did they toe the line or tow you?" And then I laughed.

"She's got you there," one said.

I squared right up to another who I'd had trouble with. Hands on my hips and close enough to hit him if I spit, I said, "What'll you have, Johnny boy?" Before he could answer I added, "Don't matter, we're serving eggs and a rasher of bacon. Think you can afford it? Put your rump down on that bench."

He did. I'd never said the word "rump" in public before.

I stomped in my boots instead of walking like a lady. Once, when someone reached as though to grab my waist, I burped, right out loud.

"She's one of us," another eater said, stopping his fork to his mouth at the sound of the burp.

And that was exactly what I had wanted. I'd act like "one of the boys," maybe even scratch my nose before I took their orders, reducing what they thought attracted them to me and cut off what gave them privilege to mistreat me. Instead of being a victim, I was in charge.

Ma grinned when I came beyond the quilt to the kitchen after my big burp. "You are quite the actress, Miss Mollie Sheehan."

I bowed and feigned picking at my nose.

She laughed out loud. "Just don't lose your lady ways when you're offstage."

"I won't. But I've put them in their place, haven't I?"

"Cutting your hair helped, I think."

I agreed. The severing of my long tresses was one less attraction—and had the added advantage of making my father livid.

FOURTEEN

WHAT WE MAY BE

There wasn't anything my father could do about my hair. I intended to grow it out again, maybe not long enough to sit on—it was a trial to care for. He had at first been speechless when he saw me, my hair short enough I couldn't even get it into a bun at my neck. I'd chopped it just below my ears.

"What 'ave ye done, lass? Cut the locks you had when your dear mother passed."

"A girl has to learn to take care of herself. My dear mum would want me to be safe."

We were near the livery where our riding horses and the Gems were kept. The equine scent soothed when his words did not.

"After all I've done for ye, after all the sacrifices I've made. Cuttin' your hair when you know it's a crown to be cherished." Disgusted, he added, "Will Shakespeare wrote, 'She has brown hair, and speaks small like a woman.' Remember that."

"But I'm no small woman, Pa. This is Shakespeare too: 'We know what we are but know not what we may be.' Maybe the stage is my future."

His eyes held pain. My heart hurt then, an intemperate tongue a drain. He was a good man and he had lived a life away from us so much of the time, when all he wanted was to be near family, to care for us. How could I see his sacrifice as anything less than loving?

I didn't apologize, but my words were soft when I said, "It was a good way for me to handle those men, Pa. It'll grow back."

"Too much commotion here," Pa said. We took down the tents, loaded the wagon, and headed south again, to San Diego where Ma Anne longed to go.

"I think you're strong enough to learn to handle the Gems," my father told me after several days on the trail. "I could use some respite now and then."

"I'm not sure I have the muscle," I said.

"Didn't you say you were no small woman?"

Our trip that autumn was in a covered wagon, seeing the future through the ears of our six mules. I thought the Gems might be pleased to be on the road and not having to haul the heavy railroad ties or drag iron scrapes full of dirt that the railroad work demanded. My father had taken extra care each evening to check for skin wounds and harness rubs, brushing the Gems and the horses while Dange lay panting in the dirt beyond the corral.

Now the dog patted beside us, whining when he wanted to be lifted up and put in the back where Ma and Jimmy sometimes sat. Kate often rode one of the horses. Mostly, I sat on the seat listening to my father's instructions about managing the reins until one day he decided I had learned enough.

"I'm going in the back to nap," he said. "You carry on."

A good thing about learning something new, a task detailed and one whose distraction from could lead to disaster, if not death, is that a mind can't meander to a lost love. I had to concentrate both for my family's sake and also to make sure the mules knew I was in charge of them, keeping them safe too. I wondered if that was how my father saw his role as a parent, the need to keep control less for his sake but for mine?

Our evening stops were different from when we'd traveled from Missouri north. We set up camp near tidy ranches owned by Mormons where we could purchase eggs and vegetables and fresh meat. My father's payment from his railroad work he'd converted into greenbacks, and he spent freely for our comfort. We rattled on toward California and came upon a stagecoach led by lads checking out a stage route. They weren't much older than me but focused on their business future.

"Now there's some boys you could pay attention to," my father said. "Let that tinker Ronan go."

Tinker? "Peter is a newspaper editor and owner, not some traveling tinsmith. Why, we're more like a tinker than Peter ever was."

"It's a state of thinking, Mollie. A man who'd make a child love him isn't thinking very far ahead himself. Those lads are. As are we. Things are booming in San Diego and we'll do well there too."

We prepared to cross the Mojave Desert, learning of the spots where there was a spring or two that we might find by following the stars. We stocked up on water in barrels. I spelled my father as we drove the night when it was coolest, though still hot. The mules led the way, as I couldn't see a thing, just hear the scrape of a cactus against the wagon bed, or the flutter of a nightbird. Sometimes the stagecoach lads would say something as they rode beside our wagon, about the stars or how warm the night was. Perhaps to keep awake or help me stay alert too. The star I was to guide the Gems toward sparkled like a torch. The mules were surefooted, never wavered in their duty.

At an oasis with two pools, a sign warned that one of the springs was contaminated.

"It's possible the other spring is bad now too," Pa said.

"We'll restrict our horses," one lad said. "Just in case."

Pa thought that wise, too, so we gave small amounts to the horses and Gems, waiting to see if they were sickened and, like the lads, staked them so they couldn't reach water on their own. We rested through the day and at dusk began again.

Not many miles into evening, Amber floundered—the mule that liked to carry a cat went down and halted any movement forward. In moonlight, we unharnessed the team. Amber lay panting on her side, and Pa took the last water in his canteen and poured it down her throat, then fondled her big head he held in his lap. "You go on ahead," my father said. "I'll catch up."

"I'll stay with you, Pa," Kate said. "We can both ride Amber when she gets up from her napping."

"No, no. You look after your ma and Jimmy. Mollie, head out now." Amber tried once to raise her head. She couldn't. A wretched cough. "Go!"

The lads had assisted with the harnessing, and they moved forward too. We really didn't know those boys, yet my father had no qualms about my taking the wagon and following them. I had time to look back in the moonlight to see him tending a sick mule. He would miss Amber. I knew there'd be no riding her to catch up.

We'd plodded on for an hour or more when Ma shouted, "I see him. Hold up, Mollie." She'd been watching too.

My father trudged along, arriving with Amber's halter on his shoulder. He pulled himself up into the wagon.

"At least she didn't die alone," Ma said. "Nothing worse than that."

When we reached the other side of the desert, the stagecoach lads moved on toward San Diego, but we stopped at a little ranchero named Los Nietos, not far from Los Angeles. We all needed the rest. We rented a house there and for several days just slept and drank water before washing and ironing to make ourselves clean and respectable. Everyone around us spoke Spanish, but still Pa learned of work plowing. His greenbacks getting low, he took the job. Who knew how long it would be before we saw the streets of San Diego?

"He does what he has to do," Ma said when I crossed my arms over my chest and asked if she wasn't disappointed.

I was. There was perhaps a happy ending for Ma Anne in that distant coastal city, and I could begin my life again, finally, settled in a place where letters could be sent and received.

"We, too, will do what we must," she said. "Our white dresses need bluing. Let's take advantage of where we are, and not lament where we are not."

FIFTEEN

ENTERTAINING ANGELS

We went neighboring. I began to pick up our town's Spanish-Mexican language, a task that occupied my mind. *Los Nietos*, I learned, meant "the grandchildren," and I thought it a happy name for a town. Many children raced around playing on the dusty streets, and Kate found friends quickly. Even Jimmy did when he walked to the market with Ma. She always wore a blazing white dress and wide sun hat, a red-dyed ribbon hanging down her back.

I stood on the sidelines, though I was polite and inquisitive and loved it when the people of the town let me practice my Spanish, never minding if I needed to repeat a word or two. We could laugh together when I realized the word for "embarrassed" was very close to the word for "pregnant." But I wasn't of a mind to make long-lasting friends here. I was sure it was temporary, and investing in a friendship took both commitment and time. I stayed backstage, so to speak, watching events unfold.

On a Sunday after we'd been in Los Nietos a week, my father asked if I wanted to ride to Los Angeles for a mass.

"Maybe Ma would like to go." I wanted to attend. It had been a long time and I needed the help of ritual to ease my heartache, know that what I suffered was nothing compared to what our Lord had. But I felt uneasy with him choosing me over his wife.

"She doesn't like to ride and I don't want to harness the wagon." I looked at her and she nodded agreement.

Anne wore the brooch my father had bought for me in Salt Lake that I had given back to him when I reminded him he'd failed to buy a "pretty" for his wife. She touched it. "You have a good time."

The City of Angels had fewer than six thousand citizens, so we found our way on the dirt streets to Our Lady of the Angels on Main. Across from the church was a plaza where people sat on benches beneath a sycamore tree and watched their children play.

The service brought me to a place of grace. I felt restored to face the uncertainty of my life ahead. My faith could keep me moored.

As we rode back to Los Nietos, I asked when we'd be moving on to San Diego.

"Ah, soon, lass."

We talked of the balmy weather, how it felt odd to be thinking of Thanksgiving without a snowfall, only enough to tip the mountains to the east. We discussed the priest's homily, his admonition to be kind to strangers, that by Scripture one might not know when one was welcoming an angel in disguise of a beggar or a tinker. He had used that very word.

We'd become so engaged by our conversation that we lost our way. We asked directions from a Mexican couple whose flat-roofed house we stopped at as the sun was setting. They were sitting in front of their home, bougainvillea blooming from a trellis over their heads. With my limited Spanish, "*Donde es* Los Nietos?" I said, hoping I asked directions to our town. They pointed and responded, and then I thought they said it was too late and we could get lost again. "They want us to spend the night."

"Stay with them?"

I tried to clarify with my mix of English and Spanish. The man stood and motioned us to lead our horses and follow him. His wife—both shorter than my father and me—tailed after us. They took us to a mustard-colored house where there were two freshly made-up beds. I slept in my underslip, hanging my white dress on the wall peg. Pa slept in his shirt and pants on top of the covers, hands crossed over his chest. "Sorry we don't have a blanket for a partition for you, Mollie. You deserve privacy."

I was surprised he even mentioned it. We'd slept as a family in single rooms so many times, in tents, too, though he was right, we often had a blanket to separate child from adult.

"Ma says 'be agile' and adapt. I'll be fine."

And I was. In the morning, I slipped on my dress. Pa was already awake and tending to the horses. Our hosts then gave us breakfast of frijoles, coffee, and tortillas, then sent us on our way toward a crossroads that we would have surely missed if we had tried to keep going in the night.

"Ma will be worried," I said, wishing there'd been a way to let them know why we hadn't come home.

"One thing I love about Anne is that she trusts that all will be well no matter the immediate circumstance. She'll have told Kate and Jimmy that we'll be home in the morning. And we'll have a story to tell of such hospitality. If I didn't know better, I'd think they were Irish."

I smiled. "We were the strangers treated like angels. If I ever have a home of my own, I want to do that too," I said. "Accept people and go beyond what is requested, give even more." I vowed to seek more occasions not only to give but to recognize kindnesses in unexpected places.

"No need to be looking for a home of your own, Mollie. You'll always have a place with us to keep you safe." He reached across the horse's neck to pat my hand holding the reins.

I moved away. I'm not sure why.

THE PLOWING JOBS FINISHED, we packed our wagon once again and headed south to San Diego. In a town called San Juan Capistrano, we stopped for the night at a campsite close to the ocean where we could see gentle waves pushing up onto sandy white beaches. Salt was in the air. We'd passed an old mission building with stone craters caved in on themselves.

"Looks like earthquake damage," Pa said.

But in another section of the ruins, we heard vespers being sung. Old olive trees with knurled trunks stood beside the chapel where red bougainvillea splashed its color against the stone wall. It was beautiful. I hoped San Diego would be as lovely.

Returning to our campsite, Ma and I prepared supper. Our neighbors in Los Nietos had shown us how to make the tortillas out of corn as well as flour. We'd finished our meal when the stagecoach lads rattled by our site, heading in the opposite direction. Pa waved them in. Ma offered them tortillas and frijoles filled with fish I'd caught.

"How was San Diego?" my father asked when the lads had been fed.

"Terrible. Things aren't booming there at all. Just a sleepy town, not sure why folks thought it wasn't. We drove our stage a long way for nothin.' You've got as good a chance to make it here as there. We're heading to Los Angeles."

"I didn't see much in that City of Angels," my father said. "The street dust is practically to my knees." He smoked his pipe. "Nothing happening in San Diego? We may as well stay right here. Yes, that's what we'll do."

"Will you just take their word for it, Da? Ma wants to go to San Diego. It was our target."

"Targets change. We'll visit one day. But for now, the Lord has led us here, to a place with a church, and I bet I can find work down the road."

I wondered if my father's willingness to take the advice of others wasn't in part his business downfall and if we were headed there once again. He'd been taken advantage of by store managers; we'd moved from gulch to gulch based on only someone else's word that gold had been discovered. He closed down our establishment only to open another in Utah. And now on the words of some lads, we weren't even going forward to where Ma had always wanted. His mind was made up, just that quickly.

OUR CAMPING SITE, with a white picket fence like most others, sat on a hill just yards from the old Capistrano ruins with its gentle arches and green palm trees soaring above them. We were high enough to see the fog roll in and watch the seagulls dip and dive over the beaches and let the sunsets paint the sky its vibrant red. It was a town for romantics, with swallows nesting in the ruins' eaves, and I decided that here I would seek the treasures Father Van Gorp had referenced would come my way if I obeyed that fourth commandment to honor my parents. I wasn't sure how, but I had to move forward even if my father no longer headed toward San Diego. At least San Juan Capistrano had a post service. I sent a letter to Mary asking of the Helena news, hoping she'd write back and tell me of the doings of one Peter Ronan. Meanwhile, I would learn the Mexican Spanish of the people who had welcomed us. I didn't do well with numbers, but languages tripped easily off my tongue.

We became even more settled in Capistrano after my father came home from a visit with an Irish hotel owner and his Mexican wife. "The US Land Commission is trying to settle title issues from when California was part of Mexico. The local mayor, an *alcalde* named Richard Egan, will help me work through the legal stuff." He was in high spirits. "I'll plow my own land for the first time."

My father set about acquiring 160 acres that he purchased at $2.25 an acre and paid the US government monthly. I remember how proud he was to be buying a ranchero. A creek flowed through it and the site was close to the olive orchard that the mission padres kept. When they used the old stone press, the scent of olive oil filled the air.

We pitched our big tent in a swale below the hills the Mexicans called *lomas*, used my quilt and ones Ma had in order to create a divide from living and bedroom space. The weather was so mild, even in early December, that we spent many more hours outside. I missed the spruce sledding of Helena.

Pa and I went to work planting corn and potatoes, both of which thrived and gave us a good crop within the season. When Ma said it might be fine for a rancher to have a real house, Pa hired a carpenter who finished the frame.

"I can help do the adobe," I said.

"Too hard a work for a girl."

My Spanish was good enough now that I had conversed with our female neighbors and learned that Mexican women always did the adobe work. They were *enjarradoras*, plasterers.

My father was unconvinced.

"Even the alcalde says it's so. Men set the beams, put up the scaffolding, and mix the mud, but women do the rest."

"They are truly home makers," Ma said. "Outside and inside."

I nodded. "The alcalde told me that some women 'like the mud, yes?' That's how he said it." I squished my fingers in and out to show my interest in the texture. "He says it is very hard work, but any girl who could manage a six-mule team through the desert can surely plaster a house."

"He knows you did that?" My father raised an eyebrow to show his interest.

"I enjoy his company."

"He would be a good husband for you."

"He's just a friend, Pa." *Why is that older man an acceptable suitor but Peter wasn't?*

"No," my father said. "It wouldn't be right for a lady to do that work despite what the alcalde says. I'll get someone to help me finish it."

But the field work kept him from that task and once again a target wasn't met.

We Sheehans celebrated Christmas in the tent, Valentine's Day, Saint Patrick's Day, and even Easter. As the days grew warmer, Ma said she was worried we would have to endure the summer heat with just a dusty canvas.

"We'll ambush him when he gets back from Los Angeles. And if he resists, we will proceed without his consent. Are you prepared for that?"

Ma Anne hesitated, then, "Yes. The time has come."

The hour grew late. Ma and Kate and Jimmy finally went to bed, but I stayed up, waiting, wondering what I'd do if something happened to him, if he didn't return. The very thought of my outliving him kept me awake until I heard the wagon rattle down the road. I grabbed the lantern and opened the gate for him. He drove past me but then stopped. He hopped from the wagon, and he hugged me, kissed the top of my head. I heard him sigh. "Mollie, you looked just like your mother standing there in the moonlight."

His embrace startled me. When he released me, I could see the tears in his eyes. Ma Anne adored him, but I saw then that it was my mother who still held his heart.

In the morning, Ma and I made our case that I be allowed to help him plaster the adobe. "It's gone on too long," Ma Anne said.

"The tents work fine."

He resisted still until I said, "You know my mother would want a real home for me, for you and any whom you say you love."

Ma Anne flinched. I had never mentioned my mother in front of her before. I hadn't meant to hurt her. I touched her shoulder.

"It's alright." She whispered the words. "I know."

My father was quiet, then, "You bring out the shame in me, lass. We'll get the house finished."

HE MIXED AND LOADED the mortar, putting it into buckets, and with a Gem's help, he hoisted it up to me on the scaffolding. Sweat dampened my head. My hands cracked from the mud. My shoulders ached as I moved along the boards to build a home. But we accomplished what we set out to do and soon had a four-room adobe house. Downstairs was a living area and a small bedroom. An outside staircase took one to the attic, we called it, with a board floor and two bedrooms. The kitchen was where it had been since we had the tent set up: in a small cabin close to the back porch. We whitewashed the adobe and our neighbors named it *Casa Blanca*. From our house, we could hear the bells calling us and could walk just down the hill to the chapel. We were in an adobe house we built ourselves on land we owned. It would have been the happy ending for my father and Anne if it had not been for the mix-up in the land titles.

THE MEXICANS BEGAN to call us "squatties" in English or *injusto occupente* in their language. They still bought our produce and they were kind to me and Kate, Jimmy and Ma too, but they kept their distance from us now, not stopping by to sit in the shade or offer suggestions for patching the adobe. We became strangers, outsiders, not angels to be welcomed. Even the alcalde said he wasn't certain about what could be done.

Once twenty men surrounded my father's wagon as he headed to Casa Blanca after a long day's work in the fields. I heard my father shouting. "Show me your deed and I will pay you as I pay the United States who says this is my land. Show me your deed!"

Their shouts grew louder. I could hear them as I watched from the window wondering what I'd do if they attacked him. I looked around. Ma's rolling pin would be my weapon.

That time, they went away, tired of his repeated "Show me your deed." I wondered if we'd soon move on.

Then the lawsuit came, the previous owners of the land moving forward with their claim. The alcalde said we must hire an attorney, an expense we had no money for. My father paced inside the cool adobe. But sometimes goodness comes from trials. And that was how, despite the anxiety of ownership and lawsuits, Peter Ronan came back into my life.

SIXTEEN

No End to That

P a hired a lawyer from Los Angeles and the case wended its way through legal meetings and barriers we had never imagined, until a year later we learned the case was to go to the Supreme Court of the United States. For this, Martin Maginnis of Montana, a lawyer and friend of my father's, agreed to argue the case before that court. Mr. Maginnis was a partner in the newspaper owned by Peter Ronan, the man who had received the Puddin-pilfered pencil. Mr. Maginnis's wife, Louise, wrote to me after my father hired her husband, but not of legal things. She told me of the "doings" in Helena.

"*Mr. Maginnis's partner, Peter Ronan, is escorting Annie Brown to dances now,*" she wrote. "*But you probably have little interest in such news with your life so full in Capistrano, or so your father writes.*"

The news of Peter faltered me. *Why shouldn't he have moved on?* Perhaps after all, my father was correct. He had suspicioned that once I was out of sight, I would soon be out of Peter's mind.

With the case awaiting its court date, the confrontations with our neighbors ceased and we were a part of the village of San Juan

Capistrano once again. I vowed to put Peter from my mind and truly enter into California life. Because of the alcalde taking notice of me, I was invited into the circle of more affluent Mexicans and Spaniards. I couldn't dress as well as they did with their lace and silks, nor reciprocate with lavish parties. But my inquisitiveness and genuine interest in their lives must have appealed, for they welcomed me, called me *La Mary* because I was American. Girls named Mary among my peers in San Juan were called *Señorita Maria*. I liked having a special name and feeling a part of old customs and happy gatherings. I pretended I belonged there.

The alcalde served as mayor in this town. People both trusted and adored him. I did as well. He allowed me the key to a small cabin he owned just above the shoreline. It faced the ocean and I could read there or walk the beach. He lived at the hotel, but the beach house he kept stocked with books and the latest newspapers. I found the *Gazette* there one afternoon and read an article of how the *Gazette* had recovered from a fire just after we'd left Helena. Peter had written the piece, printed on the anniversary of the fire. The *Gazette* had kept publishing with the help of the Republican *Montana Post*, a competitor. I could hear his voice in the rhythm of his words. I would have written my condolences for his loss if I had known. Mary turned out to be a poor correspondent and Ellen knew almost nothing of Helena, wrapped as she was in her family and those longhorns.

One day, when the alcalde dropped off newspapers while I was at his beach house, I told him about Peter, of my broken engagement at my father's insistence. "And now I have a letter from my father's attorney. Well, his attorney's wife, that Peter's found someone else. He didn't really fight for me."

"It is a difficulty when family does not see the same, yes? And the distance, it makes resolution—that is the word, yes?" I nodded. "It makes imaginings fill the holes of uncertainty in the resolution."

"Holes of uncertainty. Yes, I fill them with sadness, anger, and confusion."

"Come to the fiestas. There will be other loves for La Mary with the beautiful hair."

I'd never spent time with people of such wealth as the Castilians of San Juan, who spoke their language with the slightest lisp, after their Castilian king. My good ear claimed the difference, so *gracias* sounded like *gra-thee-us* when I expressed my thank-you. The alcalde said it was an accommodation appreciated by my hosts. *Perhaps I can find employment as an interpreter.*

I did worry about the fashion of my hostesses.

"It is the simplicity and whiteness and hot iron on the edges of your tunics that makes your statement, *si?*" the alcalde said. Dresses Ma and I made were always white, sewed with simple lines. I'd heat the irons and press seams and petticoats into crispness. I often wore a simple coral necklace that John Sweeney had sent to me at Christmas. My father had not objected to the gift nor its sender.

A colorful shawl with black fringe that reminded me of my mother's lost umbrella completed my ensemble. "They will notice not your fashion, La Mary, but your countenance, your gift of interest in others, and your kindnesses." The alcalde's words made me think of my mother.

The amusements that attending special parties promised helped push Peter from my mind. Once after a gathering moved thirty miles to yet another hacienda with musicians and tables of food spread across the flower-scented courtyard, I spent the night. In the morning I was fed chocolate and toast in what my hosts called the "little breakfast." The Bandinis' hacienda bed was so soft I imagined myself as the princess of the "Princess and the Pea" from a book in the alcalde's beach cabin called *Fairy Tales Told for Children.* A princess, who only at the end, was satisfied. I loved the fiestas celebrating a young girl turning sixteen. The Mexicans knew it was the age when reason could prevail.

My father never said a word about my being out all evening, though he always asked if the alcalde had attended too. "He'd be a fine catch, Mollie."

"Why is it you encourage some interest by men like John Sweeney or the alcalde but not Peter Ronan?"

"Don't speak that traitor's name."

"You affirm those men whom I have no interest in yet deprive me of the one love I wished for."

"You know nothing of true love."

Maybe I didn't, with Peter stepping out with others.

WE'D BEEN GONE TWO YEARS, and yet the very thought of Peter still caused me to catch my breath. I tortured myself by reading the Meagher book Peter had returned and asked me to reread. He'd underlined certain words and phrases, about "<u>faithfulness</u> to duty" or "<u>love</u> of Ireland," but put in the context of a lover to his mate, the words could take on new meaning. Yet Peter had moved on. I needed to do that too.

A letter arrived from Father Van Gorp, who once had offered comfort telling me riches awaited me if I was an obedient child and broke the engagement. *"I write at Peter Ronan's request to tell you that he still wears the gold ring you gave him and said for him to keep until you asked for it. Since you have not, he considers himself still engaged to you and prays you feel the same."*

I was astounded. We'd had no communication, nothing between us for two years. How could he imagine I'd still consider us engaged? For some reason—perhaps carrying a Shakespearean fatal character flaw of fantasizing that my father would offer comfort—I showed the priest's letter to my father. "I thought there was an end to that business. I see the two of you failed to keep your commitment, your having let him keep your silly ring. I might have known."

I didn't want to say that Peter had offered to return the ring that morning we separated.

"If I had the means, I'd go to Helena tomorrow and get that

ring and tell him to stay out of our lives." My father flicked the letter with his finger. "Now even the priest is engaged in this? It's your duty to request it back and free him. And all of us."

I cried that night, the pain as fresh as when I'd said goodbye to Peter. In the morning I wrote to Father Van Gorp. "*Please tell Mr. Ronan that he is freed of his obligation to me and to pursue other directions as Mrs. Maginnis writes he has a mind to, courting Miss Annie Brown. I'd like the ring returned.*"

Maybe I'd find respite in a convent.

IT TOOK A MONTH, but the ring arrived. It had worked its way through the envelope and some kind soul at the postal office had put it inside another and addressed it to me. I didn't recognize the handwriting when the small package appeared. The original had come from the priest, along with these words. "*How very sorry I am that you are not to marry Peter,*" he wrote. "*He is a good, faithful man who wishes you great treasures in your future.*"

How could it be that a man the priests approved of should be so disdained by the other great love of my life, my father? The priest at Capistrano, Padre Mut, had said, "God works in mysterious ways."

I wasn't fond of mysteries, only fairy tales with happy endings.

I put the little gold ring on my finger. The engagement now severed, I set about considering life without a husband, one as a dutiful daughter looking after my father and my family. Could I do so from the convent?

A week later, Mrs. Maginnis wrote expressing deep regret for any mention that might have affected my connection with Peter Ronan, "*who has asked that I write to tell you of my error in mentioning Annie Brown. Miss Brown is considering the convent—and not pursued by Mr. Ronan at all.*"

What kind of man sends his former suitors to the convent?

I wondered how old I'd need to be or what I'd need to do to satisfy the commandment of honoring my father.

"TAKE THE TEACHER'S TEST, Mollie," my father said. "It would be a huge help to our unsteady income." We were speaking after the mass with Padre Mut of San Juan.

"It would stabilize our having a teacher here," the padre said. "Your father tells me you ran a school in Montana."

I didn't want to teach, not after Jules Germain's death and my difficulty with arithmetic. I kept my father's accounts, but teaching numbers was beyond me.

Still, because I kept track of produce sold, seeds bought, equipment repair costs, doctor visits, and Ma's household expenditures, I knew that being a paid teacher would help our family. Ma had developed an ailment that brought on wheezing, so considering another "eating establishment" was out of the question to fill our meager coffers. She was exhausted fixing meals with my help. And I wanted to help. I had the recreations of parties and fiestas, dances and horseback rides along the wild Capistrano coast as pastimes. I could get away from the field work, live inside a dreamy world of others' wealth. Ma could not. She'd wait for my pa to end his working day, more often than not without a word of gratitude for her efforts at her meals and keeping house. Yet he'd praise me when I merely brought his pipe to him. "Ah, what a gift you are, Mollie."

Once I boldly mentioned my observation to Ma. "Your father loves you dearly, Mollie. He loves all his children. He takes care of us." She coughed. "You mustn't feel badly that he favors you. He wants to keep you close. You're a much bigger help to him than I can be."

"Alright," I told the padre. "I'll take the teacher's test. But only after I've had time to study."

I did study. I prayed about it. I took the test.

I failed it.

"You never had proper schooling," my father said to console me. "Those scattered years with teachers barely there a month or two in mining towns was not enough." I didn't remind him that Peter had brought about a school in Helena through the Sisters of Charity and that I could have attended if we had stayed in Helena.

"Perhaps a year in the Los Angeles school of St. Vincent de Paul would be enough that you might take the test again," Padre Mut suggested. My father and I met with him to share the humiliating test results. "I know Sister Scholastica." He tightened his rope belt around his thick waist. "We could arrange a way for you to attend and pay your fees later. They make loans. Scholarships."

I didn't imagine that even with another year of schooling I would be able to pass the test.

"Pursue it, Padre."

My father's words surprised me. "But—"

"I will sacrifice having you here with us," my father said. "In order for you to do bigger things. Become a teacher. Help your family and this little school. Don't be selfish, Mollie."

The padre lowered his eyes, threaded the rope belt through his hands. Then he brightened. "I will see if Miss Sheehan can take music lessons at the academy as well. She could direct the choir when she returns to our little village."

"And maybe those still distressed about our land issues will see us once again as neighbors rather than intruders," my father said. "You graduate and then come back to me, your papa." The padre frowned and my father added, "To all of us. To teach and play the organ and sing. For us all."

Men were always directing my path.

SEVENTEEN

Providence Moves

The convent school mesmerized. There was no need to pretend, "to take a stage." I could be quiet, observe, assist without sharing painful memories or expressing worries about my future. I loved the gardens with their orange trees scenting the air in season, begonias blooming. The synchrony of the way we girls toured the neighborhood two by two, calmed. Our uniforms took away the worries of how I dressed. Walks past grand houses built in the three years since we'd visited little Los Angeles and gotten lost, appealed. Where once were cabins with picket fences, now stood adobe homes with balconies and iron gates promising courtyards should we ever go inside. Bougainvillea cascaded like waterfalls over the lips of verandas.

In the convent, I could study, read, sing, and I was kept safe from all matter of worries. I loved the simple acts of scrubbing floors, washing tunics, helping in the kitchen. I missed the fiestas and the parties, but here was the drama of liturgy, delving into the faith, joining choirs that echoed against adobe walls.

I didn't think of Peter Ronan at all. In fact, the idea had begun in seriousness that I might truly join the order. I didn't know how

I'd repay the loan for my schooling nor how I could help my father or the village if I did, but I felt a growing call.

Sister Scholastica advised me to consider prayerfully and to give it time. "There is still a newness that greets all students who come to the school and board here, even after a year. Away from family demands, with the certainty of days, it's comforting. But to join the convent, there should be not a wish to escape but to serve."

I wasn't sure how I could serve. I was in the receiving mode and wondered if I'd always been greedy, a receiver more than a giver.

"There is evidence, too, that a great wavering over something consumes you, Mary. Such spiritual struggles must be resolved before you could take your vows."

She was insightful. My whole life I'd been trying to please my father, at the expense of finding my own path. I'd wanted his blessing, but it seemed I always failed him. It was never enough. I was never enough.

A NEW TEACHER ARRIVED—Rose Kelly. She would teach the organ. And amazingly, she came from Helena and knew all the news. Even about my life and the letter writing of Mrs. Maginnis and Father Van Gorp to me on behalf of Peter Ronan. "Oh, you're wearing the gold ring Peter sent back." She leaned into me. "So tragic and romantic. We all heard about that."

"You . . . have?"

"Peter asked the entire staff at the church and all of the Sisters to pray that you two would be reunited," Rose said.

"Well, that's all over now."

"One never knows what Providence has in store." She fairly sang the words.

A segment of Helena both knew about and cared enough to advance my romantic yearnings? I had a dozen fairy godmothers and hadn't even known it. My nights grew restless, filled with dreams.

But it wasn't Rose Kelly's news that changed my course. It was my father coming up from Capistrano for a visit. "This is a lovely place, Mollie. And you're liking it here? Learning a lot?"

"Oh yes. I'll graduate next year. I'll be twenty years old."

"You'll pass the test in good order and come back to me, to us. Kate misses you."

"And I, her."

I knew it was the moment to bring up a plan that had formed in my mind. I wouldn't take the test right away, but instead return to Helena first. I thought that was the only way to see if I was being genuinely called by God toward the sweet, orderly, studious routine of the order or if being loved by Peter was what my future held. But I knew if I told my father of my conflict, he'd be distressed. I didn't feel strong enough to withstand his disappointment. So I told him stories of Los Angeles, the Chinese Tong Wars, the places we girls were forbidden to walk by when we toured two abreast. I acted happy.

"But you like your studies?" We were in the convent gardens, a place I imagined to be like the garden of Eden with its beauty and peace.

"I do. And I'm considering . . ." I couldn't finish. Instead, I pointed out an olive tree and reminded him of when we'd first arrived at Capistrano and an old tree from the mission grove had fallen over. He'd propped it up and watered it.

"I remember," he said. "I told myself if I could keep that tree alive, it would be a sign that I could keep my family alive too, that God was blessing my decision to bring us all to California. Away from Helena and your . . . Peter." He nearly spit the name. "And here you are. Flourishing like that tree, soon to return to us."

I had permission to travel to another part of the city with my father to visit a man he'd known who had moved from Helena. He had a small ranchero, and we entered the cool of his adobe home on a hot afternoon in January. We passed a table holding a pottery bowl that looked like a gold pan. A letter lay inside. My breath caught, and before I could stop myself, I blurted, "Is that from Peter Ronan?"

My father, having preceded me through the hallway, jerked his head toward me.

"Why, yes, it is," our host answered. "You recognize his handwriting?" I nodded. "My brother is ill, and Peter's been tending to his needs in Montana. He wanted to alert me and also seek advice. He's such a good man, that Peter."

"I . . . I knew him once."

"You're trembling. This unseasonal warmth can be beastly. Would you like a glass of cool water?" He took my elbow, helped me sit. "I've put lemon twists in the pitcher from our very own tree."

I barely heard him, my thoughts so consumed by my reaction to just seeing Peter's penmanship. Was this a coincidence, luck that we came to visit when we did? I didn't believe in luck.

NOT TWO WEEKS after my father's visit, his friend left a note for me at the convent. "*Miss Sheehan. I wrote to Peter Ronan about my brother's needs and in my reply I mentioned that a friend of his was attending school here and had recognized his handwriting. He wrote back forthwith and said he was* 'glad to hear of Miss Sheehan especially as I had understood that she had not only forgotten my handwriting but my very name.' *I think you might send him a note to reassure him of your friendship.*" The note included Peter's address.

Was this divine intervention, all the little threads of faith weaving genuine love between us? Part of the riches Scripture promised by honoring my father all those years before? Or was it the devil's work of a disobedient daughter?

How I wished my mother were alive for me to talk to. Instead, I spilled my worries to Sister Scholastica.

"It is perhaps a door," she said. "You can keep it closed or walk through."

"But I don't know what's on the other side."

"We never do. It is the walk of faith."

IT WAS FEBRUARY 1872, and Valentine's Day was soon upon us. I sent handmade cards to my family. Then with trembling hands, I cut folded pieces of paper into a heart and pressed inside it a rose geranium leaf that in the language of flowers meant "preference." I signed it "*Love, Mollie*" and with a prayer sent it off to Peter.

Within the week, Peter wrote to say he knew what the rose geranium meant and that he hoped it was not some hoax another played on him, that I truly was his "preference." He ended it with "*I will not recount the pure and tender love I bear you, which neither silence nor the unhappy circumstances of our parting could efface—I still hoped on, loved on and will continue to do so until I am formally told that it is useless.*" He signed it "*Affectionately yours, Peter Ronan.*"

I danced in my small room at the school, his letter to my breast. I allowed the joy but knew then I must tell my father that I wasn't coming back to be a teacher. I'd find another way to pay back the convent's costs and help my family. I had to do it soon.

I invited my father to visit again. We took a walk, climbed a small hill, and sat on a blanket. I showed him Peter's latest letter, my heart pounding.

"I can't imagine you still care for that tinker."

"My plan is to find out if in the years we've been apart he has changed or if how I feel about him no longer warrants marriage."

"Marriage? Never."

I took a deep breath. "When I graduate, Pa, I'm going to Helena, to visit Ellen and my godchild. And Mary. And I will see Peter.

I'll either say goodbye for good or welcome him back into my heart."

"And if he no longer has this . . . this control over you and you come to your senses, what then?"

"I'll begin the process of joining the order of the Sisters of St. Vincent de Paul."

He sat silent, the letter shaking in his hand.

I took it back, folded it. "I'll find a way to pay off my debt. Maybe teach somewhere, if I pass the test." I cleared my throat. "I think at twenty I'm old enough to make up my own mind."

"Honoring your parents is a commandment that does not end at twenty."

I bristled. "Perhaps a higher commandment is to listen to God's calling of oneself, too, to find out what we may be, not just what we are."

His tears came freely and he choked the words, "Sure, Mollie, if you want to marry a slacker, I wouldn't be the one to tell you no."

I didn't hear his fractured blessing. All I heard was *slacker*! This successful businessman, this contributor to charitable causes, this kind man. There was no reaching my father on this matter. Why had I thought there might be? I was on my own. I always had been. If upon seeing Peter, there was nothing there, I could expect my father to simply say "I told you so." And should Peter and I restore our romance, it would mean a final severing from my father. I saw no other ending to this fairy tale I was living.

ONCE AGAIN, I FAILED the teacher's test. My inadequacy added to my distress that spring. I had an outstanding obligation to the Sisters that I needed a way to pay for, and I wanted that trip to Montana to affirm or deny my future with Peter.

Since my father's last visit, Peter and I had corresponded, and it was he who offered condolences for my failing the test. "*It doesn't mean you aren't an intelligent woman. God has other plans for you, I'm sure of it."*

I wrote back with gratitude and wondered if some business interest might bring him to California, as I couldn't see my way to Montana any time soon. He not only said he would come at once if I'd but set the date for our marriage, but that any amount owed to the school he would pay forthwith. He'd pay if I didn't marry him. *"And as for helping your family, I would do what you think most beneficial. A loan. A gift. Payment of attorney fees?"* My father's land case had not yet gone to court. *"A purchase of land that he might remain without fear of payment to another? Would he accept any of this from me?"*

I didn't know.

"Give me a date and I will come."

It's said that indecision is the greatest agony, that once one decides, then Providence moves. Somewhere in the Scriptures Jesus commands that we let our yes be yes and our no be no. I was in a nearly sinful state, not able to let my yes be yes while still agonizing over my father's constant no.

Despite my failing the test, I would graduate, and I was asked to give the student address. I thought about referring to that indecisive state of being and its pain, but instead my speech was titled "The Sphere and Influence of Women." It was later published in the *Los Angeles Star*, June 15, 1872. It was a heartfelt presentation of the value of women, our commitment to hearth and home, our demonstration of the faith in daily life and for others. I thought of teachers, my dear Ma Anne operating establishments in cabins and tents, the Sisters who served the poor and dedicated their lives to following God's direction. I even remembered Melody, the girl who made her living dancing. We were an agile gender. But remembering my mother who I saw reflected in Ellen's life with a loving husband, children, that's the sphere I wanted to influence on my own. I knew who I was and yet not what I could be and said that was so for all women who continue to learn, live with uncertainty, and follow quests that deepen our faith.

I had practiced this presentation before a mirror that I might do my best, all for an audience of one, sitting far back in the crowd of strangers, my dear father. How I wished that I had invited Peter to attend.

TOWARD THE END OF SUMMER, I gave Peter the date of early September. His letter outlined what lay ahead. "*We will marry in Capistrano and return to Helena after a honeymoon.*"

Marry him the same day after not seeing him for four years? Could I really do that?

He finished the letter with a line that threatened everything he'd said before. "*There is a fearful cry! The office is in flames. Adieu.*"

EIGHTEEN

WISHING FOR WHAT ISN'T

It would be the third time Peter had lost a newspaper. The one in Leavenworth to Union vandals; the fire just after we left Helena; and now this. I asked my music teacher if she'd heard anything from Helena. She had not, but then the Los Angeles paper included an article about the terrible fire in that Montana town.

I tore open Peter's letter when it arrived soon after.

I still have my health, my courage, my energy, and in a few days will again be established in business. This misfortune will not deter me from making my trip to marry you. I may be poorer than when I wrote earlier, but I know this will have no effect on us. Farewell, dear love. I will see you in a month.

Peter

I learned later the J. H. Curtis building that housed the *Gazette* was one of sixty buildings that burned in downtown Helena that August. Peter included a newspaper clip with an illustration of the burned blocks in the city, the first time a newspaper in the territory

145

had tried to illustrate a story. Sadly, it wasn't Peter's paper but the *Helena Daily Herald* instead.

Peter's *Rocky Mountain Gazette* went back to press in September—his rival's machines making it possible. There'd be no fall wedding, but Peter sent a letter to my father making a formal request for my hand. I was back in San Juan and there when Ma pressed my father to return a letter quickly giving his consent.

But Peter's hoped-for four weeks in time for the priest to say the banns turned into four months while he revived his livelihood. How I longed to go to Helena. But I had no way.

In December, Peter wrote to say a few more weeks were needed as his partner, Martin Maginnis, was heading to Washington and would bring back new presses when he returned. Maginnis had recently been elected as Montana's first non-voting representative to the US Congress and would take office the following year. He was also scheduled to argue my father's case before the Supreme Court.

On December 24, 1872, the local items section in the *Gazette* reported that "Peter Ronan was risking inclement weather, storms and snow to find a place in California where 'love wanders and orange blossoms are always in bloom.'" Someone else must have written the article, but it came in an envelope from Father Van Gorp. The priests were still involved in our affair.

Peter was on his way across the Sierra or perhaps following the desert route we'd taken in the dust of the stagecoach lads.

I could hardly wait, and yet I feared how I'd feel when he arrived, uncertainty a fragrance too familiar.

That night my mother came to me in a dream. "How will I know?" I asked her.

"You'll recognize love," she said. "Charity suffereth long, and is kind . . ." In my dream, she spoke the entire thirteenth chapter from 1 Corinthians. I knew the Scripture in Latin as my dream-mother spoke it. "Love" was what the word "charity" meant. Was our love the kind that Scripture described? I did not know. But my mother had reminded me how to recognize love's characteristics.

I knew my father loved me; but it was Peter's behavior toward me that reflected the love of Scripture.

"LA MARY. COME. I have something to show you."

I was back in San Juan, where I'd been since my graduation helping with the ranchero, helping at the mission. The alcalde drew me away from my choir rehearsal on a January morning. I met him in the arched cloister, the scent of incense blending with the orange blossoms. He sat on a stone bench, waving a telegraph in his hand. He'd established the telegraph service in Capistrano and took the messages himself. "It is from your Peter. He is in Los Angeles and awaits your invitation for him to come on the next coach to this very place."

I felt faint. After all this time, he was so close. Yet the old strain between father and fiancé commanded churning in my stomach. I was relieved that he had made it through the snows and storms and terrified of what four years apart might have done to us. I stayed silent.

"It demands a reply, La Mary. What do you wish me to say, *mi amiga?*"

"I don't know," I whispered. "I don't know what to say." I looked up at this good friend, his black hair falling across one side of his face. He brushed it aside. *What if he isn't what I thought? What if I'm not?* "You answer it." This was no stage play. I hadn't rehearsed my next line.

"But I cannot. Unless you tell me, La Mary, whether he is to come on farther or return."

Am I truly worthy of such riches? Can I live with the consequences of my decisions?

I looked out between the ancient pillars of the ruins, and I remembered the dream. "Tell him to come." If he came south from Los Angeles and I no longer saw in him the man that I would marry, I would send him back to Helena. I prayed I'd have the courage to be brave enough to be true to myself.

THE ALCALDE SENT a child to tell us Peter was now at the hotel.

"You must go to meet him, James." Ma Anne pushed him through the door.

"He has my consent, reluctant though I gave it. That's enough. There's no blessing in it. I still pray you come to your senses, Mollie."

"It's the proper thing for a father to do. Go on. Out you go." Ma Anne handed him his hat.

He stopped to pull up weeds along the way. He dawdled.

"What if Peter's changed *his* mind?" I asked.

"He's come a long way to tell you." Ma Anne smiled, patted flour tortillas she'd serve for our supper when the men returned. If they both returned.

"What if my father says something that sends him away? Or they get into a fistfight?"

Ma stopped her work then. "Your father won't go back on his word, much as he might have regretted giving his consent in the first place."

"Why is that, his unwillingness to see Peter as the good man he is? Even the priests approve of Peter."

"Don't you know?" She brushed her hands on her apron, then sat down. "Your father is envious of Peter, that he can take care of you, give you luxuries he can't."

"But he encouraged others to court me. John Sweeney. The alcalde. Why not Peter?"

"I think he saw your love for Peter as sincere and lasting. He fears you'll give your all to Peter, have no room for him. Marriage to John or the alcalde would be half felt. Your pa could keep you close." She sighed. "Perhaps he misses what he had with your mother and thought by keeping you near, he could somehow sweep away the grief he still bears at her death."

Her understanding humbled me. "It isn't right though, is it?" She stood to slice tomatoes. "Does it . . . does it bother you, Ma Anne, that my father gives some of his heart to my mother still, and so much to me?"

"Your father loves me. True love makes room for others." *Echoes of my mother's quoting Scripture in my dream.*

I would find out what kind of love I had with Peter and prayed I'd be as gracious as my stepmother.

I watched the roadway, then walked toward the gate so I could see them when they rose over the hill. And then I saw them, the two men with space between them large enough for Dange to come bounding, tail wagging as the dog trotted out to them. Peter bent to pet the old dog as I watched him through the dusk. Then he saw me. He walked more quickly, never breaking his gaze, leaving my father behind.

"Here's your . . . Peter," my father said, then brushed past us into the house.

I barely registered his presence. It was Peter who still held my heart.

Without hesitation, Peter placed his two large hands on both cheeks, looked into my eyes. "At last, Mollie, at last." Then my tears obscured his face as I felt the peace I'd prayed for. Certainty, the storehouse of treasure promised.

PETER STROKED MY HAIR as he held me to him. "I'm glad you didn't cut it. You look just the same as when I said goodbye."

"I did cut it once. But it's long enough to sit on again."

"It's beautiful. You're beautiful." My Irish Prince Charming kissed me. Then he put his arm around my waist, and we went into Casa Blanca.

Peter greeted Kate and tipped his hat to Jimmy and to Ma, who smiled then coughed. "Good to have you here, Mr. Ronan." She offered cool lemon water while my father brooded in the corner.

I didn't ask what my father said to him as they walked from the hotel to our home. He didn't tell me, at least not then. Peter was sure of himself. Gentle, kind. Told stories of his journey to make us all laugh, even Pa once. He had not changed, and I knew he'd be my happily ever after. I only hoped one day my father would see it.

Later that evening as we walked beneath a Capistrano moonlight, Peter took out a gold ring. "See if this fits you, Mollie." He slipped it on my finger.

"It's perfect." I held it up so he could see.

He took another ring of diamonds set in gold that he had on his little finger and put that ring on my finger too. "I wish I could give you the first engagement ring back," he said.

"I hoped you would."

"My sister Margaret has it, along with some little gold cufflinks I'd had monogrammed with an 'M' for 'Mollie' I never got to give you. I'd had those made for you from gold I panned myself. She enjoys them immensely." He laughed.

I laughed too.

"But this ring, it speaks of even greater love than that first one. This ring"—he rubbed his thumb across it—"this ring was given me by a circle of friends in Helena. It speaks of love of friends, but more of mine to you. That they gave it to me says we're not alone, Mollie. There are many who wanted this to be."

All those godmothers praying, I thought. Our marriage wasn't just between God and us but between us and Helena's people who had watched us dance and grow together, then apart at my father's command. Love and prayers and friends had brought us back together.

WE HAD A WEEK before we'd marry so had time to visit the mission and the sea, to have Peter meet my friends. He fit in perfectly. He stayed at the hotel and spent time with Richard Egan, the alcalde, both men liking each other at first meeting. Peter admired his beach cabin and the copies of the *Gazette* he subscribed to that he found there. In the evenings when we walked along the beach, Peter told me of the struggles getting the presses back up, how he was poorer now than when he'd asked me for my hand, but the future with me in it looked promising. He could pay my school debt, could help in other ways if my father would accept it. I shared with him stories of the day of our departure, with John Sweeney's sweet prayer in the chapel; our time in Corinne when I'd cut my hair and acted like "one of the boys" to keep their hands off me.

"A clever woman you are, Mollie. I always knew that."

And Peter gave me gifts. That gold chain I'd returned, though not with a heart but with a cross and gold earrings to match. I'd wear them on my wedding day. I returned to him that little-finger ring of gold and told him how it almost didn't make it back to me but for a postmaster who took the time to save it.

"So many kept the fires burning." He kissed me. "We'll never let that fire go out."

All would have been a time of pleasant anticipation if not for my father. He did not hide his sadness. "Anne and I will never be able to live without you, Mollie," he said as we fed the Gems together. I would miss those mules, the four that were left.

"You did just fine while I was in Los Angeles," I said. "I looked over your records. Vegetable and hay sales are excellent."

"Yes, yes, things have progressed well in that regard. But you were the mortar, Mollie. You kept it all together and now you're leaving me. Poor little Kate is awash with sadness."

"She'll come visit. You can too. It's what people do, Pa. Didn't you take my mother from her father?"

"Her pa was dead. And I am dead with your parting."

I ought to have realized it before, but it came pronounced that week. His clinging to a fantasy he held, that I would live with him forever, take care of him and give up a love like Peter's. It was his fairy tale, perhaps how he kept the memory of my mother alive. One evening at the field's edge, he called me to walk beside him while he plowed. When he finished a furrow near the gate, he bowed his head. Flies bit at Opal and she swished her tail and stomped. "Look at these fields, Mollie. You will never, never see me plow again."

I took his words to mean that he would no longer farm. "That would be sad," I said. "You have a good ranchero. You can hire others to help you if you decide not to plow. Jimmy will be old enough one day. Kate's a good helper at eleven."

"Not like you, Mollie. No one is like you." His voice cracked. "You'll be gone. You won't see your poor da working for you. You'll be gone."

I hated hurting him. "I'll always love you, Pa. But I love Peter too. Differently."

He drove the mule to the corral then, leaving me standing alone.

The night before our nuptials, an Irish stranger came by. "I've been told there's to be a wedding on the morrow. 'Tis good luck for a betrothed couple to be visited by a stranger the night before their marriage." We fed him and he went on his way. It was good luck for him—I hoped it was for us as well.

"Entertaining angels," Peter said. "We shall always welcome strangers, yes, Mollie?"

I agreed. How little I knew then of the many strangers who would come into our lives.

THE MORNING OF OUR WEDDING, my father walked with me to the church. He leaned on me, if I was honest in my description. He wept. Kate, with her red hair bound with a white ribbon, skipped ahead, holding Jimmy's hand; my brother turned around, smiling. They were happy for me. Not my father. *Do I deserve such happiness if it brings such sorrow to my father?*

But I remembered something Ma said, too, as she brushed my hair the night before. "Your pa's love for you brings him sorrow, but the pain is of his choosing, Mollie. He wants things to be different than they are and that always leads to suffering, which only he can stop by accepting what is. Time and intention will prevail."

I could not stop his sorrow. But I must not let his agony rob me of my joy. Today was my wedding day and I would rejoice in it.

It was at sunrise when Peter and I spoke our vows with only a few people in the chapel: Padre Mut, my father, sister, brother, and the alcalde too. I had dreamed of a fairy-tale wedding with a flowing dress and lace veil, but I was of modest means and chose simplicity instead. I wore a pearl-gray dress with a train and bridal veil Ma and I made ourselves. I could smell the orange blossom wreath I carried, the scent inhaled as joy.

Hand in hand Peter and I walked back to Casa Blanca where Ma had been preparing a wedding breakfast. My Capistrano friends might have wondered that we didn't have a big fiesta, but we offered a simple meal for our neighbors and some friends who came by that afternoon. We served them food Ma and I had prepared, and our neighbors and friends toasted us in English and in Spanish. Peter kept looking at me, enjoying my interpretation of our friends' good wishes spoken in Spanish, which he couldn't understand. At midnight, our friends serenaded, then bid us adios. We spent the night at the hotel. My father had gone to bed hours before.

Peter and I caught the stage the next morning at 4:00 a.m.

We were the only passengers, for which I thanked God because I cried. Peter held me. He didn't mock my sadness at leaving my family behind. "You can cry anytime you want. I'll hold you. This new path is a blend of joy and grief. But one day, the joy will win out."

"I just hoped that my father could have blessed our marriage."

"It will have to be enough that he consented to it. Give him time. Hopefully I'll prove myself adequate for his daughter."

"You're more than adequate. It's my being sufficient for him that's the lacking." *I must not wish for what isn't, but learn to love what is.*

NINETEEN

ALWAYS AN OPEN DOOR

It was dusk when we arrived in San Diego. I thought of Ma, who had wanted to come here but never did. One day I hoped my father would bring her to stay at the Horton House, an elegant hotel where Peter reserved a suite for us.

Word had gotten out that we were at the Horton, and a dozen friends from Montana and from those acquaintances of mine, mostly through the alcalde, arrived. As on our wedding evening, they serenaded us after having a supper served for all of us. It was a joyous time, though I was exhausted from the journey. We prepared for bed, this time with my husband brushing my hair while the ends nearly swept the floor below the chair I sat on.

"You attract many visitors," Peter said.

"Me attract visitors? No, they come to see you," I said. "The businessmen from Montana. I hear them talk of investments in land, in cattle and horses."

"I'm a newspaperman, that's my interest in economics. No, they came to see La Mary. The alcalde told me that's what they call you, and that you aren't American to them as much as *isleño*."

An islander. "Yes. Irish. This part of California seems to bring back memories of our island home." He finished and I twisted my hair into a braid. "I've never been to Ireland."

"You are beloved here, Mollie. In some ways, I hate to take you away from these benevolent people. But I'm heartened that you learned Spanish and Mexican—not just words, but manners and customs. I've married a smart woman."

"Not smart enough to pass the teacher's test."

"That's book larnin', ma'am," he jested. "You've the mind of a kind soul, a much higher calling. And you're a musician. The Helena Sisters can hardly wait for your return. You'll be the belle of the city. They'll welcome you back."

"Us. They'll welcome us."

I was part of an *us*, not encumbered with my father's clinging.

"Best of all, tonight you acted like you really enjoyed the company, even though I know you were tired. Our early morning departure. Sixty-five miles by stage. I remember when you were shy and retiring. Tonight, I watched as you asked after their health, their interests, their comfort. And you let acquaintances sing our praises."

"But I wasn't acting, Peter. I enjoyed them all."

ON THE TWENTIETH OF JANUARY, after a week in this balmy city of San Diego where nightly I shared my husband with visitors and guests, we took the steamer north to Los Angeles. Peter hired a carriage, and with several others from the ship, we visited the sights.

"Let's go to the academy," I said to our fellow travelers. "The convent gardens are lovely."

I introduced Peter to my instructors.

"This is the love that took you from us?" Sister Scholastica smiled.

"I'll take good care of her," Peter said.

"From what Father Van Gorp reports, I have no doubt." Her words of approval were another wedding gift.

From the convent gardens, we gathered up oranges, filling a basket for our ship journey that began anew that evening on our way to San Francisco. We spent a week there, where Peter's Montana friends—now residents of the city—found us. We joined them for the theater and concerts, dinners and dances. Peter sent me shopping with a Montana friend who took me to a modiste to have three frocks made. My new husband encouraged the purchase of a long broadcloth cloak with scalloped cape, a navy-blue ulster for coach travel, a mink stole and muff, and hats to correspond. I had my photograph made wearing the black gown with a colorful shawl hung across one shoulder as the señoritas of San Juan wore them. It was the wedding gift from my parents that Ma had handed me the night of our nuptials. That shawl draped across my black gown was the only sign of my life in Capistrano in that photograph.

Our fairy-tale time of shops and theater, companionship and conversation came to an end. We boarded the Union Pacific and raced across the desert through the rounded mountains to Corinne, Utah. The town had grown, my father's projection that it was dying out another miscalculation.

We took the stage from there toward Helena, where February mountain storms delayed us. A strange disease had affected dozens of horses, upsetting stagecoach schedules, too, and the roads were in terrible condition. We were delayed each day, sometimes not even making it between stage stops. One night we slept in a buffalo robe on the floor, all our lodging reservations long passed. Peter kept apologizing for the inconveniences.

"At least we're here together."

"You're an accommodating soul, Mollie. I'm a lucky man."

"Agile. We're agile," I said as I kissed his cheek.

We were nine days in misery before arriving at Helena and the St. Louis Hotel. Seeing it and remembering when I'd last left it in such sorrow caused a momentary catch in my heart. But this time I climbed the stairs to our room with tired delight. I began unpacking our overnight bag. Our trunks would be brought up in the morning. A knock on the door took Peter down to the desk while I unfolded our nightclothes. He returned from the lobby in a few minutes, looking sheepish.

"Ah, a few friends heard of our arrival and came to greet us. Are you up to it, Mollie?"

I saw the eagerness on his face. "Some of the ones who gave you the new engagement ring?"

He nodded. "And from Alder Gulch. They came several days ago, thinking we'd have arrived here before now. Shall I let them in?"

"Of course. What kind of wife would I be if I didn't always have an open door?"

The men pushed in as soon as Peter turned the glass doorknob. They'd been waiting just outside. More people arrived, some with their wives. I was grateful I hadn't started to undress. They filled the couches, sat on the arms of the chairs as well as in them, and on the floor. Our bed was in a separate room or they would have settled there as well.

I listened to their stories, of gold panning, of Peter's rendition of our long courtship, of our journey back from California, who we'd seen from Helena in San Diego and Los Angeles and San Francisco. Around midnight I went to the hotel kitchen and woke the cook, who frosted little cakes he'd planned for the morrow. As I offered coffee and served up the cakes, I heard the laughter and contentment in my husband's words. I wanted to go to bed. It was 2:00 a.m. But this was my life now, I imagined, acting like I wasn't tired, but instead wearing the mask of the happy hostess. I smiled as I watched my husband with love. I didn't have to act that part.

"You were a queen tonight," Peter said as we sank at last into bed. "I couldn't have asked for anyone to be so gracious to my rowdy friends. Thank you. Men talk at times about their scolding wives, and surely late-night gatherings could warrant such arguments. But you acted like it was the most natural thing in the world." He paused. "Where did you get those cakes?"

"They'll be on the hotel's bill," I told him. "Along with some extra for the sleepy cook I talked into frosting them and letting me have them. He had to bake several dozen more."

"It won't always be like this," he said. "People dropping in at all hours."

I pulled the down comforter up to my chin, then turned to kiss him. "Still, nothing makes me happier than seeing you happy. If that's cakes at two a.m., so be it."

I thought of Ma Anne as I drifted off to sleep. Maybe with me gone, my father would notice all she did for him and express his gratitude. Though my father and I had done the plastering of our Capistrano adobe, it was Ma who made Casa Blanca a home. I would do that, too, with my husband's blessing even—even if I never got my father's.

"HERE'S THE SCRAPBOOK," Peter said when he had our trunks brought in from another suite of rooms where he'd been staying since the *Gazette*'s fire. "And you need to tell me what you wrote in it and erased." He squinted. "It looks like 'other skies may bend above thee.'"

I took the scrapbook and finished writing the poem I'd written and erased that had indeed included those words.

"You kept it, though," I said.

"I was lucky to save it."

I learned that we'd be living at the hotel until the house Peter was having built for us was finished. Since the August fire had burned so many buildings, carpenters were busy.

"I have that valentine you sent me that told me we weren't finished. It was good your father made me return tomes you'd given me or they'd have been lost too."

My mother's Irish linens, her umbrella, all gone. Only my memory to hold her dear, bring her with me. "We'll open it with my poem and our marriage announcement."

Later that evening, a large but impromptu dinner had been planned by the midnight revelers of the night before. Invitations had gone out in the morning to "the city and its suburbs." It was too far for Ellen and Bill to come on such short notice—if even the invitation could have been ridden that far. And Mary had moved to a town even farther west called Missoula. She'd written to me while I was at the Sisters' academy. Our party that evening would be without any of my family—except Peter.

Two hundred attended the lavish and festive affair. Congressman and Mrs. Maginnis came. Mrs. Maginnis—I never called her Louise nor Peter's business partner Martin, though they were friends for life—hugged me, kissed each cheek. "You're the example I can give to whomever speaks of impossibilities," she said. "True love prevails. And prayers." She leaned into me. "I am so grateful you told Father Van Gorp who it was who had mentioned Peter courting Annie Brown so I could reconstruct my misunderstanding. Peter was helping the girl. I had no idea. She entered the convent, you know."

"There were things working we had no knowledge of," I said.

"We are so pleased to see you here in Helena again," Mrs. Maginnis said. She wore a tailor-made low-cut purple gown, with pearls around her neck. I wondered if she wasn't cold in such a dress. She had no cape nor shawl. "Perhaps your father and Mrs. Sheehan will return to Helena now."

The mere mention of my father caused me to pause. How would I feel about that? I had made the break, hadn't I? My father was no longer a shadow over my life.

"I think it unlikely," I said. "With Mr. Maginnis's lawyering success at the Supreme Court, my father plans to acquire forty acres more . . . to manage." I had been going to say *plow.*

"My husband's arguments won the day at the court."

"And my father is grateful. He's a full-time rancher now, not a freighter. Oh, your glass is empty. Let me fill it for you." Then I introduced her to one of Peter's friends and tended to another. We'd heard of the successful court resolution just weeks before our marriage. It was another gift that freed my father—and gave me freedom too. The only disappointment was lacking a news account to paste into our scrapbook.

THE *DAILY HERALD* sent a reporter to the gathering, whose story appeared in the February 18, 1873, issue. Of me they wrote: *"Early residents of this section of Montana knew the bride as Miss Mollie Sheehan, a modest, handsome, entertaining young lady. As Mrs. Ronan she appears the perfect matured lady whose habiliments were lovely but we make no attempt to describe them."*

But what the reporter wrote of Peter pleased me most: *"It was observed that Mr. Ronan was looking exceedingly well, and exhibited a countenance beaming in satisfaction and contentment unknown to bachelors."*

That article was the third item in the Ronan scrapbook.

I sent a copy of the news article to Kate and asked her to share it. As I folded the newsprint into the envelope, I knew the article would affirm that Peter was neither tinker nor slacker. My father was wrong about Peter, but I never expected him to admit it.

"Your father held an insalubrious love for you, at times," Father Van Gorp told me. I shared with the priest my wondering about whether I had honored my father as the commandment required. "He is unaware of it, I suspect. But you do him no dishonor by marrying Peter, nor loving your husband as a wife should."

"But he was so tragically sad, weeping as he walked me down the aisle, and even after. He was with the mules when our Capistrano friends toasted us and wished us well. He didn't even walk us to the stagecoach."

"Live your life, Mollie," the priest said. "You are in no state of disobedience. Accept the Lord's treasures and his promise to bless all your undertakings."

"I want my father's blessing."

"Keep the door open to him, love him. But it is your father's loss that he chooses to see your absence as a sorrow rather than a sign that he has raised a strong and loving daughter. It need not be your sorrow too."

AT THE SAINT PATRICK'S DAY DANCE, I wore one of my San Francisco gowns, this being an event without costumes. The black dress was Peter's choice. Again, when the musicians played "The Girl I Left Behind" and we danced to it, people moved away to let us have the floor. They saw happiness ease within the waltz, felt the satisfaction in hopes fulfilled despite our age differences, despite our separation by miles and years, despite my father's objections. Even the priests clapped their hands when we finished. Peter bowed to the applause, then swished me outside where the cool night air relieved the heat of my face brought from the attention. Others soon joined us. We were seldom alone.

TWENTY

HOSPITALITY AND HOPE

We lived three months in the Hotel St. Louis when Peter said one morning, "I'll pick you up by ten a.m."

"Riding clothes?" He shook his head.

May in Helena risks blizzards amidst tulip tips popping up. But there were no signs of a snowstorm and the sun felt warm on my face as I stepped into the carriage. "Is it ready?" I asked.

"Now don't guess away my surprise."

On the way to wherever he was taking me, I could still see burned-out buildings in the downtown section that had been abandoned. Peter had the *Gazette* offices moved inside a brick structure he said was fireproof. The road took us up higher to streets bare of trees cut for lumber and firewood. Even Mount Helena was denuded. Pockets of snow reminded us of the long winter past, a time when I found the greatest joy in being Peter's wife. I looked about. There were many new homes built in this section of the Prickly Pear Valley. At the end of Wood Street, the carriage stopped.

"Your new home, Mrs. Ronan. I'll have our things brought up from the hotel tonight."

The whitewashed boards gave off the familiar scent.

"I had bought everything—with Mrs. Maginnis's advice—once you agreed to marry me." Peter's enthusiasm bubbled. "But then the fire. Everything burned in storage. I had to reorder. Let's go inside. I hope you like it. It's only three rooms."

A black walnut settee and divan upholstered in black horsehair dominated the room we designated the parlor. Velvet curtains framed the windows. A large clock sat on the narrow table behind the divan. The kitchen had a cooking range. In cupboards were dishes, platters, three sizes of spiders where I imagined scrambling eggs and frying bacon for my spouse. The table and chairs matched. A hand pump brought water inside over the tin sink. The privy was but footsteps from the back door.

The bedroom set was of black walnut as well. I walked to the bed's edge and ran my hand across the wedding ring quilt of yellows and purples. I turned an edge back to feel the cool sheets. "Irish linen." I looked up at Peter, tears in my eyes. "You remembered."

"I know you only had the one small towel of your mother's that dressed the altar. I tried to match it with the linens I ordered from the island. They just arrived." A neighbor had come and made up the bed.

"They're perfect."

"I would invite the fabulous Mrs. Ronan to test them out for comfort and if they are the proper weight, but Mr. Ronan must return to work." He kissed me, held me close. "I'll send the carriage back to pick you up. Work keeps me from you more than I'd like." He kissed my nose. "I thought you'd enjoy the furnishings—and see what personal touches you'll want to make. I can have the hotel pack our things up."

"No, I'll do that." I put my palm on his chest, then slipped my arm into his elbow to walk out with him. "I'll pack after we drop you at the *Gazette*. We can explore our new home later, together."

TRULY, MRS. MAGINNIS had thought of everything, and she wasn't even around for me to thank, as she accompanied her husband to Washington, D.C. I placed my wedding shawl across the back of the divan, along with the photograph of me in the black gown. My father had kept the one of us together, taken in Salt Lake. I placed my mother's altar linen as a dresser runner.

I could not have been happier in that three-room house than if it had been Cinderella's castle her Prince Charming husband brought her home to.

My home "plastering" got underway. Peter loved flowers and gardening, and in late June, he planted a vegetable plot surrounded with marigolds "to keep the rabbits and deer out." His experiment at planting peanuts we laughed about, hoping there'd be no frost to claim them as sometimes happened even in July. He nurtured those mounds, covered them at night like little chicks.

We rarely disagreed and not just because I was an "accommodating soul," as he put it. I simply liked his ideas and he liked mine. Every day I asked myself how I might make his day better. It seemed that he was asking the same question of himself.

When not at home, I helped at the Sisters' school. They welcomed me back as a patron. I played the organ, directed the choir, and marveled that I replaced Miss Kelly, one of my praying fairy godmothers back in Los Angeles. New priests with their black robes had come to Helena as well. They were part of the city's social life and my own continued education in the faith. Helena produced every kind of cultural and social persuasion, and I prepared to live my life there, finding it and marriage a storehouse of riches. Only my father's acknowledgment of my choice would have made me happier.

That summer I rode out to Wisconsin Creek to spend a few days with Carrie Crane. Both friendships and family needed tending. She welcomed me though I hadn't sent word ahead. I apologized for my lapse. "Not a worry, Mollie. It's the code of the West, to welcome friends and strangers." I spent several days with Ellen and her children, too, and my godchild. Bill's investments in the longhorns had paid off, and their other operation, raising horses for the military, was prospering too.

"So long as there's Indian trouble," Bill said over supper, "the military will be around and they'll need horseflesh. We have a steady market." He wiped his mustache of biscuit bits. "Wars offer that, prosperity for those that fight them. Well, not for the Indian enemy."

"What war?"

"Those Flatheads that resist the Hellgate treaty and won't go to their reservations. They wander here and there, steal, get shot by ranchers."

He sounded callous, as though conflict was inevitable. I wanted to ask him more, but my godchild, Elizabeth, herded her little sister toward me, and I lifted her up to put her in the higher chair.

Ellen said, "It's much easier to feed Corinne in it. You'll have to get one, or borrow this, when you have your first. Any sign?"

I shook my head. I wasn't really worried that I hadn't yet conceived—we'd only been married eight months that August.

"You best spend less time on traveling to the Ruby Valley," Bill teased. "You won't get in a family way without a partner."

In September I learned that Bill was right.

Peter swung me around when I told him what I suspected, and that with my information we'd be blessed with a little one in May. "And may I order in one of those high chairs Ellen touted? That cabinetmaker can surely do it."

"Anything the princess wishes," Peter said.

I prepared by sewing baby clothes, knitting wool I spun from local sheep, and reading about what some called formula instead of breast milk to nurture a baby's growth.

Winter came on heavy, dumping two feet of snow in late November. We wouldn't see the green again until spring. But my idyllic life continued, with a loving husband, an apparently easy pregnancy, and the snows giving us excuses to read to each other in the evenings and sleep in in the mornings. I served Peter "little breakfasts" as I'd had in Capistrano. "Chocolate and toast," I told him. Until the snows delayed the delivery of chocolate. But still, my life was as I'd dreamed it might be, and I was forever grateful that I had stood up to my father and not joined the convent—and that Annie Brown had. I hoped she was as happy as I was.

It was January 9 when I was in my fifth month on a cold and blustery morning that Peter opened the window to the sunlight and said, "This is the kind of day when ships go down at sea." The sky was clear but wind whipped the treetops. He kept staring toward the downtown district. Then shouted, "No! There's a fire at the *Gazette*!"

"Peter?"

He dressed and rushed out as the wind blasted the side of the house.

The knock on the door a half hour later announced a German acquaintance who lived closer to the fire. "Your husband. He says to bring my frau and two-day-old baby to your door. You will take care, *ja*." He caught his breath. "Our house, it is threatened. You can look after Mrs. Reinig, ja?"

"Yes, of course." He lifted the infant from his mother's arms, handed him to Mollie, then carried his wife into our bedroom where he gently laid her on the Irish linens Peter and I had recently left. "I go to check on the house. *Danke, danke*."

I handed her the infant. "It'll be alright," I said to her frightened eyes.

Before long, others knocked on the door, sent by Peter, I imagined. Several brought their children bundled up for my safekeeping while they returned to fight the flames. I bustled about making tea, finding activities for the children, reassuring as I could those with worried eyes. We kept looking out the window, watching as the wind swirled the flames and the smoke turned the sky black. I wasn't worried about the press because it was in a fireproof building. Peter had also purchased $30,000 of insurance, so whatever happened to the plant, we'd be alright. I knew Peter must be safe, as he kept sending people to me. I welcomed each with open arms and gentle hugs before asking others to squeeze over and make room for more.

It was late in the day when Peter returned, smudge-faced and exhausted. People began coming for their children, had found other shelters for the night, returned to scorched but still structurally safe homes. The Reinig family remained in our bedroom.

"The *Gazette*'s safe, correct?"

He shook his head. "Only the brick interior walls remain. Everything else melted, gone. Lost. Books, files, documents, the history of Helena." He looked up at me and never had I seen such woe in my husband's optimistic eyes. "It's doubly worse, because the *Herald* lost all its files in the fire of '71. To lose all that history of a past."

"We have insurance, though. We can rebuild, yes?"

He nodded. "I'll wire them in the morning."

The last of the fire refugees came to collect their children, another mother looking bedraggled and worn. Her husband lifted his toddling daughter, who clung to his neck, her little cheek taking some of the smudge from his beard. A second child clung to his mother's skirts. They'd lost their house, looked defeated.

I put on my stage face hoping to cheer them up. "Everything is going to be fine," I said. "You have your little children. That's all that's needed in the end, isn't it?"

The mother stared at me. "Life for some of us isn't all a bed made up of Irish linen, Missus."

Her words stung. But later I wondered that in my effort to be cheerful, I had perhaps discounted the suffering that lay ahead—or even what she'd already endured. It had not been my intent. I wanted only to walk beside her and be hospitable in a time of trial.

But while I believed in the truth of my words to her, I'd failed to really see her sorrow.

True hospitality demanded more than staged optimism and definitely more attention to its timing.

While the Reinigs remained, I made up a bed for Peter and me on the parlor room floor so that the German family had a place of rest. I listened carefully to what Mrs. Reinig needed, didn't assume I knew. They remained several days and thus were there to hear the news my husband garnered from the insurance company. The fire had commenced on January 9, 1874. The insurance company had filed bankruptcy the day before.

TWENTY-ONE

THE AFTERMATH

I don't think I can do this a fourth time," Peter said. "Journalism just might not be my forte." He sat at the table, pencil in hand. The Reinigs had gone home to a repaired house, and Helena had started to rebuild the one hundred businesses and twenty residences consumed by the flames. The biggest loss came to Gans and Klein, the mercantile where ready-made frocks and other finery were sold to Helena's matrons. They estimated their losses at $160,000. Fortunately, attorney and longtime resident Colonel W. F. Sanders's diaries of early Montana days, notebooks, letters, and pamphlets were rescued by his wife and son before his office burned down. Not all Montana history had been lost.

"There are blessings to be had." I rubbed my abdomen, felt the baby move.

Peter tapped the pencil on his foolscap folio. "And we have options despite the losses. I've offers of loans and the editor from Virginia City says he'll move the *Montanan* to Helena if I'll take it over. The boys at Deer Lodge say they'll bring their operation and publish as *Helena Daily Independent* by March. I could partner with them." He ran his hands through his thick, dark hair. "But I think journalism has had enough of me."

"What will we do?" I was just beginning to experience what our neighbor had reminded me of, that not everyone slept on a bed of Irish linen. I handed Peter peanuts we'd harvested in the fall that I had roasted. I had a craving for them. "We might try cattle or horse breeding. Perhaps farming row crops. You seem to have a green thumb." I popped another peanut into my mouth.

"I did surprise a lot of Helena's citizens with that peanut plot. All things to think about."

A few days later he announced our future. "Prospecting and mining. That's Montana. I've bought into a partnership in a hydraulic placer mining operation near Blackfoot City. It's less likely than a newspaper to go up in a cloud of smoke."

"But Blackfoot City is miles away." I had visions of when my father had to leave us for long periods of time. And I found I was annoyed that he hadn't talked with me about the partnership before acting on it. But then it seemed that was his duty to be the business head. Mine was to be the plasterer, to make and keep the home.

"So it is. But I'll come back in late April, to be here for the delivery."

"And then go back to Blackfoot City, without us?"

"No. I'll bring you with me."

IT WOULD ONLY be two months before Peter returned. I filled the days making clothes, writing letters to my parents, Kate, Ellen, Mary, and Carrie. In April, a woman named Sarah arrived, a bag in hand. "I'm a nurse and your husband says I'm to stay should the babe come early." I invited her in, took her cape, and saw that her apron was as white as the eggshells a couple of our chickens laid.

It felt odd to have another woman in my home, but Peter had sent her, so I accepted her assistance. I would have words with him, though. I meant to have a say in my own household. Sarah was a chattering soul, and I was reminded at how much I liked being alone, not having to respond to questions or even smiling or laughing at her many stories when what I wanted was to sleep or read. I put on my "mask of the happy hostess" and sometimes feigned sleepiness that I might go to my bedroom for the quiet, a state I felt no need of when Peter was with me, as we shared hours of silence together.

Peter sent her away when he arrived on April 30, just in time for me to go into labor on May 1, the day our son was born. We named him Vincent (for Mother Vincent) Rankin (for a friend of Peter's). He arrived without much ado, the labor lasting long enough for the doctor to attend the delivery. Peter cut the cord, then held his blue-eyed son. Vincent's blond hair made me think of Rumpelstiltskin's work at turning straw into gold. I kissed my infant's head. *Your first grandchild*, I whispered to my mother, bringing her memory into the room and into this child's life too. I would write and tell my father.

OUR BOY WAS BAPTIZED, and then when Vincent was but five days old, Peter returned to the mine, leaving a neighbor to care for us while he was gone.

"Can't I please just have her come now and then rather than stay here?"

Peter insisted he would worry if I didn't have live-in help and so I relented. Mrs. LaCroix was a quiet woman. She even mentioned that she had helped Mrs. Maginnis pick out the furnishings.

"Your husband had asked me to do the selecting, but Mrs. Maginnis heard of it and said she thought she might bring an upper taste like the fine houses of St. Paul where she came from." She sighed. "She chose the furniture. I chose what she called the 'accoutrements,' what's in the kitchen."

"It's the details that are the most significant," I said. I never used the kitchen spider after that without thinking of Mrs. LaCroix and her accommodation.

Peter wrote on May 12 that things were going well and he would soon be making good money from the mine. On the first of June, when we were in a spring wagon making the thirty miles to Black-foot City, Ma Anne's instruction about being agile came to mind. I would plaster another house. My husband could take care of us. Would take care of us. I realized I'd been concerned and for just a moment had wondered if my father might have been right about Peter's abilities.

THE CABIN was the largest home I'd lived in, with four rooms, a spring nearby, and a view from the side of a mountain that took one's breath away, literally, as the log cabin was built a mile high. It sat a few miles from Blackfoot City, though. The mining camp was like most early gulch towns with a saloon and a small mercantile run by one of Peter's partners. A two-story hotel had a restaurant on the main floor, and what happened on the second floor was not discussed. There were no families close by, but I soon went neighboring and found a young childless couple working their claim. I invited them for supper.

I was happy in my cabin home, made cozy when our furniture arrived from Helena. Once a week when the freighter came to Blackfoot City, I carried Vincent out to the wagon and asked to use their scales for weighing out flour and cornmeal. Our boy gained a half a pound a week. Peter had planted another garden, though he had to forgo the peanuts. But we had fresh vegetables and fish, as he also loved to put a fly in for mountain trout. Game was plentiful, too, in the areas not marred by mining. The chickens cooperated.

When word reached Helena that we were settled, friends came out, often spending the night. Once again my doors were open and

I loved it, even more when doors were closed and only my husband, Vincent, and I lived out our lives behind them. That winter, Peter read to me—Shakespeare's sonnets and *Josephus*—while I nursed our baby. We sang together. He cooked and liked the creativity. It felt as though the honeymoon continued but with the addition of dear Vincent.

Once a week Peter put on snowshoes to get the mail at Blackfoot City, and sometimes we bundled ourselves up and took the sleigh to Helena for a dance or two, baby in tow. By spring, things were picking up at the mine again, and Peter arranged in the summer for me to go back to Helena and stay with Mrs. LaCroix until I delivered our second child. We'd chosen both a girl's and boy's name, and on July 8, 1875, I gave birth to Mary Ellen, whose red hair reminded me of Kate's.

Vincent and I and baby Mary Ellen were still in Helena when I felt such a strong desire to go back to our cabin. Mary Ellen was only a week old, but I was packing up with Mrs. LaCroix's help when Mrs. Maginnis, returned from Washington, D.C., stopped by, dressed in highest fashion.

"Oh, my dear," she said. "You look so strained. Do you think you should leave Helena so soon for that wretched little mining town?" We were in Mrs. LaCroix's small parlor, our hostess serving us a platter of tea she poured before leaving us alone. I wasn't sure I wanted to be alone with Mrs. Maginnis, given her pitying words. I must have looked a mess.

"We'll be fine there," I said.

"Oh, I do dread the going back and forth from Helena to Washington, D.C." She fanned herself. "Two households, it's such a trial to manage. But until children come, it's my occupation."

She and Mr. Maginnis had been married a long time and there were no babies. I wondered if she longed to trade in her summer gown with the long string of pearls for a toddler clinging to her skirts while she held a newborn in her arms. She was a woman without the attention that children required and thus had time for gossip. *Is she envious? Maybe she deliberately mentioned Annie Brown in that early correspondence that nearly separated me and Peter forever?* I prayed that babies would keep me focused on the things that truly mattered. Still, she'd been kind to us—to me— and this one lapse of etiquette would not dissolve our friendship. After all, she was the wife of my husband's partner and a woman dealing with the vicissitudes of her own frontier in faraway Washington, D.C. She, too, likely had to have an open door, perhaps put on that mask of cordiality. Maybe every hostess had to as we did our work behind our husbands. I hoped I worked beside Peter, but I wasn't really sure.

TWENTY-TWO

POLITICS AND POSSIBILITIES

We'll do the last big cleanup this week." I knew Peter referred to the end of the sluice box scouring when they'd take apart the boxes and brush out all the nooks and crannies, yielding usually hundreds if not thousands of dollars in gold. It would be added to the gold in storage we'd soon take to Helena for assay. "That'll give us what we need and there'll be plenty for you to make the trip. We all could in the fall. If you go without me now, I'll hire a traveling companion to help. But, Mollie—" He paused. "What can you really do there?"

I'd returned to our little cabin at the mining site and had gotten a letter from my father telling me that Ma Anne was ill and that I must come back to help care for her, that Kate and Jimmy missed and needed me.

"I would like to see them. And maybe I could help." The baby fussed and I picked her up. Consumption is what was suspected for Ma Anne. While the famous Dr. Benjamin Rush attributed it to smoking and said riding a good horse and leeches could help, I didn't think those would apply to Ma Anne's healing. Family and care were what she needed.

"You know he won't want you to leave once you're there."

"I know my duty," I said. I didn't relish another goodbye from my father, but I did want to help and to introduce my children to their grandparents. Chat about mothering as equals. With two children, my appreciation for Ma Anne had gone even higher. She had adapted to so many situations yet kept a cheerful heart.

But Peter was right. How could I really help? "I'll write to the alcalde to get a sense of how they're faring. Maybe he can find a nursemaid for Ma that we can hire." My father had done his best to care for his family, the cousins, me.

"Excellent idea," Peter said.

That action gave me peace, and I put off answering my father until I heard from the alcalde. The big cleanup would open possibilities. We'd have the money we needed. And if we all made the trip to California, we'd stay at the hotel or the alcalde's private residence and there'd be less concern about whether I'd extricate myself from my father's cleaving arms.

"WE'LL BE RICH TODAY, Mollie." Peter snuggled Mary Ellen's cheek as I held her in my arms, and lifted Vincent to his shoulder. "You're getting heavy, son," he said.

"Son. Son," Vincent repeated.

"Another word for his vocabulary." Peter had been keeping track. To Vincent he said, "Well done, lad."

"Lad. Lad."

Peter laughed and set him down. "I'll be back later with our count."

Since yeast was difficult to keep, I'd learned how to make sourdough biscuits with chokecherries and huckleberries in season. I imagined a celebratory meal. Maybe I'd invite the couple over the ridge. I hoped my household accounts might see an increase for trinkets for the children. I sang as I stirred up biscuits.

I saw Peter not an hour later coming up the hill. *Too soon.* "What's happened?"

"Well, Mollie, my love. We've been robbed." He sank into the chair.

"Robbed? Robbed?" I sounded like Vincent repeating new words.

"All that we accumulated this season is gone. And for that matter, the vein's run out as well, so there'll be no other season."

"What . . . what happened?"

He shook his head. "You seem to have married an unlucky man, Mollie."

A tinge of worry filled the room. "I can't go to Capistrano now. I'll write to tell my father."

"Don't . . . don't tell him of this disaster. We partners should have posed a guard. I don't want your da thinking it was stupidity that put his little girl at risk."

I wanted to assure him that he was not stupid. I wanted to say that we still had real wealth: each other, two children. He had a little put aside, I thought, and all would be well. But I didn't really know. I needed to be more assertive, to find out. "I'll not tell my father a word about it."

The sheriff began an investigation about the theft, but there were few clues. "They always suspect the Chinese," Peter said, "or if an Indian is about, they accuse them. But those I know of either race who've been panning are straight as an arrow, hard workers too."

I prayed for guidance for my husband and for me and for Ma's healing, which now I wouldn't be traveling to help with. I'd ask for forgiveness for my guilty relief at being needed at home.

WE PACKED UP and returned to Helena, taking our house back from renters. We had enough in savings to send to my father for

Ma's care, but he rejected our offer. "*She's doing better*," he had written. I hoped it wasn't his pride making that diagnosis.

Peter, meanwhile, met with his partners about what next. Congressman Maginnis was convinced that Peter should consider politics now that he had no active mine, no newspaper. "I was looking for something a little less risky," Peter told him when the four of us gathered. I'd stayed in the room, though Mrs. Maginnis had been reluctant, telling me the women needed to let men discuss important things. She baby-talked to Mary Ellen as she held her while I served up apple crisp to the men and remained in the room.

"A wife's an asset in politics," Mr. Maginnis said. "Your missus will charm the undecided, if not the opposition."

Peter was offered the job of sheriff of Deer Lodge County south of Lewis and Clark County where we lived, but he declined. The man who accepted the job appointed Peter as undersheriff anyway. "A possibility for after the election," Peter said. "Not sure I want to get into enforcing laws, but it would be interesting. A man flourishes in an intriguing job."

He wasn't interested in running for any particular office as the congressman was—and did every two years. Instead, Peter became active as a Union Democrat. He raised money for other candidates. He wrote broadsides and letters to the editor on behalf of candidates and causes. He used his wit and wisdom to speak at rallies. The goal was that the Democratic nominee for president, Tilden, would beat Hayes in the 1876 election. What would result, the men thought, would be a government appointment for Peter.

"We might well have to leave Montana," Peter told me, a prospect I didn't favor. It was after one of his events in Deer Lodge County where he'd spoken about the corruption of the current administration and a scandal involving Indian agents. The secretary of war had resigned over it. The trip had given Peter a chance to see what might be his duties as an undersheriff, if he was called upon. He'd arrived home in time for the big Fourth of

July celebration Helena always had. "Martin says there are several civil service positions or patronage appointments that change with every administration. In the postal service, the war department." Any appointment would mean a change from my beloved Helena. "Martin fancies me as the surveyor general of the Montana Territory."

"That would mean a lot of travel."

He chewed on a piece of jerked venison, a late-evening snack he often ate. "It would, but I think I'd enjoy it. Not being away from you, I wouldn't like that. But imagine the magnificent scenery, the timber, the glaciers that blind a man reflecting the morning sun. I'd have a spectacular office."

"I've never seen a glacier." I fanned the children, wiped their arms with cool water in their restless sleep. Helena had an icehouse where we could purchase such relief for hot July nights.

"We'll go north one day. That country is so amazing I think it should be designated a national park, like Yellowstone is." He took a drink of milk. "Yes, we'll camp out with the children. This Montana," he said. "It's so full of possibilities."

All lives had ups and downs, but Peter lived in the "ups" while my father dwelled in the "downs." Did we have choices for where we spent our days? "Yes," I told my children as Peter traveled once again. I made sure the children didn't feel abandoned by their father's absence. Assuring them was a way to reassure myself.

THE CAMPAIGN WAS CONTENTIOUS with the papers running political cartoons and articles that made me glad neither of our children were old enough to read. Mr. Maginnis encouraged interest in that surveyor appointment for Peter in the hoped-for Tilden administration. "You'll come to Washington, D.C.," Mrs. Maginnis said. "You'll be a charming addition to the city's hostesses." She seemed to mean it.

"If it's to be, it will be," I told her.

Our country's capital would be a new frontier, a large city where decisions were made affecting people in their homes thousands of miles away. I'd fallen in love with Capistrano, but it was here in Montana in the shadow of the snowcapped mountains where my soul soared to its greatest heights.

My father wrote, said Ma Anne was doing better, told the news of cousin Patrick's marriage and that he lived in Philadelphia, worked for the Centennial Exposition celebrating one hundred years as a nation. I'd likely never see that cousin again, our family scattered. I gave my father credit for those years he had kept returning to us. And while I had hated his taking me from Peter, the decision had resulted in his family being in one place now for years, living in the peaceful village of San Juan, and with the lawsuit settled, having secure property.

But I did miss them.

I urged my parents to visit, to come back to Helena. I could help take care of Anne and him if they were closer. His return letter reminded me that I "had made my bed": *You chose that man.*

The alcalde said my father seemed to be doing fine. The fields were planted and harvested. Kate and Jimmy were in school—the one I might have taught in if I'd ever passed the test. That failure did still sting. But it wasn't the failure that weighed on me, colored every blue sky with dark clouds on the horizon.

"It's like my many failures as a newspaperman," Peter told me when I lamented the discord between me and my father. "I have to let them go. Or that last mining disaster. I did my best. I could have done better, but I've had to take what is, accept it, and rework it into something more."

"Like throwing yourself into politics," I said.

"For now, yes. Who knows what riches lie ahead?" He lifted Mary Ellen and swung her as giggles filled the air. "Look forward, Mollie. You can't change your pa." He set his daughter safely down. "You can only change yourself."

THE PRESIDENTIAL CAMPAIGN carried on in a frenzy of parties and events throughout Montana, held at hotels or smaller gatherings, sometimes in our home. I set aside my disappointment around my father and focused on my husband, my family, turning guilt into momentum toward our future. Politics might be the stage I'd be on, helping Peter be agile in this political sphere.

People of both Republican and Democratic persuasions attended our events. There were town hall meetings where people raised their voices and spoke of carpetbaggers ruining the South or of Federal "invasions" in North Carolina and Louisiana. I didn't really understand all the nuances, but Peter did. And both sides welcomed his contributions at the meetings. He urged calm when the gatherings turned into raucous riots that led to fistfights.

"I never raise a hand," Peter assured me as I treated a cut over his eye following one volatile affair. I hadn't attended, thank goodness. There was a fire in his eyes, as though he'd been out hunting deer and brought home not only meat but a trophy to hang on the wall. He pointed to the cut above his eye. "This was from me trying to break one up." *Enthusiasm.* That's what I saw in his sparkling eyes.

"Use your words to battle," I said. "They're twice as effective and you won't need a nurse when it's over." I sounded like my mother in that moment.

He grabbed me at the waist, pulled me to him. "Ah, but I'd miss the pampering." He growled bear-like as he reached to kiss me.

I extracted myself to put the salve and bandages away. "I have things to do," I said, laughing as he chased me around the bed. "You'll wake the children."

"They'll sleep right through our therapeutics." He held me, looked into my eyes. "You're the best thing that ever happened to me, Nurse Mollie. You've given me a bright future and a legacy. What more could any man ask for?" I felt myself blush at his praise. "I know the answer to my own question." He kissed me and then whispered, "Another child."

THE CAMPAIGN WASN'T ONLY about wider national issues but about things happening close to home. Concerns about the "Indian problem" rose. Gold diggers had swarmed into the Black Hills, violating a treaty with the Sioux. Settlers staked claims on land—as Ellen and Bill had done—once roamed by Native people. Fences were torn down, to ranchers' complaints. The largest gathering of Plains Indians had come to Montana at Sitting Bull's request, making people nervous. The military was put on alert. There had been a terrible battle on June 25 between the Federal forces and the Lakota, Dakota, Northern Cheyenne, and Arapaho peoples. They called it the Battle of Greasy Grass. The military brass attending our soirees referred to it as the Battle of the Little Big Horn and sometimes as Custer's Last Stand. It took place on the Crow Reservation with the 7th Cavalry Regiment. Two hundred sixty-eight American soldiers were lost to thirty-one Natives on that June day. All of Washington was up in arms. Locally, tensions rose with white ranchers and townspeople expressing worries about safety; making sure they had ammunition in their sheds. I tried not to think about how close to us so many had lost their lives.

"The reporting of that battle was both a military and journalistic failure," Peter said. He held the *Helena Independent*, drank his coffee. "They didn't even note the army's defeat until July 6 and then referred to Bozeman's newspaper article of July 2. That's a week after it happened."

"Maybe they didn't want to upset people about the uprising." I held Mary Ellen on my hip, stirring fried potatoes with my free hand.

Peter put the paper down, monitored Vincent's eating in his high chair. Outside, the horses munched on hay in the corral, their coats already thickening. It would be an early fall.

"Maybe," he said. "But the point of a paper is to tell people the truth, even about things they might not want to hear." He was still a journalist at heart.

The truth of the election came on November 7, 1876. When

the votes were cast and counted and reported, Tilden, Peter's candidate, had won the popular vote by four hundred thousand. But he'd lost the Electoral College vote by one—and that after a compromise that itself became as controversial as the election. I hadn't spent much time thinking about voting details, but I could see Peter's frustration. The first electoral count had Tilden winning with 184 to Hayes 165. But twenty electoral votes in four Southern states were contested, throwing the election into the House of Representatives, where Martin Maginnis served as a Union Democrat.

Several weeks passed before we heard of the compromise. Congress gave all twenty disputed electoral votes to Hayes. And in return, Federal troops would leave the Southern states, ending reconstruction and efforts for a true unification of North and South. We were still dealing with the aftermath of that terrible war and President Lincoln's assassination. I wondered how my father felt about the results, him being a Lincoln supporter and this election result something Lincoln would not have wanted.

We were alone in the evening with a howling wind ripping down the east side of the Rockies and the Continental Divide, pressing Helena's finest into her stove-heated parlors. Peter had tended the stock and entered the house with fresh snow on his hat and his mustache.

"Have some cocoa." I handed him a mug.

His musings now went to the election and our own limbo. Mr. Maginnis had been reelected, but his hope to get Peter an appointment as a western surveyor for the government was now a wispy dream.

"I feel forlorn," Peter said. "Not just because Tilden lost, and Montana went for him, but that I'm not sure it is a good idea to remove Federal troops from the South. They kept the peace, protecting those freed slaves from abuses, not just on their persons, but on their rights. Since Lincoln and Congress gave the former slaves their freedom in that Thirteenth Amendment, they're protected by the Constitution, same as us."

"My father always favored the Union, even though we were from the South." I remembered the shame my father laid on me at having jigged with my school friends when word of Lincoln's assassination reached the Gulch.

He nodded. "I just don't like the way those twenty votes were allocated, all Southern states—except for that one vote from Oregon—going to Hayes. President Hayes now, I guess it is. Or will be, come March. A compromise doesn't always taste sweet. This one sure doesn't."

"Are you hungry for fresh bread? I have a loaf just out of the oven." He nodded and I served him. Good food soothed.

"One thing, in all of this, you found out about politics." I picked up my needle and thread, stitched a seam on Mary Ellen's Christmas dress before I would donate it to the Sisters who gave aid to Helena's poor. "And you're a fine speaker, a good organizer, and people on both sides respect what you have to say. You can hear opposing views without being condemning."

"My journalistic heart."

"Montana went for Tilden largely because of your efforts."

He sighed. "But because of it, Maginnis says there'll be no appointment for me in the new administration. They'll seek out Hayes supporters."

"We'll have to listen for God's guidance. Didn't you say to look forward and not back?"

He was thoughtful for many minutes. We could sit in quiet contemplation for hours. It was one of the things I loved about him, about us. Then he sat up and grinned, those twin dimples telling me he was already moving into his optimistic state. "You're right. Something will come up. There are always new possibilities."

TWENTY-THREE

THE BLESSINGS OF BABES

I sat on the sidelines at the Saint Patrick's Day dance. There'd be no squares nor even a waltz that night in my condition. Some claimed I should remain at home. But this was Montana, an expanding place, and as with the variable climate came a stretching of propriety. A woman, I decided, should be at her husband's side in all, including entertainment.

Mrs. Maginnis stood beside me at the punch bowl as we handed glass cups of ginger ale to perspiring dancers between sets. I wore a modest plaid shirtwaist with a detachable lace collar; she a red silk dress with plunging neckline. When the crowd thinned, she whispered, "Should you be here, my dear?"

I had no concern for my health. I knew that both Carrie and Ellen rode horses in the latter months of their expectancies. They had delivered without benefit of doctors. Each of my birthings had been easy, with short labors but having enough warning to bring a doctor to my door. We Montana women were sturdy in all things. As I'd said in my graduation speech those years before, "Women are strong and capable and need not be treated like fragile floral arrangements. Though being treated like precious princesses is also not a sin." There'd been laughter in the audience. I had found a husband who treated me both ways and had no problem with a very pregnant wife on his arm at a public function—or at least behind the punch bowl—while he spoke politics with friends.

"I'm quite well, Mrs. Maginnis." I changed the subject. "I'm surprised you and the congressman are here. Did you not attend the inauguration?"

"We did not. The fourth of March passed into history without our presence. Besides, where would we rather be on this Saint's day than with our Irish friends in Montana?" Then, surprising me, she said, "How fortunate that you conceive so easily."

I remembered the pity on her face when she visited me soon after Mary Ellen's birth. But now I saw a longing look that told me she had hoped for children in her life. "So it seems. Perhaps there's something fertile in the Prickly Pear's pristine waters."

She smiled. "The congressman and I should spend more time here, then."

"Ah, but his public service is a gift to all Montana, and you are his good helpmate."

"Thank you. That's most gracious of you, especially since I was so bold to mention your . . . state. I envy you." She sighed.

I grabbed at her arm. "You won't be envying my next hours." I panted before I could get the words out. "I need to find Peter."

"Are you alright? Oh!" She looked around for my husband.

I spied Peter across the dance floor, his head leaned into intense discussion with the congressman and others. "Take me there," I said and held Mrs. Maginnis's arm as I waddled to him. I waited for a good moment to interrupt him and tug him away from the conversation about the compromise and something about a Nez Perce war. *The Indians are uprising?* I couldn't wait to ask more information. I felt a second contraction. "It's time to go." The words came out hoarsely, hurried.

"Leave? We've barely arrived."

"No. It's *my* time. We need to pick up the doctor on our way. This one is coming early."

"You said April."

"I was never good with numbers, remember?"

I WAS GRATEFUL the doctor was there. I tore and bled. This baby was larger than my others so probably wasn't early at all. It was my counting that misled the delivery time. I'd taken for granted my nearness to a physician. In the past, my body gave fair warning in enough time to ensure assistance was there when needed. This delivery pressed that timing.

Just before midnight, I delivered to Peter a second son, our third child, born on Saint Patrick's Day, 1877. I hoped to name him Peter, but my husband said, "No son needs the weight of a father's name and reputation." So we named him Gerald for my brother lost to the oxen accident. And for Patrick, the saint on whose day he was born.

Gerald had olive skin, black hair, and brown eyes that sparkled like his father's. He brought something new into our family of blonds and gingers, all of us with skin the color of ivory. This child was of Ireland more than all the others. His darker skin tone was what I remembered as the coloring of my mother's. "You're still with us, Mama," I'd whispered when I first put Gerald to my breast.

I found myself bedridden in recovery, frustrated that I couldn't be out and about tending my family. Peter was a fair cook. He'd done his own meal preparation when he lived in the mines with his bachelor friends. He pampered me. I was his princess having "little breakfasts" every morning. He'd pull up a chair to sit beside me while he drank his cocoa, Mary Ellen on his knee. He'd set the chocolate cup down to rock Gerald's cradle while Vincent slept on the bed beside me. I knew how fortunate I was to have a husband both interested in and able to raise a family. "I'm so grateful," I said.

I thanked God daily in my prayers that so far I had not had to endure the hardships like those refugees from fires or military widows left without means. While I felt secure without suffrage, I knew many women didn't, and I considered important those issues in the magazines we subscribed to that wrote of women working for the vote. For now, though, I was in an idyllic place: attentive husband, healthy children, warm shelter, food enough to eat, prepared by a reasonably good cook. The future was uncertain, but we had a history: Providence moved. There were no more wishes I could ask for.

Save one: a blessing from my father who had not replied when I told him of my growing family.

I THOUGHT PETER'S FUTURE might well be back in journalism. He was a fine writer. I saved his letters written to me and often reread them. The sentiment always kindled an appreciation for the choice I'd made in marrying him. Peter's news articles were written clearly, and his editorials never carried disdain for those who might disagree with him, gently pointed out their flaws of logic. His confidence in Providence impressed me too. I hoped we could instill such faithfulness in our children.

By April, I was up and out of bed, and we'd hired a nursemaid to help with the children and who could cook. I wasn't certain, but I thought our savings might be getting thin and I mentioned it to Peter.

"Don't you worry, Mollie. God has plans."

Then one morning in early May, he went to the postal office and came home wearing dimples as parentheses to his wide grin. "I opened it right there because it looked so official. I thought it might be some sort of admonishment from the government." He showed me the return address, from the Secretary of the United States Department of the Interior. "Listen to this.

> *"Mr. Peter Ronan,*
>   *The agent at the Flathead Reservation in the Mission Valley of Western Montana has resigned prior to the end of his term. Your name has been suggested to replace him. Would you consider such an appointment? A tour of the Jocko Agency will be arranged if you will wire me of your interest.*
>
> > *Sincerely,*
> > *Carl Shurz,*
> > *Secretary of the Department*
> > *of the Interior."*

"Are you interested?"

He tapped the letter to the side of his cheek, thinking. "The agents don't have the best reputations," Peter said. "But I know there's a mission close by, St. Ignatius, run by Father Ravalli. Father Palladino spent time there too. Most of the Flathead tribes, the Salish and Pend d'Oreille, have been farmers and ranchers for years. The Kootenai still hunt more than farm. But we have things in common." He grinned. "Regardless, I'll sure take the tour. I've never seen that country. And wire Martin, to see if he's behind this or if it's come just out of the blue."

"He says it wasn't him," Peter told me after he'd heard back from Mr. Maginnis. Peter had begun packing for his horse trip across the Continental Divide to the agency, thirty miles north of Missoula, one hundred fifty miles from Helena. If we went there, it would be an entirely new terrain to adjust to, though still Montana. He'd ride through magnificent country—of course, where weren't there dramatic landscapes of mountains and meadows in all the territory?

"Martin says he's powerless in this new administration," Peter continued. "But he did find out the agent who left was under investigation for corruption and not well-liked by the Indians he was sent to serve."

"Maybe he didn't see his work there as a service."

"You could be right." He added, "Martin says that Shurz, the secretary, was a Union general and had been a newspaper editor in St. Louis before the war. Maybe he read some of my work. He also said the secretary wants civil service reform where people are appointed because of their merit and not as a plum job given because they supported the current president or was owed a favor to."

"You mean you might have gotten the offer because you're qualified for it?"

Peter laughed. "We'll see if the demands of the position are the very things I have some knowledge of."

One small worry rose. I hoped it wouldn't quell my husband's enthusiasm. Even if he didn't want the appointment after his visit, he was still excited about a new adventure, a new possibility, and I didn't want to take that eagerness away, even for a moment. But we were safe here in Helena, close to a doctor. That need was as fresh as my stitches. But what I expressed was, "Will we be closer to the Indian problems? That Nez Perce war?"

The apprehension in my voice stopped his packing, and he took my hands in his. "I'll see if it's a place I want to bring my family to, a safe place. You can count on that."

"Papa goes away?" Vincent came into the room, saw the pack, and knew something was afoot.

"Only for a little while." Peter picked him up. "Look after your mother while I'm gone."

Vincent twisted his head to stare at me. "I look."

"So you do." He put his first son down and then kissed Gerald, whom I held in my arms. Mary toddled in. She'd been walking for almost a year, though she was not yet two. He swept her up and picked Vincent back up, too, holding both against his wide chest. I wished I had a camera to capture this, babes in arms, a kind of memorial to a father's love. "I'll let you know whether to start making arrangements," Peter continued, "or fix a welcome-home meal before I start looking for something else."

As we waved him off for what I hoped would be only a few weeks, I thought about his reputation as an honest and caring man, able to see another's perspective even when it wasn't one he shared. Successful journalists looked through that window of dispassion even when they felt strongly in their personal views. Perhaps those qualities were what brought him to the Secretary of the Interior's attention. But I never for a moment imagined that if he accepted this appointment to an unknown world, that it would be anything less than an example of another of God's riches.

TWENTY-FOUR

On a Bed of Irish Linen

Peter's letter arrived a week later dated May 31, 1877, beginning with, *"My darling wife. Tomorrow will be my birthday, and tomorrow I assume the reins and will commence the discharge of duties of the Agent for the Flatheads and Confederated Tribes. I am very much taken with the place. I know you will be delighted."* He went on to write of its virtues, including that one of the Sisters at St. Ignatius had told him *"thirty-two strawberries from their garden last year weighed one pound."*

I laughed. "He would remark on garden results." To my children I said, "Your father does enjoy the growing season, and it sounds like the agency has a good one."

Peter went on to say that growth was ahead of ours in Helena, promised a milder winter in the Jocko Valley. I finished reading his letter and could feel his enthusiasm for the place. It was a gift he had as a writer, to move people's emotions and even their footsteps, as he gave me tasks I'd have to do before he arrived. By the middle of June, we'd be on to our new adventure.

He'd said the kitchen was completely furnished with the finest cookstove he'd ever seen. "*You will need your mirror, pictures, carpet, also your dishes and bedding, but you can dispose of everything else.*" There were three bedrooms, a parlor separate from the dining area, pantries, closets, a basement, and even a bathroom with a clawfoot tub. Cold water was piped into the kitchen from a stream that ran through the yard, and "*four fine government milk cows*" grazed the pasture nearby. And then perhaps the best news: "*The doctor's office is but a few feet from the house. It's well stored with all the latest apothecaries, drugs, and essentials of a country drug shoppe.*"

Who would have imagined such finery in such a remote area? I set aside my niggle of worry about living with Indians as near neighbors.

If he kept to his timetable, I had only a week to make arrangements. I met first with Mrs. Lambert who with her daughter Grace—Mary Ellen's age—would be coming with us. Her husband was the agriculturist for the agency. She'd not been there before, either, so we were going by what our husbands' letters told us about our future homes.

"My husband's new too," she told me. She was about my age and spoke happily of her life as a mother and wife. She wore her sandy-colored hair in braids twisted in a coil at the top of her head and told me that "Lambert" meant "bright landscape."

"Oh, you like words too," I said.

She nodded. She had a crooked bottom tooth one saw with her wide smile. "Better than me husband. He didn't give me such a picture of our dwelling as your husband did. Says ours has 'three rooms, mighty fine.' I hope there's a separate laundry house or that my Grace is soon out of her nappies."

We laughed at that. Peter hadn't mentioned if I could hire help for such a large house. A cook perhaps? A laundress? How many other people besides the doctor and the agriculturist did the agency employ? I had a dozen questions that would have to wait for answers while I "disposed" of everything but essentials.

Something about this packing seemed more permanent than when we'd lived in Blackfoot City and had kept the Helena house as a rental. I was to sell our home on Wood Street, so there'd be no coming back to this neighborhood. It was the enthusiasm in Peter's letter that suggested that this Jocko Agency in a valley bordered by Mission Mountains might be a place like San Juan Capistrano was for my father. A place where one could put down roots and harvest memories that didn't hold one hostage if one was vigilant, but instead, let them nurture and transform a soul.

The agency's spring wagon accommodated all our goods, the Lamberts' included. Peter and Vincent and Mary—we had dropped the Ellen when Gerald arrived—sat in the front; Mrs. Lambert with her Grace and I with Gerald, not three months old, sat in the back. We made it an adventure, the one hundred fifty miles we'd have to traverse. We shared the pleasantries of mothering. She was never cross but always gentle, which was my style too. The weather was warm but not hot, sunny. Our first night was at the town of Deer Lodge where we stayed in the hotel. A second night, at New Chicago. I loved Montana for its always hopeful names of towns, sometimes adding "city" when all that existed were two shacks and an expectation. We stopped each day for a noon lunch of bread and cheese and ham, restocking on ice at each hotel. A stage stop became our next evening's respite. Once I spelled my husband, taking the reins while he held the baby in his arms.

We had to ford the Missouri River at least twenty times before we finally reached Missoula, where friends of Peter's owned a small establishment. I hoped to see my cousin.

"Do you know of Mary Sheehan Blake's whereabouts?" I asked our hotel hosts. "My last letter to her was returned."

"I don't," the proprietor told me. "People move on and away all the time."

I counted it fortunate that I had my friendships with Carrie Crane and Cousin Ellen and the alcalde too. But as we prepared for bed that evening, I told Peter how sad I was that the morning when we broke our engagement had been the last time I'd hugged my cousin Mary. Or seen Puddin either. I hoped the agency had cats.

"Maybe Mary'll write from wherever she is," he said.

"She won't know where we are." That last goodbye rang in my ears. "I'm not sure I'm a very good friend," I said. "Aside from the Sisters and Father Van Gorp, I really had no one to say goodbye to leaving Helena, though hundreds attended the party for us." Peter was my best friend, I realized. While I missed seeing my cousins, my sister, and brother, and wrote to them often, it was Peter who I expressed deeper concerns to, Peter who heard my worries. It was Peter I allowed to comfort me and who had brought me from my shyness into being the hostess that supported his ambitions. When I wasn't with him, I wished I was.

In that moment I saw the love between my father and my mother as such an all-consuming one that when my mother died, he sank into despair for losing not only the mother of his children but his best friend. His turning to me, to keep me safe, to hold me as a reminder of what he'd lost, began to make more sense, even after he'd found Ma Anne to love. It was never as deep as how he'd loved my mother.

I vowed to make more friends, not just wear the mask of a happy hostess. I would take a lesson from Peter and truly listen and maybe even expose my interests to others than my husband now and then, speak of more than children. It might even take pressure from Peter—if he felt it—to have others who could quell my worries when they arose and he was nowhere in sight.

THE NEXT DAY we forded Finley Creek and came out of it to a grove of Ponderosa pine, tall with thick strips of bark to mark their trunks bare of needles until farther up their spines. And then beyond, the Jocko Valley of the Flathead people. The scene opened up as though a stage curtain had been drawn to unveil a glorious backdrop. But this was the real thing. Blue lupine and pink flowers mixed in with prairie grass that rose as tall as the horses' flanks. Birds chattered. A falcon cried and caught a lift. The same breeze caressed our faces. There was a whinny from the wagon's team, and up ahead a group of horses raised their heads. Then as one they raced east of us, toward a range Peter said was the Mission Mountains. The road meandered past fine-looking ranches, toward smoke-stained tepees, and then the white buildings of the agency. Snowcapped mountains rose from the valley floor. It could have been an illustration in an Irish book of fairy tales. The beauty took my breath away. But more, I felt I had come home.

"Oh, Peter. It's . . . splendid."

"I thought you'd like it."

"It fits your name, Mrs. Lambert." I turned to her. "Bright landscape."

"That it does," she said. "'Tis beautiful."

At the gate Peter pulled up the team. Harry Lambert opened it as we made quick introductions. Then Harry was handed his daughter Grace and helped his wife from the wagon. They walked before us arm in arm as Peter drove onward to a white picket fence. The scent of cooked ham and potatoes wafted from the impressive-looking whitewashed building. Peter helped me and our children step down, then put his arm around me. I brushed my skirts, adjusted the bustle, stood staring at our new home.

"Welcome to your castle," he said with dimples deep upon his face. "Compliments of the US government. And the Flathead Nation."

MY HUSBAND MAY HAVE made the decision for us, but he had my vote. This place had a peace to it, a reverence almost that made me want to bend a knee and thank God for such richness. And it went on. The sister of the miller, Miss Hoyt, had been hired to prepare the meal for us—not just that welcoming one, but as a regular cook. Her apron was white and clean, for which I was grateful. It had been a small annoyance of mine that Ma had begun to wear the same apron for several days rather than put on a clean one every day. It saved on washing duties, I knew, but I had come to appreciate the condition of a woman's apron, thinking it spoke to a virtue of cleanliness (when maybe it was simply a willingness to suffer laundry day more often).

We were weary, but tales of our travels had to be shared with Harry Lambert, who had stories of the agency to tell us. Miss Hoyt joined in, as Peter had urged her to eat at the table with us. Finally, with Vincent starting to whine as he did when he was tired and Mary falling asleep against my side and Gerald needing to nurse, I left the table. Mr. Lambert took his wife and daughter to their cottage. Hanna Hoyt began the cleanup of the dishes and prepared potatoes for the morning meal.

"We can unload tomorrow," Peter said. "Let's sleep in our travel bedrolls for the night." He laid the children's blankets out on the floor of the main bedroom.

"Oh, let's please take the trunk out now, can't we? I want to start our new life sleeping on a bed of Irish linen."

Weary as he must have been, he nodded and left, finding Harry to help him bring in the round-topped trunk. He put the sheet against his nose, inhaled. "The scent of home," he said. He helped settle the children, kissing Mary three times before she told him he'd done it right. He raised his eyebrows to me. "She has her mother's particularity."

"Or her father's."

I saw again the man for what he'd always been: faithful in the big things—bringing us to a paradise of shelter and well-being—

and faithful in the small—readying his children for bed; accommodating a wife's petty desires.

That night I prayed that our daughter would appreciate her father's gracious love and that one day she'd have such a loving husband to share her life with.

TWENTY-FIVE

A MOST HOSPITABLE PLACE

Stars paled into the morning sky when I rose before sunrise to nurse Gerald while lying like a queen, nestled in those lovely Irish linens. Peter, beside me, up on one elbow, watched this maternal tie, stroked the hair from my face.

"'Tis so good to have you here, Mollie, all of ye." An Irish lilt marked his language when he felt deeply, and I heard that in his words, just as I heard a rooster crow in the distance. I felt pampered and excited for all the newness.

Gerald was an easy child who had gained weight, so unlike Vincent. I didn't feel the need for the weekly freighter's scale. Here, the doctor would have one just across the square of buildings that made up the agency. I was anxious to meet him.

"It's like a small town you've brought us to."

"That it is. We could call it 'Jocko City' rather than the Jocko Agency. Most of the residents are in the government's employ or under agency care, the Indians included, though they seem self-sufficient."

"What do you think of them, the Indians?"

"So far, I think we've stumbled onto the finest of their race."

"I'm glad to hear that. I want to reassure my father."

Peter grunted. "Is that possible?" Then he changed the subject. "I can't figure out why the former agent left." He leaned back, arms behind his head, stared at the pinewood ceiling. "I'll check with the bookkeeper, but he might have been putting money into the agency—this house—instead of ensuring the Native people had what they needed."

"That could explain the grandeur." I handed Gerald to him while I rose to dress.

"I feel like everything I've done so far in my life, all my aptitudes and handiness, will serve me well for just this place, these people. The chief I met was happy to know there'd be children here. Now that you've arrived, my cup overfloweth." He leaned to kiss me. His lips on mine never failed to stir.

"I love you," I told him.

"And I, you."

We might have lingered longer, but Gerald fussed between us.

"Baptiste, our interpreter, says the word has gone out that you've arrived," Peter continued, "and we'll be meeting some of the chiefs, probably today."

"I've so much to learn. I want to do this well for you, Peter."

Thoughtful, he said, "One, ah, custom I'd guess you'd call it, is that they think of this house as theirs—which it is, I guess. They won't knock before coming in. The door is considered open." He chuckled. "My second morning here two Salish men"—he pronounced it *sail-ish*—"just walked right into the bedroom."

"This room?" I put my hand to my throat.

"The very same. Maybe they were just testing me to see how I'd react."

"And how did you?"

"Well"—his dimples reflected his amusement—"I shook their

hands, then rolled out, and standing in my long johns, I invited them to breakfast. What else would hospitality demand?"

"It's going to be interesting," I said.

And even that first day it was.

By sunrise, Hanna had already been up an hour preparing oatmeal, pancake batter, fried potatoes, and bacon, the aromas bringing all of us into the large dining room. I got the children up, dressed, and seated. Gerald, with his olive skin, slept in his cradle, and I hurried to help Hanna. That was how I thought of it, my helping her at that moment rather than she assisting me.

"The major likes breakfast at eight a.m.," she said, using a term for Peter I hadn't heard before. He must have been introduced that way. Perhaps some military designation went with the appointment? I'd have to ask. "Not that things go accordin' to schedule here." She scoffed. "You'll have to adapt to that. We all do."

"Be agile. Yes." I scanned the kitchen. "And I see we have a waffle maker."

"Yes, ma'am. But only cold chokecherry syrup to go with 'em. Maple's hard to come by in these parts. I don't make waffles much."

"Let's add them to this morning's menu."

She sighed. "If you're wishing it, ma'am."

She was a large girl, though quick moving between the table where she cut the potatoes and the stove where the oatmeal bubbled. There were no stains on her clean white apron.

I found a big bowl the color of adobe, cracked eggs into it, measured the flour by the handful, poured milk from the icebox, then mixed up the batter and poured the mix into the cast-iron waffle maker. I'd seen such a device, but never had one to use.

"You have to guess about when to flip it over," she said. "I say my sums from two to twenty. I'm good with numbers."

"I'll sing a verse in Gaelic, one my father taught me." No need to admit that doing sums in my head wasn't one of my talents. But like Peter, I was hopeful this place would warrant use of my endowments and become for me as it appeared to be for Peter, the place of my métier, work best suited to me, work that the world needed doing.

I WAS ANXIOUS to get our household set up but couldn't say no to my husband's offer of a tour. The morning walk set my mind buzzing. The children waddled with us, Vincent working his way toward the red-roofed barn. He had a love for horses. Mary stayed close by us as we meandered, and I carried Gerald in my arms. I did notice more than one Indian woman carrying her baby in a cloth sack on her back, going toward the granary. In the mining camps now and then when Indians were there, I'd seen babies swaddled in a board. I liked the cloth bag and thought I might just try that later. Perhaps even put up the baby hammock like our old neighbor in the gulch had.

We entered Peter's office just west of the house. "The bookshelves are filled with mostly law books and books of regulations." He had a wide window to look out of, though. A porch was shaded by an overhang.

"How pleasant it will be to have you right next door."

"When I'm not riding to far points of the reservation, I can be home for every meal." There would still be travel in his work. I hoped not for months at a time the way my father's livelihood demanded before San Juan.

Just beyond, a building stored supplies acquired for the Indians: seeds, blankets, more. Next to it was a cottage for the agency clerk who kept the records of what was distributed and what might be needed by the various tribes or the agency itself. "I'm already working on getting ammunition for the Flatheads so they can hunt buffalo this fall, scarce as I understand those animals are. Seems there's always some concern in Washington about Indians having guns. But the fall hunt is critical for them to feed their families. And there's been no trouble in the past with non-Indian neighbors as they make their way east for buffalo." He pointed in the direction of where one of the traders was licensed on the post to sell ammunition and trade with the Indians. "'Course that was before this Nez Perce war."

"What about a war?"

"It won't affect us." He patted my shoulder. "Nothing alarming."

"Where are their families?" I could see a few smoke-stained tepees, but mostly older and single Indians were within the agency except for those two mothers I'd seen walking.

"Many are on farms throughout. You saw those places with white picket fences we passed yesterday?" I nodded. "Those are Indian farms. They're all over. Can't tell them from the white ranches hereabouts. Prosperous. When we visit St. Ignatius Mission, you'll see even more how well they do."

Peter pointed out the dovecote and a barracks-like building that housed "our employees." The interpreter had his own cottage, while the miller, carpenter, stableman, and blacksmith stayed in rooms in the long narrow structure. Toward the east was both a grist mill for grinding grain and a sawmill, a barn, and the carpenter's shop. Everything was painted or washed white except for the sawmill, which was red. The doctor's residence included his office and drug dispensary. "We don't have a doctor right now," Peter said, then quickly pointed out the icehouse, milk house, chicken house, and washhouse. "I like seeing all those flowers and plantings around each building, don't you? And there's the garden, everything coming on strong."

"No doctor?" My voice squeaked.

"It's hard to recruit them, Mollie. Or so I hear."

My father might have been right. This could be a dangerous place.

"We had one when I wrote you, Mollie, but he left. We'll get another. I'm working on it. And Father Ravalli has a pharmacy at St. Ignatius only seventeen miles north. In an emergency." He rushed forward to tell me about the confederation of people who made up the Flathead Nation.

I knew he didn't want me dwelling on the lack of a physician, and I tried to listen, tried to think of other things I needed to know to quell that ping of anxiety. I spoke a silent prayer that we wouldn't need medical expertise before my husband successfully recruited a physician.

"I have to keep in mind that each tribe has their own ways," Peter continued. "And that they gave up surrounding territory when they signed the Hellgate Treaty of 1855. Well, not all signed, but that's a story I'm just learning. The Salish and Flatheads are to the south. Kootenai and Pend d'Oreille, north." He pronounced those peoples as *Coo-ten-i* and *Pon-door-ray*. "A few Nez Perce, west."

Chief of the Salish was Arlee, who lived in a cabin a mile or so from the agency buildings, my husband told me. "His mother was Nez Perce, so he held an allegiance to those people as well."

"Isn't that the group at war?"

Peter rattled on. "But there's another Salish chief, Charlo, whose father never signed the treaty and won't go to any reservation. Like Chief Victor, his son feuds with Chief Arlee because he did. He and his lodges are south of us and known as the Bitterroot Salish," he said. "He's been friendly but holds a grudge because he says his name was forged on that treaty and he doesn't recognize Arlee as chief nor the reservation as his home. He's living on traditional lands but outside the agency boundaries and has petitioned the government to stay there. It's all about tradition and land and power and who has it and how it's used," he said.

"Could it have been forged, his signature?"

He was thoughtful. "I tend to believe him. We . . . went back on an agreement made with the Nez Perce. We said they could have their homeland as a reservation in the Wallowa Mountains west of here, Idaho Territory. But then we pushed them onto a much smaller space. One of their chiefs, this Joseph, has refused to accept the tiny area. He won't go to any reservation. That's what the war is about." He turned to me. "He has alliances here. It's said he's coming in this direction."

"Should we be worried? Are the children safe?" I had written to my father, telling him of our plans, and he'd replied that I was "out of my mind" to take children to such danger.

"I hope so. The thing is, most of the white people around think all of the Indians are the same unless they have some reason to interact with them, get to know them. It'll take me years, probably, to sort out all the connections and intermarriages between groups. Like all families, people visit. It's complicated. That's what I'll have to keep in mind all the time when I'm asked to render justice here."

"You act as a judge?"

"More like a military commander. That's why the staff call me 'Major.' Startled me at first. I'm responsible for a range of things, personal justice and the functioning of the agency on behalf of the government but for the Indians settled here. Anyway," Peter continued, "the landscapes will take your breath away. Flathead Lake and a smaller lake near there you'll love too. We'll take the children picnicking."

He spoke of picnicking and war in the same breath.

Mary had been holding his hand, and she released it, squatted to watch some sort of insect cross our path. She picked it up. Peter cupped the bug in his hand when she gave it to him. "A present? For me?" She nodded, a serious little girl with freckles peppering her nose. It was a gift to me to watch this man love his children, have time for them in the work of his day. In my mind I heard my father singing Gaelic songs while he drove the Gems so long ago. There had been good times.

"Put away," Mary said, and Peter released the bug. "Carry up, Papa," she demanded then and he lifted her. This was a place that would allow the blending of family, friend, and perhaps foe, should it come to that.

"Blackfoot and Crow, traditional enemies, are east of the Divide and—"

We were interrupted then by an Indian wearing leather leggings and a colorful blanket over one shoulder. His chest was bare. He'd ridden in and said in English, "I have news." Then he spoke in another language. Peter turned to me. "I need to go with him to the interpreter. Learning Salish is on my list of must-dos." He set Mary down and she waddled toward the flowers beside the fence, nearly walking right under the horse's belly before Peter told her, "No, Mary," and guided her beneath the horse's head. She hadn't been around animals much, a city child. There'd be a dozen lessons to teach. I was glad I didn't have to teach them by myself.

"Dinner at noon?" I asked.

"That would be good." He waved me off, already walking away, tending to his duties. He really was like a major. But also like a mayor, listening to citizen needs and complaints, solving problems. And that made me the mayor's wife. I took it as one of my tasks to learn Salish, too, though I didn't know that learning one language would not open the doors to the language of all the groups living nearby. Each of the Peoples were unique, as different as Gaelic from English, as the Irish were from British.

I gathered up Vincent from the cool of the stables where the scent of grass hay took me back to early days. Striped cats, curled in the straw, stretched and meandered over for a pet. We spent a moment or two to rub the nose of a horse the stableman—a white man—said was named Nig. "He'll be good for your children to ride on."

Turning back toward the house, I saw the entire square of all the structures was bordered by a six-foot-tall white picket fence. Each side of the square was broken by a gate wide enough to drive a wagon through. The gates kept the cows out, which was why those flowers blooming in front of the doctor's house hadn't been tromped on. And it was why the garden could thrive. It was a well-thought-out plan, not unlike my Missouri uncle's plantation. But here, the workers were paid for their efforts—at least when the government kept its promises to send it or Peter's salary that he told me would be $125 per month.

On that first morning, I stopped to talk to Mrs. Lambert, who was outside with Grace. "How do you find things?"

"Pure lovely," she said. "Me mum would treasure such a place. And can you see the mountains? Like they're planted in the yard," she said. "I'll love each morning looking east at them. Or those over there." She pointed west. "Or those." The valley was cradled in mountains.

"We'll have to learn their names," I said. "How do you find your accommodations?"

"Oh la, they're as good as any I've ever been at. We were at an agency among the Hopi people for a time. I didn't like the agent there at all. But Mr. Lambert says the major is a breath of mountain air—to go with this lovely land."

"It will be perfect once we get a doctor."

We chatted for a moment longer, then both turned to see a large contingent of Indians on horseback, riding through the gateway, kicking up dust. I didn't think their presence was routine, but I wasn't certain. Women and children followed them on both horseback and afoot.

"Mollie!" I heard my husband call out as he fast-walked from the interpreter's cottage, his face grim. The children ran to him as though they hadn't just seen him moments before. When he didn't pick up Mary or brush Vincent's towhead, I knew something was amiss and I gathered my children to my skirts. Sensing my tension, they stood quiet.

The lead Indian wore an eagle feather at the top of his head, had long black braids. His beaded armband seemed to sparkle in the morning sun, but his face was stoic, dark eyes intense. Indian women and children with them milled within the picket fences, looking weary. Riders sat atop agitated horses. Was this the beginning of the war brought to our doorstep? There wasn't time to ask Peter.

I made light of their arrival when I said to Mrs. Lambert, "My husband says I must keep an open door, but I hope they aren't all planning to stay for dinner."

TWENTY-SIX

THE LAKE
OF UNCERTAINTY

I should have hustled Mary and Vincent inside, but I wanted to know what was happening. Mrs. Lambert, sensing my wish to stay with the activity, urged the children behind her fence where they commenced to play with Grace.

The horses stirred up dust that dirtied the lather on their chests. They were beautiful animals. The head man with the eagle feather dismounted and the interpreter began his work telling us they were non-treaty Nez Perce people, under Chief Eagle of the Light—whom he was. They had broken with Chief Joseph and had left behind other chiefs like White Bird and Looking Glass, all waging war against whites. Baptiste translated. "Thunder Traveling over the Mountains—this is what they call Joseph—was brought to the Christian faith by the Spaldings at Lapwai, Idaho." I'd heard of the missionaries and also of Marcus Whitman—a missionary doctor—who had died at Indian hands thirty years before.

I still held Gerald in my arms. He felt a little warm, but then he'd been carried next to me all morning and the sun bordered on hot. I'd forgotten to wear my hat.

"Chief Joseph and his band of Nez Perce have had an altercation of some seriousness with whites in Idaho. There are deaths," the interpreter continued. "Eagle of the Light says the renegade's band numbers seven hundred fifty with their women and children and twice that number of horses. This chief before us says he voted against taking revenge on the settlers in the 'Valley of the Winding Waters.' He wants no attacks for the whites' taking of Nez Perce land and the government lying." The chief used his hands and voice to tell the interpreter that Joseph would avenge these losses, wage war against the whites and the US Army. "Eagle of the Light says he tore his insignia of being a Nez Perce chief and trampled it in the council. He vows he will not take the lives of whites. Others who saw it his way joined him, and they are here now. Seeking refuge."

Baptiste swept his hand toward the many women and children sitting outside the picket fence. "They seek protection at this agency and from the army that pursues Joseph." Eagle of the Light spit when he heard Joseph's name.

"Joseph's band is being pursued by Captain Rawn and the 7th Infantry." Peter turned to me. "That's what the Indian who interrupted our tour came to tell me. They're headed toward the Bitterroot Valley, south of us."

"Armed Indians?"

"Those before us are friendlies." *How could he know?*

My husband's position authorized him to make the decision to allow these Nez Perce people before us to stay—or send them away, possibly to clash with Chief Joseph; possibly assumed to be hostile by the military, maybe shot at by fearful settlers.

"Would they risk their women and children?" I said.

"Chief Joseph apparently is, though he is in retreat. He refuses to go to the reservation." He shook his head.

A young man, maybe ten, rode up beside Eagle of the Light

and spoke. Baptiste interpreted. "He says the chief must leave. His wife gives birth."

Peter said, "Tell them they can stay if the Flathead people agree. And if they keep their word not to rejoin Joseph, should he get this far." To me he said, "We ask them to accept our terms and then we violate our own."

"He will smoke his word," the interpreter said after he'd translated. "After his child is born."

CHIEF ARLEE THEN RODE UP, holding an eagle feather in his pudgy hand. He was a formidable-looking man with a dog collar around his flat-brimmed hat. A runner had been sent to tell him that kin were at the agency. The two chiefs met with arms entwined. "He will stay on my farm," Arlee said. More Salish was exchanged. "After his child is born. The major approves?"

"I do."

Both chiefs left, my husband's first negotiation successfully completed. "How interesting that he would delay a council to be there for his child's delivery," I said.

The other horsemen began to move the women and their lodges—there were eleven in total—to Arlee's farm. Then, within the hour, the two chiefs, my husband, and the interpreter sat on the wide covered porch and smoked a pipe Arlee brought with him. "A daughter has been born," the interpreter told us.

Chief Arlee wore a calico shirt with a blanket around his chest.

Peter said, "We'll smoke and my wife will prepare us food to share, as friends."

I was a little startled, as I really didn't know what was in the larder. But I knew what we'd had for breakfast. Bacon and waffles would be on the menu.

I wanted to stay and watch the ceremony, but I had a meal to prepare and a baby to nurse as well.

Both tasks completed, I entered the porch, inviting the men toward the dining room chairs, which both chiefs accepted. Peter told me later it was an accommodation to me that they used the chairs, as Arlee preferred to squat, his back against the wainscoting. I had sent Hanna to the icehouse, and when she returned, I served them cool water first. The men lifted the mugs of water almost like a toast at some Helena party. In unison, they said a word I didn't understand and then drank. I offered the bacon and waffles next. Chief Eagle of the Light poked the waffle with his fork, looked at it this way and that, the eagle feather at the top of his black braids still as he satisfied his curiosity. Then he put the fork down, took a bite without butter or syrup. "Good," he announced.

Serving the cool water first was instinct, but later my husband said it was the perfect starter. "*Chuse* is Nez Perce for 'water,' what they hold most dear in all the elements of the natural world. You couldn't have honored them better. And we needed that." Only later did I learn how intense the world could get and how small matters tell big stories.

THE NEXT FEW DAYS were rife with uncertainty. We didn't know how far Chief Joseph's band was from the Bitterroot or whether he'd be in battle with the 7th Infantry or killing people as he came. Maybe he'd been diverted, taken another route, maybe north toward the British Miles, as Canada was often called. White ranchers rode their horses hard through the agency gates, asking for updates, expressing fears. Peter worked full-time to silence rumors. He sent out runners but wasn't sure if they returned with facts or fictions.

Charlo, the Salish chief at odds with Arlee, had told authorities once that he would only come to the Flathead Agency as a dead man, he would never come while Arlee lived. Now Peter had to gain his cooperation to at least stay neutral should Chief Joseph bring his band there.

"I guess the other agent tried and failed, so I ought not feel badly Charlo hasn't responded to my persuasions to come onto the reservation," Peter said. But after a day of talking, he said, "He'll also protect white settlers."

"That's quite an accomplishment, isn't it?" I sat on the porch drying my hair, the evening breeze warm against my neck as I lifted the heavy tresses.

"I think he knows his small band would be wiped out if they came up against the army. Charlo thinks he'll try to slip around the military and avoid capture. Apparently, he knows this land, these mountains." Peter had removed his suit coat, vest, and tie— his "uniform," he called it. It seemed formal to me, but Peter said he would always dress in his best as a way of saying he respected the people he interacted with, dealt with them officially as a representative of the government. It was only when he worked the garden or rode horses for pleasure where his cotton blousy shirt and pants marked "casual" on his fine physique.

He rose. A night owl hooted. "I'll put the children to bed. Let your hair finish drying."

When he returned, he picked up the brush and began stroking my hair. In the few weeks we'd been at the agency, the interpreter said the Indians all referred to him as "the White Chief" more than "Major." He'd gained some signing language and Salish words that I think added to our acceptance. Tomorrow, he'd ride north to see if the Pend d'Oreille had any news.

It was while Peter was off that Chief Arlee rode in again. I invited him and two others with him into the house and served them a piece of apple pie. I put a packet of sugar out for them. I didn't know what they wanted. Mary with her ginger hair walked in then. Arlee spoke. Baptiste interpreted. "He calls her *Ich-i-queel-kan*. Red Hair."

"He has a name for you," I said.

Mary scowled and stomped her foot. "He is red hair himself."
Again, Baptiste exchanged the words, but he didn't have to translate Mary's distress.

"Arlee says tell the little girl he will now call her *Khest Komkan*. Pretty Hair."

Baptiste interpreted again, and Chief Arlee spoke of the killings in the Wallowa country that had begun this time of tension. He held his eagle feather like a scepter, his voice speaking darkness as in the murky parts of a fairy tale. I turned my back to get the water pitcher when I heard moccasins behind me and felt my hair grabbed. My heart leapt into my throat.

"What!"

And then there was a second grab, my neck jerked back, but I wasn't pulled over. I felt two hands march down my tresses. "He wishes to measure your hair," Baptiste assured me, "to tell his people how many hands long it is. He has never seen such hair. Do not fear. Their hair is almost sacred."

The chief loosed me and I turned to face him, my heart beating faster than I wanted. "He says to tell you that you have pretty hair, too, like your daughter. He pays you a compliment by measuring it."

I nodded, smiled at him. I would have preferred that he ask, but like entering the house without knocking, there were different boundaries here. I would have to learn to be more agile in understanding them.

LATER THAT DAY MARY and I went out to gather up eggs and walked by the miller, Mr. Hoyt, who was painting the chicken shed. With no grain to grind, Mr. Hoyt did other work.

He nodded to us, paintbrush in hand. "Missus. Miss Mary. Good luck you bring this day."

"How is that, Mr. Hoyt?"

"Yonder is a white horse." He pointed. "If you see a white horse and a red-haired girl at the same time, you'll have good fortune." His sister, Hanna, had related superstitions to me, telling me, "Never pass anything over a babe's head or the child won't grow." When I clipped Gerald's little nails, she gasped and told me, "Oh, Missus. If you do such, he will grow up a thief. Never cut them before he's a year old." And the worst one, "Never name a child for a deceased baby or it too will die." For just a moment my heart leapt for how we'd named Gerald after my deceased brother. *Superstition.*

The wild horse herd that hovered near the agency did have one white horse that ran with it. "Very lucky," he said.

"I don't believe in luck," I told him. "God provides."

He grunted. "Have you heard the news, Missus?"

Should I continue this conversation? "What news would that be, Mr. Hoyt?" Mary carried a basket holding three eggs while my basket held a dozen. The eggs were still warm. It was a chore that Mary liked to do, and I wanted the children to participate in the work of the agency.

"Oh, such terrible news." Mr. Hoyt gestured with his brush, looking up to the heavens. Then he leaned in toward us. Mary hovered behind my aproned dress. "Of the killings. Chief Joseph taking scalps along the way." He said it with a kind of ghoulish timbre to his words. He stared at my long hair.

"It's a rumor, Mr. Hoyt. I try not to get caught up in such."

"The end times are foretold in Scripture, Missus. Foretold in Indian legend too. It's the beginning of those times. Make your peace. We must all make our peace."

"Have a good day, Mr. Hoyt." I hurried us past him, reminding myself that I would not only have to ignore thoughts of rumors, but also avoid those who embellished them.

We LIVED IN A LAKE of uncertainty, paddling through daily routines while waves pushed us here and there, threatening our journey. To compensate, I built in predictability. I scheduled mid-day meals at noon and had supper served at six. They were usually the same meal. Soup. Potatoes, some kind of meat—pork or venison or chicken—served with fresh vegetables like lettuce and cucumbers from the garden. Later, we could add fresh carrots, rutabagas. And in-season berries: huckleberries, chokecherries, strawberries, Oregon grapes, and elderberries, served in crisps and cobblers with whipped cream. The flour supply proved ample, and the government cows were quite fecund. We never lacked for butter, milk, or even ice cream. A small pond offered us cool water as well as ice in the winter, and Peter shared his idea to run the stream through the milk house to make skimming cream easier. That would come later, when "things settled down."

The employees living in the barracks-like building ate with us, as their rooms had no kitchen facilities. Our table could seat sixteen. Peter and I didn't sit at the ends but rather in the middle across from each other where I could more easily see what platters required refilling and Peter's voice could be heard by guests at both ends. It was no occasion for discussing family matters, however, and so later I asked Peter if he thought it acceptable for me to take a present to Eagle of the Light's baby, to honor the new father and mother.

"I don't see why not. It's what you'd do for any new babe, isn't it? You're just being hospitable."

The next day, Vincent, Mary, and I walked the mile to Chief Arlee's farm and gave Chief Eagle of the Light's new baby a pair of booties I'd crocheted. Here I was, taking my children into the heart of a band who had been at war but a few days before. They had broken with their colleague, Chief Joseph. Like me, they must have wondered at what the future held. Mary had picked a wild lily on our way and held it tightly.

To the new father and his wife I handed a tin of ice cream, which they ate while I held their daughter in her beaded baby board. I hadn't included the interpreter on our visit. What could bond a people more in a time of uncertainty than sharing a gift and admiring someone's child? These acts, too, were hospitality and didn't need interpretation.

"Go ahead," I urged Mary who handed the now limp lily to the new mother. I thought of those little flowers Carrie and I picked from the gulches so long ago. The words of William Wordsworth came to mind: "a genial hearth, a hospitable board." That was my duty—and my pleasure. Perhaps it was also my gift.

TWENTY-SEVEN

WE CARRY ON

Two days later I got up to the sounds of frogs croaking at the pond. We kept the windows open at night to let the cooling air in, then shut them after breakfast to keep the day's heat out. Gerald's little body felt hot even though it was a chilly night and I bathed him in cool water. Peter heard me and rose himself. "What's going on?"

"It's Gerald. See how hot he is?"

Peter traced his son's forehead with the back of his hand. Gerald cried.

Is there anything more mournful than a child's cry you cannot end? "We've got to get him to a doctor or get one to come here."

Peter winced. I hadn't meant my words to chastise. "I'll take the fastest team to Missoula," he said. "I was going to send another for supplies, but I'll go myself. I'll bring a doctor back."

Though I didn't want to have him leave with the uncertainty of the renegades' whereabouts and the danger of that route twenty-five miles to Missoula, I barely kissed my husband goodbye, I was so distraught about our baby.

My mother had lost a child just a few months old and so had Ma Anne. *How did they recover from that loss?*

One of Hanna's superstitions came to mind, the one about not naming a child for one deceased or that child, too, would die. I spoke a prayer for Gerald and for my husband's safe return.

That afternoon while trying to lower Gerald's temperature, a runner brought the news that Chief Joseph's band was near Lolo Pass, twelve miles from Missoula, and that white women and children were being brought into the courthouse with guards around them for safety. A hostile band had entered the city and were killing citizens.

Peter was there, in Missoula.

"Runners also said there were volunteers mustering to support Captain Rawn. Full-out war," Mr. Hoyt said. "At least that's the word, Missus."

I continued bathing Gerald, rubbed his body in linen-covered ice and prayed through the night. Runners came by moonlight to report to Baptiste. I was awake, cooling my son's skin. Praying his temperature would go down.

By morning, Gerald's fever seemed to have broken. I wrote in my diary of my gratitude, then asked Mrs. Lambert if she could look after my children while I spoke to Baptiste about what they might have heard either about my husband—who should have returned by now—or of Chief Joseph.

"Let me know what you find out," Mrs. Lambert said. "I need to stuff my worries with a bit of hope."

But I was more alarmed by my investigation. The carpenter, blacksmith, and Mr. Hoyt had all stopped their work and instead prepared their firearms.

"What have you heard?" Mrs. Lambert said when I returned to get my children. "Harry said this morning even the orchard trees quivered with the bad news abounding."

"It does seem like fear is in the very air." I found myself looking at every Indian who entered the agency square, wondering if this was what Mrs. Whitman had done before she and her husband died those years before.

"I'm not able to think about anything else," Mrs. Lambert said.

"My trouble too."

"What do we do this day, Mama?" Mary tugged on my apron.

This day. How can I live this day and not in the past or the future? "Let's make mud pies," I said. I spent time with my children then, let Hanna ready the noon meal. I tried to turn the conversation onto something other than war. In the meantime, I said my rosary and prayed. And I vowed to get a firearm ready too.

It was late afternoon when I heard the rattle of the wagon. I ran out into Peter's reassuring arms.

"Hey, hey." He lifted my chin. "Is it Gerald? Is he . . . ?"

"He's fine. His fever broke, thank God. But a runner said there was fighting in the streets of Missoula."

"No fighting at all. The *Missoulian* had an alarmist headline. '*Help! Help! Indians Defiant. COME RUNNING!*'" His voice gave the emphasis. "I bought the paper but read it with a jaded eye. There's been no fighting, and several volunteers working with the army are friendly Flatheads. Actually, all the Flatheads are friendly. They're all keeping their word not to harm any whites."

"But women and children, are they at the courthouse?"

"Purely a precaution. Now, Mollie,"—he took my elbow, turned me around—"that's wonderful news about Gerald. And I have more good news."

I faced a stranger.

"I want you to meet the new agency doctor, Dr. Choquette, who I'm sure is grateful Gerald's better and that he isn't walking into an emergency. My wife, Mollie Ronan."

I'd failed to notice the man not much taller than me, who removed his bowler hat and bowed slightly. When he greeted me, he had an accent. "You're from Canada?"

"Montreal, late of Ontario. And I'm not yet the agency doctor. My wife Hermine must put her stamp of approval forward, *oui?*"

He gazed around. "Which I suspect she will do as soon as her stage arrives—though she may be delayed with this Indian act-i-vi-ty." His French accent broke up the word. "But where is your baby? He's what brought me here early."

"His fever broke shortly after my husband left."

"It must have been high," the doctor said, "as your husband was quite persuasive, insisting that I come now."

"I'm sorry."

"No, no. Plans are meant to be interrupted. Hermine will be here soon enough, and this way I have a feel for the agency to help reassure her about our future home. And I leave the rumors of Missoula." He adjusted his round glasses. "It's good my first patient has recovered. Let's take a look anyway."

Reassured, Peter went off to speak to his employees, set the rumors straight. I brought Gerald to the doctor's office that I'd kept dusted while waiting for its official occupant to arrive.

Gerald's dark eyes followed Dr. Choquette's movements as he tenderly prodded the baby's tummy, looked into his eyes, held a stethoscope with two ear connections to my baby's chest. "There's a slight murmur," he said. "He might have had pneumonia or possibly rheumatic fever. Did his limbs seem tender?"

"Sometimes he cried to my touch. Yes. His legs."

He removed the instrument. "But without hearing his chest from before his fever, we cannot know. He might have been born with it."

A heart murmur? Pneumonia? Rheumatic fever? Fearsome words to any mother's ears.

"You did well, Mrs. Ronan. Bathing him in cool water."

"I made up a mustard pack and gave him water to drink, squeezed from a clean rag."

"Always helpful. Being sure he had sips of water too." The doctor re-dressed Gerald in his linen gown, his fingers adept at the tiny buttons up the back. He placed Gerald in my arms. "Hermine will enjoy having someone to trade healing potions with. I'd say your son is doing fine. We'll keep an eye on him. If he has a cough or if his fever spikes again, let me know."

"What might have caused the pneumonia or the fever?"

"We often never know, oui? Such uncertainties are the way of things." He might have been speaking to the tension of our lives. "Now I think I'll acquaint myself with the dispensary and restock when I return to pick up Hermine. We carry on."

I wrote those words of summary in my diary: *We carry on.*

ANOTHER BAND OF INDIANS arrived a few days later, camping just outside the agency fence. I watched them ride through the gate, a proud people, erect on their fine horses. No women or children were with them. *A war party?*

I was summoned to Peter's office where the Indians squatted or leaned against the wall. "Michelle, Chief of the Pend d'Oreille," Peter said, introducing him to me. He retrieved a long pipe, and the men formed a circle on the floor, passing the pipe and inhaling a long breath of smoke.

Was the war getting closer? I felt myself breathing faster, worrying for my children. My father's chastising words hovered at the surface of my mind. I smiled, hoping they couldn't see my trembling. I'd never been summoned to a council before.

Peter motioned for me to take a chair. When the pipe had made the circle, he said, "We smoke to affirm that the Pend d'Oreille will stand with their chief as well as with Chiefs Arlee and Charlo against Chief Joseph. They will protect white settlers." He nodded with his chin toward the blanketed Indian nearest him whose hair was kept long and who wore a silver cross around his neck. "Chief Michelle has sent a runner to Joseph saying that if he comes to this agency, they would fight against him, their kin, in support of the White Chief and his people."

Michelle, a man with wrinkles raining down his face, spoke

then. Baptiste interpreted. "Chief Michelle says if the wife of the White Chief would feel safer, he will post guards around the agency until the trouble with the renegade is over."

They're offering personal protection?

"What do you think, Mrs. Ronan?" Peter said. "Will their presence ease your concerns?"

I looked to my husband to shield me. Peter had quietly added weapons and ammunition to the bedroom closet. I knew how to use them. But I preferred to rely on Providence, prayers my bullets for protection.

"Will he be offended if we decline?" I didn't want people at the doorstep nor inside squatting on the floor, weapons in hand.

"I think we can say no."

"Please tell him that we'll be fine without guards that might only serve to further the rumors of a coming danger." Peter nodded. "But thank him, and tell him please that I hope he stays vigilant until Chief Joseph has passed through the Bitterroot Valley."

That Peter had left the response to the offer to me, told me he had no worry. If he'd seen the need for guards around the house, he wouldn't have brought me out. My inclusion in the council was to reduce my fears by giving me control over how I responded to the uncertainties of war. My husband knew me well.

THE ARRIVAL OF HERMINE a few days later was a cause for celebration. The doctor's wife fit in like Cinderella's foot into the slipper. She was dainty, laughed often, and peppered her speech with French. Along with Mrs. Lambert, the three of us chattered as we stitched, shared our table fare, spoke of children. It was the village I had longed for, a refuge in a time of trial. Tend and befriend, my duty and my joy.

Piercing our tender peace were rumors that the Salish would not hold true to their commitment of protection of the white people.

Peter had held several meetings with our white neighbors who worried. Then news reached us later in the month that Chief Joseph had skirted the west side of the Jocko Valley, entered the Bitterroot Valley south of us, then south of Missoula, gathering support.

"Are we in danger?" Hermine asked at our supper table.

"They'll hold," Peter said.

A runner came through the open door just then, breathing hard. Peter rose, as did the other men. Baptiste interpreted, told us that Chief Charlo had ridden into Joseph's camp and that he had refused a handshake with the renegade. "He said Joseph's palm reeked with white men's blood. That if Joseph's band shed white blood, Charlo's band would fight him. But then he allowed Joseph to follow him back to his camp for the night and offered him refuge."

"Joseph is at Charlo's?" Peter asked.

"He says Joseph must leave in the morning. He trusts he will."

I offered the runner food and water.

"Both sides of bravery," Peter said, sitting back down. "To ride into the enemy's camp and then have your adversary offer refuge."

"And perhaps brave on Joseph's part to accept such hospitality," I said.

"Indeed."

We both slept with our "eyes awake" that night, talking softly, Peter wondering if he should ride to Charlo's camp to urge a surrender by Joseph. Or try to find the military to let them know Joseph was that close. But by the time he'd send a runner or go himself, it would be morning and Joseph would be long gone.

"If he's even there. Besides," I said, "you can't fix everything."

It was advice I could take myself. Peter did. I heard his snores shortly after.

In the morning, Peter rode to Charlo's camp where he learned Joseph had moved on south, toward Yellowstone. Or so we hoped.

My husband wrote his reports, settled small disputes across the reservation, rode for the payroll to Missoula, back to the agency, met again with white ranchers to quell their fears. We fed runners, assessed whether they carried rumors or the truth. Peter's trails made a map like a spiderweb across the region.

I made soap, scented candles, knitted and crocheted, normal things while the rumors of war surrounded. Sometimes simple things bring comfort, especially when one can't fix the big things.

"I'D LIKE TO INTERVIEW her myself," I told my husband. I hadn't forgotten how he hired other women to furnish our Helena home and take care of me after childbirth. Yes, it was generous but also . . . restricting. It would be good to have a say in who was in our household. Hanna had been hired as our cook by the previous agent. And though a good worker, the omens she espoused in front of the children were worrisome. "If a fire puffs," she'd told me that very morning at the stove, "it means the neighbors are quarreling. My mother told me that." It was the only occasion I could remember when I was glad my mother hadn't been alive to share such nonsense with me. But I didn't correct her, only told the children that what Hanna shared wasn't necessarily the truth but more like fairy tales. I wanted to be sure the laundress didn't also have such jaded beliefs, so I would interview her myself.

Old doubts pushed in. Could I take the measure of this unknown woman? After all, I'd found Bart Davidson, the road agent, charming, enjoyed his attention to my sonnet-speaking and my hair. But I was younger then. Still, I had chosen Peter even though I was young and it was against my father's wishes.

The Salish woman arrived at the appointed time, carrying a child maybe a year old and "sleeping like a baby." She was as tall as me, slender, with hair as black as piano keys. The strands hung loose, clean and shiny in the afternoon sun slanting through the windows. She wore a calico dress with a beaded belt of butterflies; leggings and moccasins on her feet. She kept her eyes lowered as

I noticed most of the Indian women did, though their husbands looked directly in one's eyes. Without thinking I asked her what her name was. She answered in English before Baptiste could interpret for her in Salish. "Shows No Anger." She looked up then, her eyes welcoming. "I speak the English words, some French. I sign, but Salish falls easiest on my tongue."

I suspected she'd been taught at the St. Ignatius school, and when I asked, she nodded. "I am good in numbers."

"How fortunate. You had good teachers, then."

"My father . . . insists."

We have things in common.

"Are you willing to become our laundress? It's very hard work. And sometimes dangerous with the steaming water. I'm not sure it would be good to have your baby with you." She frowned and said something in Salish and Baptiste interpreted.

"She will place her baby in a hammock. A blanket hung from ridge-pole height, at the corner," Baptiste said. "Babies love them."

"Yes, I know."

"I will work hard," she told me in English.

"We have a lot of laundry to do." All the employees from the barracks brought their laundry to the agency laundry house. "The pay is small. My husband works to get more for the employees." Peter was paid for his work, as was Hanna, and Shows No Anger would be too. But the major's wife?

I'd put on my gracious mask and not upset my husband with what he might call my "suffrage persuasion" growing through the years. I knew my duty. Perhaps I read too many ladies' magazines.

Shows No Anger said something in Salish again and Baptiste said, "She will bring her *ship-te-ke*, her valise, ma'am, tomorrow when she starts."

"Oh, she'll be living here? Not home with her husband?"

She said something more and he interpreted. "Her husband will go with the buffalo hunters and bring back meat. This he has not done. He is not Salish. When they return, they will have their own lodge. She has told her father if she is hired at the White Chief's house, she will stay here rather than have her father make bad words about her husband. It makes it hard for her to honor him as is required for a daughter and also show no anger."

Indeed, it did. And so I made my first agency hire and added a kindred spirit.

TWENTY-EIGHT

THE PLACE
OF THE UNEXPECTED

A heavy storm rolled across the mountains, thunder and lightning playing tag beneath the bended skies. The volleys rattled the windows, the hail that followed shredding the flowers and, worse, the garden. Still more troubling was the word we received that the Salish wheat fields had been devastated by the storm. My husband would have to plead harder for ammunition for the buffalo hunts and for money for provisions of bacon, beans, peas, and other food to make up for the wheat field losses. What Indian fields could be harvested found themselves wanting too. Men rode instead to neighboring farms, discussed the rumors rather than gather sheaves. Young Salish men risked danger, riding out hoping to see the now famous Joseph, though at safe distances.

Shows No Anger's faithfulness to her father's wishes urged me to honor my father, too, and once again try to visit Capistrano. Something compelled me to go, though it was not the best time with war uncertainty. But we'd heard that another of the subchiefs traveling with Joseph had broken away, the way Eagle of the Light had. The breakaway band had surrendered all ammunition to Captain Rawn—if his people would be allowed to return to the reservation. Was that truth or fiction?

Then word came that Joseph had sneaked past Captain Rawn in the night. After the fact, we'd had news that Joseph's band had encountered the army south of the reservation at Big Hole on August 9 with many Indian casualties. None of the Flathead confederation had joined in. They had kept their word. I'd be going to California while the rumor was now that Joseph had been in Yellowstone Park, taken hostages of visitors, killed two.

Generals Howard and Miles now pursued the diminished band as they slipped toward the Bears Paw Mountains. Then we learned Joseph had halted just forty miles from the British Miles. Would he surrender there or make one last stand?

"I would take you to California," Peter said when I told him I felt I should go. "But—"

I touched my fingertips to his lips. "I can do this." My father had never met any of his grandchildren, and a part of me worried that if I didn't go soon, he might not live long enough to see them. I wanted to reassure my father. And yes, I wanted him to say that I had done well, was a good mother if still a disappointing daughter. His letters to me had pleaded for a visit, always ending with, "*You need to honor your father.*" And I thought maybe my being in California would ease Peter's worries over us, free him to go when and where he had to.

Peter would take us in the spring wagon to Missoula, where we'd catch the stage to the train at Corinne, then on to San Francisco, then a ship to Los Angeles and a stage to Capistrano. I would visit the academy and introduce my children to the Sisters, a little pride creeping into the journey.

"I go with you, Mollie." Shows No Anger touched my hand as I folded Mary's dresses, put Gerald's little shirts and trousers I'd sewn into the trunk.

"Thank you for offering, my friend." She had become a friend, one I knew would look after Peter and keep the household operating smoothly. Miller Hoyt had left, taking his sister Hanna with him. Shows No Anger didn't share superstitions. We'd hired another for the laundry, and now my friend stayed near, helping in the house. "But you're needed here."

"You are needed here too. But you go."

Her words startled me. Peter was still within his first months of employment, the ammunition and hunting issues were not resolved. There were new rumors of wars in the Columbia River basin, and our white neighbors still lived with fear and rumors that Peter was often called on to address. And there'd been the terrible storm. And what if I got to Capistrano and couldn't return before winter snows blanketed the west? Or Joseph somehow skirted the generals again and came to his cousins and uncles at our agency with some sort of confrontation and danger for this community I called home?

I looked out the window, watching Peter leave his office where he'd been before dawn. I remembered a conversation we'd had after his meeting with one of our Interior Department officials. People were constantly "dropping in." "What you do in greeting people here is important, Mollie. Our success needs both of us."

I liked it that he said "our" success.

"I just wish I could put you on the payroll." He had paused. "The next best thing is for me to stop using our personal funds to make up the difference when the commissioner fails to send adequate seed or provisions."

"We can't let people starve. It's a good reason to go into debt."

So many people depended upon him.

He came up the steps, prepared to load my trunks onto the wagon. The sun had just risen, casting a light that outlined the mountains as though they were cut with a chisel. The newly grafted crabapple trees (gleaned from Father Ravalli's work) were brushed a brilliant gold. That this man would let me leave to visit my family, spend the money, manage here alone, spoke of his generous heart. He looked so weary and the day had only just begun.

"You're right," I told Shows No Anger. "Unpack. You are needed here and so am I."

"You're not going?" Peter asked when he got inside and saw the flurry of unpacking done with more alacrity than all the folding I'd been doing filling up the trunk. "Why not?"

"Shows No Anger's husband had yet to receive ammunition to make the buffalo hunt," I said. "I'm needed here to support you in getting that to happen. I'll write to my father and encourage him with more vigor to visit here instead. My place is with you." I kissed him lightly.

I saw relief in my husband's eyes.

A commotion ensued outside. "What now?" I said, picking up my skirts so I could move faster behind Peter. A ruckus of men and horses greeted us just beyond our yard's picket fence, bringing Baptiste from his interpreter's cabin to fast-walk toward Peter. I recognized the Pend d'Oreille chief, Michelle, who earlier had offered protection for us. "Is he coming for defense?"

Several men rode with him, sitting astride healthy horses, before reining them toward the water trough.

"Ah," Chief Michelle said, dismounting his fine sorrel horse. He bowed toward me. "The White Chief's wife has not departed," Baptiste translated. To me the old chief said, "We have heard you leave and have come to ride with you, to keep you safe on your journey to the stage."

"Their camp is thirty miles out," Peter told me as he reached for the man's hand to shake it in that gentle finger-pressing way the Indians had. "Amazing that they've come so far."

"Did you tell him that I was leaving?"

"Not that I recall. They have a way of acting on things without really being certain of the outcome," Peter said.

"Please, Baptiste, tell him I have changed my mind and we are staying. Tell him thank you for anticipating my need. Invite him in. I will prepare a breakfast in gratitude for their long ride."

We stood back to let the others go into the house and Peter grabbed me and kissed me deeply. Released, I looked into his eyes. Love lived there. The kind of love that allows another to do what they thought they wanted and come to their own conclusion about its merits, rather than telling one what she could or could not do—like breaking an engagement or making her take a test that she knew she'd fail or adjusting to the unexpected. Or finding another time to go back to Capistrano.

IN LATE SEPTEMBER, Peter received permission to grant the Flatheads the right to purchase powdered lead and caps from the trader, that they might head west to hunt buffalo. Peter had urged their request be granted, but he worried out loud to me—and in letters to the commissioner—of his fears that white people in the area were still agitated by the months of war news and there might be skirmishes. He worried that upon seeing armed Indians, white ranchers would mistake them for hostile forces rather than the hunting party they were. There was yet no word about any surrender of Joseph, so agitation sat on many shoulders, Indian and white.

Preparations for the hunt consumed much attention and activity. Salish men came into the agency to confer, bought their powder, sharpened skinning knives as they talked of a hopeful hunt. Women and children would travel with them to handle the downed animals, prepare buffalo meat, and manage the hides so they did not spoil. Through the winter, some heavy hides would be made into warming robes and blankets or traded for coffee and beans. The hunt was not only a long tradition now threatened with the demise of the herds, but it defined the season and the months of labor that lay ahead.

Shows No Anger would not go, her mother taking her place. Her father had not been happy, she'd told me. "But I tell him I must earn money so we may buy meat from the trader. If there are no buffalo."

The night before they left, at Shows No Anger's invitation, we took the children and Peter drove us in the wagon to Arlee's farm where the tepees would be broken down in the morning and prepared for travel. But that evening, fires brightened the sky and drums and singing filled the senses even when one didn't know the meaning of the words. It was a great assemblage, and I was thrilled to witness it and have my children be there, Gerald pounding on his father's knee to the rhythm of the drums. Odd as it seems now, with us being among the people so short a time, I felt like I belonged there, had a home though I sojourned in a foreign land. Gratitude overwhelmed me. Peter handed me his handkerchief to wipe the tears from my eyes.

In the morning the large party moved out and were blessed by priests at St. Ignatius. Peter filled me in on that ceremony as he had decided to ride with the Salish for a few days. He hoped to tell ranchers and farmers he met that these were people who had kept their word, were prepared to defend them against warring kin, and would shed no white man's blood. And so the hunting party moved west.

And then came word of the longed-for surrender of Chief Joseph, just short of the Canadian border.

No longer would Thunder Traveling over the Mountains fight.

"Now if the government will just let him return to Idaho Territory to that shrunken piece of reservation they finally gave him," Peter said. "We never would have had a war if General Sherman had kept his word. There is sympathy for Joseph, even in Washington, D.C., Maginnis tells me. He says my letters have helped shape the conversation."

Before long, the feuding chiefs, Charlo and Arlee, both pressed Peter to offer the Flathead Reservation as refuge for the now defeated Joseph.

At the October surrender, there were only 87 warriors left of the 350 Joseph had started out with. Most of them were wounded and needed a doctor's care—as did the 184 women and 147 children in Joseph's defeated band. Peter had taken his measure of Joseph after he read what was said at his surrender speech given after nearly two thousand miles of escape. "*I am tired. My heart is sick and sad. From where the sun now stands, I will fight no more forever.*"

"It may be just the interpreter, or the army's journalist, but the man speaks poetry," Peter said. He'd repeated that portion of the speech to me. The priests, too, wrote letters of support for Joseph. The priests also wrote to allow the tribes to acquire ammunition in return for their having kept their promises to not join in the fighting. I poured my husband a second cup of coffee.

"And Charlo and Arlee both want Joseph to come here?"

"I agree with them." Joseph's defeated band could not have had a more faithful agent pressing their cause. "I'll invite the army brass to sit at our table where with your hospitality and my words I hope to convince them to let it happen." I felt again Peter's understanding that we were a matched team, dealing together with the unexpected.

MY KNUCKLES WERE RAW from scrubbing Peter's shirts. I liked to do them myself. The collars I washed separately but put my back into getting his shirts free of any food or stains of daily living. I ironed them with a vengeance, making sure each seam was flat, each pocket flap as flat as a johnnycake. And it was the very shirt I pulled out when Chief Arlee walked into the house hoping to find Peter. He sat down at the kitchen table. His calico shirt was so filthy I didn't want the children to go to him. I thought I was being hospitable when I asked the phrase, "What does your heart desire," the words Shows No Anger had suggested I open with to any Native person.

"To see the White Chief."

I poured a glass of cool water and said to him, "I have a clean shirt you can put on while you wait for my husband."

Shows No Anger let out a gasp at my words, and I knew in that instance I had made some terrible mistake.

Arlee grunted. Bits of meat stuck to his shirt along with bloodstains, dirt. He smelled bad, and I worried for his health that he wasn't clean. Well, that's what I said later had been my motivation, but Peter had other thoughts.

"I said I had a nice clean shirt for him. Of yours. And I offered him our clawfoot tub to bathe in if he wished. That I would even heat the water myself." I knew I sounded defensive. Ashamed that hospitality had not been foremost in my thoughts. "I gave him your shirt and he put it on—right over his filthy one."

"It would have been rude of him not to accept your gift," Peter said. "But—"

"I know." I rubbed my hands on my apron. "Shows No Anger's eyes got big as clenched fists. I knew I'd committed a terrible offense." I felt my face grow hot at the memory of it. "I feel so ashamed, letting cleanliness interrupt my good sense."

"He'd just come back from the hunt, probably," Peter said. "His family has to haul water from the creek some distance, that's why cleanliness of the caliber you want isn't a top priority for him."

"I hope he'll forgive me."

"I hope I get my shirt back."

CHIEF JOSEPH'S STRAGGLING BAND was not allowed to come to the Mission Valley that housed our agency. They were sent to Leavenworth, a land so flat, so far from the mountains and timber, the birds and streams that once brought him respite. Peter would write more letters—these to the Sisters who had once rescued him, asking that they intervene as they could, to help Joseph's sick and weary people. The tension of war had lessened but the threat of small skirmishes still reigned. The band was soon moved to Oklahoma, farther still from mountains and tall pines.

Then, another unexpected turn of events. After all the preparation and the importance of the buffalo hunt, it was over almost before it started. Arlee's people, including Shows No Anger's husband, had turned back. I walked to Peter's office to tell him what I'd learned, but he'd already been informed by Arlee's runner.

"They did the sacrificial thing, returning," he said. "I had hoped my riding with them for that distance and the article I wrote for the *Missoulian* about who was armed and why, would get the word out. But it didn't." He sighed. "The Indians know they have the right to hunt off the reservation and can't be compelled to remain here. But exercising their rights has consequences. They could see that. At least no one was injured, and they can hunt deer here and bear. But . . ."

"What about the winter? Their food?"

"I'm requesting more supplies. When their crops are good, they're self-sufficient. Have been for years. But things are changing. There are so few buffalo. I've even heard that a Pend d'Oreille man has lassoed and branded some buffalo and is trying to bring a few calves, bulls, and heifers to this reservation. Some sort of penance he wants to pay the priests at St. Ignatius for taking a second wife, a Blackfeet woman. Maybe it'll revive the herd."

Things were changing. It was good my husband had communication skills. It was the biggest part of his and our occupation at this place, moving between worlds, keeping tensions down while building people up. I had less good fortune with my own conversations. I'd insulted Chief Arlee—and my father wasn't happy with me either. Unlike life here, our relationship was never changing, or so it seemed.

"Are you sure you cannot come to Capistrano? I cannot express

the disappointment in your failure to visit. Ma Anne isn't well. I may not live long. You wouldn't want to have me pass without having hugged my lass one last time."

I vowed to never plant shame in my children's souls for fear it would produce anger as its fruit.

"Go to Arlee," Shows No Anger said. "Let him open his door to you. He will show you how mercy is done. You over worry about the shirt."

The Sisters had said once that a way to deal with guilt was to first pray and then take a step toward change, guilt being another fruit of shame. "Do something unexpected," she had said.

"Will you arrange it?"

Shows No Anger nodded. She tested the hot iron with her finger, pressed the linen. "I can go with you, if that is what your heart desires."

"Yes. I'd like that very much."

I was grateful I wouldn't be alone, grateful I had a friend to help scrub away my embarrassment at my lack of hospitality.

Arlee's wife, a wide woman with a wrinkled face, opened the door to their cabin and invited us in, me—carrying my baby—and Shows No Anger with her Paul. A Hudson Bay blanket, white with black-and-red stripes, covered their divan. She offered us an herbal tea with a heavenly scent. I gave her one of my fruitcakes. The room smelled smoky from the fireplace. I'm not sure what I expected, but the log home looked very much like our mining cabin. Shows No Anger made small talk in Salish while I admired photographs hanging on the wall. "Those are her people," Shows No Anger said, coming to stand beside me.

"Tell her she has a lovely family and that we have photographs of our family too. It is a pleasant thing."

"Some of our people don't like images for reasons of the spirit,

238

but Arlee is brave and does not think that he has lost himself inside the camera box."

The chief's wife added in English, "Very brave."

"Yes. He is."

Then Chief Arlee entered from the other room wearing my husband's shirt. It was spotless.

He smiled, spoke at some length, stroking the shirt with his long fingers. "He says he is grateful for the gift. He is sad he did not express gratitude at the time you gave it. He thanks you for coming to him to allow him to make amends."

I know I blushed. I curtsied. His wife cut up the fruitcake then and we ate together.

Walking back, I blinked back tears. I'd been shown grace, and the only price I'd have to pay was making a new shirt for my husband. My friend and the chief's family had erased my shame. This was a place of the unexpected.

TWENTY-NINE

WHAT GIFTS ARE THESE?

The reputation of the agency as a genial place brought visitors. Newspaper reporters from the East for whom a place called Bitterroot Valley had held little interest until they heard of the Nez Perce War and the ongoing trials of Joseph. Now, they came west, seeing western life firsthand. Fishermen, having heard that Peter could walk a mile to the Jocko River, be serenaded by a rushing waterfall, and return in half an hour with two dozen trout for dinner, came to fish, and we served them at our table. John Finerty, who was the editor of the *Irish Citizen* and wrote for the *Chicago Tribune*, spent several nights with us; after he left, Peter called a mountain peak near us "Finerty's Wart" for how the editor had described that mountain tip. I thought it was like the peak of my egg whites I beat into meringue.

Peter used these visits to press his case to visitors carrying bias about Native people. "Educating them out of ignorance," Peter called it, "not the Indians, our fellow whites." He'd explain how the individual tribes were unique, often more like us than not, gently disagreeing with others' often-jaded views. Being Irish, he had a natural bent toward the underdog, and these Indians surely were. As for stories of fishing or hunting, each visitor heard Peter's same rendition spoken without a change from the telling. They thought they were hearing it told for the first time, full of Peter's emphasis, gestures, and the ability to weave in a surprise. I'd heard the stories so many times, I could have told them in my sleep. In private I told my husband he was "story-impaired," for he never wavered in the details, never added some new mention of seeing a lynx or mountain goat, when he hadn't. "That would be fiction," he told me, smiling. "I'm a journalist, a man of facts."

"And a bit more politician than you might admit to."

I planned, cooked, and served meals and offered the hospitality that visitors spoke of hearing stories about. I varied my menu just a little, experimenting with what mysteries I could concoct with frontier basics: butter, sugar, flour, and milk. My White and Gold Cake using two dozen eggs was a favorite among repeat visitors.

We often had military men join us. When not in war, the military had more idle time than neighboring ranchers to sit at a table long after they'd finished their huckleberry cobbler. Visitors arrived unannounced, sometimes when Peter was off to other parts of the reservation or in Missoula getting the mail, perhaps conferring with the governor. I was on my own then, bringing comfort to strangers even if it meant putting on my "mask of hospitality." If I felt tired, I never let on that I was. I acted welcoming and soon discovered it wasn't a performance. I tried not to let pride visit me with a guest's praise, but inside, their words were a balm to my soul. In my prayers, I expressed gratitude for the gift of doing what I loved and receiving compliments for it. It was no fairy godmother waving a magic wand that had given me this life, the desires of my heart.

"Looking at the account," Peter said, "I think I know why the former agent left. There are unexplained expenses and odd numbers after dealing with the trader. I think he bought blankets and parfleches and pans and what the Indians didn't use, but showed he paid more than he actually did, pocketing the difference."

"No wonder they don't trust us."

First snowfalls had come and melted, but the latest had dropped a foot or more and it looked to stay. We still didn't really know how the seasons would be, and I made notes in my diary that in later years I might compare dates of the first snowfall or the first wild orchid blooming purple in the spring.

Shows No Anger had gone to live in the lodge with her husband, walking the mile to the agency each day now. Her father and husband were getting along, and she had begun what she said was "the happy season" of her marriage.

Things quieted in the winter, and we women of the agency set about preparing for the colder weather ourselves. Baking, stitching Christmas gifts. The men took time to play with the children more. I cleared out one of the storerooms, putting trunks and unused chairs in the attic, and turned the space off the kitchen into a prayer room. In the carpenter's shed, Peter built a kneeling bench (it would not be right to have a government employee do strictly personal work for the agent's wife) and a table I decorated with the altar cloth that had been my mother's. The room was a comforting addition, frequented by agency personnel as well as visiting guests.

Baptiste had given us notice, and Peter now looked for a new interpreter even while he increased his Salish and sign language lessons I often sat in on. The Choquettes stayed and the Lamberts, too, so we had quite a little compound and planned our Christmas season that we might all celebrate together.

But Peter's work brought frustration. He wrote letters to recruit and to advise the government that he needed increased salaries if he was to keep employees who had agreed to stay only for a month unless they were more fully compensated. He suggested combining two positions into one but keeping the salary for both. The commissioner wrote that he "will consider it."

Peter began reading his reports and letters to me before he sent them. I sometimes made editorial suggestions or remarked on the content. We were in Peter's office, the little woodstove heating the small room to a toasty level.

Outside the window, Vincent pulled Grace Lambert and Mary around on a piece of tin with a rope attached, swirling them in the snow where they'd get up laughing. They wore red hats I'd knitted and heavy-cord sweaters. Shows No Anger looked after Gerald while I met with Peter.

He set his letter down. "Martin Maginnis says I should sue the sheriff's office in Leavenworth for allowing my newspaper to be destroyed by those thugs while they stood by. We could use the money."

We had continued to use our personal funds to assist destitute families, to serve visitors, to make up missing wages that never got delivered.

"It would be used up in legal fees."

"Martin says he'd represent us. He won your father's case, remember."

"Something to consider. Next year," I mused.

Peter pulled out another correspondence to show me. We both wore gloves with the fingers cut out, keeping our palms warm. "I've cosigned a letter with the brother of Looking Glass and sent it to Washington asking for an end to Joseph's exile. The Jesuits urge that too. It's the humanitarian thing to do, the right thing to do, but how many times do I keep asking? It's the most grievous part of the job, writing and not being able to get a timely answer. I've come to dread the words 'will consider it.'"

"As Vincent says he dreads hearing me say 'Maybe.'"

Peter laughed. "I'm not sure his wanting a cat to live inside warrants only a 'maybe.'"

As much as I loved animals, I didn't want them inside the house.

They brought in too much dirt. "You're doing your best," I said. "Disappointments come with any position, but they can fuel new possibilities."

"My little wise woman." He stood then. "Let's make snow angels in the yard. I think that's the best way to foil frustration today."

My husband was a good man, and I marveled again that at sixteen years of age, I knew that. But I loved my father, too, and wrote anew to temper my disappointment, urging him to come visit us in the spring, a season that at the moment seemed very far away.

"WE WILL PLAY Christmas games," Hermine Choquette suggested. She pronounced it with a French accent saying "Crease-mess." We'd learned they were both natives of Montreal and they loved to speak French with Shows No Anger. "We will sing noels and carols."

My time with these women was idyllic. I couldn't recall any fairy tales that featured four female friends, but I was sure if there was one, it would be full of joyful laughter, of shared secrets as we tended our families and befriended all who came to visit. We spoke of life on this agency cradled in a setting of indescribable magnificence and yes, how blessed we were to be here.

My father's letters spoke of worry for me, danger, trouble. He lamented that my husband had taken me to this faraway place and that I had agreed to go with him. I didn't seem able to make him understand so that his worry would be lessened. Coming to Montana to see was the only way I thought might help, and so far, he'd refused to do that.

Hermine had no children but adored Grace and our three and the cobble of little ones who tagged along with their parents when they came to see the doctor. Much of our chattering as women was of our mothering and helping each other from our own chastisement when Grace stumbled over a rock and got a black eye or

Gerald wasn't yet walking at nine months. I wondered if I'd let his fever get too high before I'd started his cool baths and that now his little muscles were affected. It was good to have other women to confer with now and then, and I thought of my mother and Ma Anne, trying to remember if I'd seen women visiting. I hadn't—just our "neighboring." There was merit in time away from one's husband and best friend, time for female companionship, a trail outside of family, but directing the path toward a healthy heart.

"Let's make it a party to get our trees," I said. "All of us together."

We women prepared hot cocoa in canteens along with berry scones we'd eat at the close of our tree selections. And so the men were conscripted to get runners on a wagon, and on the appointed day, we were gifted with sunshine and a temperature of thirty. We bundled up our children and ourselves with muffs and neck scarves and caps of fur that tickled our faces. We drove the few miles to a wooded area Peter and Harry Lambert thought would give up just the right-sized trees. Smaller ones for the Lambert and Choquette cottages and a ten-foot one for the agency. And with saw in hand, the men cut our forest plunder. "This is the day that the Lord has made," Hermine said. "Let us be glad and rejoice in it."

"Indeed," Peter and I said in unison.

Christmas morning, we heard footsteps on the porch while we were still abed. Three men from Arlee's band walked right into the bedroom and shook our hands as we brushed sleep from our eyes. They offered Christmas greetings, letting us bumble with our spare Salish to greet them back. After they left, I said, "My father would be mortified."

For that first Christmas at the agency, we sang songs and celebrated, decorated the trees with strung berries, popped corn, hand-painted balls, and crosses made of twists of straw. Shows No Anger came with her husband later in the day to eat with us, riding their horses with Paul in his board attached to the side of the saddle, his face barely visible in the bundle of fur. Shows No Anger's husband handed me a beaded baby board.

"For your new one."

"But I'm not . . ."

"Soon," Shows No Anger told me.

She went on to tell of the story of the board's construction, how she soaked the alder wood so she could bend it over the top where trinkets and bits of mirror could be hung to catch the light and hold the baby's attention, how she prayed over each effort. "I will stuff the bed with moss for his head and bottom. You have no mother or grandmother, no *katsa*, to make it. I do it for you."

She beamed as I oohed and ahhed over its workmanship and uniqueness, though I had no reason to believe I'd be using it anytime soon.

I gave her a book of Shakespeare's sonnets. She had heard me reciting one when she ironed and I peeled potatoes in the kitchen one day. She'd commented about the sounds and rhythm of the words. "We do not have such to read at St. Ignatius school. You could sing to it." She held the book to her heart.

I'd knitted Paul a cap with strings on either side and pompoms of yarn at the ends. "It won't be nearly as warm as what he has now." I nodded to the boy whose dark eyes watched us from the safety of his board leaned up against the wall.

"It will be his spring and autumn cap," she said. "When the seasons are uncertain. Red is a good color."

Gifts were exchanged between the agency women and the men. The children played with their toys. We served a feast of a goose and ham and all the trimmings, including dressing with dried berries and pine nuts. It had been long in preparation, this feast, but I wasn't tired. I found that making people pleased with food and friendship lifted my spirits.

And after everyone had left, Peter and I exchanged our gifts in the bedroom without the benefit of our morning guests. He had purchased a new rosary for me in Missoula.

I kissed him and fingered the smooth beads and cross. I gave him a pair of new boots with the heels like the ranchers wore as

I'd seen Cousin Ellen's husband wear. "Better for riding since you're doing so much more of it." He smoothed the leather with his hands. "It'll be easier to keep your stirrups. The cobbler at St. Ignatius's made them."

He unlaced his brogans and immediately pulled the boots on. "A perfect fit."

I spoke the rosary prayers and then said, "It's not fair that you can buy me store-bought things. I don't get to the city to shop for you."

"That you agreed to be my wife and follow me will always be your greatest gift, Christmas after Christmas, birthday after birthday."

Those words were his greatest gift to me.

As I checked the children that evening, listened to them breathe, I thought how fortunate I was that Sister Scholastica had urged me to grow deeper in my faith to find the real reason I felt the call of the convent. This was my call, to be a wife and mother, tending daily to the small things that would help children find their own journeys, their own treasures. And if I'd never had a child of my own, to be a part of other lives, the godmother of Ellen's children. A big sister to my siblings. I didn't need to pass a teacher's test to make a difference. My father might never understand.

THIRTY

THE STORIES

"These stories are told only when snow covers the ground," Shows No Anger told me. "I have permission to tell them." It was March 1878, and snowdrifts pushed against the house, lined the paths the men dug between the root cellar, Peter's office, the storehouse, and the Lambert and Choquette cottages. They looked like deer trails breaking deep snows. Shows No Anger beaded a pair of moccasins, but she could tell stories while she worked. Vincent was spellbound. Her stories often had a character called Coyote as the instigator of various tricks but also showed how greed or anger could hurt humans.

She spent full time in the house now, and we agency women helped with laundry duties, at least until spring when I hoped to hire a new laundress—if Peter could get the wages worked out with the commissioner. Mrs. Lambert and Hermine shared the work, just as that winter we also shared many meals—and the occasions of storytelling.

Peter missed those times, having to ride out through the deep drifts to visit sections of the reservation, especially checking on food supplies. He met with Indians who asked him to settle disputes and listened to complaints of white ranchers who had come onto the reservation and begun farming in a section called Horse Plains. They built fences and then accused the Indians of tearing them down or killing their hogs and cattle for their own use.

I spent more time in my prayer room when he was gone or when the intensity of white and Indian conflicts caused his face to turn red. I wondered if he'd ask to be assigned again when he finished the former agent's term. *What would we do?* I couldn't imagine living anywhere else now. This was our home.

I found joy in unexpected places, as when rolling out dough for pies or even changing Gerald's nappies and catching those laughing eyes that sparkled like his father's. Peter spent long hours writing reports of his visits and expressing the needs of the people to those who could help address them. And he kept our larder full with venison and elk, tasks that I think acted like his prayer room—spending time in the Mission Mountains and their wooded wonders.

On a snowy day, we could look out into our world of white and see the icicles hang from the eaves like Christmas ornaments. Inside, we were "snug as a bug in a rug," a phrase I remembered my mother saying when she put me to bed. Just as I found joy in unexpected places, memories of my mother came more often, arriving with less of a feeling of loss. It was as though I carried her with me. I rubbed my belly—nurturing new life as Shows No Anger had anticipated—and I talked to my mother about this new baby forming. My mother had told me stories too.

"Are your snow stories like fairy tales, then?" I asked Shows No Anger. "Entertainment but with lessons about what happens if you don't listen to your parents or try to trick someone in order to achieve some personal gain?"

Shows No Anger worked her beads into the leather with a fat needle while I added a flounce to Mary's dress. Our only daughter was getting taller.

"Yes," she said after a pause. "They are to make us laugh and make us wonder. And to help us know where we came from. To draw a thread between our elders and our children."

"My people—the Irish—we have tales, too, about musical harps and giants and children turned into swans by terrible stepmothers. One of my mother's favorites was of the giant Finn MacCool and his wife Oonagh. She outwitted the neighbor and saved her husband. My father never liked that story, now that I remember it," I said. "He preferred tales about a magic harp that helped win a battle over one with a wise wife."

I'd once escaped inside fairy tales, lived on an imaginary stage. But here, in the shadows of mountains and in the comfort of extended family, I had no need to disappear. It was another gift.

PETER STOMPED SNOW from his fur-lined boots, handed me the mail packet. He'd been able to ride to Missoula, gone three days, but a March thaw teased. "The wages are there, at last, and I've heard from the commissioner that those two white settlers have lodged their complaints up the line. They didn't like my answers."

"Should they have even begun farming on that part of the reservation?"

"It's land not covered under the treaty, land claimed by the Kalispel, that goes all the way to the Columbia River in their experience. So I guess there's no law to stop them, but it's a bit disingenuous to take their property—again—and then complain about how their neighbors are harassing them. I'm going to write of some recent events the Pend d'Oreille complain of. Two white settlers apparently poisoned some of the Indians' dogs. And also altered their stallions. Now there's audacious for you, gelding their breeding stock. Neither denied the charges."

"Will you hold a council?"

"I'll have to."

The meeting was arranged for the agency, despite the thaw and rivers running high with ice melt. Peter hoped the trappings of the buildings would give their meeting an official status to bring greater weight to whatever the problem was. Larger gatherings like this one were expected to be held in the mill area. I was allowed to sit in, and while I did not smoke the pipe, I could breathe in the sweet scent of sage. It reminded me of my father when I'd get his pipe for him at the end of one of our traveling days. It was pleasant to have good memories of my father spring up now and then.

Offenses were spoken of by both sides, and Peter said later that he was amazed there weren't personal injuries occurring in such a remote part of the reservation. In the end, they seemed to agree that both sides were to blame and to start fresh. No threats of violence lingered.

"You've had a long day. Let's go in. Let me rub your back."

He ignored my offer. "I've got an old complaint that occurred during the last agent's time, about lost sheep and Indians chasing white women with hatchets when asked to smoke outside the house they'd barged into." He took out his corresponding file.

"The sheep ranchers want $160 in compensation. Seems fair enough and would keep tensions corralled. Do you think I can get an answer or authorization? I can see why agents don't last long. It's like the people who make the decisions live in another universe."

"Are you thinking you won't reapply when the former agent's term is finished?"

"What? No." He looked surprised. "This is my life, our life now. Despite the frustrations, there is nowhere else I'd rather be than here, with you, with these people. Every day is like being in a library where I learn new things and realize the way I see the world is not the way everyone else sees it. It takes all my skills to navigate it, but it's good work." He helped me with my shawl.

"I'll give you that back rub before supper."

"No, after I read to the children. That's my greatest ease."

"That Danish story, 'The Little Mermaid,'" I suggested.

He put his arm around my waist to steady me on the muddy

walkway. "'The Emperor's New Clothes.' It celebrates that speaking the truth is never easy. I have to remember that each time I send a letter to the commissioner."

WITH WINTER EASING BACK into its cave, wildflowers came out to play. Spring in the Jocko Valley was glorious. New birds appeared and cheered us, finches and swallows, meadowlarks and robins. Shows No Anger took me and the children out to dig camas bulbs. We could find them in the meadow by searching for pale blue flowers atop slender stems. They bowed to the earth moist from the runoff of the snow fields. She used a *kapn*, she called it, a deer antler with a fork at the end, that had been her grandmother's, handed down. I had nothing of my grandmother's and now only a little towel from my mother and that tiny piece of lace on Peter's valentine.

"Push beside the stem and find the bulb." She showed us how and said we should remove the bulb from the stems and leave them there. "So the seeds will replant." Her fingers removed the thin skin from the bulb and she put it in a basket tied at her waist. Paul was in a cloth hammock hanging from her back. After a while, he fussed and she took him down and let him waddle free.

I wore a knitted basket tied at my waist. She'd shown me her bear grass and corn husk bag, preparing me for spring and root-digging.

Gerald reached in and grabbed a bulb, started to stick it in his mouth.

Shows No Anger gently took it from his chubby hands. "It will make a big wind in his belly. Cook in the ground," she told us.

"Will they bake as well in the oven?"

She looked thoughtful, then nodded, yes. And so we added another vegetable to our dinner. We found wild asparagus growing near streams, their slender stalks tender. She pointed out wild celery, too, and I thought that this baby due in November would have the benefit of all these new foods that none of the other children had experienced. Once again I counted my blessings and took in the nurture of the landscape and my present life so free of grief and loss. I worried less about my father.

We took camping picnics to Flathead Lake, a stunning body of water, blue and depthless, where Peter caught bull trout large enough to serve all five of us—though in my pregnancy, I could have eaten one all by myself. But it was at a smaller body of water called Big Mountain Lake, a few miles west, where I truly relaxed. We camped there for three days, with Peter doing all the cooking. I think he missed the two of us in the kitchen having flour fights that led to kissing that led to more. I especially liked the cutthroat trout Peter fixed for us in a cast-iron spider over an open fire. "The only way this fish could be fresher would be if I'd walked faster from the lake to pop it in the pan." Peter inhaled the scent.

I saw my husband in his happiest of seasons. He didn't miss being a newspaper editor, miner, nor one engaged in politics, at least not in the election kind. We read of ongoing Democratic and Republican issues in the *Missoulian* and heard from Congressman Maginnis about the November election coming up, and I thought of Louise Maginnis and hoped her life was as abundant in her Washington, D.C., apartment as mine was on this frontier. It didn't seem possible it had been almost two years since the last election. Peter had declined Martin's urging he attend Democratic events, telling him he had his hands full doing a good job for the Indians and the government.

"If Martin could see me now." Peter wiped butter from his mustache. "He wouldn't believe that I had too many things on my plate besides fresh trout."

"I wish I had a camera to take a picture of you and your fish," I said. "I'd send it to my father. That would get him to visit. He does like to cast a line." I cleaned the pan while Peter let Vincent and Mary bounce on him as he lay on the quilt in the shade. Finally, in laughter, he feigned exhaustion and they fell to his side.

I felt almost guilty to be so happy, to face the May morning with streaks of colored strands writing the sunrise in the sky. Happiness was in this place where friends in Helena had been aghast at our plans to move so far away, among Indians—"with all their troubles."

Troubles found all people. Burned-out printing presses. Stolen gold from a placer mine. Failed teacher tests. Fathers pressing their will on daughters. One needed to savor the goodness when one could.

WHEN THE LETTER ARRIVED from my father in June, I felt a pang of guilt. I hadn't heard from him since Christmas, but I hadn't worried over it. Well, perhaps a little. It was out of that pressure I carried to honor thy father and thy mother that caused me to send missives to my father monthly, if not more often. I always included Ma Anne in the salutation and provided separate notes to Kate and Jimmy. The alcalde wrote back with more detailed news than any from my family. He told me first that Jimmy was fluent in Spanish now and "*likes wearing the* Traje de Charro *with its narrow waist and fitted trousers with blue-dyed laces up the side. He can dance the flamenco like he was born in Spain and performs now and then wearing his black and white sombrero. You would be proud of him and his guitar, La Mary.*" It was hard to imagine the little boy who had cried at our wedding dinner (until Peter grabbed him in a hug) as a performer. The true actor in our family.

The alcalde always had news of Kate, too, and how her hair flamed in the Capistrano sun as she helped our father in the fields. "*She says to me once that you and she are not true sisters as you have different mothers and only share your father. I assure her that the fact of that is true, but that she and you are as sisters like those born of all the same blood.*" I could almost hear him offering such comfort to Kate. And in my next letter to her I reiterated his assurance. She too had been invited but had never been allowed to visit.

The June letter in my father's hand carried no news of Kate

or Jimmy but of Ma Anne. "*She has died of consumption. Now you must come.*" I'd been summoned.

"I WANT TO HONOR HER, revere her, but I really can't go now, not with the baby only four months away." I paced the kitchen floor, all sorts of memories of Ma Anne weaving their way into my heart. Peter held Gerald on his lap. The older two ate their mush at the table.

"I can't get away now to go with you."

"Of course you can't, Peter, I understand. I'll simply have to tell him it isn't possible."

I grieved the passing of my stepmother who not once behaved like those in fairy tales. She walked a narrow path, not trying to replace my mother but stepping back when words of my mother came up in conversation. She stepped over times when I heard my father call her Ellen instead of Anne. She stepped up, supporting my father even when he didn't like admitting that he needed her to run an establishment, serve food to miners and railroad rowdies, and not complain about the cold and wet conditions. For me, she had stepped in, defending our going to dances and especially my engagement to Peter that I'd had to break. It had been Ma Anne who had pushed to allow me one last dance with him, one last morning in the hotel lobby giving Peter back the ring, saying goodbye. Had I told her thank you often enough? I likely hadn't.

I would tell Kate more of these stories, though. Kate, a daughter who had just lost her mother. We were truly sisters now, siblings in grief.

In the end, I wrote to my father to tell him of my sorrow and that I would not be coming to Capistrano. I hoped he would bring Kate and Jimmy to Montana. I didn't hear back a word.

THIRTY-ONE

THE ARRIVAL

I t's just such a joy to join you, though how you do it is beyond me." Elizabeth Custer stepped from the carriage, looking fresh as a just-bathed baby even though she'd ridden through dust and dew from Missoula. A military escort of two uniformed men accompanied her, their faces revealing no emotion as they dismounted and led their horses to the nearest trough. They eyed the various blanketed Indians crossing the square to Peter's office or the storeroom. A family entered the doctor's quarters, and Hermine waved at me as she ushered her husband's patients in.

A letter indicating Mrs. Custer's plans to visit had reached me the week before. I had no idea what to expect. Would she be the grieving widow of a man whose decisions at Little Big Horn had brought about his death and that of his brother and brother-in-law along with hundreds of other soldiers? Or would she be the gregarious army wife who had loved to travel with her husband, planning parties at the garrison in between his "Indian campaigns," as the officers who sat at our table called their assignments in the West.

I wasn't sure why she was here. But as the hospitable hostess, my task would be to read what her needs were and do my best to meet them.

"Welcome." I chose to ignore her wonder at "how I did it."

"Please, come in. Shows No Anger, would you please bring Mrs. Custer's saddlebags."

"No. My escorts will bring them in." Mrs. Custer brushed her hands at Shows No Anger as though she were a clutch of chickens needing to get out of her way.

"At least you have good help," Mrs. Custer said as she swept her way into the house, removed her wide-brimmed hat, and looked for a place to sit. She chose a chair, and the caning was soon covered with her blood-red dress of fine linen. She had tiny feet. She gazed around the room, took in the white curtains drifting in the breeze where I'd had our new Chinese cook cool two sour cream pies. "What lovely accoutrements," she said. "We never had such filigreed candleholders in most of the army camps the general and I were at."

"The agency does have a fine blacksmith."

"Not an Indian, I wouldn't imagine. I don't think they have the talent for such artistry."

"One of the Salish did those, in fact. He led a group of scouts, Company 9, in the Nez Perce War last summer."

She harrumphed and said, "Trusting them. There are perils." Then she switched to a cheerful voice. "If I may be so bold, how long have you and your major—I know that's what people call him though I don't think he was ever commissioned, was he?"

I shook my head.

"How long have you been married?"

Her forthrightness startled me, but I blurted out, "Five years." I wanted to say, "It's none of your affair," but that would of course have been rude.

"Ah, I had thirteen years with the general. It might have been more, but my father"—with vigor she pulled the fingers of her gloves to remove them—"got in the way of him at every turn, tried to get me on to other suitors." She sighed. "When I think I might have had more years but for Papa . . ."

"What is your heart's desire? Would you like some apple crisp? With fresh cream?"

"Oh, my dear, if I were to eat everything offered to me, I'd be the size of a cow. Just some water would be lovely."

I retrieved the pitcher from the icebox and poured a glass.

"So, five years," she continued. "And three lovely children. And a fourth?"

"In November."

"In the beginning I thought it fortunate we had no children, or the army never would have let me travel with him. But I so wish now I had a son to carry on his legacy and name." She took a swallow. "There's such a possibility of loss with children, don't you think? My mother and three siblings all died before I was thirteen."

"I'm . . . I'm so sorry."

"My mother's dying wish to my father was that he look after me and 'be both mother and father.' Oh my, he did. And was." She laughed, took another sip. Her nails had a clear coating on them. I looked at my own splitting nails that always happened when I was pregnant. *I should get beeswax and egg white and make a lacquer.* "I loved the doting—wealth, judgeships, and politics were my father's forte, and he did indulge me. Until I fell in love with the general. Well, he wasn't a general then and my father actually called him a tinker, imagine that." I could. In a secretive voice she said, "I met him when I was sixteen but fell in love four years later. I wrangled with my father for two more before the general distinguished himself enough at the Battle of Gettysburg and got promoted to brevet brigadier general, and my father finally gave me away at the Presbyterian Church in dear Monroe, Michigan."

She'd given me the history of her early life and courtship that was uncannily similar to my own—minus the wealth. I wondered if her mother and siblings arrived as memory when least expected.

I was astonished by her candor. It must be what people liked about her lectures and presentations when society generally prohibited women from taking public stage. Maybe she was still on a stage here, with me.

I sought to change the subject. "I assume your lecture went well in Missoula, Mrs. Custer."

"Oh, please call me Libbie. And yes, it was well attended. The audience laughed when I hoped they would and became still in the moments calling for it. I think they were moved. On second thought, I'd love a piece of that apple crisp you spoke of earlier, Mrs. Ronan."

I didn't offer to have her call me Mollie. There was something about her that seemed feigned.

The children had their demands, and I settled her in one of the bedrooms we'd reserved for guests—there were two staying here now—in the unoccupied quarters formerly used by the carpenter. Peter was busy recruiting. General Gibbon, one of our guests, had come to commend one of the thirty Salish members who had signed on as scouts to support the army the previous year. They were to receive thirty dollars for their monthlong service to protect the white community from Chief Joseph.

At supper, Libbie entertained us and our other guests with stories I suspect she told in her lectures. She spoke of their military times in Texas and Kansas and the last in the Dakota Territory at Fort Abraham Lincoln. There was no mention of his court-martial when he left a battlefield to join her and scant mention of his last deployment. She referred to a biographer she'd worked with for "details of that tragic, tragic day."

"This is a fine agency," Libbie said to the table. Heads nodded. The Lamberts and Choquettes had joined us, General Gibbon, and Alexander Matt, the to-be-honored captain of the Salish scouts. "I've seen some that were, well, not. You must have fine influence with the Interior Department, Major."

"I owe what is good to the tenor of the Flatheads," Peter answered. "A great many of us have good farms. And, of course we have a fine contingent of skilled people—present company as representative—that the government employs." He nodded toward the agriculturist, the doctor, and the Salish blacksmith.

"Were you frightened, Mrs. Ronan, with all the warring by the renegade, Chief Joseph, and that, that, vicious Sitting Bull?" Libbie asked.

"We were well defended." I caught the gaze of General Gibbon and the blacksmith captain. "The Indian police stayed vigilant, and the Pend d'Oreille chief offered to post guards around the house, but we never felt the need for it." I turned to the blacksmith captain. He held my gaze. "And brave men left their jobs, their farms, and families and volunteered to go against their kin. To protect the white people in the region."

"Still, to be right in the middle of these . . . heathens."

The blacksmith looked down. I felt I should say something in defense of what she'd called him.

"The Flathead people have been Catholics for years." Peter leaned back so the kitchen helper, a German girl we'd hired, could refill his coffee cup. "Thank you, Gretel." To Libbie he said, "We have never thought of the People here as heathens or anything other than good men and women, Indians attached to their various tribes."

"Be wary," she said.

"I find as much trouble raised by our white neighbors as by the Flatheads. It's a balancing act. Each have their grievances."

"I excuse myself," the blacksmith said, rising. "My thanks to Missus." He nodded to me.

General Gibbon, who had remained silent throughout this interchange, rose with him. "I'll take my leave as well. Good night and thank you for your hospitality, Mrs. Ronan."

"I hope it wasn't anything I said." Libbie put on a charming smile after they left. Then, "I'm sure you have stories to tell, Major. Have you thought about having your lovely wife give lectures? There's some money in it. The novelty of a woman speaking. The general's death left me destitute, but less than a year later, I have a steady income correcting my husband's tarnished image in my articles and lectures. I'm working on a book about our lives. You could do that, too, Mrs. Ronan, though your husband paints such an idyllic scene here, I'm not sure where you'd find the tension to keep audiences enthralled." She patted my hand, then said, "I'm sure you could. People speak so well of you in Helena. But then you've lived there. To capture an audience in a place not known to you, that does take a little planning and acumen, which fortunately I have."

"AMBITIOUS," PETER SAID as we readied for bed. "Her husband was as well. Some say that was his downfall in the end. Hubris. Wanting to make a name for himself."

"Why did she come here?" I brushed my hair. I'd cut it so it was only midway down my back. It took less time to dry and I didn't tangle my husband with loose strands in the night. It was also a tribute to Ma Anne in my grieving, something Shows No Anger said her people did in time of mourning.

"I'm not sure. While you were putting the children down, I asked her if she intended to go to the battlefield of the Little Big Horn where her husband died. She said she had no interest in seeing it. Said she had a sufficient view of it from the journalists who'd been there."

"To come so far."

"He's buried at West Point. No need to go to the site of his dying, I suppose." He dropped his boots beside the bed. "She is quite charming, though, don't you think?"

"Beautiful, poised, purposeful, but charming is not a word I would have thought of." But then I remembered that *charming* carried many facets, including the definition of something that didn't ring true, like the discordant notes of an out-of-tune piano or the cacophony of a gathering of finches. Her presence didn't make me want to spread my arms in joy, and I hoped my charm toward guests didn't carry such incongruity. It was something I would have to watch for, keeping the feel of a home inside a government agency that was becoming a destination for visiting dignitaries.

LIBBIE CUSTER STAYED A WEEK, asking questions, telling me stories. Her presence tested my confidence that I could be gracious no matter the strain. I looked for things we had in common. She did enjoy the children and remarked on Mary's freckles and red hair. "Chief Arlee called it that—to Mary's distress—and now he calls her 'Pretty Hair.'"

"You're that intimate with them?"

"I tend to trust until there is reason not to rather than withhold my trust until someone proves worthy. We are all worthy."

She harrumphed.

While we had guests, I directed others to the work—the cook making the meals I actually liked preparing; Gretel serving. I liked doing that, too, but I was learning to delegate. Shows No Anger helped with the children and teaching a new Salish girl to do the laundry. Instead of tending my family, I took tea with the guests. We went riding through the meadows. I took her fishing. Libbie wanted to talk, and it was my task to listen. I was more tired each night, as she was now our only guest. Fortunately, she liked to read and was writing her book, so I did get respite from her chatter each afternoon, if only for an hour.

Her questions and biases—that's what I called them—brought a pall to our meals, and I found myself deciding often whether to protest something she said to "educate her out of her ignorance" or let it pass. But I felt unfaithful to Shows No Anger when she acted as though my friend did not exist even when she sat at our table.

After one episode I followed Shows No Anger to the root cellar out of earshot of Libbie Custer and said, "I'm sorry she's so . . . demeaning is the word, I guess."

"Her husband was killed by Northern Cheyenne, Lakota, and Arapaho. She does not separate them from my people. It is wasteful for you to try to help her see with different eyes."

"I feel like I'm not defending you."

"You treat me as a friend. This is your defense." She smiled then. "Her leaving will lighten my heart."

"Mine too," I said.

We both sighed relief when she left.

But her story of her father and her relationship with him lingered. Was it grief that made our fathers behave as they did: pampering their daughters yet suggesting they must do more? And more importantly, rejecting our choices of husbands?

THIRTY-TWO

A DAUGHTER LOST

Word of the murders reached us in early July. Two men in Lewis and Clark County, two more in Deer Lodge County, four or five miners at the head of Rock Creek in Missoula County. Murdered by Indians, it was claimed, but who? Peter sent a runner and learned that a band of eighteen Nez Perce from Sitting Bull's camp near Idaho traveled on the trail through Pend d'Oreille country. Chief Michelle—whom I personally adored—told Peter that Sitting Bull told him his people must leave the reservation or join him in the killing of whites who had taken their land.

Another war?

Peter told me what he knew while we pulled weeds in the house garden. We'd been spared of the heavier grasshopper infestation we'd read about attacking much of the West. I looked forward to harvest, this year doing so in honor of Ma Anne.

"Chief Michelle thinks one of the Nez Perce chiefs has sent out marauding parties meant to kill and engage the army and that Sitting Bull will then come for the larger fight."

"Should we be . . . worried?"

"Concerned. I'm already getting claims from local authorities

264

that the deaths are from our Indians. But they aren't. Michelle says he told the runners to relay to Sitting Bull that he had long ago forgotten how to wage war, that his crops were good and nearly ready to harvest, and that they had no ammunition anyway. Then he says he told him that even a small mouse if trodden upon will turn and bite. He warns them that that's what the Pend d'Oreille would do if Sitting Bull wages war. 'We will die by our homes,' he said. They'll defend the whites."

Peter gathered up the weeds and took them to a pile he and Harry Lambert were experimenting with, creating new soil from old plants and household scraps. He told me George Washington did that sort of thing, called his trash heap a *stercorary*. He added stable dung.

Shows No Anger had approved as he collected the waste once while she watched. "We wrap seeds in fish parts before we plant. It makes the seeds stronger."

As Peter and I worked this day, I found it soothing that with my hands in dirt I could better hear of murder and danger over which I had no control. I could pull weeds. I could turn the stercorary pile with my pitchfork and use it to enrich the garden soil. It was soulful work.

"What did you and the chief decide?"

"He'll choose some scouts and I'll have a few white men to join them, and we'll arm the Indians," Peter said. "Get them blankets and other provisions." He broke up a clod of dirt. "They'll scout the trails and defend if the marauders enter the reservation. I'll have my work cut out for me trying to calm things here. And I need to make the payroll run to Missoula soon."

I always hated those trips, unannounced for security purposes. The payroll could be months late. Peter had to travel the twenty-five miles, and return carrying thousands of dollars stuffed into his shirt like my father had to.

Peter stood. "Would you look at that carrot." He held up a fat, orange root a foot long. "This soil can grow anything."

"You're a farmer at heart," I said.

"My successes in the soil keep me sane."

"That's almost lyrical," I said. He grinned.

We finished our garden stint, gathered up the children—all but Gerald, who I carried on my back in a sack—and went inside for drinks of water with dried peach pieces for flavor. All the ice was gone and even the pond that cooled the milk grew warmer in the Montana summer.

We women dealt with the facts of the murders and the rumors of more by doing what we could do: everyday things. Gardening. Laundry. Drying raspberries.

Peter sent out his scouts and then runners west toward Idaho to find out about the movements of Sitting Bull's marauding bands. He directed runners south toward Missoula to calm the neighbors and reassure them that the People of the Flathead confederation were not to be mistaken for renegades. They were as we all were, concerned for their family's safety, busy on their farms, grazing their cattle.

A MONTH LATER, while Peter was off in Missoula for the payroll, two Indians rode through the white gate. One of the men looked battered and wounded, with huckleberry juice on his calico shirt and a bloody bandanna around his head. He dismounted and eased toward the house as though carrying great pain. Wind rustled the fringe on his leggings. Through the window, I watched his companion lead their two horses to the watering trough, spotted ponies trailing behind. This man before me carried a tomahawk in a holster on his hip. *Friend or foe?*

My heart beat loudly, and I was grateful that the children—all but Gerald—were on the far side of the house, digging in a dirt pile with spoons and making castles of mud.

"What does your heart desire?" I said in Salish, hoping he could understand me. It was a phrase that could be repeated until there was a response or the visitor left.

Shows No Anger behind me whispered, "He is Nez Perce. Not from here."

Does a murderer sit at my table? I thought of Bart Davidson and felt my hands go moist. From the looks of him, he'd been in a fight.

"I am Captain George." He spoke in English. I blinked.

"I am the White Chief's wife." I nodded to him. "What would your heart desire? Water?" He lifted his chin toward the pitcher Shows No Anger held. She poured him a cup that he drank from, then pushed the cup indicating more. "My husband, the agent, is not here," I said. "Can I help you?"

I saw the temporary interpreter fast-walk toward the house. "This is Captain George," I told him as he stepped in. "He speaks English."

He said something in what must have been Nez Perce.

The interpreter turned to me, his eyes held alarm. "That means Sitting Bull will soon surround the agency. We're under attack. I need to let the major know."

I crossed myself, letting this man's panic fuel my own. "Peter's gone to Missoula."

"There is no danger for the White Chief's wife. Or any here," Captain George said. He frowned at the interpreter.

The Indian's breathing was labored as he pulled a letter from his pouch and handed it to me. "From General Miles. I work for him when they say Joseph makes his way toward Bears Paw. In a previous time. I am not to be feared."

I read the letter that gave him safe passage. But more, General Miles related that in the war, this man's daughter had been taken by Sitting Bull and "used harshly."

"I rescue her. But then I am met by white men who shoot me, leave me for dead, and take my daughter."

"Your poor child. And you, shot for trying to rescue her." I realized what I thought was a huckleberry juice stain was actually blood.

I looked at the letter again. *"He was found by Crow Indians who healed him to the state he is now."* The Crow were traditional enemies, but they'd helped. "You're trying to find your child."

"Is that letter real?" the interpreter said.

"Real enough for me," I snapped. "Dr. Choquette must look after you, Captain. Shows No Anger, will you get him, please. And you may leave," I told the interpreter.

"I'll send a runner to Missoula to meet the major. He needs to know of this."

I couldn't see any harm in that. Both left and I said to Captain George, my heart aching for him, "How old is she, your missing daughter?"

"She has sixteen summers."

Sixteen. The crucial year.

His voice cracked. "I fail her."

From what I remembered Peter telling me of the distance and travels of different factions during the Nez Perce War, this father would have ridden over two thousand miles to Sitting Bull's camp to find his daughter and bring her back. I thought of the reunion, a father rescuing his child, and remembered my father coming back to Missouri for me those years ago. How I had missed him, yet how angry I'd been to have been left behind. Did his daughter wish he'd been more protective of her in the first place? She, taken while her father was off helping white soldiers? And then to be lost a second time to white men while her father lay dying.

"Do you know where she is? Which men have her?"

"She is at Benton now, General Miles says. Held by men, they say, who are no friends of our people."

I wished Peter were here. The general's letter continued with a request that we support this man as we could and then return the ponies when able.

The doctor arrived and his kind professionalism never failed to reassure his patients—or me. "Let's get you to the clinic," Dr. Choquette said.

"As you pass, please ask his companion to come in," I said as the doctor ushered the man out. "I'll give him something to eat. Captain George, too, when you've treated him."

I wasn't sure why his daughter's status couldn't leave my mind. Perhaps a vivid imagination brought me unwarranted anxiety. I could step inside the skin of another and experience their sadness. The price I paid was remembering how my mother told me to be kind and brave. I'd lie awake at night, worrying over others' trials. Peter once told me as the clock struck 3:00 a.m., "This is not your candle to carry. It will burn or go out by itself."

AFTER I FED THE MEN, I had the two retire to a tepee set up for Indian visitors if they had no kin to welcome them at Arlee's camp. I'd offered them our guest room as I would have any traveler, but they'd declined, choosing the smoked-hide comfort of the lodge. In the morning, and perhaps with assurance this place was safe for them, Captain George came through the open door and gave me a second letter. This one was from a major of the 2nd Cavalry.

"It offers you safe passage to the town of Benton to seek your daughter," I said. "It says any who meet you are to assist in every way."

"The White Chief gives aid."

"If he was here, yes."

As time-confused as communications could be, the girl might not be at Benton anymore—or she might be safe at the fort. But if the captain traveled without white escorts, he'd likely be shot at again, riding through ranchland tense with rumors. *I don't have the authority to send an employee to go with him, do I?*

"I don't think it's safe for you to go there now."

"My daughter must know I come for her. I am delayed too long. She does not know I live."

Would Peter want me to inject myself into agency business? This wasn't just about the agency, though. It was about a father's love for his daughter.

"I will go with you or go alone to Benton and bring her back myself."

He grinned, the first time I'd seen any happy emotion on his face. "The White Chief's wife wears strong skirts."

I felt my face grow warm with the compliment. There wasn't any way to convey the years of intensity between a father and a daughter and why his dilemma so affected me. The baby stirred in my womb.

I estimated it to be two hundred fifty miles to the fort, but I knew how to ride. Mrs. Lambert would care for the children and Shows No Anger would manage the household while I was gone. *Will Peter approve?* I'd send a runner first to Benton to see what information could be gathered about the girl and then see if the interpreter had sent his runner to Missoula. I didn't know what kept Peter. It had been three days.

"I will send word to my husband, and if he does not appear within a day, I will ride with you to get word about your child. Time here will build your strength."

In the interim, I brought sugar cookies to the two men, made sure they knew they were welcome at every meal. I saw to their comforts. I walked with them to the river and showed them the best fishing holes, though they smiled as if they already knew them. We served the trout they caught, and after others left the table that evening, that father lingered to speak of his daughter. I'd put the older children in their beds.

"Walks with Wisdom is a lovely name," I said when he told me.

"My sister's name. She dies young."

"Your daughter must have been wise to have survived all she

has." I knew many had died in Joseph's battles, which she'd been present for as a hostage.

He nodded. "She knows a great pool of love from which to dip."

"That's a picturesque thing to say."

He looked puzzled. "I do not know this word you say, pick-tur-esque."

"It describes how she gained her strength in a way I can see with my eyes. A large pool of love." I expanded my arms. "Maybe she draws on such love as you search for her for many months and miles."

"She is worthy of such seeking." He went on to tell me of how her mother had nearly died at her birth, but his prayers had brought them both to this living day. That she had chosen a man to marry.

"And do you approve of him?"

"I approve when he was a child as old as yours." He nodded to Gerald in his hammock. "She takes sixteen years to see her parents' wisdom. She resists for a time."

"Young girls are prone to do that. He doesn't travel with you to rescue her, her intended husband?"

"He does not know yet that he's been chosen."

"Ah," I said. "Is she your only child?"

"The only one who lives."

I had heard tales of white children being taken by Indians, but here was a tragedy about a Nez Perce girl abducted by white men. I prayed for their happy ending.

PETER RETURNED the next day in the presence of the runner. I started to tell him about Captain George and my plans to ride myself to find his daughter.

"Come with me." Peter's expression—after he kissed me—gave no indication whether he carried good news or ill. "Let's find our grieving father."

"Captain George," Peter called out. We stood outside the smoke-stained tepee, and both Nez Perce men bent through the hide opening and stood tall before us, eyes squinting to adjust to the bright sunshine. "I am glad to see you are alive. I come to lighten your heart."

I exhaled, hadn't realized I'd been holding my breath.

He introduced himself, then said, "I encountered a group of Idaho Indians camped. One of them, John Hill whom you know as Ta-Netchet, was there."

"Hands Shot-Off." The father's face offered a smile. "He is my friend."

"He tells me about you and your daughter. He says that she is at home. He has seen her there."

"She is at home?"

Peter nodded. "Some Flathead Indians—John didn't know who—went to Benton and took back your daughter from the white men who had her and rode with her back to Idaho. He believed you had died."

The man's countenance went from dark to light, as bright as a kerosene lamp lightens the night. Tears poured down Captain George's face. I found my own cheeks wet.

Was it coincidence that Peter encountered men who had knowledge before Peter knew he'd need it? Or just another act of Providence? I had no part in this except to make Captain George comfortable while they waited. But I felt as though I'd done more. And maybe I had, by walking beside him, letting me hear him talk about his daughter and his hoped-for happy ending. Trusting in Providence to make things happen when we couldn't. What a reunion there would be, the daughter discovering her father was still alive and the father once again holding his rescued child in his arms.

Weeks later, Captain George sent a letter to us confirming that his daughter was indeed safe. He thanked us for our help in caring for him while he healed and for what part we played in getting him back to his family. Peter had sent a letter requesting safe passage. He'd returned the ponies to the general.

My own father would have traveled two thousand miles if I was in harm's way. But I couldn't get him to travel half that distance to this agency where I might show him how Peter had provided a good life for us and was a kind and generous father, where he might meet his grandchildren and hug his daughter who had done her best to honor him all her life.

"*You did all that my heart desired*," Captain George ended his letter. Another rich blessing in that father's words—just as Father Van Gorp had once predicted.

THIRTY-THREE

WHAT THE
HEART DESIRES

The crocks of sauerkraut scented the root cellar, while dried apple rings hung from their strings, giving the dank place an almost festive air. I let my eyes adjust to the darkness, checked for snakes who liked to cool themselves when hot August danced across the valley stage. This baby I carried didn't seem to like the heat much, and its restlessness would settle while I inhaled the earthy scents, brought dried berries for storage, and stacked slabs of smoked fish that Shows No Anger had helped me smoke to preserve.

Dr. Choquette was extra busy in the heat, seeing dozens of patients suffering with breathing difficulties or babies with heat rash. I watched mothers bring their children all day long, worried looks upon their faces. He often used an herbal remedy of rosemary to relieve the rash. He visited Arlee's camp and spoke with Indian doctors, not threatened by their knowledge but finding ways to learn from them—and in return they seemed willing to add a few of his suggestions to their treatments.

The doctor particularly liked obstetrics. "Nothing better than a bouncing baby," he told me as he examined me in my sixth month. "A smaller child, oui?"

"I've noticed that. But it's active."

"You are busy too. Perhaps more time resting, feet up. To slow the ankle swellings."

I had been concerned about this baby, tried to set it aside. I didn't want to alarm Hermine, who expected a baby in the spring, nor Mrs. Lambert. She had told me that very morning that she, too, was pregnant. Shows No Anger was also with child. We women celebrated together over tea, joking about our respective tummies in various stages of protuberance.

"I feel like a seal, my whole body burgeoned like one," Hermine said.

"Oh, you haven't even begun," Mrs. Lambert told her, laughing.

"It's funny you should say 'seal,'" I said. "That's what Ronan means in Gaelic: little seal."

"*Bébé phoque*," Hermine said in French.

"Perhaps a nickname for your baby," Mrs. Lambert told me.

"Choquette means the collector of taxes, on wine and food." Hermine had the loveliest French accent. "I won't be choosing such a nickname for my *enfant*." She rubbed her still flat abdomen, her wrapper garment loose. "Will you pick a name for your child before it is born?" she asked Shows No Anger.

"We will wait to see how the baby makes its choices. The priests will give him a Christian name, early. When he is older, he may take another name, from a grandfather of long ago. Some of us have many names."

"All our children's names have family connections too," I said.

None of us expressed outwardly any worry about our deliveries, something women in mining or frontier towns or on remote ranches like Cousin Ellen often did. Shows No Anger said she would deliver with her mother's help. It was her father's wish.

THAT FALL, Peter worked again to get permission for ammunition for the buffalo hunt and at the agency, making sure the fields we harvested were raked up and the straw tied into bales for possible feed in the winter. None of the People put hay up, as farmers had in Iowa or like Ellen's Bill did in the Ruby Valley. Cattle could graze throughout the season here, the winters being milder. Heavy snows tended to coat the mountains, and when it reached the valley floor, it didn't seem to stay long. Ice caked the dirt roads, making travel treacherous. Peter tried to think ahead for the colder season, hoping to ward off horse and cattle starvation.

He still had not found a permanent interpreter, a position critical to the agency and our success. Such a person required not only the necessary language skills but the ability to read the nuances, the hand gestures, the blink of an eye, the lifting of the chin. He—and it would have to be a he—had to create trust not just between Peter and the agency staff but with the Native people who relied on their translations to carry the weight of their grievances or the lightness of their joys. Having respect for all the People was of utmost importance.

I often prayed about these business issues, feeling I had no other way of helping.

Then Shows No Anger told me of a French and Pend d'Oreille man with a Salish wife and two children. "The Jesuits train him, but he has the gift of learning many tongues. He speaks the language of all the Flatheads. And French." She ironed Peter's shirt while I urged Gerald to use his spoon instead of his hands to eat his oatmeal. *What a mess he makes.* "Michel Rivais is a good father too."

"He sounds perfect. Can you get him to come and see Peter?"

"He says he cannot do this work, as his sight leaves him."

"He's blind?"

"Soon. His heart causes this . . . decline, as you might say. He has the pneumonia."

I looked at Gerald. Was blindness in his future?

I told Peter about Mr. Rivais anyway. "Rheumatism can cause eye problems," Peter said.

"Maybe Dr. Choquette or a physician in Missoula or Helena could help."

"I'll ride out to him. Someone local who can speak so many languages in addition to English could be a real boon here."

Michel (pronounced like "Michael") was such a boon. His Indian wife—who was so clean and tidy—and two children came with him to live in the cottage at the agency. His Indian name was The Man Who Walks Alone, which he rarely did because his wife Maria was often his guide. He had a musical way of speaking, played the violin, and doted on his two children. Two previous children had died, I learned. He was an indulgent father who would often defer to his son and daughter, asking how he should take his wages.

"A silk handkerchief, Papa."

"A shawl for Mama? Or sugar for us?" The two would giggle— they were eight and nine years old—fingers covering their mouths in shyness.

When Michel took cash, he often spent it at the trader's on velvet and leggings and whatever things he might give to them. The Choquettes especially liked having someone else they could communicate with in their Canadian French, and I often heard them with Shows No Anger, chattering like old friends.

Peter set about getting him to see a specialist that his fading eyesight might be halted or even reversed. He corresponded with a Missouri senator he knew to help. It became another issue for Peter to work on, one he said made him feel that he was doing God's work in the midst of paradise. "He's the best interpreter I've encountered, Mollie. I'm so glad you found him."

AND SO OUR PARADISE GREW and grew again when our third son and fourth child arrived on November 1, 1878. Unlike the hard labor with Gerald, Matthew James—named for both grandfathers—came easily into this world. He was smaller than my others, seemed more fragile to me.

I was still abed with my baby when Chief Michelle of the Pend d'Oreille arrived with six men dressed in colorful blankets, as much to mark the occasion of our son's birth as to ward off the November chill. Our interpreter eased his way through the door behind the Pend d'Oreille, who had entered the sitting room next to our bedroom. Peter joined their circle, pulling on his suit coat and buttoning his britches. The door was ajar, and I could see some of the activity that included the men squatting in a circle, passing the pipe. They pulled the smoke with their hands toward their throat to represent their commitment to the truthful words they would share, carried on the whisper of smoke. When the pipe reached Peter, he inhaled, too, and then the chief spoke through our interpreter.

"The chief has heard of the new white child and wishes to adopt him into his People."

Michelle nodded, spoke more. The interpreter continued, "He would give him his very own name—*Whee-eat-sum-khay*. It means 'Plenty Grizzly Bear.' Michelle is his baptismal name. He keeps it but wishes to give your baby the bear name." The chief nodded in agreement. He spoke more, and the interpreter informed us that such a name was of the highest compliment, as the grizzly was the most feared, respected, and noble of all creatures. "The name does not come from a brave encounter with a grizzly," Michel told us, "but as a tribute to his own courage. The name is a gift from the Lower Kalispel and once belonged to a hereditary chief there."

"How much did you hear?" Peter asked as he came into the bedroom.

"Plenty Grizzly Bear? It sounds so officious for this little seal of a child." I'd gotten dressed and stood next to the baby's cradle, the blue eyes watching me, hands clasped, both legs jerking together as I brushed soft brown curls.

"It's quite an honor."

"We must accept it," I said.

"Oh, I agree."

Peter returned and gave his consent from the two of us that our baby be adopted into the Pend d'Oreille tribe and receive the name given as a gift. Each participant then made a speech of honor that Michel translated, taking quite some time. Then, "They would like to see the baby."

"Yes, of course." I had planned to carry him out, but Peter waved them into our bedroom.

They filed past, each pressing soft fingers to our baby's heart as the infant watched in wonder at the feathers and the blankets and the tender eyes of these fine men. They each said, "*Shay*," meaning "good," when they finished their baby greeting. The precious moment reminded me that my father had warned me about frightening "injuns." And my son would now have many adopted fathers promising to look after him, that he might live up to his honored name, Plenty Grizzly Bear.

Gretel and I prepared a breakfast for twelve, then I nursed my baby.

"The chief will go nameless," Shows No Anger told me when she arrived and I described the morning's activity.

"But he is still Chief Michelle."

"This is not his Indian name. He will be in mourning now."

And she was right. When Peter saw the chief the next day, he told him as much and that until he had another name bestowed on him, grief would separate him from us.

"I had no idea we'd be the cause of such distress. Should we have declined the honor?" I ground coffee beans while Peter stoked the fire in the cookstove. It heated the entire kitchen well enough we found ourselves—children and guests—congregating at the long table for nearly every meal. The parlor with its fireplace just didn't carry the warmth of this kitchen.

"It would be a great dishonor if you had said no," Shows No

Anger said as she separated peanuts from the hulls in a burlap bag. "He will find another name. There will be a big ceremony."

"The last thing I want is a hassle over this," Peter said. "How would I explain that to the commissioner?"

The next day our interpreter told us that the chief had sent runners to the Lower Kalispel camp where an underchief had died. The runner was to see if the chief might be given the loan of the deceased's name—Man Who Regrets His Country. "It is what my heart desires," he told Peter, as solemn as though he spoke of death.

It was early December before we had word that the request had been granted so long as Flatheads and the Pend d'Oreille would send the Lower Kalispel six ponies they claimed had been stolen from them eight years before.

This was apparently accomplished, for on Christmas Day, Peter was summoned to St. Ignatius, and there, in the company of Chief Michelle and members of all the tribes, our son was officially adopted into the Confederated Tribes of the Flathead, with the name of Plenty Grizzly Bear. The chief of the Pend d'Oreille also received a blessing. He would henceforth be known by his now loaned name of Man Who Regrets His Country.

"The old chief took off that hang-dog look he's had for weeks like it was a mask," Peter said when he returned. "And donned the biggest grin you've ever seen." He ate a piece of fruitcake I'd prepared. It was a special recipe, one adapted from Ma Anne's.

"I wish our baby could have been there to greet his large new family."

"Vincent stood in for him. It's a ceremony I suspect he'll remember all his life."

"I wish I could have been there too. I do like a little pomp and circumstance now and then."

"Like the princess you are. But motherhood suits you best and there's little ceremony in that." He lifted Plenty Grizzly Bear from my arms, held him.

"Oh, but there is great ceremony in motherhood. Celebrating the first tooth. When they learn to use the potty chair. Pull their own trousers up. And the magnificence of a newborn nursing and being blessed with enough milk to feed him."

I wondered if my mother's life was such that she could see the glory over the grime in the few years she had to be a mother. I hoped so. And that Ma Anne had felt like a princess when she held Kate and Jimmy in her arms.

"I NEED TO WRITE to the commissioner about employee wages. Again," Peter told me a few days later. "The last man I hired in the carpenter shop agreed to stay only a month unless the pay was increased. I'd like to get a clerk on board. They can all make more money working in Missoula or Frenchtown." Retaining help was always a problem. "During the Nez Perce War, the army wanted the Pend d'Oreille to scout for them but didn't want to pay them." Peter shook his head. "I fail to understand some of the thinking of this government I work for." He leaned against the sink, long legs crossed at the ankle, watching me iron. It was a soothing task I liked to do.

"I don't really think of Shows No Anger as an employee, though perhaps I should," I said. I tested the sadiron with a wet finger before I pressed it to the linen altar cloth, Peter's shirt now pressed and hung. "I enjoy her company." Through the window I saw her holding Mary's hand as they moved through the geese flock surveilling the yard. "And most of all, my friend. Her troubles between her father and her husband remind me of our trials—not recently, of course—between you and me and Pa. It causes me to wonder what got in his way of seeing you the way I do, the way people in Helena did."

"Might never know for sure, Mollie. Don't dwell."

"It still saddens me that the two of you were friends for all those years and then it was severed. I don't think I remember my father having many friends."

"You always see the good, so you're willing to overlook my warts. Your father saw them all and wanted to protect you from them."

"But isn't that what love is, seeing only the good?"

"Between a couple, yes. But fathers who love their daughters have a jaded eye to any who would take them away. I expect one day poor Mary's beaus will feel scrutinized unfairly. We fathers only want what's best."

I hadn't heard from Kate of late and wondered what trials she might be going through following Ma Anne's death. I felt a little guilty that six-week-old Matthew James was at my breast. All was splendid in my world. I had four healthy children, a husband who loved me, friends close by, people who welcomed us into their valley, and a landscape to soothe and inspire. If only I could accept that I might never have my father's blessing.

THIRTY-FOUR

GIFTS IN THE WILDERNESS

O f course, I wrote to my father telling him of his namesake, Matthew James, and once again invited him to visit, to "stay a year. Let me look after you here."

I heard nothing.

Valentine's Day approached, a favorite time. I helped the children make cards for their father, our interpreter's children, for Grace Lambert and for Hermine and for Paul and Shows No Anger's unborn baby. I'd already sent cards to my father, Kate, and Jimmy and had one for Peter I hoped to add to our scrapbook.

It was Hermine who came to tell me after her husband returned that Shows No Anger's baby had died. "It occurs before Dr. Choquette can make his way to her lodge, before her mother acting as midwife could turn the baby." Hermine cried as she shared the details. I held her. *Before prayers could uncurl the cord wrapped around the infant's neck.*

"It is so tragic." Hermine dabbed at her tearful eyes. "Little Paul cries beside his brother. His father weeps. The entire lodge, they all wail. They do not come for my husband until too late, but he does not tell them this. It would only add to their remorse. His tears fall too." She began to cry again, and that led to my tears falling too.

"Can we go to Shows No Anger? What is the custom?" I asked Michel, grateful to have an interpreter who could "educate us out of our ignorance." I had gone to his cottage, something I rarely did.

"There will be a dressing of the infant by his aunties and *katsa*, wrapping the baby in a colorful blanket. The men will make the coffin, and they will stand beside the father like a stake holds up a young tree, there, before it is needed. There will be a feast after. A gathering, with time to send runners. A priest has already been summoned. When the drummers finish, when the mourning dances are complete, when the food is served and eaten, there will be an entourage." He said the word with a French lilt. "The entourage will take the coffin with l'enfant to the cemetery at St. Ignatius. It is customary for mourners to come when the family is ready."

"I'd like to be with her."

"Friends put aside their desires."

I wiped my eyes. "I understand. Can you go and tell her that I put my arms around her in my prayers, if not in person?"

He nodded then after a pause. "Perhaps it is acceptable for the wife of the White Chief to go when her heart tells her to. But do not bring your babies."

And so Peter and I went together, leading our nearly blind interpreter. We entered the tepee where Shows No Anger sat against pillows of fur, her husband holding Paul, both beside her. I smelled sage burning and knew it was a cleansing act not unlike the incense burned by the priests to purify and sanctify. The room felt like a holy place. A bundle near Shows No Anger's mother I took to be the child. The woman frowned. *We violate the custom.*

Paul jabbered when he recognized us, his face lit up. I think he might have looked for Gerald, but Mrs. Lambert had kept all the children. "Maybe we should go," I whispered to Peter. But when she saw us, Shows No Anger lifted her arms, and I sank to my knees to hold her. I could think of nothing to say. Among friends in grief, no words are needed.

THINGS CHANGED at the agency after the funeral of Angel's Heart, the name they'd given the baby. Shows No Anger's father said the name could not be spoken by Shows No Anger or her husband for a year. It was the requirement. And the parents must give away all the gifts given for the baby. There was to be no sign that Angel's Heart had ever been there, his spirit being lifted from this place to heaven with no attachments to keep him on this earth. I thought then maybe it was good I had so few items from my mother. She had gone straight to heaven, though I still held her in my heart.

Shows No Anger was also prohibited for that year from working at the agency and she could not hold Matthew, our newborn. But I was allowed to go camas digging with her in the spring and berry picking. And I could bring her gifts of baked goods, trinkets for Paul. And we could sit outside her lodge while a house was being built for her family. Her husband had brought the logs to the agency mill, and soon they would have their own place to be. "And when I am with child again, my husband will come for the doctor even if my father says he is not needed." She would be brave in defiance, she said, "as a daughter must sometimes be."

THE WAGON RATTLED into the yard through the picket fence main gate in September, late afternoon. It carried my father, Kate, Jimmy, and two cats. I recognized two of the six mules and nearly dropped the soup tureen I'd gotten from the pantry at the sight of them.

"Oh, blessed saints," I cried and fairly flew out the door. "You've come. I've waited so long." I hugged Kate, who had jumped down from the wagon, copper-colored hair shining in the setting sun. Jimmy, too, let me hug him. He was now a lean twelve-year-old, my height, wearing Spanish-looking clothes, including a wide sombrero I knocked off in my exuberant embrace.

And then my father. When I saw him stand beside the wagon, I gasped. He was missing his right arm.

"WHAT HAPPENED? Why didn't you tell me?" Then thinking it didn't matter, I said, "You're here. That's all that matters." I stepped back to look at him.

"And would you have dropped everything and come? Kate looked after me, didn't you, lass."

"Yes, Pa, I did." Kate stood taller than my father, taller than me. Her moves were fluid, and she had a husky voice that sounded sultry. "He needed little attention once he was home from the hospital. You know how stubborn he can be." She patted his shoulder. "We didn't know what had happened for a week."

"Come inside and tell me all," I said. "We'll wash the salted beef and get you fed." Peter came out of his office about then and I said, "Look who's here. They've come at last."

"Cousin Ellen says to tell you hello," Jimmy said. "We stopped there for a time. They have a big ranch. But not as much activity as here." His eyes scanned the yard with Indians bringing logs for milling, others going into the doctor's office, the sounds of the blacksmith's anvil, the scents of horses being led past us. Pounding by the carpenters adding a second story to our house made it hard to hear. Because of the many guests that came, the department had authorized the addition of more bedrooms. We would have eleven when the addition was completed. I tried to see our home as he might. "Your house is as big as a castle."

Chickens clucked and got out of the way as a Salish boy led the mules and wagon toward the stable.

"You be careful with those animals." My father raised his voice. "Don't ignore me."

I reassured the boy in Salish and told my father, "He can't understand you."

"He's very good with the animals," Peter said. "They'll be well treated." Then to my father, "Welcome, James. You've made your daughter a happy soul." He reached to take my father's left hand to shake it.

My father looked around instead, acted like he didn't see the welcoming gesture. "Good horseflesh about. I guess they'll be alright. Let's head inside this . . . castle."

"Pa," I began, but Peter shook his head. He hugged Kate, shook Jimmy's hand, and moved us all toward the inside of the house. I knew the time would come for confrontation, for my speaking up for my husband and how my father treated him. But Peter had signaled now was not that time. I was relieved and knew I'd have to overcome the guilt I felt at seeing my father's missing arm and my not having been there to help him recover.

"It's quite a story," my father said when Vincent was introduced to his grandad for the first time and asked him why he only had one arm. Children are so direct. I love that. We were in the kitchen eating pickled cucumbers and bites of cheese, enough to calm hunger until supper. Gee Duck, our new Chinese cook, and Gretel prepared our meal and would tell us when the soup was ready.

"He's learned to write with his left hand," Kate said. "That took some trial and error."

He smiled at her. "Aye, that it did. But I can still run the team with one line." He raised his arm to show off his muscles. Then to Mary, who was petting one of the cats they'd brought with them, "Don't touch her ears, lass. Bandit's not partial to people handling her head. But she likes her tail stroked."

"You always liked cats," I said. I wasn't sure they were clean enough to be inside the house, but I stepped over my concern.

"But what happened to your arm, Grandad?" Vincent's question reminded me of the day Ma Anne told me not to ask personal questions of others.

My father took a chair away from the table. "I was driving the team back from Anaheim and went to set the brake when it broke and I fell forward, lad. Fell right out of the box and the wagon rolled right over my arm. I don't remember that. I fell headfirst and knocked myself out. Or maybe the mule kicked me when I invaded its space." He made light of it as Vincent stared. "The mules stayed. The wagon blocked the road, I guess, and someone came along and found me. Like a Good Samaritan, they took me to the hospital in Anaheim. Me arm was so infected, they had to cut it off. I don't remember that either. Told me they had to keep me soul here on earth by taking my arm. I can do quite a bit with just one." He reached out and fluffed Vincent's blond hair.

"It must have been a terrifying time for you two," I said. Both Jimmy and Kate nodded.

"We didn't know where he was." Kate buttered a thick slice of bread. "The Samaritan took care of the mules, too, and when Da finally came to and could tell them who he was and that he had a home in Capistrano, he sent word. The alcalde brought the telegram to us."

"Praise God for the kindness of strangers," I said.

"You came a long way," Peter said. "Must have been a challenge."

"I told him we should take the train and the stage," Jimmy said. "I haven't ever ridden on a train. But you know Da."

"Well, I'm glad you're here." I patted Jimmy's sleeve. "And while it's not good form to ask how long you might be able to stay, how long might you be able to stay?"

"As long as we feel safe," my father said. "I've worried over all the warring Indian news in the papers. This agency has been in the thick of it."

"No safer place in the country," Peter said.

"It's true, Pa. Why, the chief of the Pend d'Oreille offered to post guards for us. And he once rode thirty miles to say goodbye when he heard I planned to come to California to see you."

"Which you didn't do."

I winced but stumbled on. "He gave his name Plenty Grizzly Bear to your namesake, Matthew James, and adopted him into the tribe. We're a big family here."

"The way the Mexicans and Spanish took us in," Jimmy said.

"Very similar."

"We don't live with 'em," my father said.

"Perhaps your loss," Peter said.

My father jerked his head toward Peter. "Wouldn't be my biggest loss. You made that happen, Ronan."

A thick silence stilled the conversation.

We were rescued by the call for dinner and the arrival of several of the bachelors joining us for soup and fresh-baked bread and my latest mincemeat pie.

"It's like the establishment," Kate said as we made room for others around the table.

"You remember that?"

"A little. How lovely to have someone else cook supper."

"It is," I said. "But we women all tend to cleanup."

"It's what women do." She winked at me while she helped my father from the horsehair chair he'd sunk into, walked him to the caned chair at the head of the table. I hoped he'd feel honored.

"You're still wearing that gold ring Mollie gave you." Kate nodded to Peter.

"That I am. It was almost lost in the mail when Mollie asked for it back." He wiggled his little finger. "I've kept it here ever since."

"You kept your word," she said. "As a good husband should."

My father grunted. Peter said the table grace, and lifting my eyes at the end, I smiled at my little sister who I saw as a kindred soul.

MY FAMILY HAD BEEN with us a month, with us walking on tiptoes to keep any tensions down, when word reached us that the Archbishop Charles John Seghers of Oregon was coming to the valley. He would stay with us for a night.

"You'll get to meet an archbishop," I told my father. "Imagine that."

The prelate brought a large party with him, and much flurry and fluster swept through the agency. He would hold a mass in the agency mill for the Flathead people, then travel on to St. Ignatius for another gathering and service in the church there. We would all attend the second one, we women staying with the Sisters at the school and Peter and the men with the priests. Tomorrow we would join the entourage heading to the mission, but tonight we had a respite after supper that had included not only the arch-bishop's party but the Hogans, a ranching family whom we'd become acquainted with. I thought Kate might enjoy the company of their son Philip. He was a little older than Kate but had struck up a conversation with her when he'd brought timber to be milled. He was building a house for himself on his father's ranch near the reservation. The two had lingered after supper and sat out on the porch in the lamplight.

Despite my family having been with us a month, my father and I had had little time to talk privately. There were always people about. The archbishop's arrival took planning time. It also seemed my father avoided time alone with me, devoting his interest to riding horses with the children and going fishing. He had yet to hold me.

This evening I carved out time for my father and me. We sat in the parlor. The next day we'd all head for St. Ignatius.

"How did it feel to share a meal with an archbishop?" I asked.

My father smoked his pipe. I'd filled it for him just as I had as a child. "Not something I'd have thought would happen in my time. Especially not on some remote Indian agency."

"We've had so many wonderful opportunities here."

"And you're not afraid."

"I'm not. You see how the People are. Everything runs smoothly. Peter's a fine manager."

He snorted. "Not so smoothly you could leave it to mourn your stepmother. Or visit your family. Apparently, your husband couldn't arrange that for you. Looks to me like he controls you, Daughter, not protects you."

"Peter never stood in my way of coming to see you. I made those decisions."

"I find that hard to believe."

"Do you?" I swallowed. "It took me a long time to decide to defy you and tell Peter I'd marry him, but I did it. Just as I decided I was needed here, with my husband and children. It's my job—one I have come to enjoy—to manage the household, hire the people we need. I'm advertising now for a teacher for Vincent and Mary."

"Your husband should be handling those affairs."

"Pa. First you say Peter's controlling me and that's deplorable and then you say he should be managing more. The truth is, we are a partnership. We make decisions together. But about my family, you, he defers to me. That's why I never visited. I felt I was needed here."

"You broke my heart, lass, sayin' you'd be marryin' the man."

He knocked tobacco out of his pipe, continued to chew on the stem.

"I wish you could see Peter as you once did, when he was your friend. You admired his love of books and respected his devotion to the faith. Even his compassion you once commented on. But then he fell in love with me—"

"He betrayed my friendship going behind my back to court you, just a child."

"I was sixteen. I knew what love was then, and while I struggled later whether four years of separation had erased it, I'll always be sure that what I once knew to be true was true, despite your efforts to dissuade me."

"I did it for your own good."

"And good came from it. I got a fine education at the Los Angeles academy."

"But you never took the teacher's test again. It would have been of great help to your family if you'd earned money. 'Honor thy father and thy mother.'" He shook his pipe at me. "Whatever happened to that?"

I felt a sourness in my stomach. He could be lauded for his persistence, for freighting all those years, discovering ranching, his endurance in caring for Ma while she was sick, for learning how to write with his left hand. He could adapt and carry on. Admirable qualities. But he also had the skill of laying guilt like bricks to build a rigid wall.

"Pa, I won't let you do this."

"What?"

"Hang on to old grievances and claim I dishonored you. I never did. What greater honor could I give but to let faith guide me and live the life I felt called to. To be a wife and mother. That was all I ever wanted to be. The only little footnote in my fairy-tale life is that I have somehow displeased the man I loved first, my father."

"Loved first, but not best."

I sighed. "I've said all I can for now." I patted his left hand lying in his lap. "I love you, Pa. I always have. Can't we build on that?"

He clutched my fingers and let me have the final word.

THE NEXT MORNING we traveled with the archbishop's ensemble and were met a couple of miles from St. Ignatius by two hundred mounted men of the Flathead confederation. As we passed, they formed a line on either side of our carriages.

"It feels like we're royalty," Kate whispered.

"It's for the archbishop," I reminded her.

"Oh, I know. But doesn't it make your feet tingle just a little? I mean, out here in the wilderness to have such pageantry and—"

She was interrupted by a volley of gunshots, then ululating with high-pitched voices, yet another part of the extravaganza. As we came over the rise toward the mission, what must have been a thousand or more Indians greeted us, some in full regalia with feather headdresses and others with blankets around their chests held with beaded belts. The women carried their children on their backs, dressed in white buckskins adorned with flowers and animals, the cut beads glistening in the sun.

"Their dresses are gorgeous," Kate said.

"Shows No Anger made these." I wore beaded hair bands four inches wide separated by twists of hair above smaller beaded bands. I'd chosen braids and these gifts to wear rather than my hat.

Our carriage was pulled to the side then. Peter and my father and the boys (except little Matthew) were in one together. I wondered if Peter and my father might come to some civil resolution forced inside the carriage space these past three hours.

Arrived, the archbishop stepped down and walked beneath a canopy of silk and rich embroidery that four Flathead men held up. Eight Jesuits walked behind him, all dressed in full vestments, carrying thuribles of incense they swung out, smoke-like mist scenting the air. Two girls walked backward in front of them, tossing dried flowers to mark their path. Then the thousand or more Indians trailed behind the shaded archbishop, and we Anglos walked, bringing up the very end. I had put Matthew in his brother's beaded board and carried him sleeping on my back. At the church, the prelate spoke a prayer translated into many languages. The sweetest sound of a girls' choir sang the responses.

And then as one exhaled breath, the People all bowed down in silence to receive the archbishop's blessing.

We bowed down, too, cradled in the magnificence of the mountains, kneeling on grasses as grand and soft as velvet, a soft breeze lifting the incense as the Jesuits shook the thuribles on their chains. To the side, I saw Peter kneel next to my father; Vincent and Jimmy kneeling beside their respective fathers. Gerald sat before Peter, cocooned in safety. Fathers praying with their sons. For me that day, that scene, was more moving than the archbishop's blessings.

I took Mary's hand and Kate's. "Remember this," I whispered. "God's gift in the wilderness."

THIRTY-FIVE

TRANSLATIONS

I was telling him about the clay from that dry lake bed and that we mix it with flour and water. It makes a better and more long-lasting whitewash," Peter told me. "Your father found it interesting. He wants to see how it's done. He even suggested it might be packaged and sold as a product."

Peter and I were in our bedroom where we had a semblance of privacy, though there always seemed to be a baby in the cradle too. Pa and Kate and Jimmy were still with us as we approached a year since their arrival the previous fall. It was late summer of 1880.

"It's actually a good idea," Peter continued.

"He had a number of good ideas through the years, but somehow getting them implemented didn't always work," I said, remembering. "He lost the stores at Bannack and Virginia City. A poor judge of character cost him." Peter had endured many mishaps, fires, the stolen gold, but he'd always come back stronger.

"Part of living. By the way, remember that theft in Blackfoot, on the final sluice day cleaning, when someone got all our gold? When we should have posted a guard?"

"I remember."

Peter removed his boots and trousers, shirt and tie. "Well, Maginnis tells me he heard that the young couple over the ridge—I can't remember their names but we had them for supper once or twice—they were the culprits. She was expecting a child when we were waiting on Mary."

"A quiet couple. You said something about entertaining angels."

"I did. Well, it seems he did quite well for himself after we left Blackfoot. And Martin thinks he might have been our thief. Something he heard. The young man managed to escape out of the country without any suspicion on him."

"Will you pursue it?"

"Naw." He put his boots away. "There's no real evidence and our lives—and the partners'—have gone forward."

"My father once spent weeks going after one of the men he'd hired to run the store who sold his goods and kept the money."

"He told me about that, how his wife didn't want him to go after him. He said he should have listened."

"Really? He confessed that to you? At least you're having conversations with my da," I said. "That's progress."

"He's a good man, Mollie."

"I know that. He's just bossy as that lead cow butting everyone to where she wants them to go." I was thoughtful. "I come by the same behavior naturally, I guess." I finished nursing Matthew and laid him satisfied in his cradle.

"You're the least domineering person I know," my husband told me as he brushed my hair. It was easier to care for with it just below my shoulders.

"I'm not sure your children would agree." I checked on Gerald in his crib in the room next door. I always listened carefully to his breathing after that episode of pneumonia. Peter kissed his forehead and then Matthew's too. "Pa told me he wondered why we'd named this child for your father—Matthew as his first name and his name, James, second."

"Did he."

"I think he's gotten petty in his old age," I said.

"I have that to look forward to." Peter braided my hair, the single plait over my shoulder. Then he crawled between our Irish linens into bed.

"But the two of you have resolved your differences?"

"I doubt he'll ever admit that he was wrong about me, and it isn't needed. He did it for you. He thought you were too young, and he didn't imagine I'd ever do great things in life. And I haven't."

"I don't think we're put here to do great things. But to do small things bravely and with gratitude and kindness."

"That, my pretty Mollie, is a profound statement."

"It is."

I blew out the lantern and joined him in bed, more exhausted than I'd been. Dr. Choquette had just confirmed that we'd have another baby—or rather two babies—in the spring. I was about three months along and he'd told me he could hear two heartbeats beside my own.

"I have to step over those little things that annoy me about Da. When I suggested he sell Casa Blanca and live here permanently, he told me he couldn't. 'Mark my words'"—I mimicked his brogue—"'ye'll need it one day when things fall apart, lass. Your Peter isn't the Prince Charming you believe him ta be.'" I smoothed the sheets over my chest. "Maybe it's just as well that he doesn't want to live here full-time. I might kill him."

Peter laughed. "That you'd never do. But if he does stay, you'll have to find a way to not let his comments pierce you like a knife."

"Perform the small things with great faith. Step over big things when I must, is that how?" Silence greeted me. "You do know that Philip Hogan and Kate are getting serious. I don't know what Pa will say about that."

Still more silence and then I realized Peter was asleep. I'd have to deal with my father as I always had—on my own but knowing Peter backed me with whatever stand I took.

SHOWS NO ANGER took us once again camas digging and Kate joined in. She had a few memories of Montana and loved this landscape. She fell in love too with a certain wheat rancher, her eyes alight when she talked of him—even more when she spoke to him. I had to be careful that I didn't impose Peter's and my early relationship onto theirs, though we were of similar ages when we fell in love. I liked Philip. I hoped my father did too.

The cherry trees Peter had planted the previous fall had leafed out in March, and now in August, we expected a spare but promising first crop. The summer had been sublime—the weather temperate, thunderstorms without hail, just the magnificence of towering clouds and warm rain. We rode horseback, took picnics, and stayed two or three days camping at Big Mountain Lake, setting up tents beneath the fir trees. That fall we were thrilled by the beauty of the larch turning a raging gold. The sunsets stunned across a bending sky. It was pure Montana to me.

Peter had brought hogsheads of trout from Denver, first by train, then wagons, to stock this remote lake that wasn't as cold as the Flathead nor as deep. Wildflowers abounded, and we'd see deer and elk and mountain goats in the distance. At any sign of bears, we'd pack up, even though we had Plenty Grizzly Bear— Matthew James—with us.

The dog that Chief Michelle had given us that year barked at the children running along the shoreline, his tail in a happy wag. The children picked bouquets the way I had with Carrie Crane. I loved the site, this lake, and was pleased I could share it with my extended family. My father relaxed here, marveled with Vincent when he found elk horn sheds we'd take back with us. Vincent wanted to use them as a fence around the kitchen garden. We listened to the squeals of children splashing, and I was full of memories when my father sang Gaelic songs and taught us one or two. He still had a fine voice. My mother would have loved spoiling the children; Ma Anne would have too. Pa seemed happy here and I began to hope that he might stay forever. If he did, it would be the blessing I longed for. I didn't need his words.

AT THE AGENCY, all the buildings had been whitewashed—Jimmy had helped—with the special clay mixture. Peter was still trying to get the commissioner to approve the purchase of more flour to mix with the dirt from the dry lake bed. At my suggestion, he'd sent a bag of the mixture to Washington, D.C., ("Just add water") to help them see the potential of sales of the product off the reservations. Increased income for the confederation.

"He doesn't want the reservation to compete with the producers of whitewash in Missoula and around the country, not even for use on other federal buildings," Peter told me after the latest correspondence. "The Flathead could make some money, but no, they aren't to compete." It was another of my husband's frustrations. But he remained faithful in supporting the People, being their translator to the federal government and decoding government talk back to them.

We lived a life of translation, I was coming to see. Deciphering the meaning of actions of the People and the government—and actions we take as part of a family.

That fall, the silver maple tree on the front lawn turned its leaves to red. I enjoyed autumn, even though it meant increased pressure on Peter dealing with ammunition issues for the buffalo hunters; then the fallout when the buffalo hunters turned back, both because of declining numbers of animals and because there were always altercations with white ranchers or city folk seeing hostiles everywhere. More white people encroached within the reservation boundaries, hunting and farming. Peter had meetings with the ranchers and with traders licensed to buy and sell on the reservation. But we could see that fewer buffalo meant Peter had to request more allocations of beef and beans. But more, it meant things were changing for these tribes and white encroachment was a part of it.

We welcomed more guests that fall too. Fishermen now, and "trophy" hunters who killed deer and elk not for the meat—they gave the hides and meat to the agency for distribution—but usually kept the antlers. And railroad people—as the Northern Pacific, surveyed in the 1870s, hoped to push into Montana. A reporter from the St. Paul, Minnesota, *Pioneer Press* spent several days asking questions, letting herself be "educated out of her ignorance." I was grateful for the second-story bedrooms. My father engaged in the conversations, animated, happy. My hopes rose that this could be his forever place.

"PHILIP HAS ASKED ME to marry him," Kate told me. We were sitting in the new two-holer privy my father had built with Jimmy and the agency carpenter's help. He'd said I needed a "decent" outhouse. It was helpful, I had to admit. We had a bathroom with a bathtub inside the house and each bedroom had a slop pail that had to be emptied daily. That was part of Gretel's task. But it was quiet in this little refuge where I placed used coffee grounds and vinegar to contain the smells.

"That's a rather auspicious subject for our inauspicious setting," I said.

"It's the first time I've had you alone for days," Kate said. "Doesn't it tire you?"

"It does. But it's what I do here, isn't it? Most of the time I love it. My husband next door, home for almost every meal. But let's talk about your news. What does your heart desire?"

"I told Phil yes, of course." Her blue eyes sparkled in the shaft of sunlight pouring through the cutout of a cat in the outhouse door. "But I need your advice about how to tell Pa. Philip's not a Catholic."

"I suspect it's less his faith than that you'll be staying here and sending him back home with Jimmy—unless he decides to remain here too."

"I wish he would. I'd feel so much better about saying yes to Phil."

"You can't make your decision based on what Pa wants. You have to know your own heart."

She swatted a fly with a rolled newspaper we kept for various purposes in the privy. "Pa says you dishonored him by becoming engaged to Peter. And later, by marrying him and leaving Pa. He's warned me for years not to do what 'Mollie did to me.' It got worse after Mama died."

My face felt hot.

"Were there other proposals?"

"Just one. And Da was right about him." She sighed. "But I didn't appreciate his pushing me to see it before I was ready. Philip is different. I don't want Da interfering, though I've told Phil how he might be, how he came between you and Peter."

"Would you like me to talk to him, run interference for you?"

She was quiet. A bumblebee hovered at the cat cutout but moved on. "No. I need to tell him myself."

"That's wise. And brave."

"But I'd like you there with me, praying while I do the talking."

"It will be my honor. I'll start now."

THIRTY-SIX

THIS DAY

A parlor conversation," my father said. "Must be serious." Kate had arranged for us to sit together with our father in the wainscoted room. November stuck its feet inside the valley, leaving cold footprints in the night, so Peter started a small fire, then left us Sheehans alone, though he'd offered to stay.

"It is important," Kate's husky voice answered our father. "Won't you sit?"

"I'll stand." He looked wary, his two daughters forming a wall before him. He stood at the fireplace, hand behind his back. I sat on the divan. "Let's have it, then."

Kate cleared her throat. "Philip Hogan has asked me to marry him, and I've said yes. Of course, he'll officially ask you for your blessing, but I wanted you to know about it first, so you wouldn't be caught off guard. Or injure him." She made her voice light but firm.

"My blessing? My permission, you mean. You're only sixteen."

"I'm nineteen, Da. We don't need your permission."

"No, you're not. You're sixteen and too young. That tinker

302

doesn't even have his own place. Will you live with his family? No. Sixteen is too young." He paced.

"She knows her own age, Pa. I was the one who upset you at sixteen. And as Ma Anne tried to defend me then, I'm defending Kate now."

He stomped two steps, glared in front of me. "You will not defy me. Not dishonor me again." I saw the anger in his eyes, the hurt and disappointment, almost as though it was all those years ago.

"Da." Kate touched his shoulder. He jerked as though struck. "It's me. I'm the one planning to marry Philip, with or without your permission. Mollie has nothing to do with this."

"You set this up." He shook his finger at me. "You let an older man steal a young girl's love."

"Phil's but a year older than me."

"She . . . she fell in love, Pa, just the way you did with Ma and with Kate's ma." *Should I just stay quiet?* "It's natural. It's not meant to hurt those who also love us that we will leave behind. She won't stop loving you. I'll never stop loving you."

To Kate he said, "And if I say no?"

"I'll be sad, but I'll still say yes to Philip. And hard as it will be, I'll ask someone else to give me away."

"Peter, I suppose. You'd ask that traitor to do it."

"Jimmy," she said.

He frowned. "You've thought of everything. Except hurting your pa, piercing what is left of my heart after my Ellen died, my babies, your mother. And your sister left me, who dishonors me still."

"How do I do that, Pa?" I should have kept quiet.

"Right under my nose you let your sister meet up with a man she thinks she wants to marry. She doesn't know what she wants."

"I think she does. You were wrong about Peter and me and I knew it. But I honored your wishes anyway." My heart throbbed at my ears. My breath came short, but I knew I needed to be kind—to him and to Kate. I wanted to list all the wrongs I felt he'd done to me, how he'd kept me from Peter, looked after himself. But such words would only fuel a fire better left to go out.

I felt the tears. "I know you love Kate just as you love me. She deserves a life that she helps create. We all do. Blessing her marriage could be your greatest kindness. Ma Anne would be pleased, and I think my mother would be too." I felt my babies shift inside me and told myself to stay calm. "We honor our fathers and our mothers when we are true to ourselves, Pa. When how you raised us gives us confidence to step out on our own, face the consequences of our decisions, maybe even be there to prop us up and send us out again, knowing you believe in us."

His shoulders sank. Tears fell on his cheeks, and I waited for him to sob as he did on my wedding day, say he was sorry. But he didn't. He walked out instead. It was a defeated gait, his head hung low.

"DID HE EVER TELL YOU why he resisted our marriage so much?" I'd never asked my husband what transpired between them when they met at the hotel in San Juan Capistrano where my father at last gave his consent. But now, seven years later, on this day, I wondered.

Peter and I sat on the porch, bundled up on the swing. "He loves you. I knew that. And you were young at sixteen. I gave him that and reminded him that we'd honored his wishes until you were older and reached out, and even the priests and Sisters supported our long-distance affair. I urged him to grant his consent, or he'd risk losing your love—"

"I'd never stop loving him."

"I know. But you'd go away with me against his will, and that would cause a breach that might not be bridged. He thought about that and, reluctant, gave his consent. It was all contingent on how you felt. At that point you hadn't seen me for four years. I was more nervous that you might change your mind. Never been more grateful that you didn't.'"

Gerald wandered outside and put his head on my lap. The new screen door flapped. "Mommy and Daddy make face sounds," he said.

We laughed. "Kissing," Peter said, then grabbed Gerald and kissed his nose. "Why aren't you in bed?" He lifted our son and he squealed as Peter popped him onto his shoulder and took him to the room he shared with Vincent.

Kate joined me then and sat in the rattan chair that looked out toward the Mission Mountain range.

"It won't matter," Kate said. "I'm going to marry Philip." She dabbed at her tear-swollen eyes with what Mary called her "bless-you cloth." "Pa said he wouldn't survive when you left, but we did. And he'll make it. He's resilient."

"I am that, lass." Our father had stepped out on cat feet, quiet as the night. "And I give my consent."

"You do?" Kate stood quickly, faced him.

"I think you're too young. But if he asks, I'll give my blessing."

Kate rushed to him and held him. His left arm patted her back as she thanked him. "Oh, Da, you've made me so happy."

"Not as happy as your Philip does, I guess."

Kate laughed. "No. But close. And what would really make me happy is that you'd stay in Montana, here with Mollie. I know she and Peter have invited you. You could see Mollie every day, and us and Cousin Ellen now and then. Maybe do a circuit of living with each of us for three or four months."

"Planning my life for me."

The way you planned out ours. I was glad I didn't say that out loud nor the other thing I wanted to blurt out.

"I have my place in Capistrano. And Jimmy's a California boy. Why, he even speaks English with a Spanish accent." He chuckled. "No, I belong at Casa Blanca. You'll need it one day. Wheat-ranching is a risky business." He turned to me. "And you never know how long a government job might last. Very perilous."

"Like being a freighter into gold camps," I said, but I saw a grin begin. "But we're made to risk, aren't we, Pa? To fall down and get back up, just as you have done over and over. And to savor this day that the Lord has made, those treasures that he's placed inside our storehouses. A cat riding on the back of a mule. An altar with a dirt floor in a mining camp. The love of our lives for as long as we have them."

"A daughter plastering an adobe house." He squeezed my shoulder, said to Kate, "And another patching it up. I'll try to hang my hat on those. When's your Phil going to come and see me?"

"Just as soon as I let him know the door is open."

He winked at me. It was a hummingbird flutter of a blessing.

THE WEDDING on January first took place in our living room with a St. Ignatius priest administering the sacrament of marriage.

"At least Phil won't ever forget his anniversary," Peter whispered.

There'd been one glitch when our father learned Phil wasn't a Catholic, but the banns were read for three weeks and he agreed that he and Kate would raise the children Catholic, which calmed our father down. That the priests approved of Kate's young man made all the difference to my father's acceptance.

We had a large gathering afterward with lots of food. In the afternoon, though it was cold, a procession of Kootenai, Salish, and Pend d'Oreille families came into the house with fur leggings, wearing buckskin clothing lined with lynx and ermine fur. Many were swathed in buffalo robes for warmth. They softly shook the hands of the newlyweds, offered beaded gifts and blankets for the sister of the White Chief's wife. When Old Michelle arrived, he wrapped the couple in a single blanket he removed from around his shoulder. "It is a custom," Michel translated. "A wedding blessing, that you will always sleep under one blanket."

As they tramped through, I served them little wedding cakes and cookies, pieces of my fruitcake wrapped in tissue paper. I smiled—no mask of the smiling hostess needed. They were welcome guests in our home. My eyes must have gone to the muddy tracks on the floor at various times because the ever-observant Shows No Anger whispered to me, "We will tend to the mud in the morning. Now, we love. This time comes only on this day." She poured cups of hot cider.

And she was right.

"You've excelled again," Peter said as he surveyed the activity in the parlor, the living area, the kitchen filled with friends both Indian and non-Indian. Our older Ronan children spoke with Flathead friends, and the Lamberts' children—joined by the Choquettes' child—lifted cookies from the table when they thought no one was looking.

"It is a lovely party. Nice that Phil's friends came even though they looked a little wary."

"Ignorance breeds discomfort." Peter put his arm around my waist. "Those twins will be here soon."

"To join our happily ever after."

I watched my father give my sister's hand in her marriage. Tears fell, but he smiled too. Both of his daughters had marriages they wanted blessed by God, first. What greater way of honoring a parent could there be? I could live without my father's blessing. I would have to.

It was a full blending of my family with our lives here in the Mission Valley. What happened after Prince Charming woke Sleeping Beauty with his kiss, after the villains were assailed, after the memories of a hundred years had been put to rest? Happiness.

THIRTY-SEVEN

LEAVINGS

Jimmy and my father prepared to leave in March when some of the roads were clear of snow. They would travel by stage-coach to Corinne, Utah, then to Los Angeles by rail—reversing the journey Peter and I had made after our marriage—taking a ship to San Francisco, then by stage to Capistrano. The Gems he would leave behind with us. He no longer plowed—he leased out his land, including the additional acres he'd bought after the lawsuit was settled.

"I like my warm winters," Pa told me. "It isn't bad here in your valley but"—he shivered—"there was a thin layer of ice on my washbowl this morning. I can leave that behind."

"Thank you for coming." I kissed his cheek, my unborn babies preventing a full hug. He reached his arm around me, held me. "We'll miss you," I whispered. "The children adore you."

"Maybe you'll visit."

"We will."

The stage now came as far as the agency, so it would be here soon. We stood on the porch, his arm light on my shoulder.

"I know you might like something of Anne's," he said then.

"And of your mother's." I thought of the lost umbrella, the stolen Irish linen sheets taken the night before we left Denver. "I had some brooches of your ma's that Anne wore now and then." I remembered seeing them. "And the one I bought you in Salt Lake that you had me give to her."

"Because you forgot to buy her a gift."

He nodded. "The truth is, Mollie, I had to sell all of them. Things got a little tight."

"Oh, Pa, I wish you'd said something."

"Pride can be a troubling thing."

"I have the memories," I said. "I'm discovering that those are more important than physical things. They can't be sold or stolen. They lie inside a basket in my heart, and I can draw on them for strength anytime I want."

"I do have these." He handed me a small box. Inside were locks of hair: one the color of sunrise; another the color of earth.

"Anne's? And my mother's?" He nodded. Two had ribbons on them.

"Your little sister who died at birth and your brother Gerald."

"Don't you want to keep them?"

"It's time," he said. "I thought you might wish to weave them and put them in a frame. Ellen had one such hanging on her wall."

"I'll do that," I said. "And send it to you."

"Bring it," he said. He touched my hair, stroked it in its snood and tucked my shawl tighter. The wind was chilly. "And maybe add a lock of your own."

The stage pulled up. Pa shouted for Jimmy, who had finished putting the two cats into a covered basket with a lid he'd punched air holes in. I hugged Jimmy goodbye. "Adios," he said, then lifted my palm and brushed his lips the way the alcalde would have. My father shook Peter's hand, tipped his hat at me, and the Sheehan pair stepped into the stage to cats meowing their discontent. I wasn't as sad as I might have been. The leavings—residue and remnants of lives—I held in my heart as well as my hands. And

I knew how to elevate the good memories over the bad now and how to make nurturing new ones.

ON MARCH 18, I gave birth to twins. Dr. Choquette attended the delivery. Mrs. Lambert spent the week after helping as I had done with the arrival of her latest babe. The priests came and baptized the girls. Louise Anne and Katherine Josephine we named them. They were tiny, but Katherine especially had good lungs she used frequently to express her opinion. I sent word to Kate that her namesake was hearty and strong and to come meet them both when she could. She and Phil lived but an hour away.

Louise wasn't as hardy as her sister. While I nursed Katherine, I watched my husband nurture this tiny life, hold Louise to his chest, keeping her warm before the fire. I saw in him those qualities of my father that I most loved: attentiveness, hopefulness, perseverance. He sang Gaelic songs to his newest daughters but whispered special encouragement to Lovely Louise as we called her. She lived only fifteen days.

Shows No Anger came to comfort me. We shared a grief, one known to my mother and my stepmother, too, and to dozens of other mothers through the years. I wept for this child, too soon an angel. Shows No Anger reminded me that we women survive great losses, giving me courage that I could too.

Chief Arlee called Katherine *Es-nees-e-lil*, meaning "The Twin," and later added a Salish word that translated as "Good Looking." Our Native friends accepted us, overlooked our mistakes, loved us, I believe, as we loved them. But only Matthew— Plenty Grizzly Bear—was ever adopted into the tribe. Still, dozens bowed their heads at the funeral of Lovely Louise. We now had another connection to the people: the grave among many of their ancestors. Life and death to bind us, gardens and graves a part of this life.

As the Northern Pacific route entered the reservation, timbers were sold, giving a small boon to the agency economy for use for the Flathead people. The railroad needed twenty-five hundred crossties per mile. Because Peter had seen how the railroad affected surrounding communities with camp followers and gamblers and tent saloon operators (who were not to sell alcohol to the Indians but did), ex-convicts seeking work and escape and "fallen women," he arranged for something different. He hired Mormon work crews to lay tracks across the reservation and thus avoided some of the altercations he would otherwise have had to police.

Margaret Theresa was born on the day before the golden spike went in at Gold Creek, marking the completion of the Northern Pacific Railway. And four years later, Isabel—whom the Indians called Sunshine—arrived, followed by my husband's namesake, Peter. He was born in September 1890, in the midst of Peter taking the census.

I saw my father for the last time in the summer of 1888. Isabel was fifteen months old when I traveled with her to see him. Vincent, our oldest, joined us too.

We boarded the train to Portland, then by steamboat headed down the Columbia and followed the coast to San Francisco, then by train to Santa Ana. Our firstborn was alive with a hundred questions, still asking when my father picked us up, driving two spirited horses with his one arm.

"I always preferred mules," Pa told us as he maneuvered the reins with his crippled hand. "I didn't know how much I'd miss those Gems. How are they?"

"Pearl is still with us, gentle as a lamb."

"She has a cat to look after," Vincent said.

"These horses don't take to cats," my father said as the team jerked forward. He made an awkward motion.

"May I take the reins?" I asked.

"What?" He looked at me. "Aye, that would be good, Mollie. I'll hold your babe. Isabel?"

I nodded and he handed me the reins.

Something in his act of accepting help touched me. He wasn't teaching me how to do something, wasn't seeing me as a stand-in for my mother. I was a daughter doing what I could to help, while carrying on my own life as a woman should.

We passed the ruined mission walls with swallows darting in and out, and as we came up the lane toward Casa Blanca, memories breathed in and out like the ocean on the beach. The gate I'd opened for him where in the lamplight he said I reminded him so of my mother. The old plow beside the field. The house I'd helped my father build and where Peter and I had our wedding breakfast prepared with love by Ma Anne. I blinked back tears.

"Right there, Vincent, that's the house I helped your grandpa build," I said.

"You built a house?" Vincent's incredulous voice made me laugh.

"I did. We did."

"It's what women do," my father said. "She mixed the mud and I got it to her so she could plaster. And it's still standing."

Vincent blinked. "It looks like a fairy-tale house with flowers all over it. I never knew you could do such a thing, Ma. Look, someone's left the door open."

"I did," my father said. "To let fresh air in."

I flicked the reins on the horses' backs, and we sped up the hill toward old memories and the nurture of new ones. It was good to be back, even without my father's stated blessing. ·

THIRTY-EIGHT

Family Legacy

We had more guests with the railroad's presence, more visitors as my husband's operation of the agency became a beacon for congressmen and senators, military and government officials. They liked to bring interested people to a showplace of accord between Indian and white. The visitors required tending, but I considered them boons to our little household. While we employed teachers now who lived in a cottage at the agency, the presence of guests of all persuasions proved to act as added animated classrooms.

Libbie Custer, for example, returned with a signed copy of *Boots and Saddles*, her book about her life with her husband. I found her less strident during that visit, her having lived with her husband's death for more than ten years now. She never remarried. She appeared to relax in our hospitality, entertaining the children with her stories of her life as a general's wife. "You know," she said, "I hadn't wanted to visit here that first time. It was so soon after . . . The general had suggested it and provided the escort. But it was your kindnesses to me, your acceptance of where I was in my puddle of grief, that truly blessed me. I'm not sure I thanked you."

"I offered hospitality."

"Ah, but so much more."

"Time, intention, and kindness heal," Peter said when I shared with him what Libbie had experienced with us. Arm in arm we walked beneath the cherry trees, the orchard looking healthy. "She has a life without his physical presence but one very much wrapped up in shaping who he was. With all her lectures and now her book promotion, she probably has to be onstage most of the time. Here, she could be herself."

"That's exactly how I hope everyone who comes here feels."

"You make it so, Mollie."

I loved these small moments with my husband and always said an extra prayer of gratitude for the privilege to live in paradise, to share it with a love more charming than any fairy tale could tell. I had a purpose and a path.

We still weathered disappointments. Chief Joseph—who Peter had met and counted as a friend—had not been allowed to return to his beloved Idaho nor our agency. But he was finally moved to the Columbia region to the Colville Reservation in Washington Territory. At least it had rushing streams, mountains, meadows, and tall trees, it was said. Nothing like the flat land of Leavenworth or Oklahoma.

A new provision—the Code of Offenses—had been passed by the government in 1883, meant to assimilate more Indians into American life. Peter and I saw it as a means to wipe out the culture of Native people, and he rarely enforced it. He saw trouble in trying to implement its provisions prohibiting the People singing or dancing, doing those things that had always been allowed, that made them who they were. "You'd think after all these years here I'd be more sanguine about the craziness I see of certain government regulations. Sometimes I can make a small dent in it, but meanwhile a man could go bald pulling his hair out."

"You implement with an eye to real justice," I said.

"Something that has evaded the Indians for years."

"You should maybe take a little rest now and then," I said. "I don't want you keeling over from overwork."

He laughed. "I've hired a new clerk, that'll help. And I need to go fishing more. Which I can do. Is there a break in the guest list? Maybe we can all go to the Big Mountain Lake."

"Yes, let's do that. I love that place."

"This will be Peter's first camping trip," Peter said. "Though he won't remember much of it at nine months."

"I've always been impressed that you can recall the birthdays of each of our children," I said. "Not a lot of fathers do. Mine didn't."

"None of their births have come with the memory of a loss," he said, "the way your da experienced. Except for Lovely Louise for us. But we have her twin to remind us of the goodness when they arrived." He paused. "March 18, 1881."

"It will be good to camp out. Let's plan for it." I looked at my calendar. "We have another author coming. She writes for the *St. Paul Pioneer Press*. After she leaves, we'll make our trek to that pretty lake."

The author of *The Rainbow's End*, Alice Palmer Henderson, brought her book she signed for Margaret, an early reader. That daughter especially loved to bury herself in stories as I had when I was her age. The author was gracious and kind and laughed about the open door we had to Indians who walked right in without knocking.

"What's the phrase you're saying?" she asked after two Salish men came in and then left with a bit of sugar.

"What does your heart desire?"

"And aren't those generous words."

"My friend Shows No Anger introduced me to that greeting here, but it is also found in the Psalms. 'Delight thyself in the Lord and he shall give thee the desires of thine heart.'"

"Which psalm is that?" She had her notepad and pencil out.

"Thirty-seven, verse four. I find myself saying it with our visitors too. 'What does your heart desire?' It is, after all, my hope, that we can know and meet their wishes. Yours as well."

"You certainly have."

After she left, she sent us a copy of what she'd written about her visit. Peter pasted the news article in our scrapbook. She wrote of Katherine and Margaret bringing her bouquets of morning wildflowers and a breakfast of fresh trout and venison, of the bear rugs, the laughter of children, the large table that included guests and residents of the agency and Flathead people. All in a landscape so magnificent with its mountains and meadows framed by bending skies.

She described our storehouse of riches.

At the end she added, "The visitor is greeted with the gracious question, 'What does your heart desire?' The keynote to receiving it is a household harmony of helpfulness and courtesy made at an always open door."

⪜ EPILOGUE ⪛

I remembered that author's words as I helped load our passel of children into the wagon. We rattled toward that idyllic mountain lake, in a setting that was pure Montana. Shows No Anger came with us, as did her husband, both riding fine horses. Paul sat astride a horse of his own. Shows No Anger expected a new baby soon. Kate and Phil planned to join us the next day.

Peter seemed especially excited. He hummed a tune.

"You're in a good mood," I said.

"I have a surprise for your birthday."

"It's not for another week."

"I was going to have a ceremony, gather in the priests, but decided not to wait."

"A ceremony? Goodness, what could it be?"

We pulled the wagon up next to the Big Mountain Lake, and he took my hand to help me out. We looked out over the water, a view that never failed to lift my spirit. I spied a white dot in the distance I thought might be a bighorn sheep, but before I could point it out to Peter, he spread his arms. "Meet Lake Mary Ronan."

"What?"

"The Transcontinental Survey Commission has approved my request to call this body of water you so love 'Lake Mary Ronan.'"

"Oh, Peter. That's . . . precious." But it disturbed me too.

"Please don't be offended if I still think of it as how the Kootenai call it, Big Mountain Lake."

Peter nodded. I could see I'd disappointed him.

"I don't mean to be ungrateful. To have something in Montana named for me, it's . . . it's quite an honor."

"Women's names aren't often given to the jewels of the land-scape. I thought you deserved it. You've given so much to this place and the people. The chief agreed."

The chief's acceptance made me feel better. I rested my head on Peter's shoulder. The waters of the Big Mountain Lake—Lake Mary Ronan—shimmered in the afternoon sun. Around me was everything my heart could desire: family, friends, the beauty of the land, the laughter of children, a husband I adored. An osprey dipped overhead, its presence adding to my storehouse of riches. I wished my father had stayed in Montana, but he had at least visited. And we had found our own happy ending between a loving father and an honoring daughter, a blessed relationship, even if he never blessed my marriage with his words. I would treasure that.

⪩ Author's Notes ⪨

I don't know how or when I acquired *Girl from the Gulches:
The Story of Mary Ronan* as told to Margaret Ronan, edited by Ellen Baumler, and published by the Montana Historical
Society, but I'm grateful I did. Mary—Mollie—was an ordinary
Montana woman who lived an extraordinary life. And though I
read her memoir at least five years ago, it never left me. It's said
that a memoir is the "story we tell ourselves about ourselves,"
so there were spaces to speculate about Mollie's life within her
remembrances.

Mollie's memoir told of the trials with her father, her love for
him, and how he intervened in her life, with some exploration of
why he might have behaved in these ways. Her disappointment at
being left behind, the joy of her cousins' arrival, the initial surprise and trepidation in meeting Ma Anne, the many moves and
struggles, her teaching tragedies, life in San Juan Capistrano in the
1870s, and the circumstances of her return to Helena, Montana,
are all founded in fact. The details of the engagement, the dances
at Last Chance Gulch, the establishments and James's orders to
close them down (except in Corinne), the rowdies of Corinne, the
trip to Salt Lake City, the encounter with road agents, the role of
the religious community of Helena and Los Angeles creating a

path for Peter and Mary's fascinating life—these are all chronicled in *Girl from the Gulches*. So are their times in San Juan, the alcalde's influence, fires, the mining mishaps, and Peter's political adventures. Most interesting is the surprising and splendid life they found on the Jocko Agency serving the Confederated Salish, Pend d'Oreille, and Kootenai tribes, as they are known today.

Mollie was intrigued early on by Native American history and did memorize Chief Black Hawk's surrender speech to recite along with poems and sonnets, one of which brought her interest from a road agent. I have created Bart Davidson based loosely on that desperado Jack Gallagher, who had complimented Mollie's sonnet-sharing and had charmed. But the timing didn't fit for my having Mollie meet him later on, so Bart became a composite of vigilante actions in the 1860s and early 1870s Montana.

The Ronans' involvement with the Nez Perce War of 1877—during their first years at the agency—did occur, including the Flathead Indians' offer of protection for the Ronans both then and when Mollie had planned to visit her father. In 2020, while I was working on this book, the Nimiipuu people, descendants of Chief Joseph, purchased 148 acres near Joseph, Oregon, land where Joseph's band had departed from, as they made their way through the Bitterroot Valley toward Canada, creating the tensions of 1877. The small acreage in Oregon is a remnant of the 1.7 million acres originally promised by the 1855 Treaty that had been reduced to 770,000 acres in the Treaty of 1865 by what the Nez Perce call the "Steal Treaty." For a government account of the retreat, see "Flight of the Nez Perce," Yellowstone National Park, National Park Service (tinyurl.com/atpwtwpn).

The Ronans and the St. Ignatius priests did support Joseph coming to the Flathead Reservation, but this was not allowed. He and his people were sent to Leavenworth briefly where Peter had once been imprisoned, then to Oklahoma and finally to the Colville Reservation of eastern Washington State, where he died. His life is celebrated annually at Chief Joseph Days in Joseph,

Oregon, a town named for him, where the 148 acres of the traditional tribal campsite belong again to the People.

The Ronan encounters with Chiefs Arlee, Charlo, and Michelle—who did give his name to Matthew James—are all based on facts. The hiring of the exquisite blind linguist Michel is recounted in Mollie's memoir. So is Mollie's interaction with Captain George, who tried to rescue his daughter, lost her, and was left for dead. This Nez Perce father's devotion to his daughter I think had a profound effect on Mollie Ronan. Aspects of it are also included in Peter's agency reports published as *"A Great Many of Us Have Good Farms," Agent Peter Ronan Reports on the Flathead Indian Reservation, Montana, 1877–1887*, edited by Rober J. Bigart and published by Salish Kootenai College Press in Pablo, Montana.

James Sheehan did bring his brother and Mollie's three cousins from Kentucky to Iowa, then to Missouri, Colorado, and Montana before California in 1869. Mollie's brother Gerald's death was as described. Mollie lost touch with cousins Patrick and Mary, but Ellen and Bill had a ranch in the Ruby Valley and Carrie Crane did live on the Wisconsin Creek where Mollie attended that quilting bee. Mollie did love plays and performances, and the encounter in Salt Lake City with the actress is recounted in her memoir, along with the play based on a father's search for his daughter. The theft of the Irish linen, the lost umbrella, the scrapbook entries and erasures, and Mollie's poem, are all a part of her story, as is her struggle to honor her father, pass the teaching test, be educated at the Los Angeles academy, and give the graduation address. And her nearly entering the convent following Mrs. Maginnis's report about Peter and Annie Brown. The religious community's role in their engagement is as described. Her father's behavior at the wedding is from Mollie's recollections, as is her father's accident and Kate's later engagement and marriage.

The Ronans' many moves, the gold theft, Peter's dabbling in politics as a Union Democrat, his relationship with Congressman

Maginnis, the nature of his agency appointment, are based on fact, as is the congressman's arguing James Sheehan's case at the Supreme Court (and winning). Shows No Anger and Paul are products of my imagination, but the difficulty with buffalo hunting, allocating ammunition, and the encroachment of white settlers onto the reservation are based on Peter's reports and other histories of the time. After ranching was opened to nontribal people legally in 1904, the Native peoples lost more than half of their original reservation. Peter did not live to see it.

Peter Ronan's journalistic experience served him well on the reservation. He had been a printer, was imprisoned in Leavenworth where Sister Vincent tended him, and he lost his presses three other times to fires. The Salish Kootenai College published several years of Peter Ronan's letters and reports as an agent in a second book, *Justice to Be Accorded to the Indians*, edited by Robert Bigart, covering 1888 to 1893, up to the final year when Peter Ronan died of a heart attack. He was fifty-one. Copies of these reports are available through the Montana Historical Society, to which I am also most grateful. Of special note was the gracious reading of this manuscript by Montana writer and historian Ellen Baumler, who had edited *Girl from the Gulches* and taught Mollie's story at the university level. She saved me from a number of geographical and historical errors that any Montanan would have cringed at. I'm so grateful. I also extend gratitude to Cary Heskett, friend and resident of Kalispell, who helped put me in touch with important resources early on and who also read the manuscript, catching things like my assertion that "May was balmy in Helena." You won't see that phrase included. I am so grateful, yet I bear full responsibility for errors still found within this work.

Peter's reports chronicle the Flathead people transitioning from a buffalo-hunting and gathering economy to farming, though the Flathead people were self-supporting from early on. For details about historical buffalo as a part of the community, see *"I Will Be Meat for My Salish": The Buffalo and the Montana Writers Project*

322

Interviews on the Flathead Indian Reservation, written by Bon I. Whealdon and others and edited by Robert Bigart. A dissatisfaction is noted in the book by the Selis Qlispe Culture Committee Elders Cultural Advisory Council. It addresses the value of the memories of the elders but decries the translations from "stilted 'primitive' English used in place of articulate Salish," and that some of the language used is "offensive to Indian people."

The agency was often visited by officials, the military, and writers, including Elizabeth Custer more than once. The whitewashed buildings, the reputation of Mollie's hospitality, and the history of peaceful interactions made the agency a showcase.

The conflicts with white settlers encroaching and the challenges of managing a large organization while working respectfully with three separate tribes are also documented. Peter did get the lake named Lake Mary Ronan, which is how it is listed on present-day maps. It is part of Lake Mary Ronan State Park. The mountain peak he affectionately referred to as "Finerty's Wart" was officially named for Peter and is known today as Mt. Ronan. I tried to discover how the Native people might have felt about the naming of the mountain and the lake after the Ronans. Uncertain, I gave Mollie pause in accepting Peter's "gift," as I think that out of respect for the Flathead people, she would have had at least a moment's hesitation with the survey commission's naming of Big Mountain Lake for her.

There is also a town named Ronan and others named Arlee and Charlo, based on these Native leaders of the 1800s. A 2021 nonfiction book about the Arlee Warriors basketball team of Arlee, Montana, by *New York Times* writer Abe Streep, offers a contemporary reflection on descendants of people Mollie and Peter might have known. Titled *Brothers on Three: A True Story of Family, Resistance, and Hope on a Reservation in Montana*, it followed the 2017 state championship team members and their community struggles and triumphs. It was serendipitous to have discovered the book before I'd finished my manuscript.

St. Ignatius, also on Montana maps, was one of the earliest missions in the West and is listed on the National Register of Historic Places. Following a fire in 1919, little of the community remains, but the brick church still stands with the Mission Mountains towering behind it. The archbishop did present a mass there, and Mollie writes of an earlier one held in the mill at the Jocko Agency as well.

At Peter's death, his clerk, Joseph P. Carter, was appointed interim agent. Carter and Mary Ellen—Pretty Hair—married in 1895, and Mollie and her young children continued to live at the agency for a few more years. When Carter was appointed to a full term, Vincent became the agency clerk.

Mollie eventually moved to Missoula, Montana, to be closer to the university, she wrote, so that her younger children might one day attend. She spent the remainder of her life in Missoula. Her house on Pine Street still stands.

Peter did remove the little gold ring, Mary reports in her memoir. He let one of his girls play with it . . . and it was lost. But she still had the memory; those can never be lost.

In an epilogue of her memoir, Mary writes that her greatest joys in life came as wife and mother. "In their suffering, failures, and sorrows I have felt anguish unutterable, not to have been endured but for the faith that through our many tribulations we enter into the kingdom of God." I found Mollie to be a remarkable woman of faith and fortitude, and it's my hope that you, dear reader, do as well. She died in 1940 and is buried next to Peter in St. Mary's Cemetery in Missoula.

⟩⟩ Acknowledgments ⟨⟨

Thanks go to the Bitterroot Salish, Upper Pend d'Oreille, and the Kootenai tribes—also known as the Confederated Salish and Kootenai Tribes of the Flathead Nation—for preserving their history and culture and to their extensive materials available online. Writing during a time of COVID prevented travel, so I relied heavily on Mary's memoir, books about Montana, and online resources. Of special note is the official website of the Confederated Salish and Kootenai Tribes (www.csktribes.org), the Kootenai Culture Committee, and the Selis Qlispe Culture Committee Elders Cultural Advisory Council, who work to preserve and shape the direction of the stories told of tribal people. The Three Chiefs Cultural Center (threechiefs.org), formerly the People's Center, allows access to the story of this confederation of tribes as told through "a museum, an exhibit gallery, educational programs and a quality giftshop." In a temporary setting at St. Ignatius, Montana, it has now reopened for visitors. Nine Pipes Museum (ninepipesmuseum.org) at Charlo is an equally important museum that tells the history of the reservation but also that of the Jocko Agency—where the Ronans lived—specifically.

I tried to stay true to the stories as told through Mollie's eyes as relayed in her memoir. This included her spellings of Salish and Kootenai and Pend d'Oreille words and her remembrance of events such as the gifts of names, the visits by the archbishop, blind Michel, and the offers of protection during the Nez Perce War. It would not surprise me if her memory at times conflicts with the Flathead Nation's perspectives, though I found no evidence of such. I tried to be sensitive to contemporary understandings as well as honoring the story of this woman and her husband who spent seventeen years of their lives in service—which is how they saw their work—to the Native people they were allowed to live among.

Gratitude for individuals who assisted me goes especially to Ellen Baumler, editor of Mollie's memoir and my source book. And to Cary Heskett of Kalispell, Montana, who came into my life through her daughter Hilary whom we had the pleasure of hosting for several months some years ago while she served a physical therapy internship for her doctorate. Mollie's story was in the back of my mind then, and when I told Hilary, she told her mom, who caught my enthusiasm and to whom we are also now connected for life. Such are the ways stories bring us gifts. Cary connected with genealogists, contacted people from the Family History Center, gleaning information shared with her and ultimately with me. Cary also read a version of this book and helped correct and direct me toward making it an authentic Montana story. Research can be a spiderweb of connections. Hilary Heskett, through a friend, put me in touch with John Fraley, author of *Rangers, Trappers, and Trailblazers* and *A Woman's Way West, In and Around Glacier National Park from 1925 to 1990*. In a phone conversation, he graciously shared wisdom of his forty years with the Montana Wildlife Agency. Another researcher to whom I'm indebted is CarolAnne Tsai of Portland, who first provided me with connections about Mary Catherine Fitzgibbon Sheehan Ronan and who continues to be a support for writing whatever subject claims me. I'm also grateful to my friend Laurie Koski, who grew up in Fort Benton, Montana, and who now lives in Bend, Oregon. She graciously answered questions and told me how to pronounce the Ronan name (Row-NAN).

A number of books about Montana served me well. *Montana* by Clark C. Spence; *F. Jay Haynes, Photographer*, published by the Montana Historical Society; *The Last Best Place, A Montana Anthology*, edited by William Kittredge and Annick Smith; *Montana Women Homesteaders: A Field of One's Own*, edited by Sarah Carter; *This House of Sky* by Ivan Doig; and the volumes of Peter's agency reports detailing issues about payroll delays, recruitment challenges, ranching, even the whitewash packaging efforts. Despite the wisdom of these writers and these researchers, mistakes can be made, and they belong to me.

Especially helpful for understanding Mollie's life and her relationship with her father is the book *The AfterGrief: Finding Your Way Along the Long Arc of Loss* by Hope Edelman. Through the author's research and insights, I gained understanding about Mollie's loss of her mother at an early age and the separations from her father and how those may have affected her as both a child and an adult—and how loss affects us all, each in unique ways.

Thanks are in order for my pre–copyediting friend Janet Meranda who catches so many details while I can still correct them; to Revell editor Andrea Doering who always makes the stories better bringing wisdom and insight; to Barb Barnes who finds the mistakes I overlook and who wins diplomatic awards for how she tells me about them. Thank you to the full team at Revell—Michele Misiak, Karen Steele, and to the fabulous sales team. To Leah Apineru of Colorado who left the publicity business but who still does social media stuff for me, and to Anji Verlaque, my webmaster, much gratitude. Thank you tons! To many others who bring these stories to readers through Baker Publishing Group and to my agent of thirty years, Joyce Hart of Hartline Literary: I couldn't have done it without you. Thank you.

I extend gratitude to my prayer team, to my family who put up with me, and especially to Jerry who offers careful comments as I read early drafts out loud to him. I hope to discover errors and to make corrections to the rhythm, tasks that seem only to be found in reading from paper and out loud. He never falls asleep, for which I'm eternally grateful.

Last, and perhaps deepest gratitude, goes to readers for making room in your lives for these stories.

Of special note are the librarians, museum staff, and bookstore fairy godmothers who have carried my titles, many all forty of them, hand sold them, and spread the word. Thank you. Of special note:

Paulina Springs Books, Sisters, OR
Sunriver Books and Music, Sunriver, OR
Klindt's Books, The Dalles, OR (the oldest bookstore in Oregon)
Deschutes County Library, Bend, OR
. . . And Books Too, Clarkston, WA
Wacoma Books, Hood River, OR
Powell's Books, Beaverton, OR
Chaparral Books, Portland, OR
The High Desert Museum Gift Shop, Bend, OR
Hood River Historical Museum, Hood River, OR
Walla Walla Library, Walla Walla, WAisto
Aurora Colony Museum, Aurora, OR
The Pacific Northwest Booksellers

And the Sherman County Museum of Moro, Oregon, county population 1800, where I held my first book signing in 1991, and we sold out all 75 copies they'd ordered in.

If not already, please consider joining my Story Sparks newsletter at www.jkbooks.com, which I hope brings monthly inspiration into your lives as your many responses to it bring joy to mine. I am thankful to many more unnamed people who continue to walk beside me on this journey, writing stories that inform and strengthen my own faith and I hope do yours as well.

Warmly,
Jane

≋ Book Group Discussion ≋ Questions

1. Did Mollie honor her mother and father? How did she do that or where did she fail?

2. Why did fairy tales appeal to Mollie? How do such childhood stories help define us? Do you have a favorite fairy tale?

3. Mollie spoke of memorizing Chief Black Hawk's speech. What did she gain by reciting his speech or Shakespeare's sonnets for people eating at the establishment? How did her wish to be dutiful—as Chief Black Hawk spoke of doing his duty—affect Mollie's decision-making?

4. Was James Sheehan a good father? Why or why not? Was Mollie a good daughter? Why or why not?

5. Mollie says she was a shy child, so shy she was afraid to ask her father what to call her stepmother. How did grieving the loss of her mother affect her shyness? How did confusion by the absences of her father and being left with others affect her confidence?

6. How did Peter's absences during their marriage (at the

mine, his political travel, supply missions to Missoula, etc.) differ from Mollie's father's absences? Or did she tell herself different stories?

7. What gifts of Mollie's gave her the most confidence? Her faith? Her facility with languages? Her love for Peter and her children? Her ability to anticipate another's needs and attempt to meet them? Her trust in the promise of the "storehouse of riches"? Others?

8. What are your gifts? What's in your storehouse of riches?

9. How would you describe the relationship between Mollie and Shows No Anger? Were they employer/employee? Friends? What events played a role in the changing of those relationships? Have you ever walked the path that transcended employer/employee into a friendship? How did that happen?

10. How would you characterize the stepparenting of Anne? Did she make the best decisions to stay behind while James took Mollie to plays and on trips? What else might she have done to be the mother Mollie longed for?

11. Why did Captain George's mission to rescue his daughter so affect Mollie despite her being powerless to do much to bring about a positive resolution?

12. Did Mollie ever feel that she was enough in the eyes of her father?

13. How did Mollie's life as the wife of an agent encourage others? Or did it? How do everyday acts of kindness and bravery translate into blessings?

She came to the West for rest . . .

WHAT SHE FOUND
WAS A PASSION.

Award-winning author Jane Kirkpatrick weaves
yet another lyrical tale based on a true story that
will keep readers captivated to the very end.

Read on for a sneak peek at
Natalie Curtis's story . . .

FROM BROKEN THINGS

Autumn—1902, Three Years Earlier

Though she had not seen the desert-bronzed face of her brother for two years, Natalie Curtis recognized in the sparkle of his eyes what was different. "You've found yourself," she said.

"And you haven't."

George Curtis dropped his leather travel pack in the vestibule of the New York family home, shaking the umbrellas in the brass stand. He held Natalie's shoulders, and she looked into blue eyes that matched her own. They shared the same wispy blond hair. George pulled her to his chest. "Come here. Let me hug my little sister."

Natalie leaned into the scent of leather as her shoulders relaxed for the first time in months. She hadn't realized how much she'd missed him. George was like an apparition arriving from the exotic West.

Natalie backed away first, looked her brother up and down. "You're brown as a walnut. You look . . . rested."

"I am, but for the train ride." He flipped his hat to the hat rack, then ran his hands through his hair. "It's so good to see you. So good." His voice carried warmth and wistfulness, but his eyes said *pitiful*. And she was.

The chambermaid appeared from nowhere to take his long coat. "Shall I place your bag in your room, Master George?"

"No, leave it here. I'll take it up later, Bella. Thank you."

"Very good, sir." She curtsied and disappeared.

"Your years away have fortified you." Natalie watched his easy smile expand to his warm eyes.

"Asthma, gone." He paused. "Wish I could say the same for you."

She'd put on weight in her malaise and she knew her skin was pale as a piano key. Simply getting out of bed exhausted her. Fortunately, she'd had the day to get ready for her brother's return.

"Are you feeling any . . . stronger?" George asked.

"I'm not sure it's about strength so much as overcoming the doubt."

"About never playing again?"

She forced her voice higher. "Come on." She slipped her arm through his. "They're all waiting, but I begged them to let me see you first, before you put on any western airs."

He laughed, didn't move. "No airs. But I do feel the confinement here between the brownstones, all the cabs, the hawkers on the streets." He shook himself like a dog of rain. "The desert, Natalie." His eyes grew distant. "It's astonishingly magnificent."

"Astonishingly." She smiled. "Do your cowboy friends mind the way you talk?"

"They tolerate my vocabulary, now that I'm a good hand. That's all that matters on a ranch. Whether you can stay on a horse while moving cattle through greasewood and sage, up and out of arroyos. That's how you're graded. I call the cows 'bovines of a recalcitrant nature.' My cowboy colleagues wondered if those words were a form of foreign profanity." He smiled. "A few have picked up on calling them recalcitrant."

"Oh, you." She punched his shoulder. *Solid muscle.*

"It's been the best thing I ever did, Nat. Leave here. Head west. The postcards I've sent don't say the half of it."

"But why did you have to go in the first place?" Natalie had a little girl's voice rather than a whine.

He lifted her chin. He was nearly a foot taller than her. "You should come back with me."

She stepped away. "I couldn't. Mimsey would never permit it nor Bogey either. And I'm not strong. I'm so very tired almost all of the time. I cough. There are other things . . ."

"You're twenty-six years old. Old enough to be an independent woman, I'd say."

"There's no such thing as an independent woman in this era. At my age. I'm a woman with nothing to consume her life. The doctor says I . . . still have healing to do to rid myself of the . . ." She squeezed his arm. "I'm struggling a little, that's all. Bogey says it'll get better."

"It's been nearly five years, Nat." The kindness in his voice, not pitying but sympathizing, caused her to blink back tears.

"I know, I know."

He patted her fingers as he pulled them through his bent elbow. "Promise me we'll talk about it later."

She nodded assent.

They were the closest of the Curtis children. Though George was four years older than Natalie, he understood her. He lived in an inner world of words as she lived in an inner sphere of music. But then he'd headed to the West and he had changed.

As had she five years before.

"They're waiting for you," she said.

Arm in arm they sauntered into the dining room where siblings and parents greeted George with joyous shouts. Mimsey, as the Curtis children called their mother, usually so organized and proper, fluttered with tears in her eyes as she clung to George, welcoming home her wayward son. "Come, come. Tell us all about your latest adventures. How was the train ride?" Mimsey took his hands in hers. "You're chilled." Then, releasing them, "Are you home for good, one can only hope?"

"I'm used to desert heat." George rubbed his palms, as though before a fire.

"My friends are all atwitter wanting a luncheon with you to hear your stories. We'll get that on the schedule." She pronounced it *shed-ule*. Natalie remembered she'd picked that up on that last trip to Europe. The *healing tour* that didn't heal.

"In due course, Mimsey." Her father intervened. "Let's let the lad have a bite to eat. Cook's prepared something healthy for you." Their father—called Bogey by his children and friends—stood with hands clasped behind his back, warming himself at the fireplace in the living room. "A little food will warm you up. Just what the doctor ordered."

Their father was a prominent physician, currently an emeritus professor. As a major in the army, he had attended President Lincoln's bedside during his final hours and helped with the autopsy. He'd known sorrow, and Natalie knew he grieved for her current emotional state that he seemed powerless to change. She couldn't change it either. Or hadn't.

Bogey herded his family into the dining room. Natalie held back as the siblings crowded around George at the table, passing him the silver saltshaker, the platters with cheeses and cold chicken and ham that the cook brought in. Pickles and coarse brown bread were next. George told his stories with wide swathes of his arms. He was more animated than Natalie remembered him being. He'd always been the shy one, along with her. She'd been bold only in her music, excelling at everything she tried, especially the piano. Until that day.

Laughter. Oohs and ahhs and exclamations. She scanned the room of her brothers and sisters. Except for George, they all lived together, still. Constance was nearly forty. Natalie supposed they were considered "old maids," or "at home" as the latest census described single women. She as well. She had hoped for a life beyond, maybe one day marrying and managing a household staff—after her career. She'd been on the road toward that when her life—like shattered silk—ripped apart.

She shook her head of the painful memory. She focused instead on the light in George's eyes, noted the tiny crow's-feet, the tanned face with laugh lines. He was thirty-one and wore the look of an explorer, someone who had gone beyond expectations, even his own.

"Don't you think so, Nat?" George spoke.

She hadn't heard what he'd said.

"About what?"

"About coming to Arizona with me. And California. And New Mexico. Some people seem to think New Mexico is still a part of Mexico."

"Isn't it?" This from Marian, the youngest Curtis at twenty-two.

Her siblings teased Marian for not knowing such a fact of geography, and Natalie was grateful the subject had changed as she watched them chatter. George had a broken canine tooth. There was probably a story about what happened to cause that. She'd have to ask.

"You haven't answered my question." George returned to her.

"She couldn't possibly make such a trip," Mimsey said. "She's not strong enough."

"And what would she do there?" Mirian asked. "Sign on as a ranch—what did you call yourself—a ranch hand?"

"Let her breathe in the air. That alone will heal her. Look what it did for my asthma."

"You do look healthy," their father-doctor said. "Good to see that, son. Good to see." He appeared to consider George's offer. "It might benefit Natalie."

"No." Mimsey's word was dressed in finality. Her husband frowned and she added, "She's simply not strong enough."

"The West could heal her. Why, I've—"

"I am here." Natalie spoke more forcefully than she'd intended. "In front of you all. Please, don't talk about me as though I'm not present."

Silence like an early morning fog filled the formerly boisterous room. Her siblings looked away, caught each other's eyes. *Pity. They pity me.*

George cleared his throat. "I nearly forgot. I brought gifts for you." He wiped his mouth with the linen napkin. "Let me get my pack."

"Bella can fetch it for you." Her father motioned to the maid who'd been standing by the sideboard. She curtsied, then moved into the hall and returned with the leather knapsack while the cook entered and cleared away George's dishes. George thanked her for the meal and the maid for his bag and set it on the dining room table, plopping it with a sturdy *thump!*

He unlatched the buckles, reached inside, and pulled out treasures. Colorfully woven lengths of cloth that could be table runners or a dresser scarf. "Navajo," George said. A red sash he described as part of a Katsina regalia. "Katsina dolls are Hopi. And dancers represent Katsina spirits which are powerful helpers in everyday life and who carry their prayers. The red sash represents the earth in blossom after rain clouds have made their way to the desert." He pulled out a rattle made from a gourd, something he described as a musical instrument. A selection of turquoise stones. A silver bracelet. A coral necklace.

"So beautiful. Such smooth stones." His siblings passed the items to each other.

"It's like Christmas in October," Mirian said.

Then he unwrapped from sheepskin a piece of smooth pottery that he set at the end of the woven runner displaying his gifts. The pot could be held in the palm of a woman's hand. It was bowl-shaped with a small nozzle-like protuberance at the top. George pointed to that feature. "It's a seed pot. For corn, mostly."

"They're all precious." Natalie reached out as though to touch the pottery, then pulled back.

"Go ahead and pick something, each of you. Mimsey too."

"You pick ours then, Bogey. Or we can take what's left. Yes, go ahead, children. Natalie, you first, dear."

Mirian pouted. "She always goes first."

"Shush." Mimsey motioned Natalie to proceed.

Natalie chose the pottery bowl. She held it in both hands. The clay felt warm almost, though she knew that must be just a feature of its artistry as it was October and the outside air cool. "The design. It's so delicate. And such lovely colors."

"It's Acoma, from a pueblo in New Mexico. They work with an aloe tip dipped in the paint they make themselves from insects and seeds. Then they draw the designs using the plant rather than a brush."

"With a very steady hand," Constance said. "Not a wavy line in sight." She donned the coral necklace, turned to look at herself in the mirror above the sideboard.

"An aloe plant," Natalie said. "Like the one Cook has in the kitchen? The one we break open to heal burns?"

"The same," George said.

"And you say they were done by aboriginal people?" This from Bridgham, the only other Curtis son.

"They're natives to that land. American Indians."

"And you brought this all the way from the West. And it didn't break." Natalie examined the pottery piece with red and green designs artfully arranged, crossing each other in a delicate pattern around the entire pot, including the throat, as she thought of the protuberance. "Such thin clay walls."

"About that," George said. "They use pots for everything, the way some tribes use baskets for storage or how we use glass containers to hold salts or buttons. What I learned about the Acoma pot is that long ago, when they made them from the local clay, the pots would be quite beautiful after painting and firing, but they were fragile, easily broken. They tossed the broken shards out onto the desert and made more." Storytelling and enthusiasm brightened his eyes. *Telling stories is what he did at the library before he moved west.* "The tale goes, that some ancient grandmothers were out on the desert and began picking up the broken pieces and pounding them back into powder. One ingenious potter added the old clay to the new clay, and those pots when fired became strong." He clicked his fingernail on the side of the piece Natalie had chosen. "Very strong. And beautiful. Both."

"And the broken pieces mixed in the new clay, that's what brought the resiliency?" Natalie asked.

"That's what they say."

Natalie turned her pot around in her small hands. "And these are used for storing seeds, and then the throat allows but one seed out at a time during planting?"

"Supposedly. They walk across the fields and drop them in, singing as they go."

"Singing."

"So the traders tell me. I've never been there," George said.

"Could be a good sales pitch for gullible outsiders," Bridgham said. "Everyone likes a story to go with their purchases."

"I love that story." Natalie felt tears she blinked away. "That out of broken things, already gone through fire, when mixed with new clay, something totally different is created. Something stronger."

The family chatter over their gifts and George's stories faded as Natalie held the art piece: practical yet a metaphor too. New purpose could come out of what was broken. Natalie imagined herself as a cracked and damaged piece of clay. What was the "new" she could blend it with to grow stronger?

"Are there other Indian artists like the one who made this?" Natalie asked.

"Dozens of tribes, so I'd suspect so," George said. "They're not all in New Mexico. They're scattered around California and Arizona and have names like Zuni and Taos. Apache, Navajo. Many others. It's like stepping into another world there, Nat. Anthropologists, even some women, descend on certain ruins during the cooler season because the artifacts there are so old. It's our nation's history written in clay and stone."

"Women?" Mimsey said. "Oh yes, I think I did read about a Mr. and Mrs. Stevenson spending six months among the Pueblo

340

people, she called them, some twenty years ago. They were looking for patrons—remember, Bogey?"

Natalie's father nodded agreement.

Natalie said, "It must have been very interesting work."

"Surely not for a single woman though. Unchaperoned? Egads," Constance said. She stood, holding the ceramic piece Natalie had handed to her. "Whatever will you do with this? We've no garden to plant."

"It's art," Natalie said. "Beautiful in its own right. And it's . . . history." She looked at all the items George had brought back. Each was singularly precious. Handcrafted.

"My bedtime is long overdue," Mirian said, standing. "And I imagine you're exhausted, George. You'll be here for a while, won't you, dear Brother? To regale us with more adventures?"

"A week or so." He hesitated, then added, "Long enough to talk Natalie into going back with me."

"It'll take longer than a week for a negotiation that's going nowhere." Mimsey put her arms around Natalie's shoulders. She felt her mother's warmth but also the containment. "I have all my chicks at home for the first time in two years, and I'm not going to let you spend one moment trying to break up the flock, George."

Natalie's heart beat a little faster. She caught her breath and stepped away from her mother's arms, the cloying of family suddenly suffocating in a way she hadn't known before. "I could go at least for a visit, couldn't I?" She answered her own question. "Yes. I will go, for a visit."

"Good for you, Nat!" George said.

"We'll see," Mimsey said.

"I have to go back to Arizona in a week, but I'll come back for Christmas and we'll head west for the New Year, you and me, Nat."

Natalie rubbed the pottery as if a genie might pop out and grant her three wishes. "I want to meet the person who made this."

"It'll be our goal."

"Bogey, say something?" Mimsey pleaded. "She's not up to this."

"I see a little spark in Natalie's eyes I haven't seen for years. I won't put that out."

Natalie let them discuss her. She had something more important to engage her heart. A glorious work of art crafted from the clay of broken things had found its way into her hands. George had found himself in the West. *Maybe there's hope for me.*

Jane Kirkpatrick is the *New York Times* and CBA bestselling and award-winning author of forty books, including *Something Worth Doing*, *One More River to Cross*, *Everything She Didn't Say*, *All Together in One Place*, *A Light in the Wilderness*, *The Memory Weaver*, *This Road We Traveled*, and *A Sweetness to the Soul*, which won the prestigious Wrangler Award from the Western Heritage Center. Her works have won the WILLA Literary Award, the Carol Award for Historical Fiction, and the 2016 Will Rogers Gold Medallion Award. And been short-listed for the Christy, Spur, and Oregon Book Awards. Jane divides her time between Central Oregon and California with her husband, Jerry, and Cavalier King Charles Spaniel, Caesar. Learn more at www.jkbooks.com.

"Once again, Jane Kirkpatrick creates a bold and inspiring woman out of the dust of history. Jennie's triumph, in the skilled hands of one of the West's most beloved writers, leaves its mark on your heart."

—SANDRA DALLAS, *New York Times* bestselling author

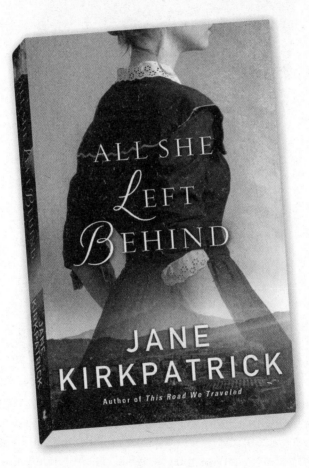

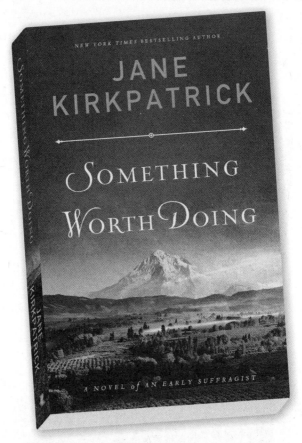

Adversity can squelch the human spirit . . .
or it can help us discover strength we
NEVER KNEW WE HAD.

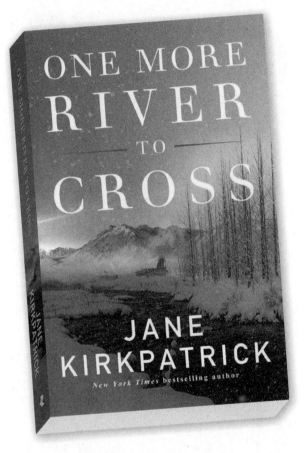

Based on true events, this compelling survival story by award-winning novelist Jane Kirkpatrick is full of grit and endurance. Beset by storms, bad timing, and desperate decisions, eight women, seventeen children, and one man must outlast winter in the middle of the Sierra Nevada in 1844.

THERE IS MORE THAN ONE WAY TO TELL A STORY . . .

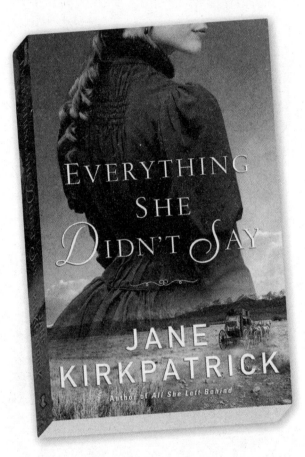

In 1911, Carrie Strahorn wrote a memoir sharing some of the most exciting events of twenty-five years of shaping the American West with her husband, railroad promoter and writer Robert Strahorn. Nearly ten years later, she's finally ready to reveal the secrets she hadn't told anyone—even herself.

Tabitha Brown refuses to be left behind
in Missouri when her son makes the decision
to strike out for Oregon—even if she has to
hire her own wagon to join the party.

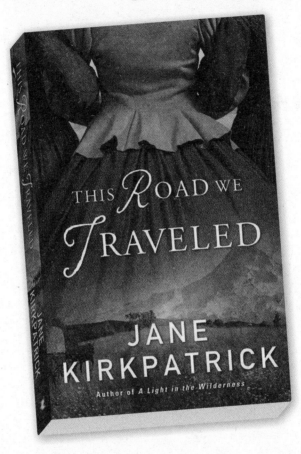

With her signature attention to detail and epic style, *New York
Times* bestselling author Jane Kirkpatrick invites you to travel
the deadly and enticing Oregon Trail. Based on actual events,
This Road We Traveled inspires the pioneer in all of us.

Jane Kirkpatrick

WEAVING THE STORIES OF OUR LIVES

Get to know Jane at

JKBooks.com

Sign up for the *Story Sparks* newsletter
Read the blogs
Learn about upcoming events